PENGUIN TWENTIETH-CENTURY CLASSICS

APOCALYPSE

AND THE WRITINGS ON REVELATION

David Herbert Lawrence was born into a miner's family in Eastwood, Nottinghamshire, in 1885, the fourth of five children. He attended Beauvale Board School and Nottingham High School, and trained as an elementary schoolteacher at Nottingham University College. He taught in Croydon from 1908. His first novel, *The White Peacock*, was published in 1911, just a few weeks after the death of his mother to whom he had been extraordinarily close. His career as a schoolteacher was ended by serious illness at the end of 1911.

In 1912 Lawrence went to Germany with Frieda Weekley, the German wife of the Professor of Modern Languages at the University College of Nottingham. They were married on their return to England in 1914. Lawrence had published *Sons and Lovers* in 1913; but *The Rainbow*, completed in 1915, was suppressed, and for three years he could not find a publisher for *Women in Love*, completed in 1917.

After the war, Lawrence lived abroad, and sought a more fulfilling mode of life than he had so far experienced. With Frieda, he lived in Sicily, Sri Lanka, Australia, New Mexico and Mexico. They returned to Europe in 1925. His last novel, *Lady Chatterley's Lover*, was published in 1928 but was banned in England and America. In 1930 he died in Vence, in the south of France, at the age of forty-four.

Lawrence's life may have been short, but he lived it intensely. He also produced an amazing body of work: novels, stories, poems, plays, essays, travel books, translations, paintings and letters (over five thousand of which survive). After his death Frieda wrote that, 'What he had seen and felt and known he gave in his writing to his fellow men, the splendour of living, the hope of more and more life . . . a heroic and immeasureable gift.'

Dr Mara Kalnins is Fellow in English at Corpus Christi College and Staff Tutor in Literature for the Board of Continuing Education, University of Cambridge. She has written widely on D. H. Lawrence and

edited a collection of critical essays for his centenary year as well as a selection of his poetry. She has also edited three volumes for the definitive Cambridge edition of his works.

John Worthen is advisory editor for the works of D. H. Lawrence in Penguin Twentieth-Century Classics. Currently Professor of D. H. Lawrence Studies at the University of Nottingham, he has published widely on Lawrence; his acclaimed biography, *D. H. Lawrence: The Early Years 1885–1912*, was published in 1991. He has also edited a number of volumes in the authoritative Cambridge Lawrence Edition whose texts Penguin Twentieth-Century Classics are reproducing.

D. H. LAWRENCE

———————

APOCALYPSE

AND THE WRITINGS ON REVELATION

EDITED WITH AN INTRODUCTION AND
NOTES BY MARA KALNINS

PENGUIN BOOKS

PENGUIN BOOKS

Published by the Penguin Group
Penguin Books Ltd, 27 Wrights Lane, London w8 5TZ, England
Penguin Books USA Inc., 375 Hudson Street, New York, New York 10014, USA
Penguin Books Australia Ltd, Ringwood, Victoria, Australia
Penguin Books Canada Ltd, 10 Alcorn Avenue, Toronto, Ontario, Canada M4V 3B2
Penguin Books (NZ) Ltd, 182–190 Wairau Road, Auckland 10, New Zealand

Penguin Books Ltd, Registered Offices: Harmondsworth, Middlesex, England

First published 1931
Cambridge University Press edition published 1980
Published with new editorial matter in Penguin Books 1995
1 3 5 7 9 10 8 6 4 2

Copyright © the Estate of Frieda Lawrence Ravagli, 1980
Introduction and Notes copyright © Mara Kalnins, 1995
Chronology copyright © John Worthen, 1994

Typeset by Datix International Limited, Bungay, Suffolk
Printed in England by Clays Ltd, St Ives plc

Contents

Note on the Penguin Lawrence Edition

D. H. Lawrence stands in the very front rank of English writers this century; unlike some other famous writers, however, he has always appealed to a large popular audience as well as to students of literature, and his work still arouses passionate loyalties and fervent disagreements. The available texts of his books have, nevertheless, been notoriously inaccurate. The Penguin Lawrence Edition uses the authoritative texts of Lawrence's work established by an international team of scholars engaged on the *Cambridge Edition of the Works of D. H. Lawrence* under its General Editors, Professor James T. Boulton and Professor Warren Roberts. Through rigorous study of surviving manuscripts, typescripts, proofs and early printings the Cambridge editors have provided texts as close as possible to those which Lawrence himself would have expected to see printed. Deletions deliberately made by printers, publishers or their editors, accidentally by typists and printers – at times removing whole pages of text – have been restored, while house-styling introduced by printers is removed as far as is possible. The Penguin Lawrence Edition thus offers both general readers and students the only texts of Lawrence which have any claim to be the authentic productions of his genius.

Chronology

1885   David Herbert Richards Lawrence (hereafter DHL) born in Eastwood, Nottinghamshire, the fourth child of Arthur John Lawrence, collier, and Lydia, née Beardsall, daughter of a pensioned-off engine fitter.

1891–8   Attends Beauvale Board School.

1898–   Becomes first boy from Eastwood to win a County Council
1901   scholarship to Nottingham High School, which he attends until July 1901.

1901   Works three months as a clerk at Haywood's surgical appliances factory in Nottingham; severe attack of pneumonia.

1902   Begins frequent visits to the Chambers family at Haggs Farm, Underwood, and starts his friendship with Jessie Chambers.

1902–5   Pupil-teacher at the British School, Eastwood; sits the King's Scholarship exam in December 1904 and is placed in the first division of the first class.

1905–6   Works as uncertificated teacher at the British School; writes his first poems and starts his first novel 'Laetitia' (later *The White Peacock*, 1911).

1906–8   Student at Nottingham University College following the normal course leading to a teacher's certificate; qualifies in July 1908. Wins *Nottinghamshire Guardian* Christmas 1907 short-story competition with 'A Prelude' (submitted under name of Jessie Chambers); writes second version of 'Laetitia'.

1908–11   Elementary teacher at Davidson Road School, Croydon.

1909   Meets Ford Madox Hueffer (later Ford), who begins to publish his poems and stories in the *English Review* and recommends rewritten version of *The White Peacock* (1911) to William Heinemann; DHL writes *A Collier's Friday Night* (1934) and first version of 'Odour of Chrysanthemums' (1911); friendship with Agnes Holt.

1910   Writes 'The Saga of Siegmund' (first version of *The Trespasser*, 1912), based on the experiences of his friend, the Croydon teacher Helen Corke; starts affair with Jessie Chambers; writes first version of *The Widowing of Mrs. Holroyd* (1914); ends affair with Jessie Chambers but continues friendship; starts to write 'Paul Morel' (later *Sons and Lovers*, 1913); death of Lydia Lawrence in December; gets engaged to his old friend Louie Burrows.

1911   Fails to finish 'Paul Morel'; strongly attracted to Helen Corke; starts affair with Alice Dax, wife of an Eastwood chemist; meets Edward Garnett, publisher's reader for Duckworth, who advises him on writing and publication. In November falls seriously ill with pneumonia and has to give up school-teaching; 'The Saga' accepted by Duckworth; DHL commences its revision as *The Trespasser*.

1912   Convalesces in Bournemouth; breaks off engagement to Louie; returns to Eastwood; works on 'Paul Morel'; in March meets Frieda Weekley, wife of Ernest, Professor at the University College of Nottingham; ends affair with Alice Dax; goes to Germany on a visit to his relations on 3 May; travels however with Frieda to Metz. After many vicissitudes, some memorialized in *Look! We Have Come Through!* (1917), Frieda gives up her marriage and her children for DHL; in August they journey over the Alps to Italy and settle at Gargnano, where DHL writes the final version of *Sons and Lovers*.

1913   *Love Poems* published; writes *The Daughter-in-Law* (1965) and 200 pp. of 'The Insurrection of Miss Houghton' (abandoned); begins 'The Sisters', eventually to be split into *The Rainbow* (1915) and *Women in Love* (1920). DHL and Frieda spend some days at San Gaudenzio, then stay at Irschenhausen in Bavaria; DHL writes first versions of 'The Prussian Officer' and 'The Thorn in the Flesh' (1914); *Sons and Lovers* published in May. DHL and Frieda return to England in June, meet John Middleton Murry and Katherine Mansfield. They return to Italy (Fiascherino, near Spezia) in September; DHL revises *The Widowing of Mrs. Holroyd*; resumes work on 'The Sisters'.

1914   Rewrites 'The Sisters' (now called 'The Wedding Ring') yet again; agrees for Methuen to publish it; takes J. B. Pinker as agent. DHL and Frieda return to England in June, marry on 13 July. DHL meets Catherine Carswell and S. S. Koteliansky; compiles short-story collection *The Prussian Officer* (1914). Outbreak of war prevents DHL and Frieda returning to Italy; at Chesham he first writes 'Study of Thomas Hardy' (1936) and then begins *The Rainbow*; starts important friendships with Ottoline Morrell, Cynthia Asquith, Bertrand Russell and E. M. Forster; grows increasingly desperate and angry about the war.

1915   Finishes *The Rainbow* in Greatham in March; plans lecture course with Russell; they quarrel in June. DHL and Frieda move to Hampstead in August; he and Murry bring out *The Signature* (magazine, three issues only) to which he contributes 'The Crown'. *The Rainbow* published by Methuen in September, suppressed at the end of October, prosecuted and banned in November. DHL meets painters Dorothy Brett and Mark Gertler; he and Frieda plan to leave England for Florida; decide to move to Cornwall instead.

1916   Writes *Women in Love* between April and October; publishes *Twilight in Italy* and *Amores*.

1917   *Women in Love* rejected by publishers; DHL continues to revise it. Makes unsuccessful attempts to go to America. Begins *Studies in Classic American Literature* (1923); publishes *Look! We Have Come Through!* In October he and Frieda evicted from Cornwall on suspicion of spying; in London he begins *Aaron's Rod* (1922).

1918   DHL and Frieda move to Hermitage, Berkshire, then to Middleton-by-Wirksworth; publishes *New Poems*; writes *Movements in European History* (1921), *Touch and Go* (1920) and the first version of 'The Fox' (1920).

1919   Seriously ill with influenza; moves back to Hermitage; publishes *Bay*. In the autumn, Frieda goes to Germany and then joins DHL in Florence; they visit Picinisco and settle in Capri.

1920   Writes *Psychoanalysis and the Unconscious* (1921). He and Frieda move to Taormina, Sicily; DHL writes *The Lost Girl* (1920), *Mr Noon* (1984), continues with *Aaron's Rod*; on summer visit to Florence has affair with Rosalind

Baynes; writes many poems from *Birds, Beasts and Flowers*
(1923). *Women in Love* published.

1921   DHL and Frieda visit Sardinia and he writes *Sea and
Sardinia* (1921); meets Earl and Achsah Brewster; finishes
Aaron's Rod in the summer and writes *Fantasia of the
Unconscious* (1922) and 'The Captain's Doll' (1923); plans
to leave Europe and visit USA; puts together collection of
stories *England, My England* (1922) and group of short
novels *The Ladybird, The Fox* and *The Captain's Doll*
(1923).

1922   DHL and Frieda leave for Ceylon, stay with Brewsters,
then travel to Australia; he translates Verga. In Western
Australia meets Mollie Skinner; in Thirroul, near Sydney,
he writes *Kangaroo* (1923) in six weeks. Between August
and September, he and Frieda travel to California via
South Sea Islands, and meet Witter Bynner and Willard
Johnson; settle in Taos, New Mexico, at invitation of
Mabel Dodge (later Luhan). In December, move up to
Del Monte Ranch, near Taos; DHL rewrites *Studies in
Classic American Literature.*

1923   Finishes *Birds, Beasts and Flowers.* He and Frieda spend
summer at Chapala in Mexico where he writes 'Quetzal-
coatl' (first version of *The Plumed Serpent*, 1926). Frieda
returns to Europe in August after serious quarrel with
DHL; he journeys in USA and Mexico, rewrites Mollie
Skinner's *The House of Ellis* as *The Boy in the Bush*
(1924); arrives back in England in December.

1924   At dinner in Café Royal, DHL invites his friends to come
to New Mexico; Dorothy Brett accepts and accompanies
him and Frieda in March. Mabel Luhan gives Lobo (later
renamed Kiowa) Ranch to Frieda; DHL gives her *Sons
and Lovers* manuscript in return. During summer on
ranch he writes *St. Mawr* (1925), 'The Woman Who
Rode Away' (1925) and 'The Princess' (1925); in August,
suffers his first bronchial haemorrhage. His father dies in
September; in October, he, Frieda and Brett move to
Oaxaca, Mexico, where he starts *The Plumed Serpent* and
writes most of *Mornings in Mexico* (1927).

1925   Finishes *The Plumed Serpent*, falls ill and almost dies of
typhoid and pneumonia in February; in March diagnosed

as suffering from tuberculosis. Recuperates at Kiowa Ranch, writes *David* (1926) and compiles *Reflections on the Death of a Porcupine* (1925). He and Frieda return to Europe in September, spend a month in England and settle at Spotorno, Italy; DHL writes first version of *Sun* (1926); Frieda meets Angelo Ravagli.

1926   Writes *The Virgin and the Gypsy* (1930); serious quarrel with Frieda during visit from DHL's sister Ada. DHL visits Brewsters and Brett; has affair with Brett. Reconciled, DHL and Frieda move to Villa Mirenda, near Florence, in May and visit England (his last visit) in late summer. On return to Italy in October he writes first version of *Lady Chatterley's Lover* (1944); starts second version in November. Friendship with Aldous and Maria Huxley; DHL starts to paint.

1927   Finishes second version of *Lady Chatterley's Lover* (1972); visits Etruscan sites with Earl Brewster; writes *Sketches of Etruscan Places* (1932) and the first part of *The Escaped Cock* (1928). In November, after meetings with Michael Arlen and Norman Douglas, works out scheme for private publication with Pino Orioli, and starts final version of *Lady Chatterley's Lover* (1928).

1928   Finishes *Lady Chatterley's Lover* and arranges for its printing and publication in Florence; fights many battles to ensure its despatch to subscribers in Britain and USA. In June writes second part of *The Escaped Cock* (1929). He and Frieda travel to Switzerland (Gsteig) and the island of Port Cros, then settle in Bandol, in the south of France. He writes many of the poems in *Pansies* (1929); *Lady Chatterley's Lover* pirated in Europe and USA.

1929   Visits Paris to arrange for cheap edition of *Lady Chatterley's Lover* (1929); unexpurgated typescripts of *Pansies* seized by police; exhibition of his paintings in London raided by police. He and Frieda visit Majorca, France and Bavaria, returning to Bandol for the winter. He writes *Nettles* (1930), *Apocalypse* (1931) and *Last Poems* (1932); sees much of Brewsters and Huxleys.

1930   Goes into Ad Astra Sanatorium in Vence at start of February; discharges himself on 1 March; dies at Villa

Robermond, Vence, on Sunday 2 March; buried on 4
March.

1935   Frieda sends Angelo Ravagli (now living with her at
Kiowa Ranch – they marry in 1950) to Vence to have
DHL exhumed, cremated, and his ashes brought back to
the ranch.

1956   Frieda dies and is buried at Kiowa Ranch.

John Worthen, 1994

Introduction

Apocalypse is D. H. Lawrence's last book. It is a vigorously iconoclastic work, a radical and searching criticism of the political, religious and social structures which have shaped our materialistic and technological age. Like many modern writers, Lawrence sought to articulate two of the major currents of thought and feeling that have found expression in the imaginative literature of the twentieth century. Firstly, the fascination with the psychological, internal world of man – what he called in one of his poems the *terra incognita* of the self[1] – and in his fiction, essays and poems he explored the unknown places of the human psyche so that they could be understood and become the basis for renewal in human relationships. Secondly, his works chart the profound unease many writers have felt faced with a world in which creative human values seem increasingly to be sacrificed to materialism and to empty social and intellectual forms, impoverishing the quality of life and threatening to dehumanize the individual. But his works also reveal Lawrence to be, as he called himself, 'a passionately religious man',[2] not in the narrow sense of belonging to a particular creed, for early on he had rejected the Nonconformist Christian upbringing of his youth, but in the sense of seeing and reverencing divine creativity in the universe and in man. *Apocalypse* is therefore also a statement of hope. It expresses Lawrence's belief in humanity's power to 're-establish the living organic connections, with the cosmos, the sun and earth, with mankind and nation and family' (149:32–4), to regain the imaginative and spiritual values which alone can revitalize our world. Ranging over his entire system of thought on God and man, on psychology, science, politics and art, *Apocalypse* is Lawrence's last testament, his final attempt to convey his vision of man and of the cosmos to posterity.

From his youth Lawrence had been familiar with the Bible and with apocalyptic literature. Its language had the 'power of echoing and re-echoing in my unconscious mind' (55:1), and the imagery of the Old and New Testaments, their language and symbolism, deeply influenced the formation of his style and vision. But it was not until

1923 when he was living in Taos, New Mexico, that Lawrence first thought about writing on the Book of Revelation. He was contacted by the English painter and mystic Frederick Carter, who asked him to look at his manuscript and drawings on the symbolism of Revelation. Lawrence liked Carter's work and offered to help with its publication,[3] though his own interests lay not in astrology but in the way he felt the symbols of Revelation revealed fundamental truths about human psychology: 'Myself I am more interested in the microcosm than in the macrocosm, and in the gates to the psyche rather than the astrological houses.'[4] It was a period when his own work on psychology was flourishing. In the previous year he had completed *Fantasia of the Unconscious*, and in the winter of 1922–3 he was rewriting the early versions of *Studies in Classic American Literature* which, like the earlier 'Study of Thomas Hardy' and 'The Crown', were as much explorations of human nature as studies of literature. He believed that Apocalypse was 'a revelation of Initiation experience',[5] symbolically showing the way to the liberation of the self, a manual of esoteric lore derived from the pre-Christian world which had later been altered and reinterpreted by Jewish and Christian writers, yet which still held, in its story of the opening of the seven seals and the rebirth of the soul, the clue to a profound psychical experience in man, beyond rational or scientific explanation.

Revelation, he argued, was a symbolic account of how to attain inner harmony as well as a sense of living connection with the greater universe. The central emblem of this process was the heavenly figure of Zodiac man, whose body was composed of the twelve signs of the Zodiac, symbolizing the powers governing the various parts of man, and himself an emblem of the mystic correspondence between the individual and the universe, the microcosm and the macrocosm. St John's imagery 'started primarily from the physical psyche, the organic and the nervous and cerebral psyche, and expanded into the stars'.[6] Thus Revelation gives us a 'cypher-account of the process of the conquest of the lower or sensual dynamic centres by the upper or spiritual dynamic consciousness, a conquest affected centre by centre, towards a culmination in the *actual* experience of spiritual infinitude'.[7] This process, however, did not involve a postponed spiritual salvation, as in Christian doctrine, still less the crude conquest of the physical by the spiritual, a notion that Lawrence, with his deep belief in the primacy of the instinctual and emotional self over the rational, would have dismissed. Rather, man held the key to fulfilment in the here and now, within himself, in what Lawrence called the 'physical psyche' or the 'biological psyche'. He resolved the apparent semantic contradiction of this term by defining it as the union of spirit and body through the life-energy informing both: 'the psyche comprising our whole consciousness, physical, sensual, spiritual, pre-cerebral as well as cerebral'.[8] The initiation process in Revelation showed how the psyche could both relate to and interpret the objective, material universe and understand the subjective, inner world, integrating them for its own development and enrichment. In this respect, as in others, Lawrence's insights paralleled, and in some cases anticipated, those of modern psychology.

During the war years Lawrence had read many books on the esoteric and the occult, though his critical sense made him doubtful of such writers as the Russian-born theosophist Helena Blavatsky, whose *Isis Unveiled* and *The Secret Doctrine* he had rated as 'not *very* much good'.[9] The importance of his extensive reading in such areas as well as in psychology and anthropology, however, lay in the stimulus they offered to his imagination as an artist, rather than in the validity of their particular doctrines, as indeed Lawrence himself recognized.

> I am not a proper archaeologist nor an anthropologist nor an ethnologist. I am no 'scholar' of any sort. But I am very grateful to scholars for their sound work. I have found hints, suggestions for what I say here in all kinds of scholarly books, from the Yoga and Plato and St. John the Evangel and the early Greek philosophers like Herakleitos down to Frazer and his 'Golden Bough,' and even Freud and Frobenius. Even then I only remember hints – and I proceed by intuition.[10]

Similarly, Lawrence's reading of James Pryse's *The Apocalypse Unsealed* at this time had been important not because it offered a complete and intellectually satisfying account of the Book of Revelation, but because its interpretation of St John's symbols stimulated his imagination. Pryse wrote that the opening of the seven seals in Apocalypse represented the liberation of a latent power in the self; through the controlled awakening of the seven principal nerve centres, or 'chakras', of the spine, each of which is a centre of psychic energy, a life-enhancing force could be released. It was a notion immediately congenial to Lawrence, who explored similar ideas in *Fantasia* where he called this vortex of energy a 'plexus'. In yoga, too, this power, termed *kundalini*, is represented by the symbol of the serpent or dragon lying coiled at the base of the spine. When awakened, it releases latent psychic energy and stimulates the regeneration of the spirit. Lawrence later called it 'That startled life which runs through us like a serpent, or coils within us potent and waiting, like a serpent' (123:7–9), and the opening of the seven seals of Revelation represents 'the opening, and conquest of the great psychic centres of the human body' (101:11–12).

Lawrence's interest in Apocalypse and its symbols also prompted him to read and review Dr John Oman's newly published account of St John, *Book of Revelation*, in 1923.[11] The review, though short, is significant for two reasons. Firstly, Lawrence's description of St John's 'passionate and mystic hatred of the civilization of his day, a hatred so intense only because he knew that the living realities of men's being were displaced by it' (41:13–16) epitomizes his passionate feeling about his own time, but Lawrence's quest for 'the living realities of men's being' never faltered and was always the impulse behind the growth and development of his life, thought and art. Secondly, the review reveals Lawrence's fundamental ideas about the inexhaustible nature of symbols, a notion he was to develop later in *Apocalypse*. For Lawrence, the symbols of Revelation were not there to be explicated and definitively explained through scholarly exegesis. Rather, their value lay in their irreducible complexity. True symbols – as distinct from allegorical ones with their one-to-one reference – suggested the many possibilities co-existent in narrative interpretation, and set up fruitful ambiguities. The symbols of archetypal myths, he argued, were valid for all times and places and thus could give shape and meaning to modern man's existence.

The imagery, symbols and myths of Revelation continued to fascinate Lawrence, but for the moment his correspondence with Frederick Carter and his reading of apocalyptic literature lapsed, and it was not until the end of his life that he resumed the idea of writing about St John's vision. In the intervening years he had travelled widely in Old and New Mexico and throughout Europe, but in September 1929, in failing health, he moved to Bandol in the south of France where he was to write his late poems, a handful of reviews (including an introduction to a new book on Revelation by Carter), some essays, and his last book, *Apocalypse*.

At this time Carter, hearing that Lawrence was again in Europe, resumed their correspondence, and Lawrence again offered to help with the publication of Carter's original manuscript and write a foreword to it. In the meantime, however, Carter had published a much-revised and shortened version of the 1923 document as *The Dragon of the Alchemists* (1926), but he sent Lawrence some rewritten material for a new book, suggesting a collaboration. Lawrence agreed and enthusiastically returned to his study of Revelation and apocalyptic literature, ordering a formidable reading list from his London bookseller, which included editions of the Bible, R. H. Charles's scholarly *A Critical and Exegetical Commentary on the Revelation of St. John*, *L'Apocalypse de Jean* by A. Loisy, Hesiod, Plutarch and Dean Inge's lectures on Plotinus, which he read for their accounts of ancient cosmology and cosmogony.[12] But undoubtedly the works that were most important to him and to his interpretation of the Book of Revelation were Gilbert Murray's *Five Stages of Greek Religion* and John Burnet's *Early Greek Philosophy*, which he had read and reread over the years and which had profoundly influenced the evolution of his thought. In particular the ideas on science, religion and philosophy of the pre-Socratic philosopher Heraclitus had a lasting influence on nearly all his writing after July 1915, as Lawrence himself had acknowledged: 'I shall write all my philosophy again. Last time I came out of the Christian Camp. This time I must come out of these early Greek philosophers' and 'I shall write out Herakleitos, on tablets of bronze'.[13]

He found Heraclitus's notion that all creation is dual but emerges from a primary absolute – the 'Boundless' – which itself transcends these contraries, immediately congenial: 'All existence is dual, and surging towards a consummation into being,'[14] and 'the Infinite, the Boundless, the Eternal . . . [is] the real starting point'.[15] Heraclitus also taught that the universe only exists by virtue of opposition, through the power of conflict, or 'strife', the creative principle that separated out the primary substance. Thus: 'Homer was wrong in saying: "Would that strife might perish from among gods and men!" He did not see that he was praying for the destruction of the universe; for, if his prayer were heard, all things would pass away.'[16] Creation is therefore dual, in a continual state of flux, a ceaseless conflict of opposites coming into being and passing away. Lawrence explored Heraclitus's doctrine in essays like 'The Crown' and in some of the late poems, such as 'Strife', where he also draws a distinction between the creative conflict of contraries and the destructive dominance of single power, which is evil.

There are two eternities fighting the fight of Creation, the light projecting itself into the darkness, the darkness enveloping herself within the embrace of light. And then there is the consummation of each in the other, the consummation of light in darkness and darkness in light, which is absolute: our bodies cast up like foam of two meeting waves, but foam which is absolute, complete, beyond the limitation of either infinity, consummate over both eternities. The direct opposites of the Beginning and the End, by their very directness, imply their own supreme relation. And this supreme relation is made absolute in the clash and the foam of the meeting waves. And the clash and the foam are the Crown, the Absolute.[17]

In his fiction, too, Lawrence depicts his characters not so much as 'stable egos', in the sense of established personalities whose actions can be rationally analysed and understood, but rather as mysterious beings, in a continual process of self-creation, evolving or destroying themselves through the conflict of deep inner forces as well as through pressures from the external world. Burnet's philosophical study, therefore, was of the greatest importance in shaping Lawrence's thoughts about human nature and the cosmos.

In the pre-Socratic teaching that 'All things are full of gods'[18] and in Murray's analysis of ancient Greek myth and religion, Lawrence found a kindred vision to his own belief in God. As early as 1911, after he had rejected his Nonconformist upbringing, he had written: 'There still remains a God ... a vast, shimmering impulse which wavers onwards towards some end',[19] and at the end of his life, in 1929, he reaffirmed this belief:

There is Almighty God ... The cosmos brought forth all the world, and brought forth me. It brought forth my mind, my will, and my soul ... there must be that in the cosmos which contains the essence, at least, or the potentiality, of all things, known and unknown ... And this terrific and frightening and delighted potency I call Almighty God (175:16–27).

The question that seemed to Lawrence to face humanity in every age – and never more so than in our century of scientific materialism – was 'How shall man put himself into relation to God, into a living relation?'[20] In our era, he felt, 'the long light of Christianity is guttering to go out, and we have to get at new resources in ourselves'.[21] His late writings are a renewed and urgent search for the archetypal myths and symbols that would help humanity to find those 'new resources'. It was a search that took him back to ancient religions and civilizations, not because he advocated a return to primitive forms for modern man, but because he recognized the enduring validity of concepts which had nourished humanity in the past; these, he felt, must also have value for our time.

> We can never recover an old vision, once it has been supplanted. But what we can do is to discover a new vision in harmony with the memories of old, far-off, far, far-off experience that lie within us. (54:16–19)

Lawrence's later writings on the Aztecs, the American Indians, the Etruscans and, at the end of his life, on the Book of Revelation were therefore not simply nostalgia for a golden age – though the longing for a lost coherence seems to be a deeply rooted psychological need in many societies – but rather an active enquiry into ancient beliefs and systems which seemed to offer a more vital way of conceptualizing the universe and man's place in it.

Lawrence's collaboration with Carter continued during the autumn of 1929, and indeed the latter visited him in mid-November at Bandol and stayed until the end of the month. By the time he left, Lawrence had written 20,000 words on Revelation and in mid-December he wrote to Carter: 'I have roughly finished my introduction, and am going over it, working it a bit into shape.'²² He was still revising the manuscript before Christmas, but between then and 6 January 1930 he abandoned the original plan of recasting what now totalled nearly 25,000 words (with another 20,000 words of deleted material, some of which is in the Appendix to this volume) into an introduction for Carter's new book. Instead, he had the manuscript typed over the Christmas holidays and early in January wrote a new, short introduction for Carter. However, Carter did not include it in his book, now called *The Dragon of the Apocalypse*,²³ and the introduction was finally published posthumously as a separate essay in *The London Mercury* of July 1930. The long first introduction became Lawrence's last book, *Apocalypse*. He did not live to revise it. On 15 January he wrote: 'I shall lay my longer introduction by – not try to publish it now',²⁴ and although he was still writing a few poems and correcting some proofs, his vitality was diminishing rapidly. Weakened by the tuberculosis and pneumonia that were to kill him, Lawrence entered the Ad Astra Sanatorium at Vence on 6 February, where only the very late review of Eric Gill's *Art Nonsense and Other Essays* was still to be written before he died on 2 March.

Apocalypse, then, was the last sustained work of any length that Lawrence wrote. It is a strenuous enquiry into the forces that have shaped Western civilization and a final attempt to transmit his understanding of the complexity of human psychology to posterity. Like Nietzsche before him, Lawrence condemned the failure of Christian and democratic ideals in Western civilization, criticizing in particular Christianity's emphasis on renunciation, love and equality, which he felt denied the highly complex nature of the individual: 'Man is a being of power, and then a being of love' with a need 'to get a living balance between his nature of power and his nature of love, without denying either' (163:30, 35–6). In *Apocalypse* he explored this dual nature, the collective and individual selves as he termed them, arguing that by relinquishing earthly power and focusing only on love, Christ inevitably surrendered power to the mediocre and created a religion that would foster the self-glorification of the weak.

> One of the obscurest but profoundest needs of man is this need to belong to a group, a group called a church, or a nation, or an empire, and to feel the power thereof. And the chief reason for the profound dissatisfaction of today is that man is unhappy in his collective self. Modern nations no longer give adequate expression to the deeper, collective feelings of the men of the nation. They no longer express our true nature, the nature of power which is in us. (161:40–162:6)

Modern man must redress the balance, acknowledge the need for earthly splendour and power as embodied in the authority and greatness of the hero, the natural leader, one who 'transmits the life of the universe'.[25] In contemporary terms, Lawrence's views may seem to verge on the dangerously authoritarian, yet he detested any political system, 'whether it represent one man ... or a whole mass of people, a Demos',[26] which threatened to deny the freedom of the individual. In his exploration of political, social and religious systems he could be, and often was, infuriatingly contradictory, but the contradictions were always a way of exploring alternatives, part of a process of coming to a fuller understanding of the forces that move people and nations. He was especially fond of drawing a distinction between the aristocrat and the democrat, not in the sense of political or social categories, but rather as types of individuals, recognizing and confirming the innate differences that characterize human beings: 'mankind falls forever into the two divisions of aristocrat and democrat . . . We are speaking now not of political parties, but of the two sorts of human nature: those that feel themselves strong in their souls, and those that feel themselves weak' (65:6–7, 15–17). Essentially his view of man, then, is not political at all, but spiritual. The aristocrat is he who embodies the sense of divinity informing humanity, who can interfuse the earthly and the spiritual for the enrichment of the community. Lawrence argued that the goal for humanity must be to create a state where each individual can at once fully achieve his own potential and recognize and give homage to the different gifts in other men. And throughout his life and works he explored ways in which mankind could achieve this.

Central to Lawrence's thinking was his perception of man as a creature of dual consciousness, perpetually in conflict with himself, with the claims of emotion, instinct and the senses on the one hand, and those of the intellect and reason on the other. This is revealed in our two ways of knowing the universe: 'in terms of apartness, which is mental, rational, and scientific, and knowing in terms of togetherness, which is religious and poetic'.[27] The split into these two forms of knowledge, he believed, arose in classical times and is today especially manifested in man's increasing alienation from the natural world. Like the Romantics of the previous century, Lawrence was keenly alive to the mystery and beauty of the non-human universe and to the sense that the human species is a part of a vast creative pattern. At the same time he saw modern man as wilfully divorcing himself from that world through the products of human intellectual consciousness; all too often the quest for material gain and technological advance violate the integrity of the world of nature and thwart creative human impulses. It was for this reason that he so emphatically criticized the division between body and spirit, the flesh and the word, which he felt had arisen in classical Greece, Rome and Christianity. He argued for the end of the dominance of the Logos, the word, and the re-establishment of a balance between the spiritual and sensual planes of existence. Only through such re-integration could modern man attain inner harmony and regain a sense of living connection with the universe.

In *Apocalypse* Lawrence exemplifies the two forms of knowledge by drawing a distinction between the kind of understanding achieved by self-conscious mental activity and the deeper emotional awareness generated by sense-consciousness:

We have lost almost entirely the great and intricately developed sensual awareness, or sense-awareness, and sense-knowledge, of the ancients. It was a great depth of knowledge arrived at direct, by instinct and intuition, as we say, not by reason. It was a knowledge based not on words but on images. The abstraction was not into generalisations or into qualities, but into symbols. And the connection was not logical but emotional. The word 'therefore' did not exist. Images or symbols succeeded one another in a procession of instinctive and arbitrary physical connection – some of the Psalms give us examples – and they 'get nowhere' because there was nowhere to get to, the desire was to achieve a consummation of a certain state of consciousness, to fulfill a certain state of feeling-awareness ... Man thought and still thinks in images. But now our images have hardly any emotional value. (91:26–38, 93:1–2)

Here Lawrence's ideas about image and symbol also illuminate his own idiosyncratic method of interpreting Revelation, a method which eschews intellectual and scholarly analysis and instead relies on insights yielded by an imaginative response to the accumulation of images. His way of reading Revelation exemplifies the tendency of the creative mind, as he believed, to move naturally in cycles in its effort to attain full interpretation and understanding. He defines this method in *Apocalypse* as one which 'starts with an image, sets the image in motion, allows it to achieve a certain course or circuit of its own, and then takes up another image' (96:29–30) and allows 'the mind to move in cycles, or to flit here and there over a cluster of images' (97:1–2). The images, and the reader's responsive thoughts, then, modulate into one another in an associative process which is mimetic of the way the consciousness operates. It is also an apt description of Lawrence's own artistic style – the continual, slightly modified repetition, the vision and revision, which characterize his effort to articulate an idea or an impression.

By extension, this process is also particularly appropriate to the interpretation of an esoteric text such as Apocalypse. It may be that the scholarly attempt to recover an original meaning or original sources, though fascinating in itself, is ultimately an illusory quest, for each uncovered earlier myth would itself be based on some previous narrative or fable. Rather, the value of interpreting such texts may lie in their achievement as literature, in the stimulus they offer to the imagination, rather than in their validity as historical documents. Reading and interpreting a text is itself a creative action which can enrich our understanding. In biblical narrative, as Frank Kermode has pointed out, narrative and imagery are often characterized by gaps whose meaning must be actively supplied by the reader,[28] as the eye supplies the absent detail in an Impressionist painting. There is an absence of 'therefore', as Lawrence put it. It is a process that can also be seen at work in some of Lawrence's late poems, which often form clusters and show the working-out of a thought in several forms. The mutations these poems pass through reveal the habit of the poetic mind to move cyclically in the effort to articulate its insights. Of course, the very spontaneity of such a process has its dangers. It has been pointed out by many critics that at times Lawrence's writing becomes repetitive to an extent which threatens to damage the integrity of his art. Indeed, the stricture can be applied to *Apocalypse*, which is essentially a first draft, but in the freshness and beauty of its prose and in its powerful engagement with fundamental questions about the human and the divine and how these inform our lives, it remains one of Lawrence's most important works. In this respect his words on Carter's book are perhaps even more appropriate for his own:

> And so the value of these studies in the Apocalypse. They wake the imagination and give us at moments a new universe to live in . . . What does it matter if it is confused? What does it matter if it repeats itself? What does it matter if in parts it is not very interesting, when in other parts it is intensely so, when it suddenly opens doors and lets out the spirit into a new world, even if it is a very old world! (54:14–15, 24–7)

On a deeper level Lawrence's enquiry into the nature and function of image and symbol in *Apocalypse* may be seen as an expression not only of his deepening understanding of human consciousness but also of his effort to reconcile the disparate elements of the psyche within himself. His fascination with apocalyptic images, which he felt belong to an ancient matrix of mythopoeic imagination which modern man, with his emphasis on reason and science, has lost, is strikingly similar in some respects to the ideas of Jung, whose *Psychology of the Unconscious* Lawrence had read. Jung believed that there was a myth-creating level of mind, which he termed the collective unconscious, common to all civilizations and individuals, which gives form to emotional experience and hence meaning and significance to existence. Although he used different terms and examples, Jung, like Lawrence, felt that modern man has somehow become alienated from this mythopoeic aspect of his being. The result is that malaise of our century, the sense of futility, brought on by the decline of religion and the myths by which human existence had traditionally been shaped. For Jung, too, the psyche naturally seeks to resolve the contraries within itself, to integrate the disparate aspects of the inner, subjective self and bring them into harmony with the outer, objective world. To the achievement of this, and the sense of wholeness which it brings, Jung gave the name 'integration'. Similarly, for Lawrence the goal of every individual, analogous to that of the artist, is to 'create that work of art, the living man, achieve that piece of supreme art, a man's life'.[29] In a still wider sense, this activity was at once the means and aim of all existence, the creation and achieving of the self by its own powers: 'The final aim of every living thing, creature, or being is the full achievement of itself.'[30]

The spiritual journey towards integration and the sense of purpose and value which it brings, then, is the basic aim of human existence, but it is a journey most urgently undertaken in the second half of life and is thus also a preparation for death. Viewed in this way, Lawrence's analysis of the symbols of Revelation takes on new significance: the meeting of contraries such as the red and green dragons – the Agatho and Kako Daimon – the twin aspects of the woman as Cosmic Mother and Whore of Babylon, exemplify the psychic process of harmonizing the contraries within to attain wholeness. Moreover, it is significant that Lawrence should diverge from his analysis of the images in the first half of St John's narrative and turn to discuss the importance of number symbolism instead. He derived some of the examples of ancient numerological systems he uses here from his reading of Burnet and the latter's account of the pre-Socratic mathematician Pythagoras; in particular he cites Pythagoras's mathematical triangle of ten, the tetraktys of the dekad. This, as Jung points out, is a mandala, an emblem standing for the wholeness and integration of the self: 'Psychologically, the rotundum or mandala is a symbol of the self. The self is the archetype of order par excellence. The structure of the mandala is arithmetical, for "whole numbers" are likewise archetypes of order. This is true particularly of the Pythagorean tetraktys.'[31] Numbers, then, in mythology and in the consciousness are 'an aspect of the physically real as well as of the psychically imaginary' and are 'vehicles for psychic processes in the unconscious'.[32]

The direction and implications of Lawrence's approach to Revelation are now perhaps a little clearer. The creative energy of the psyche should be directed towards the attainment of integration, but our rational age, by so often diminishing the importance of the mythic substratum of the consciousness and its manifestations in art and religion, has impoverished human existence. By denying that anything has or can have numinous significance, we limit our understanding of reality itself. It was in this sense that Lawrence railed against the achievements of rational thought and scientific advance.

> I would like to know the stars again as the Chaldeans knew them, two thousand years before Christ . . . But our experience of the sun is dead, we are cut off. All we have now is the thought-form of the sun. He is a blazing ball of gas, he has spots occasionally, from some sort of indigestion, and he makes you brown and healthy if you let him . . . And that is all we have, poor things, of the sun . . . Where, for us, is the great and royal sun of the Chaldeans? Where even, for us, is the sun of the Old Testament, coming forth like a strong man to run a race? We have lost the sun. We have lost the sun, and we have found a few miserable thought-forms . . .
>
> Do you think you can put the universe apart, a dead lump here, a ball of gas there, a bit of fume somewhere else? How puerile it is, as if the universe were the back yard of some human chemical works! . . . The Chaldeans described the cosmos as they found it: magnificent. We describe the universe as we find it: mostly void, littered with a certain number of dead moons and unborn stars, like the back yard of a chemical works.
>
> Is our description true? Not for a single moment, once you change your state of mind . . . Our state of mind is becoming unbearable. We shall have to change it. And when we have changed it, we shall change our description of the universe entirely . . . We shall not get back the Chaldean vision of the living heavens. But the heavens will come to life again for us, and the vision will express also the new men that we are.
> (51:22–52:11, 53:31–54:13)

Lawrence's dislike of the limited concept of a tidy, post-Newtonian universe – one which acts by predictable laws that can be rationally discovered – anticipates the more recent findings of modern physics on unpredictability in chaos boundary conditions and the uncertainty principle in quantum mechanics. He would have found Fritjof Capra's *The Tao of Physics*, a fascinating account of parallels between physics and Eastern mysticism, eminently congenial. More recently,

Introduction

Murry Gell-Mann's *The Quark and the Jaguar* seeks to demonstrate the similarities between simple and complex systems in physics and the biological sciences, exploring different kinds of creativities which can encompass the birth of suns and the mind of man.[33] Lawrence's plea for a new vision based on a synthesis between science on the one hand and religion and the arts on the other foreshadows an important area of contemporary thinking. In this new synthesis there would need to be a reconciliation between the two forms of knowledge, as indeed he believed there had been in the far past: 'The religious systems of the pagan world . . . gave the true correspondence between the material cosmos and the human soul. The ancient cosmic theories were exact, and apparently perfect. In them science and religion were in accord.'[34] At the heart of this integrating process lay the recognition that rational thought and intuitive understanding were both ultimately manifestations of the same creative activity of the imagination. Quite early on, in the 'Study of Thomas Hardy' and the early versions of *Studies in Classic American Literature*, Lawrence had glimpsed the possibility of a 'harmony between the two halves of the psyche', the emotional and rational selves, and 'between religion and science',[35] but it was not until the late poems and his exploration of the two kinds of knowledge in the *Apocalypse* essays that he came to see them as aspects of the same basic faculty in the consciousness. In his discussion he first explores the contrary ways of seeing:

> . . . man has two ways of knowing the universe: religious and scientific. The religious way of knowledge means that we accept our sense-impressions, our perceptions, in the full sense of the word, complete, and we tend instinctively to link them up with other impressions, working towards a whole. The process is a process of association, linking up, binding back (religio) or referring back towards a centre and a wholeness. This is the way of poetic and religious consciousness, the instinctive act of synthesis . . .
>
> Science is only the contrary method . . . The scientific instinct breaks up or analyses the direct impression: that is the first step: and then logical reason enters, and makes inferences. Religion starts from impressions accepted whole and referred back to other impressions. Science starts from questioning an impression, and comparing it, *contrasting* it with another impression . . .
>
> There we see the two processes of the human consciousness.
> (190:14–191:14)

However, just as Lawrence came to see the body and soul as conceptually distinct but actually integrated (as we have seen, he called this self the 'biological psyche' or the 'physical psyche'), so the intellectual and intuitive selves were part of the same integral consciousness which he called the 'emotional mind'[36] or the 'emotional consciousness'. In the *Apocalypse* fragments (printed in this volume) he suggests that the scientific and religious states of mind are essentially manifestations of the same primary imaginative faculty.

> Anyone who knows the condition of supreme religious consciousness knows that the true modern physicist and mathematician ... is in a precisely similar state of mind or soul, or has passed through such a state, and builds his science on a description of this state ...
>
> Both ways end in the same place, the absolute somewhere or the absolute nowhere. But the method of approach is different. There is the method of association and unison, and the method of contrast and distinction ...
>
> The point of all this is that there need be no quarrel between our two ways of consciousness. (193:27–194:2)

This notion is of course a development of ideas Lawrence had suggested earlier in his writings, but it finds its most complete expression in the late poems and essays, where he describes this central function of human consciousness in different ways, calling it variously 'the sense of wonder', 'intrinsic naïveté', 'the essential act of attention'. In *Apocalypse* he also calls it 'the poetic intelligence', but it is always in essence the creative power that enables the psyche to imagine reality, to create those moments of insight and understanding that are its closest approach to the unknown power which informs the universe and which all cultures and times have seen as divine.

It has become a commonplace to say that we live in an age of crisis. Indeed, crisis appears to be a recurrent way of thinking about one's own time, as if there is something in the mind which predisposes us to see ourselves living at the end of an era, passing through a transitional state towards a new phase. One explanation of this habit may lie in the way we perceive time as a linear, forward flow and impose a fixed order on the past, seeing it as immutable, whereas we speak of the infinite possibilities of the future. In thermodynamic theory the arrow of time began with the compact single event (the Big Bang as it is popularly called) which formed the universe, and proceeds through its expansion and running down (entropy). In biological life this arrow moves inexorably from birth via the ageing of all living things to their dissolution. An associative pattern would seem to arise in the consciousness, of order arising from order in the past but not of course predictable for the future, so that the sense of being in the present is a sense of being poised between the known and the unknown, in a transitional stage between pattern (or knowledge) and chaos (the unknown), a chaos however which is pregnant with the possibilities of creativity and new patterning. In his late essay 'Chaos in Poetry', a review of Harry Crosby's *Chariot of the Sun*, Lawrence clarifies some of his ideas on the nature of the poetic imagination and the way humanity manufactures reality and imposes order on primordial chaos, in ways that both illuminate his later discussion of science and religion in *Apocalypse* and have considerable relevance to contemporary ideas about the nature of reality.

Using Crosby's book as a focus, much as he was to use the Book of Revelation for the exploration of analogous issues, Lawrence analyses the mind's predisposition to impose order on the chaos of the phenomenal world:

> Man, and the animals, and the flowers, all live within a strange and for ever surging chaos. The chaos which we have got used to we call a cosmos. The unspeakable inner chaos of which we are composed we call consciousness, and mind, and even civilization . . . But man cannot live in chaos . . . Man must wrap himself in a vision, make a house of apparent form and stability, fixity . . . Man fixes some wonderful erection of his own between himself and the wild chaos, and gradually goes bleached and stifled under his parasol. Then comes a poet, enemy of convention, and makes a slit in the umbrella; and lo! the glimpse of chaos is a vision, a window to the sun.[37]

It is also the habit of the scientific mind to replace one paradigm of reality, one set of theories, with another; and this process – of continually arriving at knowledge which modifies previous forms – determines man's understanding of the universe. The twentieth century in particular has recognized the dangers of reducing cosmic theory to a set of fixed formulae and the necessity to remain open to fresh insights. At another level this ability lies at the heart of all creativity; Lawrence called it an intuitive apprehension, a 'moment of inception in the soul, before the germs of the known and the unknown have fused to begin a new body of concepts'.[38] Such moments of insight, as Jung has pointed out, also reveal the mind's ability to grasp realities normally beyond human consciousness. He draws a distinction between consciously understood experience and the way 'our intuitions point to things that are unknown and hidden – that by their very nature are secret', to aspects of that objective world which exists in its own right but is only imperfectly known.[39] The imagination, then, is not an ephemeral state or condition, but basic to human consciousness itself and its way of perceiving and understanding the universe and humanity's place in it.

The discoveries of mathematics and physics in the second half of this century would also appear to bear out Lawrence's recognition that humanity is itself part of that dance of energies, the interconnected web, which is the cosmos. When Lawrence writes 'I am part of the sun as my eye is part of me. That I am part of the earth my feet know perfectly, and my blood is part of the sea' (149:20–22), he is not merely speaking metaphorically, but expressing the modern perception of nature as a dynamic network of relationships, of which the human observer, too, is an integral part.[40] In recent years this understanding has generated a significant shift in awareness, which embeds the human species much more firmly in the natural world and its workings. We have given popular names to this sense, speaking of the biosphere or Gaia, for example, seeing the coming era as one which will be based on a more holistic vision of the world rather than as a series of disassociated parts. We speak of the 'New Age' and 'The Age of Aquarius', in reference to the movement of the equinoctial sun out of the constellation of Pisces (which it entered 2,000 years ago, coinciding with the rise of Christianity) into that of Aquarius, the water-carrier: 'we are passing over the border of Pisces, into a new sign and a new era'[41] (98:18–19). The New Age may stimulate a renaissance of the intuitive and spiritual as modes of understanding, may move away from technological advance and the squandering of the earth's resources towards a new awareness of ecological issues, recognizing the mutual dependence of all natural phenomena. To speak of that New Age is a symbolic way of describing what may well be a major shift in humanity's perception of itself, as Capra and Gell-Mann have suggested[42] and as indeed Lawrence's essays in *Apocalypse* anticipated. Far from being an esoteric enquiry into an obscure book of the Bible, with which few people nowadays are familiar, Lawrence's exploration of the human psyche and human knowledge radiates into the heart of advances today in the fields of physics and psychology. In its exploration of the fluid, inner life of the imagination and in the connections it makes between that world and the outer worlds discovered by science, *Apocalypse* focuses on issues which we ignore at our peril: the need to re-create viable concepts of morality – uniting social and individual psychology, scientific advances and the creative arts – to give contemporary life the ethical meaning it appears increasingly to lack. For us, living at the close of the twentieth century and the opening of the twenty-first, these issues take on new urgency. But any evolving system of values, whether based on scientific or religious forms, which seeks to give coherence and meaning to existence must be founded on man's emotional need to envisage those values and his place in 'the living, incarnate cosmos' (149:20). If we are to preserve the delicate ecological system of this green earth, control the deadly technological innovations of the twentieth century, and enable our species to continue to evolve, we will need to foster those imaginative powers and non-material values which alone can give direction to mankind's adventure into the unknown. For that adventure in our time, as in Lawrence's, Blake's words are a fitting epitome: 'The Imagination is not a State: it is the Human Existence itself.'[43]

NOTES ON THE INTRODUCTION

1. Vivian de Sola Pinto and Warren Roberts, eds., *The Complete Poems of D. H. Lawrence*, 2 volumes (Heinemann, 1964), p. 666.

2. George J. Zytaruk and James T. Boulton, eds., *The Letters of D. H. Lawrence*, volume II (Cambridge University Press, 1982), 165. (Hereafter referred to as *Letters*, ii.)

3. Although DHL never wrote an introduction for it as originally planned, he and Carter met several times and corresponded, discussing ancient astrology, the validity of religious myths and the enduring relevance of Apocalypse and apocalyptic symbols. The immediate fruits of these discussions were DHL's two essays 'On Being Religious' and 'On Human Destiny', published in the *Adelphi* magazine in February and March 1924. Their discussion of the dragon emblem in Revelation clearly influenced DHL to make it the central symbol of his next novel, *The Plumed Serpent*.

4. Warren Roberts, James T. Boulton and Elizabeth Mansfield, eds., *The*

Letters of D. H. Lawrence, volume IV (Cambridge University Press, 1987), 405. (Hereafter referred to as *Letters*, iv.)

5. *Letters*, iv. 460.

6. Ibid.

7. 'Fenimore Cooper's Anglo-American Novels', in Armin Arnold, ed., *The Symbolic Meaning: The Uncollected Versions of Studies in Classic American Literature* (Centaur Press, 1991), p. 75.

8. Ibid.

9. James T. Boulton and Andrew Robertson, eds., *The Letters of D. H. Lawrence*, volume III (Cambridge University Press, 1984), 299. (Hereafter referred to as *Letters*, iii.)

10. 'Foreword' to D. H. Lawrence, *Fantasia of the Unconscious* (1922).

11. Throughout, DHL adds the definite article to the title *Book of Revelation*. The review was published in the April 1924 issue of the *Adelphi* magazine under the pseudonym L. H. Davidson.

12. See Keith Sagar and James T. Boulton, eds., *The Letters of D. H. Lawrence*, volume VII (Cambridge University Press, 1993), 515, 519, 560, 578, 589. (Hereafter referred to as *Letters*, vii.)

13. *Letters*, ii. 367, 364.

14. D. H. Lawrence, *Reflections on the Death of a Porcupine and Other Essays*, ed. Michael Herbert (Cambridge University Press, 1988), p. 359.

15. *Letters*, ii. 363.

16. John Burnet, *Early Greek Philosophy* (Black, 1892; 1925), p. 136.

17. *Reflections on the Death of a Porcupine*, p. 259.

18. Burnet, p. 48.

19. James T. Boulton, ed., *The Letters of D. H. Lawrence*, volume I (Cambridge University Press, 1979), 256. (Hereafter referred to as *Letters*, i.)

20. *Reflections on the Death of a Porcupine*, pp. 189–90.

21. Ibid., p. 208.

22. *Letters*, vii. 599.

23. 'I did about 6,000 words for Carter's Apocalypse book', *Letters*, vii. 618. Carter later changed the title to *The Dragon of Revelation* (1931), and later still the book was revised and reissued as *Symbols of Revelation* (1934).

24. *Letters*, vii. 622.

25. James T. Boulton and Margaret H. Boulton, with Gerald M. Lacy, eds., *The Letters of D. H. Lawrence*, volume VI (Cambridge University Press, 1991), 114. (Hereafter referred to as *Letters*, vi.)

26. *Reflections on the Death of a Porcupine*, p. 270.

27. D. H. Lawrence, *A Propos of 'Lady Chatterley's Lover'*, in *Lady Chatterley's Lover* (Penguin, 1994), p. 331.

28. See Frank Kermode, *Poetry, Narrative, History* (Blackwell, 1990), pp. 34–6.

29. *Letters*, ii. 299.

30. D. H. Lawrence, *Study of Thomas Hardy and other essays*, ed. Bruce Steele (Cambridge University Press, 1985), p. 12.

31. C. G. Jung, *Civilization in Transition, The Collected Works*, volume 10, trans. R. F. C. Hull (Routledge, 1964), p. 424.

32. Ibid., p. 409.

33. With apologies to Professor Gell-Mann, who rightly warns the reader: 'It seems to be characteristic of the impact of scientific discovery on the literary world and on popular culture that certain items of vocabulary, interpreted vaguely or inaccurately, are often the principal survivors of the journey from the technical publication to the popular magazine or paperback. The important qualifications and distinctions, and sometimes the actual ideas themselves, tend to get lost along the way.' *The Quark and the Jaguar* (W. H. Freeman, 1994), p. 27.

34. D. H. Lawrence, 'The Two Principles', in Warren Roberts and Harry T. Moore, eds., *Phoenix II: Uncollected, Unpublished and other Prose Works by D. H. Lawrence* (Heinemann, 1968), p. 227.

35. D. H. Lawrence, 'Nathaniel Hawthorne I', in *The Symbolic Meaning*, p. 138.

36. 'The Two Principles', in *Phoenix II*, p. 237.

37. Edward D. McDonald, ed., *Phoenix: The Posthumous Papers of D. H. Lawrence* (Heinemann, 1936), p. 255.

38. Ibid., p. 259.

39. C. G. Jung, *Modern Man in Search of a Soul*, trans. C. F. Baynes (Harcourt Brace, 1933), p. 157. Although Jung is speaking here of the visionary poet, his distinction between the kinds of imaginative insight is equally illuminating for the creative workings of the scientific mind.

40. For Fritjof Capra the perception of this interconnectedness 'enforces the similarities between the views of physicists and mystics; it also raises the intriguing possibility of relating subatomic physics to Jungian psychology . . . and it sheds new light on the fundamental role of probability in quantum physics'. Fritjof Capra, *The Tao of Physics* (Shambhala Publications, rev. edn 1991), p. 341.

41. See also *The Complete Poems*, p. 616: 'Dawn is no longer in the house of the Fish'. Interestingly, Jung speaks of the psychic changes in the collective psyche when one set of archetypes is replaced by another, 'which always appear at the end of one Platonic month and at the beginning of another . . . This transformation started in the historical era and left its traces first in the passing of the aeon of Taurus into that of Aries, and then of Aries into Pisces, whose beginning coincides with the rise of Christianity. We are now nearing that great change which

may be expected when the spring-point enters Aquarius.' Jung, *Civiliza-tion in Transition*, p. 311.

42. See the concluding paragraphs to Capra, *The Tao of Physics*, pp. 371–5 and Gell-Mann, *The Quark and the Jaguar*, p. 375.

43. William Blake, *Milton*, Book 2, Plate 32.

Note on the Texts

'A Review of The Book of Revelation by Dr. John Oman' and 'Introduction to The Dragon of the Apocalypse by Frederick Carter'

This edition reprints the 'Review' as it was published in the *Adelphi* magazine for April 1924, since there is no surviving manuscript or typescript. The base-text for the 'Introduction', however, is the manuscript DHL sent around 6 January 1930 to his agent, who placed it with *The London Mercury*, where it appeared in the July 1930 issue.

Apocalypse

There are only two complete versions of *Apocalypse*: the holograph manuscript, written in the autumn of 1929, and the typescript made over the Christmas holidays of 1929–30, which is extensively revised in DHL's handwriting. This typescript is the final stage in the production of *Apocalypse* that has any textual authority, since DHL did not live to see the publication of his last book. It is the base-text for the Cambridge Edition (1980) which is reproduced here.

The first edition, published in Florence by Giuseppe Orioli on 3 June 1931, contains many compositor's misreadings and errors of omission, punctuation and spelling. For example, DHL's habit of stylistic repetition, which sometimes caused his typists difficulty, here encouraged the printer's eye to jump between the lines, thus generating mistakes such as: 'mystification, and of all' when the typescript actually reads 'mystification. On the whole the modern mind dislikes mystification, and of all' (59:4–5). Similarly the Orioli edition reads 'On and on we go, for the mental consciousness', which makes no sense, whereas the text should read: 'On and on we go, for the mental consciousness labours under the illusion that there is somewhere to go to, a goal to consciousness' (93:7–9). The first edition has many wrong substantives, for example: 'Sion' for 'Sin' (63:10), 'sin' for 'six' (105:22) and 'reserved' for 'reversed' (69:16).

Moreover, Orioli himself, living as he did in Fascist Italy, altered the text. Alarmed by the references to Mussolini he deleted 'Mussolini is also a martyr' (146:16–17) and 'like Mussolini' (146:19), replacing the phrases with 'others also are martyrs' and 'like these'. This edition, based on DHL's final corrected text, restores the deletions made by Orioli and corrects the errors made in that edition and compounded by all subsequent editions.

Appendixes

The texts in these Appendixes are three draft manuscript portions of *Apocalypse* which DHL wrote in November 1929 but later deleted. Fragments 1 and 2 were part of the *Apocalypse* notebook (which was the basis for the typescript), and the third fragment, bearing the separate title *Apocalypsis II*, was written in a separate notebook. The texts reproduced here are those published in the Cambridge Edition (1980).

Advisory Editor's Note

I would like to thank Professor James T. Boulton and Professor F. Warren Roberts, General Editors of the *Cambridge Edition of the Works of D. H. Lawrence*, for their advice and planning in the preparation of this edition.

John Worthen, 1995

Facsimile of the title page of the First edition.

APOCALYPSE

BY

D. H. LAWRENCE

G. ORIOLI

FLORENCE

1931

A Review of
The Book of Revelation
by Dr. John Oman

The Apocalypse is a strange and mysterious book. One therefore welcomes any serious work upon it. Now Dr. John Oman (*The Book of Revelation*, Cambridge University Press, 7s. 6d. net) has undertaken the arrangement of the sections into an intelligible order. The clue to the order lies in the idea that the theme is the conflict between true and false religion, false religion being established upon the Beast of world empire. Behind the great outward happenings of the world lie the greater, but more mysterious happenings of the divine ordination. The Apocalypse unfolds in symbols the dual event of the crashing-down of world-empire and world-civilization, and the triumph of men in the way of God.

Dr. Oman's rearrangement and his exposition give one a good deal of satisfaction. The main drift we can surely accept. John's passionate and mystic hatred of the civilization of his day, a hatred so intense only because he knew that the living realities of men's being were displaced by it, is something to which the soul answers now again. His fierce, new usage of the symbols of the four Prophets of the Old Testament gives one a feeling of relief, of release into passionate actuality, after the tight pettiness of modern intellect.

Yet we cannot agree that Dr. Oman's explanation of the Apocalypse is exhaustive. No explanation of symbols is final. Symbols are not intellectual quantities, they are not to be exhausted by the intellect.

And an Apocalypse has, must have, is intended to have various levels or layers or strata of meaning. The fall of World Rule and World Empire before the Word of God is certainly one stratum. And perhaps it would be easier to leave it at that. Only it is not satisfying.

Why should Doctor Oman oppose the view that, besides the drama of the fall of World Rule and the triumph of the Word, there is another drama, or rather several other concurrent dramas? We gladly accept Dr. Oman's interpretation of the two Women and the Beasts. But why should he appear so unwilling to accept any astrological reference? Why should not the symbols have an astrological meaning, and the drama be also a drama of cosmic man, in terms of the stars?

Apocalypse

As a matter of fact, old symbols have many meanings, and we only define one meaning in order to leave another undefined. So with the meaning of the Book of Revelation. Hence the inexhaustibility of its attraction.

— L. H. Davidson.

Introduction to
The Dragon of the Apocalypse
by Frederick Carter

It is some years now since Frederick Carter first sent me the manuscript of his *Dragon of the Apocalypse*. I remember it arrived when I was staying in Mexico, in Chapala. The village post-master sent for me to the post-office: Will the honourable Señor please come to the post-office. I went, on a blazing April morning, there in the northern tropics. The post-master, a dark, fat Mexican with moustaches, was most polite: but also rather mysterious. There was a packet—did I know there was a packet? No, I didn't. Well, after a great deal of suspicious courtesy, the packet was produced; the rather battered typescript of the *Dragon*, together with some of Carter's line-engravings, mainly astrological, which went with it. The post-master handled them cautiously. What was it? What was it? It was a book, I said, the manuscript of a book, in English. Ah, but what sort of a book? What was the book about? I tried to explain, in my hesitating Spanish, what the *Dragon* was about, with its line-drawings. I didn't get far. The post-master looked darker and darker, more uneasy. At last he suggested, was it *magic*? I held my breath. It seemed like the Inquisition again. Then I tried to accommodate him. No, I said, it was not magic, but the *history* of magic. It was the history of what magicians had thought, in the past, and these were the designs they had used.—Ah! The postman was relieved. The history of magic! A scholastic work! And these were the designs they had used!—He fingered them gingerly, but fascinated.

And I walked home at last, under the blazing sun, with the bulky package under my arm. And then, in the cool of the patio, I read the beginning of the first *Dragon*.

The book was not then what it is now. Then, it was nearly all astrology, and very little argument. It was confused: it was, in a sense, a chaos. And it hadn't very much to do with St. John's Revelation. But that didn't matter to me. I was very often smothered in words. And then would come a page, or a chapter, that would release my imagination and give me a whole great sky to move in. For the first time I strode forth into the grand fields of the sky. And it was a real experience, for which I have been always grateful. And always the sensation comes back to me, of the dark shade on the veranda in Mexico, and the sudden release into the great sky of the old world, the sky of the zodiac.

I have read books of astronomy which made me dizzy with the sense of illimitable space. But the heart melts and dies, it is the disembodied mind alone which follows on through this horrible hollow void of space, where lonely stars hang in awful isolation. And this is not a release. It is a strange thing, but when science extends space *ad infinitum*, and we get the terrible sense of limitlessness, we have at the same time a secret sense of imprisonment. Three-dimensional space is homogeneous, and no matter *how* big it is, it is a kind of prison. No matter how vast the range of space, there is no release.

Why then, this sense of release, of marvellous release, in reading the *Dragon?* I don't know. But anyhow, the *whole* imagination is released, not a part only. In astronomical space, one can only *move*, one cannot *be*. In the astrological heavens, that is to say, the ancient zodiacal heavens, the whole man is set free, once the imagination crosses the border. The whole man, bodily and spiritual, walks in the magnificent fields of the stars, and the stars have names, and the feet tread splendidly upon—we know not what, but the heavens, instead of untreadable space.

It is an experience. To enter the astronomical sky of space is a great sensational experience. To enter the astrological sky of the zodiac and the living, roving planets is another experience, another *kind* of experience; it is truly imaginative, and to me, more valuable. It is not a mere extension of what we know: an extension that becomes awful, then appalling. It is the entry into another world, another kind of world, measured by another dimension. And we find some prisoned self in us coming forth to live in this world.

Now it is ridiculous for us to deny any experience. I well remember my first real experience of space, reading a book of modern astronomy. It was rather awful, and since then I rather hate the mere suggestion of illimitable space.

But I also remember very vividly my first experience of the astrological heavens, reading Frederick Carter's *Dragon:* the sense of being the macrocosm, the great sky with its meaningful stars and its profoundly meaningful motions, its wonderful bodily vastness, not empty, but all alive and doing. And I value this experience more. For the sense of astronomical space merely paralyses me. But the sense of the living astrological heavens gives me an extension of my being, I become big and glittering and vast with a sumptuous vastness. I am the macrocosm, and it is wonderful. And since I am not afraid to feel my own nothingness in front of the vast void of astronomical space, neither am I afraid to feel my own splendidness in the zodiacal heavens.

The *Dragon* as it exists now is no longer the *Dragon* which I read in Mexico. It has been made more—more argumentative, shall we say. Give me the old manuscript and let me write an introduction to that! I urge. But: No, says Carter. It isn't *sound*.

Sound what? He means his old astrological theory of the Apocalypse was not sound, as it was exposed in the old manuscript. But who cares? We do not care, vitally, about theories of the Apocalypse: what the Apocalypse means. What we care about is the release of the imagination. A real release of the imagination renews our strength and our vitality, makes us feel stronger and happier. Scholastic works don't release the imagination: at the best, they satisfy the intellect, and leave the body an unleavened lump. But when I get the release into the zodiacal cosmos my very feet feel lighter and stronger, my very knees are glad.

What does the Apocalypse matter, unless in so far as it gives us imaginative release into another vital world? After all, what meaning *has* the Apocalypse? For the ordinary reader, not much. For the ordinary student and biblical student, it means a prophetic vision of the martyrdom of the Christian Church, the Second Advent, the destruction of worldly power, particularly the power of the great Roman Empire, and then the institution of the Millennium, the rule of the risen Martyrs of Christendom for the space of one thousand years: after which, the end of everything, the Last Judgment, and souls in heaven; all earth, moon and sun being wiped out, all stars and all space. The New Jerusalem, and Finis!

This is all very fine, but we know it pretty well by now, so it offers no imaginative release to most people. It is the orthodox interpretation of the Apocalypse, and probably it is the true superficial meaning, or the final intentional meaning of the work. But what of it? It is a bore. Of all the stale buns, the New Jerusalem is one of the stalest. At the best, it was only invented for the Aunties of this world.

Yet when we read Revelation, we feel at once there are meanings behind meanings. The visions that we have known since childhood are not so easily exhausted by the orthodox commentators. And the phrases that have haunted us all our life, like: And I saw heaven opened, and behold! A white horse!—these are not explained quite away by orthodox explanations. When all is explained and expounded and commented upon, still there remains a curious fitful, half-spurious and half-splendid wonder in the work. Sometimes the great figures loom up marvellous. Sometimes there is a strange sense of incomprehensible drama. Sometimes the figures have a life of their own, inexplicable, which cannot be explained away or exhausted.

And gradually we realize that we are in the world of symbol as well as of allegory. Gradually we realize the book has no one meaning. It has meanings. Not meaning *within* meaning: but rather, meaning against meaning. No doubt the last writer left the Apocalypse as a sort of complete Christian allegory, a Pilgrim's Progress to the Judgment Day and the New Jerusalem: and the orthodox critics can explain the allegory fairly satisfactorily. But the Apocalypse is a compound work. It is no doubt the work of different men, of different generations and even different centuries.

So that we don't have to look for *a meaning*, as we can look for a meaning in an allegory like *Pilgrim's Progress*, or even like Dante. John of Patmos didn't *compose* the Apocalypse. The Apocalypse is the work of no one man. The Apocalypse began probably two centuries before Christ, as some small book, perhaps, of Pagan ritual, or some small pagan-Jewish Apocalypse written in symbols. It was written over by other Jewish apocalyptists, and finally came down to John of Patmos. He turned it more or less, rather less than more, into a Christian allegory. And later scribes trimmed up his work.

So the ultimate intentional, Christian meaning of the book is, in a sense, only plastered over. The great images incorporated are like the magnificent Greek pillars plastered into the Christian Church in Sicily: they are not merely allegorical figures: they are symbols, they belong to a bigger age than that of John of Patmos. And as symbols they defy John's superficial allegorical meaning. You can't give a great symbol a "meaning", any more than you can give a cat a "meaning". Symbols are organic units of consciousness with a life of their own, and you can never explain them away, because their value is dynamic, emotional, belonging to the sense-consciousness of the body and soul, and not simply mental. An allegorical image has a *meaning*. Mr. Facing-both-ways has a meaning. But I defy you to lay your finger on the full meaning of Janus, who is a symbol.

It is necessary for us to realize very definitely the difference between allegory and symbol. Allegory is narrative description using, as a rule, images to express certain definite qualities. Each image means something, and is a term in the argument and nearly always for a moral or didactic purpose, for under the narrative of an allegory lies a didactic argument, usually moral. Myth likewise is descriptive narrative using images. But myth is never an argument, it never has a didactic nor a moral purpose, you can draw no conclusion from it. Myth is an attempt to narrate a whole human experience, of which the purpose is too deep, going too deep in the blood and soul, for mental explanation or description. We *can* expound the myth of Kronos very easily. We can explain it, we can even draw the moral conclusion. But we only look a little silly. The myth of Kronos lives on beyond explanation, for it describes a profound experience of the human body and soul, an experience which is never exhausted and never will be exhausted, for it is being felt and suffered now, and it will be felt and suffered while man remains man. You may explain the myths away: but it only means you go on suffering blindly, stupidly, "in the unconscious" instead of healthily and with the imaginative comprehension playing upon the suffering.

And the images of myth are symbols. They don't "mean something". They stand for units of human *feeling*, human experience. A complex of emotional experience is a symbol. And the power of the symbol is to arouse the deep emotional self, and the dynamic self, beyond comprehension. Many ages of accumulated experience still throb within a symbol. And we throb in response. It takes centuries to create a really significant symbol: even the symbol of the Cross, or of the horse-shoe, or the horns. No man can invent symbols. He can invent an emblem, made up of images: or metaphors: or images: but not symbols. Some images, in the course of many generations of men, become symbols, embedded in the soul and ready to start alive when touched, carried on in the human consciousness for centuries. And again, when men become unresponsive and half dead, symbols die.

Now the Apocalypse has many splendid old symbols, to make us throb. And symbols suggest schemes of symbols. So the Apocalypse, with its symbols, suggests schemes of symbols, deep underneath its Christian-allegorical surface meaning of the Church of Christ.

And one of the chief schemes of symbols which the Apocalypse will suggest to any man who has a feeling for symbols, as contrasted with the orthodox feeling for allegory, is the astrological scheme. Again and again the symbols of the Apocalypse are astrological, the movement is star-movement, and these suggest an astrological scheme. Whether it is worth while to work out the astrological scheme from the impure text of the Apocalypse depends on the man who finds it worth while. Whether the scheme *can* be worked out remains for us to judge. In all probability there was once an astrological scheme there.

But what is certain is that the astrological symbols and suggestions are still there, they give us the lead. And the lead leads us sometimes out into a great imaginative world where we feel free and delighted. At least, that is my experience. So what does it matter whether the astrological scheme can be restored intact or not? Who cares about explaining the Apocalypse, either allegorically or astrologically or historically or any other way. All one cares about is the lead, the lead that the symbolic figures give us, and their dramatic movement: the lead, and where it will lead us to. If it leads to a release of the imagination into some new sort of world, then let us be thankful, for that is what we want. It matters so little to us who care more about life than about scholarship, what is correct or what is not correct. What does "correct" mean, anyhow? *Sanahorias* is the Spanish for carrots: I hope I am correct. But what are carrots correct for?

What the ass wants is carrots; not the idea of carrots, nor thought-forms of carrots, but carrots. The Spanish ass doesn't even know that he is eating *sanahorias*. He just eats and feels blissfully full of carrot. Now does *he* have more of the carrot, who eats it, or do I, who know that in Spanish it is called a *sanahoria* (I hope I am correct) and in botany it belongs to the *umbelliferæ*?

We are full of the wind of thought-forms, and starved for a good carrot. I don't care *what* a man sets out to prove, so long as he will interest me and carry me away. I don't in the least care whether he proves his point or not, so long as he has given me a real imaginative experience by the way, and not another set of bloated thought-forms. We are starved to death, fed on the eternal sodom-apples of thought-forms. What we want is *complete* imaginative experience, which goes through the whole soul and body. Even at the expense of reason we want imaginative experience. For reason is certainly not the final judge of life.

Though, if we pause to think about it, we shall realize that it is not Reason herself whom we have to defy, it is her myrmidons, our accepted ideas and thought-forms. Reason can adjust herself to almost anything, if we will only free her from her crinoline and powdered wig, with which she was invested in the eighteenth and nineteenth centuries. Reason is a supple nymph, and slippery as a fish by nature.

She had as leave give her kiss to an absurdity any day, as to syllogistic truth. The absurdity may turn out truer.

So we need not feel ashamed of flirting with the zodiac. The zodiac is well worth flirting with. But not in the rather silly modern way of horoscopy and telling your fortune by the stars. Telling your fortune by the stars, or trying to get a tip from the stables, before a horse-race. You want to know what horse to put your money on. Horoscopy is just the same. They want their "fortune" told: never their misfortune.

Surely one of the greatest imaginative experiences the human race has ever had was the Chaldean experience of the stars, including the sun and moon. Sometimes it seems it must have been greater experience than any god-experience. For God is only a great imaginative experience. And sometimes it seems as if the experience of the living heavens, with a living yet not human sun, and brilliant living stars in *live* space must have been the most magnificent of all experiences, greater than any Jehovah or Baal, Buddha or Jesus. It may seem an absurdity to talk of *live* space. But is it? While we are warm and well and "unconscious" of our bodies, are we not all the time ultimately conscious of our bodies in the same way, as live or living space? And is not this the reason why void space so terrifies us?

I would like to know the stars again as the Chaldeans knew them, two thousand years before Christ. I would like to be able to put my ego into the sun, and my personality into the moon, and my character into the planets, and live the life of the heavens, as the early Chaldeans did. The human consciousness is really homogeneous. There is no complete forgetting, even in death. So that somewhere within us the old experience of the Euphrates, Mesopotamia between the rivers, lives still. And in my Mesopotamian self I long for the sun again, and the moon and stars, for the Chaldean sun and the Chaldean stars. I long for them terribly. Because *our* sun and *our* moon are only thought-forms to us, balls of gas, dead globes of extinct volcanoes, things we *know* but never feel by experience. By *experience*, we should feel the sun as the savages feel him, we should "know" him as the Chaldeans knew him, in a terrific embrace. But our experience of the sun is dead, we are cut off. All we have now is the thought-form of the sun. He is a blazing ball of gas, he has spots occasionally, from some sort of indigestion, and he makes you brown and healthy if you let him. The first two "facts" we should never have known if men with telescopes, called astronomers, hadn't told us. It is obvious, they are mere thought-forms. The third "fact", about being brown and healthy, we believe because the doctors have told us it is so. As a matter of fact, many neurotic people become more and more neurotic, the browner and "healthier" they become by sun-baking. The sun can rot as well as ripen. So the third fact is also a thought-form.

And that is all we have, poor things, of the sun. Two or three cheap and inadequate thought-forms. Where, for us, is the great and royal sun of the Chaldeans? Where even, for us, is the sun of the Old Testament, coming forth like a strong man to run a race? We have lost the sun. We have lost the sun, and we have found a few miserable thought-forms. A ball of blazing gas! with spots! he browns you!

To be sure, we are not the first to lose the sun. The Babylonians themselves began the losing of him. The great and living heavens of the Chaldeans deteriorated already in Belshazzar's day to the fortune-telling disc of the night skies. But that was man's fault, not the heavens'. Man always deteriorates. And when he deteriorates he always becomes inordinately concerned about his "fortune" and his fate. While life itself is fascinating, fortune is completely uninteresting, and the idea of fate does not enter. When men become poor in life then they become anxious about their fortune and frightened about their fate. By the time of Jesus, men had become so anxious about their fortunes and so frightened about their fates, that they put up the grand declaration that life was one long misery and you couldn't expect your fortune till you got to heaven; that is, till after you were dead. This was accepted by all men, and has been the creed till our day, Buddha and Jesus alike. It has provided us with a vast amount of thought-forms, and landed us in a sort of living death.

So now we want the sun again. Not the spotted ball of gas that browns you like a joint of meat, but the living sun, and the living moon of the old Chaldean days. Think of the moon, think of Artemis and Cybele, think of the white wonder of the skies, so rounded, so velvety, moving so serene; and then think of the pock-marked horror of the scientific photographs of the moon!

But when we have seen the pock-marked face of the moon in scientific photographs, need that be the end of the moon for us? Even rationally? I think not. It is a great blow: but the imagination can recover from it. Even if we have to believe the pock-marked photograph, even if we believe in the cold and snow and utter deadness of the moon—which we *don't* quite believe—the moon is not therefore a dead nothing. The moon is a white strange world, great, white, soft-seeming globe in the night sky, and what she actually communicates to me across space I shall never fully know. But the moon that pulls the tides, and the moon that controls the menstrual periods of women, and the moon that touches the lunatics, she is not the mere dead lump of the astronomist. The moon is the great moon still, she gives forth her soft and feline influences, she sways us still, and asks for sympathy back again. In her so-called deadness there is enormous potency still, and power even over our lives. The Moon! Artemis! the great goddess of the splendid past of men! Are you going to tell me she is a dead lump?

She is not dead. But maybe we are dead, half-dead little modern worms stuffing our damp carcasses with thought-forms that have no sensual reality. When we describe the moon as dead, we are describing the deadness in ourselves. When we find space so hideously void, we are describing our own unbearable emptiness. Do we imagine that we, poor worms with spectacles and telescopes and thought-forms, are really more conscious, more vitally aware of the universe than the men in the past were, who called the moon Artemis, or Cybele, or Astarte? Do we imagine that we really, livingly know the moon better than they knew her? That our knowledge of the moon is more real, more "sound"? Let us disabuse ourselves. We know the moon in terms of our own telescopes and our own deadness. We know everything in terms of our own deadness.

But the moon is Artemis still, and a dangerous goddess she is, as she always was. She throws her cold contempt on you as she passes over the sky, poor, mean little worm of a man who thinks she is nothing but a dead lump. She throws back the cold white vitriol of her angry contempt on to your mean, tense nerves, nervous man, and she is corroding you away. Don't think you can escape the moon, any more than you can escape breathing. She is on the air you breathe. She is active within the atom. Her sting is part of the activity of the electron.

Do you think you can put the universe apart, a dead lump here, a ball of gas there, a bit of fume somewhere else? How puerile it is, as if the universe were the back yard of some human chemical works! How gibbering man becomes, when he is really clever, and thinks he is giving the ultimate and final description of the universe! Can't he see that he is merely describing himself, and that the self he is describing is merely one of the more dead and dreary states that man can exist in? When man changes his state of being, he needs an entirely different description of the universe, and so the universe changes its nature to him entirely. Just as the nature of our universe is entirely different from the nature of the Chaldean cosmos. The Chaldeans described the cosmos as they found it: magnificent. We describe the universe as we find it: mostly void, littered with a certain number of dead moons and unborn stars, like the back yard of a chemical works.

Is our description true? Not for a single moment, once you change your state of mind: or your state of soul. It is true for our present deadened state of mind. Our state of mind is becoming unbearable. We shall have to change it. And when we have changed it, we shall change our description of the universe entirely. We shall not call the moon Artemis, but the new name will be nearer to Artemis than to a dead lump or an extinct globe. We shall not get back the Chaldean vision of the living heavens. But the heavens will come to life again for us, and the vision will express also the new men that we are.

And so the value of these studies in the Apocalypse. They wake the imagination and give us at moments a new universe to live in. We may think it is the old cosmos of the Babylonians, but it isn't. We can never recover an old vision, once it has been supplanted. But what we can do is to discover a new vision in harmony with the memories of old, far-off, far, far-off experience that lie within us. So long as we are not deadened or drossy, memories of Chaldean experience still live within us, at great depths, and can vivify our impulses in a new direction, once we awaken them.

Therefore we ought to be grateful for a book like this of the *Dragon*. What does it matter if it is confused? What does it matter if it repeats itself? What does it matter if in parts it is not very interesting, when in other parts it is intensely so, when it suddenly opens doors and lets out the spirit into a new world, even if it is a very old world! I admit that I cannot see eye to eye with Mr. Carter about the Apocalypse itself. I cannot, myself, feel that old John of Patmos spent his time on his island lying on his back and gazing at the resplendent heavens; then afterwards writing a book in which all the magnificent cosmic and starry drama is deliberately wrapped up in Jewish-Christian moral threats and vengeances, sometimes rather vulgar.

But that, no doubt, is due to our different approach to the book. I was brought up on the Bible, and seem to have it in my bones. From early childhood I have been familiar with Apocalyptic language and Apocalyptic image: not because I spent my time reading Revelation, but because I was sent to Sunday School and to Chapel, to Band of Hope and to Christian Endeavour, and was always having the Bible read at me or to me. I did not even listen attentively. But language has a power of echoing and re-echoing in my unconscious mind. I can wake up in the night and "hear" things being said—or hear a piece of music—to which I had paid no attention during the day. The very sound itself registers. And so the sound of Revelation had registered in me very early, and I was as used to: "I was in the Spirit on the Lord's day, and heard behind me a great voice, as of a trumpet, saying: I am the Alpha and the Omega"— as I was to a nursery rhyme like Little Bo-Peep! I didn't know the meaning, but then children so often prefer sound to sense. "Alleluia: for the Lord God omnipotent reigneth". The Apocalypse is full of sounding phrases, beloved by the uneducated in the chapels for their true liturgical powers. "And he treadeth the winepress of the fierceness and wrath of Almighty God".

No, for me the Apocalypse is altogether too full of fierce feeling, fierce and moral, to be a grand disguised star-myth. And yet it has intimate connexion with star-myths and the movement of the astrological heavens: a sort of submerged star-meaning. And nothing delights me more than to escape from the all-too-moral chapel meaning of the book, to another wider, older, more magnificent meaning. In fact, one of the real joys of middle age is in coming back to the Bible, reading a new translation, such as Moffatt's, reading the modern research and modern criticism of some Old Testament books, and of the Gospels, and getting a whole new conception of the Scriptures altogether. Modern research has been able to put the Bible back into its living connexions, and it is splendid: no longer the Jewish-moral book and a stick to beat an immoral dog, but a fascinating account of the adventure of the Jewish—or Hebrew or Israelite nation, among the great old civilized nations of the past, Egypt, Assyria, Babylon, and Persia: then on into the Hellenic world, the Seleucids, and the Romans, Pompey and Anthony. Reading the Bible in a new translation, with modern notes and comments, is more fascinating than reading Homer, for the adventure goes even deeper into time and into the soul, and continues through the centuries, and moves from Egypt to Ur and to Nineveh, from Sheba to Tarshish and Athens and Rome. It is the very quick of ancient history.

And the Apocalypse, the last and presumably the latest of the books of the Bible, also comes to life with a great new life, once we look at its symbols and take the lead that they offer us. The text leads most easily into the great chaotic Hellenic world of the first century: Hellenic, not Roman. But the symbols lead much further back.

They lead Frederick Carter back to Chaldea and to Persia, chiefly, for his skies are the late Chaldean, and his mystery is chiefly Mithraic. Hints, we have only hints from the outside. But the rest is within us, and if we can take a hint, it is extraordinary how far and into what fascinating worlds the hints can lead us. The orthodox critics will say: Fantasy! Nothing but fantasy! But then, thank God for fantasy, if it enhances our life.

And even so, the "reproach" is not quite just. The Apocalypse has an old, submerged astrological meaning, and probably even an old astrological scheme. The hints are too obvious and too splendid: like the ruins of an old temple incorporated in a Christian chapel. Is it any more fantastic to try to reconstruct the embedded temple, than to insist that the embedded images and columns are mere rubble in the Christian building, and have no meaning? It is as fantastic to deny meaning when meaning is there, as it is to invent meaning when there is none. And it is much duller. For the invented meaning may still have a life of its own.

Apocalypse

I

Apocalypse means simply Revelation, though there is nothing simple about this one, since men have puzzled their brains for nearly two thousand years to find out what, exactly, is revealed in all its orgy of mystification. On the whole, the modern mind dislikes mystification, and of all the books in the Bible, it finds Revelation perhaps the least attractive.

That is my own first feeling about it. From earliest years right into manhood, like any other nonconformist child I had the Bible poured every day into my helpless consciousness, till there came almost a saturation point. Long before one could think or even vaguely understand, this Bible language, these "portions" of the Bible were *douched* over the mind and consciousness, till they became soaked in, they became an influence which affected all the processes of emotion and thought. So that today, although I have "forgotten" my Bible, I need only begin to read a chapter to realise that I "know" it with an almost nauseating fixity. And I must confess, my first reaction is one of dislike, repulsion, and even resentment. My very instincts *resent* the Bible.

The reason is now fairly plain to me. Not only was the Bible, in portions, poured into the childish consciousness day in, day out, year in, year out, willy nilly, whether the consciousness could assimilate it or not, but also it was day in, day out, year in, year out expounded, dogmatically, and always morally expounded, whether it was in day-school or Sunday School, at home or in Band of Hope or Christian Endeavour. The interpretation was always the same, whether it was a Doctor of Divinity in the pulpit, or the big blacksmith who was my Sunday School teacher. Not only was the Bible verbally trodden into the consciousness, like innumerable foot-prints treading a surface hard, but the foot-prints were always mechanically alike, the interpretation was fixed, so that all real interest was lost.

The process defeats its own ends. While the Jewish poetry penetrates the emotions and the imagination, and the Jewish morality penetrates the instincts, the mind becomes stubborn, resistant, and at last

59

repudiates the whole Bible authority, and turns with a kind of repugnance away from the Bible altogether. And this is the condition of many men of my generation.

Now a book lives as long as it is unfathomed. Once it is fathomed, it dies at once. It is an amazing thing, how utterly different a book will be, if I read it again after five years. Some books gain immensely, they are a new thing. They are so astonishingly different, they make a man question his own identity. Again, other books lose immensely. I read *War and Peace* once more, and was amazed to find how little it moved me, I was almost aghast to think of the raptures I had once felt, and now felt no more.

So it is. Once a book is fathomed, once it is *known*, and its meaning is fixed or established, it is dead. A book only lives while it has power to move us, and move us *differently*; so long as we find it *different* every time we read it. Owing to the flood of shallow books which really are exhausted in one reading, the modern mind tends to think every book is the same, finished in one reading. But it is not so. And gradually the modern mind will realise it again. The real joy of a book lies in reading it over and over again, and always finding it different, coming upon another meaning, another level of meaning. It is, as usual, a question of values: we are so overwhelmed with *quantities* of books, that we hardly realise any more that a book can be valuable, valuable like a jewel, or a lovely picture, into which you can look deeper and deeper and get a more profound experience every time. It is far, far better to read one book six times, at intervals, than to read six several books. Because if a certain book can call you to read it six times, it will be a deeper and deeper experience each time, and will enrich the whole soul, emotional and mental. Whereas six books read once only are merely an accumulation of superficial interest, the burdensome accumulation of modern days, quantity without real value.

We shall now see the reading public dividing again into two groups: the vast mass, who read for amusement and for momentary interest, and the small minority, who only want the books that have value to themselves, books which yield experience, and still deeper experience.

The Bible is a book that has been temporarily killed for us, or for some of us, by having its meaning arbitrarily fixed. We know it so thoroughly, in its superficial or popular meaning, that it is dead, it gives us nothing any more. Worse still, by old habit amounting almost to instinct, it imposes on us a whole state of feeling which is now repugnant to us. We detest the "chapel" and the Sunday School feeling which the Bible must necessarily impose on us. We want to get rid of all that *vulgarity*—for vulgarity it is.

Perhaps the most detestable of all these books of the Bible, taken superficially, is Revelation. By the time I was ten, I am sure I had heard, and read, that book ten times over, even without knowing or taking real heed. And without ever knowing or thinking about it, I am sure it always roused in me a real dislike. Without realising it, I must, from earliest childhood have detested the pie-pie, mouthing, solemn, portentous, loud way in which everybody read the Bible, whether it was parsons or teachers or ordinary persons. I dislike the "parson" voice through and through my bones. And this voice, I remember, was always at its worst when mouthing out some portion of Revelation. Even the phrases that still fascinate me I cannot recall without shuddering, because I can still hear the portentous declamation of a nonconformist clergyman: "And I saw heaven opened, and behold a white horse; and he that sat upon it was called"—there my memory suddenly stops, deliberately blotting out the next words: "Faithful and True". I hated, even as a child, allegory: people having the names of mere qualities, like this somebody on a white horse, called "Faithful and True". In the same way I could never read *Pilgrim's Progress*. When as a small boy I learnt from Euclid that: "The whole is greater than the part", I immediately knew that that solved the problem of allegory for me. A man is more than a Christian, a rider on a white horse must be more than mere Faithfulness and Truth, and when people are merely personifications of qualities they cease to be people for me. Though as a young man I almost loved Spenser and his *Faerie Queen*, I had to' gulp at his allegory.

But the Apocalypse is, and always was from earliest childhood, to me antipathetic. In the first place its splendiferous imagery is distasteful because of its complete unnaturalness. "And before the throne there was a sea of glass like unto crystal: and in the midst of the throne and round about the throne were four beasts full of eyes before and behind.

"And the first beast was like a lion, and the second beast like a calf, and the third beast had a face as a man, and the fourth beast was like a flying eagle.

"And the four beasts had each of them six wings about him; and they were full of eyes within: and they rest not day and night, saying, Holy, holy, holy, Lord God Almighty, which was, and is, and is to come—".

A passage like that irritated and annoyed my boyish mind because of its pompous unnaturalness. If it is imagery, it is imagery which cannot be imagined: for how can four beasts be "full of eyes before and behind", and how can they be "in the midst of the throne and round about the throne"? They can't be somewhere and somewhere else at the same time. But that is how the Apocalypse is.

Again, much of the imagery is utterly unpoetic and arbitrary, some of it really ugly, like all the wadings in blood, and the rider's shirt dipped in blood, and people washed in the blood of the Lamb. Also such phrases as "the wrath of the Lamb" are on the face of them ridiculous. But this is the grand phraseology and imagery of the nonconformist chapels, all the Bethels of England and America, and all the Salvation armies. And vital religion is said to be found, in all ages, down among the uneducated people.

Down among the uneducated people you will still find Revelation rampant. I think it has had, and perhaps still has more influence, actually, than the Gospels or the great Epistles. The huge denunciation of kings and Rulers, and of the whore that sitteth upon the waters, is entirely sympathetic to a Tuesday evening congregation of colliers and colliers' wives, on a black winter night, in the great barn-like Pentecost chapel. And the capital letters of the name: MYSTERY, BABYLON THE GREAT, THE MOTHER OF HARLOTS AND ABOMINATIONS OF THE EARTH thrill the old colliers today as they thrilled the Scotch Puritan peasants and the more ferocious of the early Christians. To the underground early Christians, Babylon the great meant Rome, the great city and the great empire which persecuted them. And great was the satisfaction of denouncing her and bringing her to utter, utter woe and destruction, with all her kings, her wealth and her lordliness. After the Reformation Babylon was once more identified with Rome, but this time it meant the Pope, and in Protestant and nonconformist England and Scotland out rolled the denunciations of John the Divine, with the grand cry: "Babylon the great is fallen, is fallen, and is become the habitation of devils, and the hold of every foul spirit, and a cage of every unclean and hateful bird—". Nowadays the words are still mouthed out, and sometimes still they are hurled at the Pope and the Roman Catholics, who seem to be lifting their heads up again. But more often, today, Babylon means the rich and wicked people who live in luxury and harlotry somewhere in the vague distance, London, New York, or Paris worst of all, and who never once set foot in "chapel", all their lives.

It is very nice, if you are poor and *not* humble—and the poor may be obsequious, but they are almost *never* truly humble, in the Christian sense—to bring your grand enemies down to utter destruction and discomfiture, while you yourself rise up to grandeur. And nowhere does this happen so splendiferously as in Revelation. The great enemy in the eyes of Jesus was the Pharisee, harping on the letter of the law. But the Pharisee is too remote and subtle for the collier and the factory-worker. The Salvation Army at the street corner rarely raves about Pharisees. It raves about the Blood of the Lamb, and Babylon, Sin, and Sinners, the great harlot, and angels that cry Woe, Woe, Woe! and Vials that pour out horrible plagues. And above all, about being Saved, and sitting on the Throne with the Lamb, and reigning in Glory, and having Everlasting Life, and living in a grand city made of jasper, with gates of pearl: a city that "had no need of the sun, neither of the moon, to shine in it". If you listen to the Salvation Army you will hear that they are going to be very grand, very grand indeed, once they get to heaven. *Then* they'll show you what's what. *Then* you'll be put in your place, you superior person, you Babylon: down in hell and in brimstone.

This is entirely the tone of Revelation. What we realise when we have read the precious book a few times is that John the Divine had, on the face of it, a grandiose scheme for wiping out and annihilating everybody who wasn't of the elect, the chosen people, in short, and of climbing up himself right on to the throne of God. With nonconformity, the chapel people took over to themselves the Jewish idea of the chosen people. They were "it", the elect, or the "saved". And they took over the Jewish idea of ultimate triumph and reign of the chosen people. From being bottom dogs they were going to be top dogs: in Heaven. If not sitting actually on the throne, they were going to sit in the lap of the enthroned Lamb. It is doctrine you can hear any night from the Salvation Army or in any Bethel or Pentecost Chapel. If it is not Jesus, it is John. If it is not Gospel, it is Revelation. It is popular religion, as distinct from thoughtful religion.

II

Or at least, it was popular religion when I was a boy. And I remember, as a child, I used to wonder over the curious sense of self-glory which one felt in the uneducated leaders, the men especially of the Primitive Methodist Chapels. They were not on the whole pious or mealy-mouthed or objectionable, these colliers who spoke heavy dialect and ran the "Pentecost". They certainly were not humble or apologetic. No, they came in from the pit and sat down to their dinners with a bang, and their wives and daughters ran to wait on them quite cheerfully, and their sons obeyed them without overmuch resentment. The home was rough yet not unpleasant, and there was an odd sense of wild mystery or power about, as if the chapel men really had some dispensation of rude power from above. Not love, but a rough and rather wild, somewhat "special" sense of power. They were so *sure*, and as a rule their wives were quite humble to them. They ran a chapel, so they could run their household. I used to wonder over it, and rather enjoy it. But even I thought it rather "common". My mother, who was Congregationalist, never set foot in a Primitive Methodist chapel in her life, I don't suppose. And she was certainly not prepared to be humble to her husband. If he'd been a real cheeky chapel man, she would no doubt have been much meeker with him. Cheek, that was the outstanding quality of chapel men. But a special kind of cheek, authorised from above, as it were. And I know now, a good deal of this special kind of religious cheek was backed up by the Apocalypse.

It was not till many years had gone by, and I had read something of comparative religion and the history of religion, that I realised what a strange book it was that had inspired the colliers on the black Tuesday nights in Pentecost or Beauvale Chapel to such a queer sense of special authority and of religious cheek. Strange marvellous black nights of the north Midlands, with the gas-light hissing in the chapel, and the roaring of the strong-voiced colliers. Popular religion: a religion of self-glorification and power, forever! and of darkness. No wailing "Lead kindly Light"! about it.

The longer one lives, the more one realises that there are two kinds of Christianity, the one focussed on Jesus and the Command: Love one another!—and the other focussed, not on Paul or Peter or John the Beloved, but on the Apocalypse. There is the Christianity of tenderness. But as far as I can see, it is utterly pushed aside by the Christianity of self-glorification: the self-glorification of the humble.

There's no getting away from it, mankind falls forever into the two divisions of aristocrat and democrat. The purest aristocrats during the Christian era have taught democracy. And the purest democrats try to turn themselves into the most absolute aristocracy. Jesus was an aristocrat, so was John the Apostle, and Paul. It takes a great aristocrat to be capable of great tenderness and gentleness and unselfishness: the tenderness and gentleness of *strength*. From the democrat you may often get the tenderness and gentleness of weakness: that's another thing. But you usually get a sense of toughness.

We are speaking now not of political parties, but of the two sorts of human nature: those that feel themselves strong in their souls, and those that feel themselves weak. Jesus and Paul and the greater John felt themselves strong. John of Patmos felt himself weak, in his very soul.

In Jesus' day, the inwardly strong men everywhere had lost their desire to rule on earth. They wished to withdraw their strength from earthly rule and earthly power, and to apply it to another form of life. Then the weak began to rouse up and to feel *inordinately* conceited, they began to express their rampant hate of the "obvious" strong ones, the men in worldly power.

So that religion, the Christian religion especially, became dual. The religion of the strong taught renunciation and love. And the religion of the weak taught *down with the strong and the powerful, and let the poor be glorified*. Since there are always more weak people than strong, in the world, the second sort of Christianity has triumphed and will triumph. If the weak are not ruled, they will rule, and there's the end of it. And the rule of the weak is *Down with the strong!*

The grand biblical authority for this cry is the Apocalypse. The weak and pseudo-humble are going to wipe all worldly power, glory and riches off the face of the earth, and then they, the truly weak, are going to reign. It will be a millennium of pseudo-humble saints, and gruesome to contemplate. But it is what religion stands for today: down with all strong, free life, let the weak triumph, let the pseudo-humble reign. The religion of the self-glorification of the weak, the reign of the pseudo-humble. This is the spirit of society today, religious and political.

III

And this was pretty well the religion of John of Patmos. They say he was an old man already when he finished the Apocalypse in the year 96 A.D.: which is the date fixed by modern scholars, from "internal evidence".

Now there were three Johns in early Christian history: John the Baptist, who baptised Jesus, and who apparently founded a religion, or at least a sect of his own, with strange doctrines that continued for many years after Jesus' death; then there was the Apostle John, who was supposed to have written the Fourth Gospel and some Epistles; then there was this John of Patmos who lived in Ephesus and was sent to prison on Patmos for some religious offence against the Roman State. He was, however, released from his island after a term of years, returned to Ephesus and lived, according to legend, to a great old age.

For a long time it was thought that the Apostle John, to whom we ascribe the Fourth Gospel, had written the Apocalypse also. But it cannot be that the same man wrote the two works, they are so alien to one another. The author of the Fourth Gospel was surely a cultured "Greek" Jew, and one of the great inspirers of mystic, "loving" Christianity. John of Patmos must have had a very different nature. He certainly has inspired very different feelings.

When we come to read it critically and seriously, we realise that the Apocalypse reveals a profoundly important Christian doctrine which has in it none of the real Christ, none of the real Gospel, none of the *creative* breath of Christianity, and is nevertheless perhaps the most effectual doctrine in the Bible. That is, it has had a greater effect on second-rate people throughout the Christian ages, than any other book in the Bible. The Apocalypse of John is, as it stands, the work of a second-rate mind. It appeals intensely to second-rate minds in every country and every century. Strangely enough, unintelligible as it is, it has no doubt been the greatest source of inspiration to the vast mass of Christian minds—the vast mass being always second-rate—since the first century. And we realise, to our horror, that this is what we are up against today: not Jesus nor Paul, but John of Patmos.

The Christian doctrine of love even at its best was an evasion. Even Jesus was going to reign "hereafter", when his "love" would be turned into confirmed power. This business of reigning in glory hereafter went to the root of Christianity: and is, of course, only an expression of frustrated desire to reign here and now. The Jews would not be put off: they were determined to reign on earth, so after the Temple of Jerusalem was smashed for the second time, about 200 B.C., they started in to imagine the coming of a Messiah militant and triumphant, who would conquer the world. The Christians took this up as the Second Advent of Christ, when Jesus was coming to give the gentile world its final whipping, and establish a rule of saints. John of Patmos extended this previously modest rule of saints (about forty years) to the grand round number of a thousand years, and so the Millennium took hold of the imagination of man.

And so there crept into the New Testament the grand Christian enemy, the Power-spirit. At the very last moment, when the devil had been so beautifully shut out, in he slipped, dressed in Apocalyptic disguise, and enthroned himself at the end of the book as Revelation.

For Revelation, be it said once and for all, is the revelation of the undying will-to-power in man, and its sanctification, its final triumph. If you have to suffer martyrdom, and if all the universe has to be destroyed in the process, still, still, still, O Christian, you shall reign as a king and set your foot on the necks of the old bosses!

This is the message of Revelation.

And just as inevitably as Jesus had to have a Judas Iscariot among his disciples, so did there have to be a Revelation in the New Testament.

Why? Because the nature of man demands it, and will always demand it.

The Christianity of Jesus applies to a part of our nature only. There is a big part to which it does not apply. And to this part, as the Salvation Army will show you, Revelation does apply.

The religions of renunciation, meditation, and self-knowledge are for individuals alone. But man is individual only in part of his nature. In another great part of him, he is collective.

The religions of renunciation, meditation, self-knowledge, pure morality are for individuals, and even then, not for complete individuals. But they express the individual side of man's nature. They isolate this side of his nature. And they cut off the other side of his nature, the collective side. The lowest stratum of society is always non-individual, so look there for the other manifestation of religion.

The religions of renunciation, like Buddhism or Christianity or Plato's philosophy, are for aristocrats, aristocrats of the spirit. The aristocrats of the spirit are to find their fulfilment in self-realisation and in service. Serve the poor. Well and good. But whom are the poor going to serve? It is the grand question. And John of Patmos answers it. The poor are going to serve themselves, and attend to their own self-glorification. And by the poor we don't mean the indigent merely: we mean the merely collective souls, terribly "middling", who have no aristocratic singleness and aloneness.

The vast mass are these middling souls. They *have* no aristocratic individuality, such as is demanded by Christ or Buddha or Plato. So they skulk in a mass and secretly are bent on their own ultimate self-glorification. The Patmossers.

Only when he is alone, can man be a Christian, a Buddhist, or a Platonist. The Christ statues and Buddha statues witness to this. When he is with other men, instantly distinctions occur, and levels are formed. As soon as he is with other men, Jesus is an aristocrat, a master. Buddha is always the lord Buddha, Francis of Assisi, trying to be so humble, as a matter of fact finds a subtle means to absolute power over his followers. Shelley could not *bear* not be the aristocrat of his company. Lenin was a Tyrannus in shabby clothes.

So it is! Power is there, and always will be. As soon as two or three men come together, especially to *do* something, then power comes into being, and one man is a leader, a master. It is inevitable.

Accept it, recognise the natural power in the man, as men did in the past, and give it homage, then there is a great joy, an uplifting, and a potency passes from the powerful to the less powerful. There is a stream of power. And in this, men have their best collective being, now and forever. Recognise the flame of power, or glory, and a corresponding flame springs up in yourself. Give homage and allegiance to a hero, and you become yourself heroic. It is the law of men. Perhaps the law of women is different.

But act on the reverse, and what happens? Deny power, and power wanes. Deny power in a greater man, and you have no power yourself. But society, now and forever, must be ruled and governed. So that the mass must grant *authority* where they deny power. Authority now takes the place of power, and we have "ministers" and public officials and policemen. Then comes the grand scramble of ambition, competition, and the mass treading one another in the face, so afraid they are of power.

A man like Lenin is a great evil saint who believes in the utter destruction of power. It leaves men unutterably bare, stripped, mean, miserable, and humiliated. Abraham Lincoln is a half-evil saint who *almost* believes in the utter destruction of power. President Wilson is a quite evil saint who quite believes in the destruction of power—but who runs himself to megalomania and neurasthenic tryanny. Every saint becomes evil—and Lenin, Lincoln, Wilson are true saints so long as they remain purely individual;—every saint becomes evil the moment he touches the collective self of men. Then he is a perverter: Plato the same. The great saints are for the *individual* only, and that means, for one side of our nature only, for in the deep layers of ourselves we are collective, we can't help it. And the collective self either lives and moves and has its being in a full relationship of power: or it is reversed, and lives a frictional misery of trying to destroy power, and destroy itself.

But nowadays, the will to destroy power is paramount. Great kings like the late Tsar—we mean great in position—are rendered almost imbecile by the vast anti-will of the masses, the will to negate power. Modern kings are negated till they become almost idiots. And the same of any man in power, unless he be a power-destroyer and a white-feathered evil bird: then the mass will back him up. How can the anti-power masses, above all the great middling masses, ever have a king who is more than a thing of ridicule or pathos?

The Apocalypse has been running for nearly two thousand years: the hidden side of Christianity: and its work is nearly done. For the Apocalypse does not worship power. It wants to murder the powerful, to seize power itself, the weakling.

Judas had to betray Jesus to the powers that be, because of the denial and subterfuge inherent in Jesus' teaching. Jesus took up the position of the pure individual, even with his disciples. He did not *really* mix with them, or even really work or act with them. *He was alone all the time.* He puzzled them utterly, and in some part of them, he let them down. He refused to be their physical power-lord. The power-homage in a man like Judas felt itself betrayed! So it betrayed back again: with a kiss. And in the same way, Revelation had to be included in the New Testament, to give the death-kiss to the Gospels.

IV

It is a curious thing, but the collective will of a community really reveals the *basis* of the individual will. The early Christian Churches, or communities, revealed quite early a strange will to a strange kind of power. They had a will to destroy all power, and so usurp themselves the final, the ultimate power. This was not quite the teaching of Jesus, but it was the inevitable implication of Jesus' teaching, in the minds of the vast mass of the weak, the inferior. Jesus taught the escape and liberation into unselfish, brotherly love: a feeling that only the strong can know. And this, sure enough, at once brought the community of the weak into triumphant being; and the will of the community of Christians was anti-social, almost anti-human, revealing from the start a frenzied desire for the end of the world, the destruction of humanity altogether; and then, when this did not come, a grim determination to destroy all mastery, all lordship, and all human splendour out of the world, leaving only the community of saints as the final negation of power, and the final power.

After the crash of the Dark Ages, the Catholic Church emerged again a *human* thing, a complete, not a half-thing, adjusted to seed-time and harvest and the solstice of Christmas and of midsummer, and having a good balance, in early days, between brotherly love and natural lordship and splendour. Every man was given his little kingdom in marriage, and every woman her own little inviolate realm. This Christian marriage guided by the church was a great institution for true freedom, true possibility of fulfilment. Freedom was no more, and can be no more than the possibility of living fully and satisfactorily. In marriage, in the great natural cycle of church ritual and festival, the early Catholic Church tried to give this to men. But alas, the Church soon fell out of balance, into worldly greed.

Then came the Reformation, and the thing started over again: the old will of the Christian community to destroy human worldly power, and to substitute the *negative* power of the mass. The battle rages today, in all its horror. In Russia, the triumph over worldly power was accomplished, and the reign of saints set in, with Lenin for the chief saint.

And Lenin was a saint. He had every quality of a saint. He is worshipped today, quite rightly, as a saint. But saints who try to kill all brave power in mankind are fiends, like the Puritans who wanted to pull all the bright feathers out of the chaffinch. Fiends!

Lenin's rule of saints turned out quite horrible. It has more thou-shalt-nots than any rule of "Beasts", or emperors. And this is bound to be so. Any rule of saints must be horrible. Why? Because the nature of man is not saintly. The *primal* need, the old-Adamic need in a man's soul is to be, in his own sphere and as far as he can attain it, master, lord, and splendid one. Every cock can crow on his own muck-heap, and ruffle gleaming feathers, every peasant could be a glorious little Tsar in his own hut, and when he got a bit drunk. And every peasant was consummated in the old dash and gorgeousness of the nobles, and in the supreme splendour of the Tsar. The supreme master, and lord and splendid one: their own, their own splendid one: they might see him with their own eyes, the Tsar! And this fulfilled one of the deepest, greatest and most powerful needs of the human heart. The human heart needs, needs, needs splendour, gorgeousness, pride, assumption, glory, and lordship. Perhaps it needs these even more than it needs love: at last, even more than bread. And every great king makes every man a little lord in his own tiny sphere, fills the imagination with lordship and splendour, satisfies the soul. The most dangerous thing in the world is to show man his own paltriness as a hedged-in male. It depresses him, and *makes* him paltry. We become, alas, what we think we are. Men have been depressed now for many years in their male and splendid selves, depressed into dejection and almost into abjection. Is not that evil? Then let men themselves do something about it.

And a great saint like Lenin—or Shelley or St. Francis—can only cry *anathema! anathema!*, to the natural proud self of power, and try deliberately to destroy all might and all lordship, and leave the people poor, oh, so poor! Poor, poor, poor, as the people are in all our modern democracies, though nowhere so absolutely impoverished in life as in the most absolute democracy, no matter how they be in money.

The community is inhuman, and less than human. It becomes at last the most dangerous because *bloodless* and insentient tyrant. For a long time, even a democracy like the American or the Swiss will answer to the call of a hero, who is somewhat of a true aristocrat: like Lincoln: so strong is the aristocratic instinct in man. But the willingness to give the response to the heroic, the true aristocratic call, gets weaker and weaker in every democracy, as time goes on. All history proves it. Then men turn against the heroic appeal, with a sort of venom. They will only listen to the call of mediocrity wielding the insentient bullying power of mediocrity: which is evil. Hence the success of painfully inferior and even base politicians.

Brave people add up to an aristocracy. The democracy of thou-shalt-not is bound to be a collection of weak men. And then the sacred "will of the people" becomes blinder, baser, colder and more dangerous than the will of any tyrant. When the will of the people becomes the sum of the weakness of a multitude of weak men, it is time to make a break.

So today. Society consists of a mass of weak individuals trying to protect themselves, out of fear, from every possible imaginary evil, and, of course, *by their very fear*, bringing the evil into being.

This is the Christian Community today, in its perpetual mean thou-shalt-not. This is how Christian doctrine has worked out in practice.

V

And Revelation was a foreshadowing of all this. It is above all what some psychologists would call the revelation of a thwarted "superiority" goal, and a consequent inferiority complex. Of the positive side of Christianity, the peace of meditation and the joy of unselfish service, the rest from ambition and the pleasure of knowledge, we find nothing in the Apocalypse. Because the Apocalypse is for the non-individual side of a man's nature, written from the thwarted collective self, whereas meditation and unselfish service are for pure individuals, isolate. Pure Christianity anyhow *cannot* fit a nation, or society at large. The Great War made it obvious. It can only fit individuals. The collective whole must have some other inspiration.

And the Apocalypse, repellant though its chief spirit be, does also contain another inspiration. It is repellant only because it resounds with the dangerous snarl of the *frustrated*, *suppressed* collective self, the frustrated power-spirit in man, vengeful. But it contains also some revelation of the true and positive Power-spirit. The very beginning surprises us: "John to the seven churches in Asia: grace be to you and peace from HE WHO IS AND WAS AND IS COMING, and from the seven Spirits before his throne, and from Jesus Christ the faithful witness, the first-born from the dead, and the prince over the kings of the earth; to him who loves us and has loosed us from our sins by shedding his blood—he has made us a realm of priests for his God and Father,—to him be glory and dominion for ever and ever, Amen. Lo, he is coming on the clouds, to be seen by every eye, even by those who impaled him, and all the tribes of earth will wail because of him: even so, Amen",—I have used Moffatt's translation, as the meaning is a little more explicit than in the authorised version.

But here we have a curious Jesus, very different from the one in Galilee, wandering by the lake. And the book goes on: "On the Lord's day I found myself rapt in the Spirit, and I heard a loud voice behind me like a trumpet calling, 'Write your vision in a book'.—So I turned to see whose voice it was that spoke to me; and on turning round I saw seven golden lampstands and in the middle of the lampstands One who resembled a human being, with a long robe, and a belt of gold round his breast; his head and hair were white as wool, white as snow; his eyes flashed like fire, his feet glowed like burnished bronze, his voice sounded like many waves, in his right hand he held seven stars, a sharp sword with a double edge issued from his mouth, and his face shone like the sun in full strength. When I saw him, I fell at his feet like a dead man; but he laid his hand on me, saying: 'Do not be afraid; I am the First and Last, I was dead and here I am alive for evermore, holding the keys that unlock death and Hades. Write down your vision of what is and what is to be hereafter. As for the secret symbol of the seven stars which you have seen in my right hand, and of the seven golden lampstands: the seven stars are the angels of the seven churches, and the seven lampstands are the seven churches. To the angel of the church at Ephesus write thus:—"These are the words of him who holds the seven stars in his right hand, who moves among the seven golden lampstands—"'".

Now this being with the sword of the Logos issuing from his mouth and the seven stars in his hand is the Son of God, therefore, the Messiah, therefore Jesus. It is very far from the Jesus who said in Gethsemane: "My heart is sad, sad even unto death; stay here and watch".—But it is the Jesus that the early Church, especially in Asia, prominently believed in.

And what is this Jesus? It is the great Splendid One, almost identical with the Almighty in the visions of Ezekiel and Daniel. It is a vast Cosmic lord, standing among the seven eternal lamps of the archaic planets, sun and moon and five great stars around his feet. In the sky his gleaming head is in the north, the sacred region of the Pole, and he holds in his right hand the seven stars of the Bear, that we call the Plough, and he wheels them round the Pole star, as even now we see them wheel, causing the universal revolution of the heavens, the roundwise moving of the cosmos. This is the lord of all motion, who swings the cosmos into its course. Again, from his mouth issues the two-edged sword of the Word, the mighty weapon of the Logos which will smite the world (and in the end destroy it). This is the sword indeed that Jesus brought among men. And lastly, his face shines like the sun in full strength, the source of life itself, the dazzler, before whom we fall as if dead.

And this is Jesus: not only the Jesus of the early churches, but the Jesus of popular religion today. There is nothing humble nor suffering here. It is our "superiority goal", indeed. And it is a true account of man's *other* conception of God; perhaps the greater and more fundamental conception: the magnificent Mover of the Cosmos! To John of Patmos, the Lord is *Kosmokrator*, and even *Kosmodynamos*: the great Ruler of the Cosmos, and the Power of the Cosmos. But alas, according to the Apocalypse man has no share in the ruling of the Cosmos until after death. When a Christian has been put to death by martyrdom, then he will be resurrected at the Second Advent and become himself a little Kosmokrator, ruling for a thousand years. It is the apotheosis of the weak man.

But the Son of God, the Jesus of John's vision, is more even than this. He holds the keys that unlock death and Hades. He is Lord of the Underworld. He is Hermes, the guide of souls through the death-world, over the hellish stream. He is master of the mysteries of the dead, he knows the meaning of the holocaust, and has final power over the powers below. The dead and the lords of death, who are always hovering in the background of religion away down among the people, these Chthonioi of the primitive Greeks, these too must acknowledge Jesus as a supreme lord.

And the lord of the dead is master of the future, and the god of the present. He gives the vision of what was, and is, and shall be.

Here is a Jesus for you! What is modern Christianity going to make of it? For it is the Jesus of the very first communities, and it is the Jesus of the early Catholic Church, as it emerged from the Dark Ages and adjusted itself once more to life and death and the cosmos, the whole great adventure of the human soul, as contrasted with the little petty personal adventure of modern Protestantism and Catholicism alike, cut off from the cosmos, cut off from Hades, cut off from the magnificence of the Star-mover. Petty little personal salvation, petty morality instead of cosmic splendour, we have lost the sun and the planets, and the Lord with the seven stars of the Bear in his right hand. Poor, paltry, creeping little world we live in, even the keys of death and Hades are lost. How shut in we are! All we can do, with our brotherly love, is to shut one another in. We are so afraid somebody else might be lordly and splendid, when we can't. Petty little bolshevists, every one of us today, we are determined that *no* man shall shine like the sun in full strength, for he would certainly outshine us.

Now again we realise a dual feeling in ourselves with regard to the Apocalypse. Suddenly we see some of the old pagan splendour, that delighted in the might and the magnificence of the Cosmos, and man who was as a star in the cosmos. Suddenly we feel again the nostalgia for the old pagan world, long before John's day, we feel an immense yearning to be freed from this petty personal entanglement of weak life, to be back in the far-off world before men became "afraid". We want to be freed from our tight little automatic "universe", to go back to the great living cosmos of the "unenlightened" pagans!

Perhaps the greatest difference between us and the pagans lies in our different relation to the cosmos. With us, all is personal. Landscape and the sky, these are to us the delicious background of our personal life, and no more. Even the universe of the scientist is little more than an extension of our personality, to us. To the pagan, landscape and personal background were on the whole indifferent. But the cosmos was a very real thing. A man *lived* with the cosmos, and knew it greater than himself.

Don't let us imagine we see the sun as the old civilisations saw it. All we see is a scientific little luminary, dwindled to a ball of blazing gas. In the centuries before Ezekiel and John, the sun was still a magnificent reality, men drew forth from him strength and splendour, and gave him back homage and lustre and thanks. But in us, the connection is broken, the responsive centres are dead. Our sun is a quite different thing from the cosmic sun of the ancients, so much more trivial. We may see what we call the sun, but we have lost Helios forever, and the great orb of the Chaldeans still more. We have lost the cosmos, by coming out of responsive connection with it, and this is our chief tragedy. What is our petty little love of nature— Nature!!—compared to the ancient magnificent living with the cosmos, and being honoured by the cosmos!

And some of the great images of the Apocalypse move us to strange depths, and to a strange wild fluttering of freedom: of true freedom, really, an escape to *somewhere*, not an escape to nowhere. An escape from the tight little cage of our universe; tight, in spite of all the astronomists' vast and unthinkable stretches of space; tight, because it is only a continuous extension, a dreary on and on, without any meaning: an escape from this into the vital Cosmos, to a sun who has a great wild life, and who looks back at us for strength or withering, marvellous, as he goes his way. Who says the sun cannot speak to me! The sun has a great blazing consciousness, and I have a little blazing consciousness. When I can strip myself of the trash of personal feelings and ideas, and get down to my naked sun-self, then the sun and I can commune by the hour, the blazing interchange, and he gives me life, sun-life, and I send him a little new brightness from the world of the bright blood. The great sun, like an angry dragon, hates the nervous and personal consciousness in us. As all these modern sunbathers must realise, for they become disintegrated by the very sun that bronzes them. But the sun, like a lion, loves the bright red blood of life, and can give it an infinite enrichment if we know how to receive it. But we don't. We have lost the sun. And he only falls on us and destroys us, decomposing something in us: the dragon of destruction instead of the life bringer.

And we have lost the moon, the cool, bright, ever-varying moon. It is she who would caress our nerves, smooth them with the silky hand of her glowing, soothe them into serenity again with her cool presence. For the moon is the mistress and mother of our watery bodies, the pale body of our nervous consciousness and our moist flesh. Oh the moon could soothe us and heal us like a cool great Artemis between her arms. But we have lost her, in our stupidity we ignore her, and angry she stares down on us and whips us with nervous whips. Oh beware of the angry Artemis of the night heavens, beware of the spite of Cybele, beware of the vindictiveness of horned Astarte.

For the lovers who shoot themselves in the night, in the horrible suicide of love, they are driven mad by the poisoned arrows of Artemis: the moon is against them: the moon is fiercely against them. And oh, if the moon is against you, oh beware of the bitter night, especially the night of intoxication.

Now this may sound nonsense, but that is merely because we are fools. There is an eternal vital correspondence between our blood and the sun: there is an eternal vital correspondence between our nerves and the moon. If we get out of contact and harmony with the sun and moon, then both turn into great dragons of destruction against us. The sun is a great source of blood-vitality, it streams strength to us. But once we resist the sun, and say: It is a mere ball of gas!—then the very streaming vitality of sunshine turns into subtle disintegrative force in us, and undoes us. The same with the moon, the planets, the great stars. They are either our makers or our unmakers. There is no escape.

We and the cosmos are one. The cosmos is a vast living body, of which we are still parts. The sun is a great heart whose tremors run through our smallest veins. The moon is a great gleaming nerve-centre from which we quiver forever. Who knows the power that Saturn has over us, or Venus? But it is a vital power, rippling exquisitely through us *all the time*. And if we deny Aldebaran, Aldebaran will pierce us with infinite dagger-thrusts. He who is not with me is against me!—that is a cosmic law.

Now all this is *literally* true, as men knew in the great past, and as they will know again.

By the time of John of Patmos, men, especially educated men, had already almost lost the cosmos. The sun, the moon, the planets, instead of being the communers, the comminglers, the life-givers, the splendid ones, the awful ones, had already fallen into a sort of deadness, they were the arbitrary, almost mechanical engineers of fate and destiny. By the time of Jesus, men had turned the heavens into a mechanism of fate and destiny, a prison. The Christians escaped this prison by denying the body altogether. But alas, these little escapes! especially the escapes by denial!—they are the most fatal of evasions. Christianity and our ideal civilisation has been one long evasion. It has caused endless lying and misery, misery such as people know today, not of physical want but of far more deadly *vital* want. Better lack bread than lack life. One long evasion, whose only fruit is the machine!

We have lost the cosmos. The sun strengthens us no more, neither does the moon. In mystic language, the moon is black to us, and the sun is as sackcloth.

Now we have to get back the cosmos, and it can't be done by a trick. The great range of responses that have fallen dead in us have to come to life again. It has taken two thousand years to kill them. Who knows how long it will take to bring them to life.

When I hear modern people complain of being lonely then I know what has happened. They have lost the cosmos.—It is nothing human and personal that we are short of. What we lack is cosmic life, the sun in us and the moon in us. We can't get the sun in us by lying naked like pigs on a beach. The very sun that is bronzing us is inwardly disintegrating us—as we know later. Process of katabolism. We can only get the sun by a sort of worship: and the same the moon. By *going forth* to worship the sun, worship that is felt in the blood. Tricks and postures only make matters worse.

VI

And now we must admit that we are also grateful to St. John's Revelation for giving us hints of the magnificent cosmos and putting us into momentary contact. The contacts, it is true, are only for moments, then they are broken by this other spirit of hope-despair. But even for the moments we are grateful.

There are flashes throughout the first part of the Apocalypse of true cosmic worship. The cosmos became anathema to the Christians, though the early Catholic Church restored it somewhat after the crash of the Dark Ages. Then again the cosmos became anathema to the Protestants after the Reformation. They substituted the non-vital universe of forces and mechanistic order, everything else became abstraction, and the long slow death of the human being set in. This slow death produced science and machinery, but both are death products.

No doubt the death was necessary. It is the long, slow death of society which parallels the quick death of Jesus and the other dying gods. It is death none the less, and will end in the annihilation of the human race—as John of Patmos so fervently hoped—unless there is a change, a resurrection, and a return to the cosmos.

But these flashes of the cosmos in Revelation can hardly be attributed to John of Patmos. As an apocalyptist he uses other people's flashes to light up his way of woe and hope. The grand hope of the Christians is a measure of their utter despair.

It began, however, before the Christians. Apocalypse is a curious form of literature, Jewish and Jewish Christian. This new form arose somewhere about 200 B.C., when the Prophets had finished. An early Apocalypse is the Book of Daniel, the latter part at least: another is the Apocalypse of Enoch, the oldest parts of which are attributed to the second century B.C.

The Jews, the Chosen People, had always had an idea of themselves as a grand imperial people. They had their try, and failed disastrously. Then they gave it up. After the destruction of the temple by Antiochus Epiphanes, the national imagination ceased to imagine a great natural

Jewish Empire. The prophets became silent forever. The Jews became a people of *postponed destiny*. And then the seers began to write Apocalypses.

The seers had to tackle this business of postponed destiny. It was no longer a matter of prophecy: it was a matter of vision. God would no longer *tell* his servant what would happen, for what would happen was almost untellable. He would show him a vision.

Every profound new movement makes a great swing also backwards to some older, half-forgotten way of consciousness. So the apocalyptists swung back to the old cosmic vision. After the second destruction of the Temple the Jews despaired, consciously or unconsciously, of the *earthly* triumph of the Chosen People. Therefore, doggedly, they prepared for an unearthly triumph. That was what the apocalyptists set out to do: to vision forth the unearthly triumph of the Chosen.

To do this, they needed an all-round view: they needed to know the end as well as the beginning. Never before had men wanted to know the end of creation: sufficient that it was created, and would go on for ever and ever. But now, the apocalyptists had to have a vision of the end.

They became then cosmic. Enoch's visions of the cosmos are very interesting, and not very Jewish. But they are curiously geographical.

When we come to John's Apocalypse, and come to know it, several things strike us. First, the obvious scheme, the division of the book into two halves, with two rather discordant intentions. The first half, before the birth of the baby Messiah, seems to have the intention of salvation and renewal, leaving the world to go on renewed. But the second half, when the Beasts rouse up, develops a weird and mystic hate of the world, of worldly power, and of everything and everybody who does not submit to the Messiah out and out. The second half of the Apocalypse is flamboyant hate and a simple lust, lust is the only word, for the end of the world. The apocalyptist *must* see the universe, or the known cosmos, wiped out utterly, and merely a heavenly city and a hellish lake of brimstone left.

The discrepancy of the two intentions is the first thing that strikes us. The first part, briefer, more condensed or abbreviated, is much more difficult and complicated than the second part, and the feeling in it is much more dramatic, yet more universal and significant. We feel in the first part, we know not why, the space and pageantry of the pagan world. In the second part is the individual frenzy of those early Christians, rather like the frenzies of chapel people and revivalists today.

Then again, we feel that in the first part we are in touch with great old symbols, that take us far back into time, into the pagan vistas. In the second part, the imagery is Jewish allegorical, rather modern, and has a fairly easy local and temporal explanation. When there is a touch of true symbolism, it is not of the nature of a ruin or a remains embedded in the present structure, it is rather an archaic reminiscence.

A third thing that strikes us is the persistent use of the great pagan, as well as Jewish power-titles, both for God and for the Son of Man. *King of Kings and Lord of Lords* is typical throughout, and Kosmokrator, and Kosmodynamos. Always the titles of power, and never the titles of love. Always Christ the omnipotent conqueror flashing his great sword and destroying, destroying vast masses of men, till blood mounts up to the horses' bridles. Never Christ the Saviour: never. The Son of Man of the Apocalypse comes to bring a new and terrible *power* on to the earth, power greater than that of any Pompey or Alexander or Cyrus. Power, terrific, smiting power. And when praise is uttered, or the hymn to the Son of Man, it is to ascribe to him power, and riches, and wisdom, and strength, and honour, and glory, and blessing—all the attributes given to the great kings and Pharaohs of the earth, but hardly suited to a crucified Jesus.

So that we are left puzzled. If John of Patmos finished this Apocalypse in 96 A.D., he knew strangely little of the Jesus legend, and had just none of the spirit of the Gospels, all of which preceded his book. A curious being, this old John of Patmos, whoever he was. But anyhow he focussed the emotions of certain types of men for centuries to come.

What we feel about the Apocalypse is that it is not one book, but several, perhaps many. But it is not made up of pieces of several books strung together, like Enoch. It is one book, in several layers: like layers of civilisation as you dig deeper and deeper to excavate an old city. Down at the bottom is a pagan substratum, probably one of the ancient books of the Aegean civilisation: some sort of a book of a pagan Mystery. This has been written over by Jewish apocalyptists, then extended, and then finally written over by the Jewish-Christian apocalyptist John: and then, after his day, expurgated and corrected and pruned down and added to by Christian editors who wanted to make of it a Christian work.

But John of Patmos must have been a strange Jew: violent, full of the Hebrew books of the Old Testament, but also full of all kinds of pagan knowledge, anything that would contribute to his passion, his unbearable passion, for the Second Advent, the utter smiting of the Romans with the great sword of Christ, the trampling of mankind in the winepress of God's anger till blood mounted to the bridles of the horses, the triumph of the rider on a white horse, greater than any Persian king: then the rule of Martyrs for one thousand years: and then oh then the destruction of the entire universe, and the last Judgment. "Come, Lord Jesus, Come"!

And John firmly believed He was coming, and coming *immediately*. Therein lay the trembling of the terrific and terrifying hope of the early Christians: that made them, naturally, in pagan eyes, the enemies of mankind altogether.

But He did not come, so we are not very much interested. What does interest us is the strange pagan recoil of the book, and the pagan vestiges. And we realise how the Jew, when he *does* look into the outside world, has to look with pagan or gentile eyes. The Jews of the post-David period have no eyes of their own to see with. They peered inward at their Jehovah till they were blind: then they looked at the world with the eyes of their neighbours. When the prophets had to see visions, they had to see Assyrian or Chaldean visions. They borrowed other gods to see their own invisible God by.

Ezekiel's great vision, which is so largely repeated in the Apocalypse, what is it but pagan, disfigured probably by jealous Jewish scribes: a great pagan concept of the Time Spirit and the Kosmokrator and the Kosmodynamos! Add to this that the Kosmokrator stands among the wheels of the heavens, known as the wheels of Anaximander, and we see where we are. We are in the great world of the pagan cosmos.

But the text of Ezekiel is hopelessly corrupt—no doubt deliberately corrupted by fanatical scribes who wanted to smear over the pagan vision. It is an old story.

It is none the less amazing to find Anaximander's wheels in Ezekiel. These wheels are an ancient attempt to explain the orderly yet complex movement of the heavens. They are based on the first "scientific" duality which the pagans found in the universe, namely, the moist and the dry, the cold and the hot, air (or cloud) and fire. Strange and fascinating are the great revolving wheels of the sky, made of dense air or night-cloud and filled with the blazing cosmic fire, which fire peeps through or blazes through at certain holes in the felloes of the wheels, and forms the blazing sun or the pointed stars. All the orbs are little holes in the black wheel which is full of fire: and there is wheel within wheel, revolving differently.

Anaximander, almost the very first of the ancient Greek thinkers, is supposed to have invented this "wheel" theory of the heavens in Ionia in the sixth century B.C. Anyhow Ezekiel learnt it in Babylonia: and who knows whether the whole idea is not Chaldean. Surely it has behind it centuries of Chaldean sky-knowledge.

It is a great relief to find Anaximander's wheels in Ezekiel. The Bible at once becomes a book of the human race, instead of a corked-up bottle of "inspiration". And so it is a relief to find the four Creatures of the four quarters of the heavens, winged and starry. Immediately we are out in the great Chaldean star-spaces, instead of being pinched up in a Jewish tabernacle. That the Jews managed, by pernicious anthropomorphising, to turn the four great Creatures into Archangels, even with names like Michael and Gabriel, only shows the limit of the Jewish imagination, which can know nothing except in terms of the human ego. It is none the less a relief to know that these policemen of God, the great Archangels, were once the winged and starry creatures of the four quarters of the heavens, quivering their wings across space, in Chaldean lore.

In John of Patmos, the "wheels" are missing. They had been superseded long ago by the spheres of the heavens. But the Almighty is even more distinctly a cosmic wonder, amber-coloured like sky-fire, the great Maker and the great Ruler of the starry heavens, Demiurge and Kosmokrator, the one who wheels the cosmos. He is a great *actual* figure, the great dynamic God, neither spiritual nor moral, but cosmic and vital.

Naturally or unnaturally, the orthodox critics deny this. Archdeacon Charles admits that the seven stars in the right hand of the "Son of Man" are the stars of the Bear, wheeling round the Pole, and that this is Babylonian: then he goes on to say "but our author can have had nothing of this in mind".

Of course, excellent clergymen of today know exactly what "our author" had in mind. John of Patmos is a Christian saint, so he *couldn't* have had any heathenism in mind. This is what orthodox criticism amounts to. Whereas as a matter of fact we are amazed at the almost brutal paganism of "our author", John of Patmos. Whatever else he was, he was not afraid of a pagan symbol, nor even, apparently, of a whole pagan cult. The old religions were cults of vitality, potency, and power: we must never forget it. Only the Hebrews were moral: and they only in patches. Among the old pagans, morals were just social manners, decent behaviour. But by the time of Christ all religion and all thought seemed to turn from the old worship and study of vitality, potency, power, to the study of death and death-rewards, death-penalties, and morals. All religion, instead of being religion of *life*, here and now, became religion of postponed destiny, death, and reward *afterwards*, "if you are good".

John of Patmos accepted the postponement of destiny with a vengeance, but he cared little about "being good". What he wanted was the *ultimate* power. He was a shameless power-worshipping pagan Jew, gnashing his teeth over the postponement of his grand destiny.

It seems to me he knew a good deal about the pagan value of symbols, as contrasted even with the Jewish or Christian value. And he used the pagan value just when it suited him, for he was no timid soul. To suggest that the figure of the Kosmodynamos wheeling the heavens, the great figure of cosmic Fire with the seven stars of the Bear in his right hand, could be unknown to John of Patmos is beyond even an Archdeacon. The world of the first century was full of star-cults, the figure of the Mover of the Heavens must have been familiar to every boy in the east. Orthodox critics in one breath relate that "our author" had no starry heathenism in mind, and in the next they expatiate on how thankful men must have been to escape, through Christianity, from the senseless and mechanical domination of the heavens, the changeless rule of the planets, the fixed astronomical and astrological fate. "Good heavens!" we still exclaim: and if we pause to consider, we shall see how powerful was the idea of moving, fate-fixing heavens, half-cosmic, half-mechanical, but still not anthropomorphic.

I am sure not only John of Patmos, but St. Paul and St. Peter and St. John the Apostle knew a great deal about the stars, and about the pagan cults. They chose, perhaps wisely, to suppress it all. John of Patmos did not. So his Christian critics and editors, from the second century down to Archdeacon Charles, have tried to suppress it for him. Without success: because the kind of mind that worships the divine *power* always tends to think in symbols. Direct thinking in symbols, like a game of chess, with its king and queen and pawns, is characteristic of those men who see power as the great desideratum— and they are the majority. The lowest substratum of the people still worships power, still thinks crudely in symbols, still sticks to the Apocalypse and is entirely callous to the Sermon on the Mount. But so, apparently, does the highest superstratum of church and state still worship in terms of power: naturally, really.

But the orthodox critics like Archdeacon Charles want to have their cake and eat it. They *want* the old pagan power-sense in the Apocalypse, and they spend half their time denying it is there. If they *have* to admit a pagan element, they gather up the skirts of their clerical gowns and hurry past. And at the same time, the Apocalypse is a veritable heathen feast for them. Only they must swallow it with pious appearances.

Of course the dishonesty, we can call it no less, of the Christian critic is based on fear. Once start admitting that *anything* in the Bible is pagan, of pagan origin and meaning, and you are lost, you won't know where to stop. God escapes out of the bottle once and for all, to put it irreverently. The Bible is so splendidly full of paganisms and therein lies its greater interest. But once admit it, and Christianity must come out of her shell.

Once more then we look at the Apocalypse, and try to sense its structure vertically, as well as horizontally. For the more we read it, the more we feel that it is a section through time, as well as a Messianic mystery. It is the work of no one man, and even of no one century. Of that we feel sure.

The oldest part, surely, was a pagan work, probably the description of the "secret" ritual of initiation into one of the pagan Mysteries, Artemis, Cybele, even Orphic: but most probably belonging there to the east Mediterranean, probably actually to Ephesus: as would seem natural. If such a book existed, say two or perhaps three centuries before Christ, then it was known to all students of religion: and perhaps it would be safe to say that every intelligent man in that day, especially in the east, was a student of religion. Men were religious-mad: not religious-sane. The Jews were just the same as the gentiles. The Jews of the dispersion certainly read and discussed everything they could lay their hands on. We must put away forever the Sunday School idea of a bottled-up Jewry with nothing but its own God to think about. It was very different. The Jews of the last centuries B.C. were as curious, as widely read, and as cosmopolitan as the Jews of today: saving, of course, a few fanatical sets and sects.

So that the old pagan book must quite early have been taken and written over by a Jewish apocalyptist, with a view to substituting the Jewish idea of a Messiah and a Jewish salvation (or destruction) *of the whole world*, for the purely individual experience of pagan initiation. This Jewish Apocalypse, written over perhaps more than once, was surely known to all religious seekers of Jesus' day, including the writers of the Gospels. And probably, even before John of Patmos tackled it, a Jewish-Christian apocalyptist had re-written the work once more, probably had already extended it in the prophetic manner of Daniel, to foretell the utter downfall of Rome: for the Jews loved nothing in the world so much as prophesying the utter downfall of the gentile kingdoms. Then John of Patmos occupied his prison-years on the island in writing the whole book over once more, in his own peculiar style. We feel that he invented little, and had few ideas: but that he did indeed have a fierce and burning passion against the Romans who had condemned him. For all that, he shows no hatred of the pagan Greek culture of the east. In fact, he accepts it almost as naturally as his own Hebrew culture, and far more naturally than the new Christian spirit, which is alien to him. He rewrites the older Apocalypse, probably cuts the pagan passages still shorter, simply because they have no Messianic anti-Rome purport, not for any objection to their paganism; and then he lets himself go in the second half of the book, where he can lash the Beast called Rome (or Babylon), the Beast called Nero, or Nero redivivus, and the Beast called Antichrist, or the Roman priesthood of the Imperial cult. How he left the final chapters about the New Jerusalem we don't know, but they are now in a state of confusion.

We feel that John was a violent but not very profound person. If he invented the letters to the seven churches, they are a rather dull and weak contribution. And yet it is his curious fervid intensity which gives to Revelation its lurid power. And we cannot help liking him for leaving the great symbols on the whole intact.

But after John had done with it, the real Christians started in. And them we really resent. The Christian fear of the pagan outlook has damaged the whole consciousness of man. The one fixed attitude of Christianity towards the pagan religious vision has been an attitude of stupid denial, denial that there was anything in the pagans at all, except bestiality. And all pagan evidence in the books of the Bible had to be expurgated, or twisted into meaninglessness, or smeared over into Christian or Jewish semblances.

This is what happened to the Apocalypse after John left it. How many bits the little Christian scribes have snipped out, how many bits they have stuck in, how many times they have forged "our author's" style, we shall never know: but there are certainly many evidences of their pettifogging work. And all to cover up the pagan traces, and make this plainly unchristian work passably Christian.

We cannot help hating the Christian *fear*, whose method, from the very beginning, has been to deny everything that didn't fit: or better still, suppress it. The system of suppression of all pagan evidence has been instinctive, a fear-instinct, and has been thorough, and has been, really, criminal, in the Christian world, from the first century until today. When a man thinks of the vast stores of priceless pagan documents that the Christians have wilfully destroyed, from the time of Nero to the obscure parish priests of today, who still burn any book found in their parish that is unintelligible, and therefore possibly heretical, the mind stands still!—and we reflect with irony on the hullabaloo over Rheims Cathedral. How many of the books we would give our fingers to possess, and can't, are lost because the Christians burnt them on purpose! They left Plato and Aristotle, feeling these two kin. But the others—!

The instinctive policy of Christianity towards all true pagan evidence has been and is still: suppress it, destroy it, deny it. This dishonesty has vitiated Christian thought from the start. It has, even more curiously, vitiated ethnological scientific thought the same. Curiously enough, we do not look on the Greeks and the Romans after about 600 B.C., as *real* pagans: not like Hindus or Persians, Babylonians or Egyptians or even Cretans, for example. We accept the Greeks and Romans as the initiators of our intellectual and political civilisation, the Jews as the fathers of our moral-religious civilisation. So these are "our sort". All the rest are mere nothing, almost idiots. All that can be attributed to the "barbarians" beyond the Greek pale: that is, to Minoans, Etruscans, Egyptians, Chaldeans, Persians and Hindus, is, in the famous phrase of a famous German professor: *Urdummheit*. Urdummheit, or primal stupidity, is the state of all mankind before precious Homer, and of all races, all, except Greek, Jew, Roman and—ourselves!

The strange thing is that even true scholars, who write scholarly and impartial books about the early Greeks, as soon as they mention the autochthonous races of the Mediterranean, or the Egyptians, or the Chaldeans, insist on the childishness of these peoples, their perfectly trivial achievement, their necessary Urdummheit. These great civilised peoples knew nothing: all *true* knowledge started with Thales and Anaximander and Pythagoras, with the Greeks. The Chaldeans knew no true astronomy, the Egyptians knew no mathematics nor science, and the poor Hindus, who for centuries were supposed to have invented that highly important reality, the arithmetical zero, or nought, are now not allowed even this merit. The Arabs, who are almost "us", invented it.

It is most strange. We can understand the *Christian* fear of the pagan way of knowledge. But why the scientific fear? Why should science betray its fear in a phrase like Urdummheit? We look at the wonderful remains of Egypt, Babylon, Assyria, Persia, and old India, and we repeat to ourselves: *Urdummheit!* Urdummheit? We look at the Etruscan tombs and ask ourselves again, *Urdummheit?* primal stupidity? Why, in the oldest of peoples, in the Egyptian friezes and the Assyrian, in the Etruscan paintings and the Hindu carvings we see a splendour, a beauty, and very often a joyous, sensitive intelligence which is certainly lost in our world of *Neufrecheit*. It it is a question of primal stupidity or new impudence, then give me primal stupidity.

The Archdeacon Charles is a true scholar and authority in Apocalypse, a far-reaching student of his subject. He tries, without success, to be fair in the matter of pagan origins. His predisposition, his terrific prejudice, is too strong for him. And once, he gives himself away, so we understand the whole process. He is writing in time of war—at the end of the late war—so we must allow for the fever. But he makes a bad break, none the less. On page 86 of the second volume of his commentary on Revelation, he writes of the Antichrist in the Apocalypse that it is "a marvellous portrait of the great god-opposing power that should hereafter arise, who was to exalt might above right, and attempt, successfully or unsuccessfully for the time, to seize the sovereignty of the world, backed by hosts of intellectual workers, who would uphold all his pretensions, justify all his actions, and enforce his political aims by an economic warfare, which menaced with destruction all that did not bow down to his arrogant and godless claims. And though the justness of this forecast is clear to the student who approaches the subject with some insight, and to all students who approach it with the experience of the present world war, we find that as late as 1908, Bousset in his article on the "Antichrist" in Hastings' *Encyclopedia of Religion and Ethics*, writes as follows: 'The interest in the (Antichrist) legend...is now to be found only among the lower classes of the Christian community, among sects, eccentric individuals, and fanatics.'

"No great prophecy receives its full and final fulfilment in any single event, or single series of events. In fact, it may not be fulfilled at all in regard to the object against which it was primarily delivered by the prophet or Seer. But, if it is the expression of a great moral and spiritual truth, it will of a surety be fulfilled at sundry times and in divers manners and in varying degrees of completeness. The present attitude of the Central Powers of Europe on this question of might against right, of Caesarism against religion, of the state against God, is the greatest fulfilment that the Johannine prophecy in XIII has as yet received. Even the very indefiniteness regarding the chief Antichrist in XIII is reproduced in the present upheaval of evil powers. In XIII the Antichrist is conceived as a single individual, i.e. the demonic Nero; but even so, behind him stands the Roman Empire, which is one with him in character and purpose, and in itself the Fourth Kingdom or the Kingdom of the Antichrist—in fact, the Antichrist itself. So in regard to the present war, it is difficult to determine whether the Kaiser or his people can advance the best claims to the title of a modern Antichrist. If he is a present-day representative of the Antichrist, so just as surely is the empire behind him, for it is one in spirit and purpose with its leader—whether regarded from its military side, its intellectual, or its industrial. They are in a degree far transcending that of ancient Rome 'those who are destroying the earth'".

So there we have Antichrist talking German to Archdeacon Charles, who, at the same moment, is using the books of German scholars for his work on the Apocalypse. It is as if Christianity and ethnological science alike could not exist unless they had an opposite, an Antichrist or an Urdummheit, for an offset. The Antichrist and the Urdummheit are just the fellow who is different from me. Today Antichrist speaks Russian, a hundred years ago he spoke French, tomorrow he may speak cockney or the Glasgow brogue. As for Urdummheit, he speaks any language that isn't Oxford or Harvard or an obsequious imitation of one of these.

VII

It is childish. What we have now to admit is that the beginning of the new era (our own) coincided with the dying of the old era of the true pagans or, in the Greek sense, barbarians. As our present civilisation was showing the first sparks of life, say in 1000 B.C., the great and ancient civilisation of the older world was waning: the great river civilisations of the Euphrates, the Nile and the Indus, with the lesser sea-civilisation of the Aegean. It is puerile to deny the age and the greatness of the three river civilisations, with their intermediary cultures in Persia or Iran, and in the Aegean, Crete or Mycene. That any of these civilisations could do a sum in long division we do not pretend. They may not even have invented the wheel-barrow. A modern child of ten could lick them hollow in arithmetic, geometry, or even, maybe, astronomy. And what of it?

What of it? Because they lacked our modern mental and mechanical attainments, were they any less "civilised" or "cultures", the Egyptians and the Chaldeans, the Cretans and the Persians and the Hindus of the Indus, than we are? Let us look at a great seated statue of Rameses, or at Etruscan tombs, let us read of Assiburnipal or Darius, and then say. How do our modern factory workers show beside the delicate Egyptian friezes of the common people of Egypt? or our khaki soldiers, beside the Assyrian friezes? or our Trafalgar Square lions beside these of Mycene? Civilisation? it is revealed rather in sensitive life than in inventions; and have we anything as good as the Egyptians of two or three thousand years before Christ, as a people? Culture and civilisation are tested by vital consciousness. Are we more vitally conscious than an Egyptian 3000 years B.C. was? Are we? Probably we are less. Our conscious range is wide, but shallow as a sheet of paper. We have no depth to our consciousness.

A rising thing is a passing thing, says Buddha. A rising civilisation is a passing civilisation. Greece rose upon the passing of the Aegean: and the Aegean was the link between Egypt and Babylon. Greece rose as the passing of the Aegean civilisation, and Rome rose as the same, for the Etruscan civilisation was a last strong wave from the Aegean, and Rome rose, truly, from the Etruscans. Persia arose from between the great cultures of the Euphrates and the Indus, and no doubt, in the passing of these.

Perhaps every rising civilisation must fiercely repudiate the passing civilisation. It is a fight within the self. The Greeks fiercely repudiated the barbarians. But we know now, the barbarians of the east Mediterranean were as much Greeks as most of the Greeks themselves. They were only Greeks, or autochthonous Hellenes who adhered to the old way of culture instead of taking on the new. The Aegean must always have been, in the primitive sense, Hellenic. But the old Aegean culture is different from what we call Greek, especially in its religious basis. Every old civilisation, we may be certain of it, had a definitely religious basis. The nation was, in a very old sense, a church, or a vast cult-unit. From cult to culture is only a step, but it took a lot of making. Cult-lore was the wisdom of the old races. We now have culture.

It is fairly difficult for one culture to understand another. But for culture to understand cult-lore is extremely difficult, and, for rather stupid people, impossible. Because culture is chiefly an activity of the mind, and cult-lore is an activity of the senses. The pre-Greek ancient world had not the faintest inkling of the lengths to which mental activity could be carried. Even Pythagoras, whoever he was, had no inkling: nor Herakleitos nor even Empedokles or Anaxagoras. Socrates and Aristotle were the first to *perceive* the dawn.

But on the other hand, we have not the faintest conception of the vast range that was covered by the ancient sense-consciousness. We have lost almost entirely the great and intricately developed sensual awareness, or sense-awareness, and sense-knowledge, of the ancients. It was a great depth of knowledge arrived at direct, by instinct and intuition, as we say, not by reason. It was a knowledge based not on words but on images. The abstraction was not into generalisations or into qualities, but into symbols. And the connection was not logical but emotional. The word "therefore" did not exist. Images or symbols succeeded one another in a procession of instinctive and arbitrary physical connection—some of the Psalms give us examples—and they "get nowhere" because there was nowhere to get to, the desire was to achieve a consummation of a certain state of consciousness, to fulfill a certain state of feeling-awareness. Perhaps all that remains to us today of the ancient way of "thought-process" are games like chess and cards. Chess-men and card-figures are symbols: their "values" are fixed in each case: their "movements" are non-logical, arbitrary, and based on the power-instinct.

Not until we can grasp a little of the working of the ancient mind can we appreciate the "magic" of the world they lived in. Take even the sphinx conundrum: *What is it that goes first on four legs, then on two and then on three?*—The answer is: Man.—To us it is rather silly, the great question of the sphinx. But in the uncritical ancient who *felt* his images, there would spring up a great complex of emotions and fears. The thing that goes on four legs is the animal, in all its animal difference and potency, its hinterland consciousness which circles round the isolated consciousness of man. And when, in the answer, it is shown that the baby goes on four legs, instantly there springs up another emotional complex, half fear, half amusement, as man realises himself as an animal, especially in the infantile state, going on all fours with face to the ground and belly or navel polarised to the earth's centre, like a true animal, instead of navel polarised to the sun, as in the true man, according to primitive conception. The second clause, of the two-legged creature, would bring up complex images of men, monkeys, birds and frogs, and the weird falling into relationship of these four would be an instant imaginative act, such as is very hard for us to achieve, but which children still make. The last clause, of the three-legged creature, would bring wonder, faint terror, and a searching of the great hinterlands beyond the deserts and the sea for some still-unrevealed beast.

So we see that the emotional reaction to such a conundrum was enormous. And even kings and heroes like Hector or Menelaus would make the same reaction, as a child now does, but a thousandfold stronger and wider. Men were not fools for so doing. Men are far more fools today, for stripping themselves of their emotional and imaginative reactions, and feeling nothing. The price we pay is boredom and deadness. Our bald processes of thought no longer are life to us. For the sphinx-riddle of man is as terrifying today as it was before Oedipus, and more so. For now it is the riddle of the dead-alive man, which it never was before.

VIII

Man thought and still thinks in images. But now our images have hardly any emotional value. We always want a "conclusion", an *end*, we always want to come, in our mental processes, to a decision, a finality, a full-stop. This gives us a sense of satisfaction. All our mental consciousness is a movement onwards, a movement in stages, like our sentences, and every full-stop is a mile-stone that marks our "progress" and our arrival somewhere. On and on we go, for the mental consciousness labours under the illusion that there is somewhere to go to, a goal to consciousness. Whereas of course there is no goal. Consciousness is an end in itself. We torture ourselves getting somewhere, and when we get there it is nowhere, for there is nowhere to get to.

While men still thought of the heart or the liver as the seat of consciousness, they had no idea of this on-and-on process of thought. To them a thought was a completed state of feeling-awareness, a cumulative thing, a deepening thing, in which feeling deepened into feeling in consciousness till there was a sense of fulness. A completed thought was the plumbing of a depth, like a whirlpool, of emotional awareness, and at the depth of this whirlpool of emotion the resolve formed. But it was no stage in a journey. There was no logical chain to be dragged further.

This should help us to appreciate the prophetic method of the past, and also the oracular method. The old oracles were not supposed to say something that fitted plainly in the whole chain of circumstance. They were supposed to deliver a set of images or symbols of the real dynamic value, which should set the emotional consciousness of the enquirer, as he pondered them, revolving more and more rapidly, till out of a state of intense emotional absorption the resolve at last formed; or, as we say, the decision was arrived at. As a matter of fact, we do very much the same, in a crisis. When anything very important is to be decided we withdraw and ponder and ponder until the deep emotions are set working and revolving together, revolving, revolving, till a centre is formed and we "know what to do". And the fact that no politician today has the courage to follow this intensive method of "thought" is the reason of the absolute paucity of the political mind today.

IX

Well then, let us return to the Apocalypse with this in mind: that the Apocalypse is still, in its movement, one of the works of the old pagan civilisation, and in it we have, not the modern process of progressive thought, but the old pagan process of rotary image-thought. Every image fulfills its own little cycle of action and meaning, then is superseded by another image. This is specially so in the first part, before the birth of the Child. Every image is a picture-graph, and the connection between the images will be made more or less differently by every reader. Nay, every image will be understood differently by every reader, according to his emotion-reaction. And yet there is a certain precise plan or scheme.

We must remember that the old human conscious-process has to *see something happen*, every time. Everything is concrete, there are no abstractions. And everything *does* something.

To the ancient consciousness, Matter, Materia, or Substantial things are God. A great rock is God. A pool of water is God. And why not? The longer we live the more we return to the oldest of all visions. A great rock *is* God. I can touch it. It is undeniable. It is God.

Then those things that move are doubly God. That is, we are doubly aware of their godhead: that which is, and that which moves: twice godly. Everything is a "thing": and every "thing" acts and has effect: the universe is a great complex activity of things existing and moving and having effect. And all this is God.

Today, it is almost impossible for us to realise what the old Greeks meant by god, or *theos*. Everything was *theos*; but even so, not at the same moment. At the moment, whatever *struck* you was god. If it was a pool of water, the very watery pool might strike you: then that was god; or the blue gleam might suddenly occupy your consciousness: then that was god; or a faint vapour at evening rising might catch the imagination: then that was *theos;* or thirst might overcome you at the sight of the water: then the thirst itself was god; or you drank, and the delicious and indescribable slaking of thirst was the god; or you felt the sudden chill of the water as you touched it: and then another god came into being, "the cold": and this was not a *quality*, it was an existing entity, almost a creature, certainly a *theos*: the cold; or again, on the dry lips something suddenly alighted: it was "the moist", and again a god. Even to the early scientists or philosophers, "the cold", "the moist", "the hot", "the dry" were things in themselves, realities, gods, *theoi*. And they *did things*.

With the coming of Socrates and "the spirit", the cosmos died. For two thousand years man has been living in a dead or dying cosmos, hoping for a heaven hereafter. And all the religions have been religions of the dead body and the postponed reward: eschatological, to use a pet word of the scientists.

It is very difficult for us to understand the pagan mind. When we are given translations of stories from the ancient Egyptian, the stories are almost entirely unintelligible. It may be the translations' fault: who can pretend really to *read* hieroglyph script? But when we are given translations from Bushman folk-lore, we find ourselves in almost the same puzzled state. The words may be intelligible, but the connection between them is impossible to follow. Even when we read translations of Hesiod, or even of Plato, we feel that a meaning has been arbitrarily *given* to the work, which is not its own meaning. It is the movement that is wrong, the inner connection. Flatter ourselves as we may, the gulf between Professor Jowett's mentality and Plato's mentality is almost impassable; and Professor Jowett's Plato is, in the end, just Professor Jowett, with hardly a breath of the living Plato. Plato divorced from his great pagan background is really only another Victorian statue in a toga—or a chlamys.

To get at the Apocalypse we have to appreciate the mental working of the pagan thinker or poet—pagan thinkers were necessarily poets—who starts with an image, sets the image in motion, allows it to achieve a certain course or circuit of its own, and then takes up another image. The old Greeks were very fine image-thinkers, as the myths prove. Their images were wonderfully natural and harmonious. They followed the logic of action rather than of reason, and they had no moral axe to grind. But still they are nearer to us than the orientals, whose image-thinking often followed no plan whatsoever, not even the sequence of action. We can see it in some of the Psalms, the flitting from image to image with no essential connection at all, but just the curious image-association. The oriental loved that.

To appreciate the pagan manner of thought we have to drop our own manner of on-and-on-and-on, from a start to a finish, and allow the mind to move in cycles, or to flit here and there over a cluster of images. Our idea of time as a continuity in an eternal straight line has crippled our consciousness cruelly. The pagan conception of time as moving in cycles is much freer, it allows movement upwards and downwards, and allows for a complete change of the state of mind, at any moment. One cycle finished, we can drop or rise to another level, and be in a new world at once. But by our time-continuum method, we have to trail wearily on over another ridge.

The old method of the Apocalypse is to set forth the image, make a world, and then suddenly depart from this world in a cycle of time and movement and even, an *epos;* and then return again to a world not quite like the original one, but on another level. The "world" is established on twelve: the number twelve is basic for an established cosmos. And the cycles move in sevens.

This old plan still remains, but very much broken up. The Jews always spoilt the beauty of a plan by forcing some ethical or tribal meaning in. The Jews have a moral instinct against design. Design, lovely plan, is pagan and immoral. So that we are not surprised, after the experience of Ezekiel and Daniel, to find the *mise en scène* of the vision muddled up, Jewish temple furniture shoved in, and twenty-four elders or presbyters who no longer quite know what they are, but are trying to be as Jewish as possible, and so on. The sea as of glass has come in from the Babylonian cosmos, the bright waters of heaven, as contrasted with the bitter or dead waters of the earthly sea: but of course it has to be put in a dish, a temple laver. Everything Jewish is *interior*. Even the stars of heaven and the waters of the fresh firmament have to be put inside the curtains of that stuffy tabernacle or temple.

But whether John of Patmos actually left the opening vision of the throne and the four starry Creatures and the twenty-four elders or witnesses, in the muddle we find them in, or whether later editors deliberately, in true Christian spirit, broke up the design, we don't know. John of Patmos was a Jew, so he didn't much mind whether his vision was imaginable or not. But even then, we feel the Christian scribes smashed up the pattern, to "make it safe". Christians have always been "making things safe".

The book had difficulty in getting into the Bible at all: the eastern Fathers objected to it so strongly. So if, in Cromwellian fashion, the heathen figures had their noses and hands knocked off, to "make them safe", we can't wonder. All we can do is to remember that there is probably a pagan kernel to the book: that this was written over, perhaps more than once, by Jewish apocalyptists, before the time of Christ: that John of Patmos probably wrote over the whole book once more, to make it Christian: and after that Christian scribes and editors tinkered with it to make it safe. They could go on tinkering for more than a hundred years.

Once we allow for pagan symbols more or less distorted by the Jewish mind and the Christian iconoclast, and for Jewish temple and ritual symbols arbitrarily introduced to make the heavens fit inside that precious Israelitish tabernacle, we can get a fairly good idea of the *mise en scène*, the vision of the throne with the cosmic beasts giving praise, and the rainbow-shrouded Kosmokrator about whose presence the prismatic glory glows like a rainbow and a cloud: "Iris too is a cloud". This Kosmokrator gleams with the colour of jasper and the sardine stone: the commentators say greenish yellow, whereas in Ezekiel it was amber yellow, as the effulgence of the cosmic fire. Jasper equates with the sign *Pisces*, which is the astrological sign of our era. Only now are we passing over the border of Pisces, into a new sign and a new era. And Jesus was called The Fish, for the same reason, during the first centuries. Such a powerful hold had star-lore, originally Chaldean, over the mind of man!

From the throne proceed thunders and lightnings and voices. Thunder indeed was the first grand cosmic utterance. It was a being in itself: another aspect of the Almighty or the Demiurge: and its voice was the first great cosmic noise, betokening creation. The grand Logos of the beginning was a thunderclap laughing throughout chaos, and causing the cosmos. But the Thunder, which is also the Almighty, and the Lightning, which is the Fiery Almighty putting forth the first jet of life-flame—the fiery Logos—have both also their angry or sundering aspect. Thunder claps creative through space, Lightning darts in fecund fire: or the reverse, destructive.

Then before the throne are the seven Lamps, which are explained as the seven Spirits of God. Explanations are fishy, in a work like this. But the seven lamps are the seven planets (including sun and moon) who are the seven Rulers from the heavens over the earth and over us. The great sun that makes day and makes all life on earth, the moon that sways the tides and sways our physical being, unknown sways the menstrual period in women and the sexual rhythm in a man, then the five big wandering stars, Mars, Venus, Saturn, Jupiter, Mercury, these, which are also our days of the week are as much our

Rulers now as ever they were: and as little. We know we live by the sun: how much we live by the others, we don't know. We reduce it all to simple gravitation-pull. Even at that, strange fine threads hold us to the moon and stars. That these threads have a psychic pull on us, we know from the moon. But what of the stars? How can we say? We have lost that sort of awareness.

However, we have the *mise en scène* of the drama of the Apocalypse: call it heaven, if you like. It really means the complete cosmos as we now have it: the "unregenerate" cosmos.

The Almighty has a book in his hand. The book is no doubt a Jewish symbol. They were a bookish people: and always great keepers of accounts: reckoning up sins throughout the ages. But the Jewish symbol of a book will do fairly well, with its seven seals, to represent a cycle of seven: though how the book is to be *opened* piece by piece, after the breaking of each seal, I myself cannot see: since the book is a rolled up scroll, and therefore could not *actually* be opened till all seven seals were broken. However, it is a detail: to the apocalyptist and to me. Perhaps there is no intention of opening it, till the end.

The Lion of Judah is supposed to open the book. But Lo! when the kingly beast comes on to the stage, it turns out to be a Lamb with seven horns (of power, the seven powers or potencies) and seven eyes (the same old planets). We are always hearing a terrific roaring as of lions, and we are always seeing a Lamb exhibiting this wrath. John of Patmos' Lamb is, we suspect, the good old lion in sheep's clothing. It behaves like the most terrific lion. Only John insists that it is a Lamb.

He has to insist on the Lamb, in spite of his predilection for lions, because Leo must now give way to Aries; for, throughout the whole world, the God who, like a lion, was given blood sacrifice must be shoved into the background, and the sacrificed god must occupy the foreground. The pagan mysteries of the sacrifice of the god for the sake of a greater resurrection are older than Christianity, and on one of these mysteries the Apocalypse is based. A Lamb it has to be: or with Mithras, a bull: and the blood drenches over the initiate from the cut throat of the bull (they lifted his head up as they cut his throat) and makes him a new man.

> "Wash me in the blood of the Lamb
> And I shall be whiter than snow—"

shrieks the Salvation Army in the market place. How surprised they would be if you told them it might just as well have been a bull. But perhaps they wouldn't. They might twig at once. In the lowest stratum of society religion remains pretty much the same, throughout the ages.

(But when it was for a hecatomb, they held the head of the bull downwards, to earth, and cut his throat over a pit. We feel that John's Lamb was for a hecatomb).

God became the animal that was slain, instead of the animal that does the slaying. With the Jews, then, it had to be a lamb, partly because of their ancient paschal sacrifice. The Lion of Judah put on a fleece: but by their bite ye shall know them. John insists on a Lamb "as it were slain": but we never see it slain, we only see it slaying mankind by the million. Even when it comes on in a victorious bloody shirt at the end, the blood is not its *own* blood: it is the blood of inimical kings.

> "Wash me in the blood of my enemies
> And I shall be that I am—"

says John of Patmos in effect.

There follows a paean. What it is is a real pagan paean of praise to the god who is about to demonstrate. The elders, those twice twelve of the established cosmos, who are really the twelve signs of the zodiac on their "seats", keep getting up and bowing to the throne, like the sheaves to Joseph. Vials of sweet odour are labelled: Prayers of the saints; probably an after-touch of some little Christian later on. Flocks of Jewish angels flock in. And then the drama begins.

X

With the famous four horsemen, the real drama begins. These four horsemen are obviously pagan. They are not even Jewish. In they ride, one after the other—though why they should come from the opening of the seals of a *book*, we don't know. In they ride, short and sharp, and it is over. They have been cut down to a minimum.

But there they are: obviously astrological, zodiacal, prancing in to a purpose. To what purpose? This time, really individual and human, rather than cosmic. The famous book of seven seals in this place is the body of man: of a man: of Adam: of any man: and the seven seals are the seven centres or gates of his dynamic consciousness. We are witnessing the opening, and conquest of the great psychic centres of the human body. The old Adam is going to be conquered, die, and be re-born as the new Adam: but in stages: in seven-fold stages: or in six stages, and then a climax, seven. For man has seven levels of awareness, deeper and higher: or seven spheres of consciousness. And one by one these must be conquered, transformed, transfigured.

And what are these seven spheres of consciousness in a man? Answer as you please, any man can give his own answer. But taking a common "popular" view, they are, shall we say, the four dynamic natures of man and three "higher" natures. Symbols mean something: yet they mean something different to every man. Fix the meaning of a symbol, and you have fallen into the commonplace of allegory.

Horses, always horses! How the horse dominated the mind of the early races, especially of the Mediterranean! You were a lord if you had a horse. Far back, far back in our dark soul the horse prances. He is a dominant symbol: he gives us lordship: he links us, the first palpable and throbbing link with the ruddy-glowing Almighty of potency: he is the beginning even of our godhead in the flesh. And as a symbol he roams the dark underworld meadows of the soul. He stamps and threshes in the dark fields of your soul and of mine. The sons of God who came down and knew the daughters of men and begot the great Titans, they had "the members of horses", says Enoch.

Within the last fifty years man has lost the horse. Now man is lost.

Man is lost to life and power—an underling and a wastrel. While horses thrashed the streets of London, London lived.

The horse, the horse! the symbol of surging potency and power of movement, of action, in man. The horse, that heroes strode. Even Jesus rode an ass, a mount of humble power. But the horse for true heroes. And different horses for the different powers, for the different heroic flames and impulses.

The rider on the white horse! Who is he then? The man who needs an explanation will never know. Yet explanations are our doom.

Take the old four natures of man: the sanguine, the choleric, the melancholic, the phlegmatic! There you have the four colours of the horses, white, red, black, and *pale*, or yellowish. But how should sanguine be white?—Ah, because the blood was the life itself, the very life: and the very power of life itself was white, dazzling. In our old days, *the blood was the life*, and visioned as power it was like white light. The scarlet and the purple were only the clothing of the blood. Ah the vivid blood clothed in bright red!—itself it was like pure light.

The red horse is choler: not mere anger, but natural fieryness, what we call passion.

The black horse was the black bile, refractory.

And the phlegm, or lymph of the body was the pale horse: in excess it causes death, and is followed by Hades.

Or take the four planetary natures of man: jovial, martial, saturnine and mercurial. This will do for another correspondence, if we go a little behind the *Latin* meaning, to the older Greek. Then Great Jove is the sun, and the living blood: the white horse: and angry Mars rides the red horse: Saturn is black, stubborn, refractory and gloomy: and Mercury is really Hermes, Hermes of the Underworld, the guide of souls, the watcher over two ways, the opener of two doors, he who seeks through hell, or Hades.

There are two sets of correspondence, both physical. We leave the cosmic meanings, for the intention here is more physical than cosmic.

You will meet the white horse over and over again, as a symbol. Does not even Napoleon have a white horse? The old meanings control our actions, even when our minds have gone inert.

But the rider on the white horse is crowned. He is the royal me, he is my very self, and his horse is the whole *mana* of a man. He is my very me, my sacred ego, called into a new cycle of action by the Lamb and riding forth to conquest, the conquest of the old self for the birth of a new self. It is he, truly, who shall conquer all the other "powers" of the self. And he rides forth, like the sun, with arrows, to conquest, but not with the sword, for the sword implies also judgment, and this is my dynamic or potent self. And his bow is the bended bow of the body, like the crescent moon.

The true action of the myth, or ritual-imagery, has been all cut away. The rider on the white horse appears, then vanishes. But we know why he has appeared. And we know why he is paralleled at the end of the Apocalypse by the last rider on the white horse, who is the heavenly Son of Man riding forth after the last and final conquest over the "kings". The son of man, even you or I, rides forth to the small conquest: but the Great Son of Man mounts his white horse after the last universal conquest, and leads on his hosts. His shirt is red with the blood of monarchs, and on his thigh is his title: King of Kings and Lord of Lords. (Why on his thigh? Answer for yourself. Did not Pythagoras show his golden thigh in the temple? Don't you know the old and powerful Mediterranean symbol of the thigh?) But out of the mouth of the final rider on the white horse comes that fatal sword of the logos of judgment. Let us go back to the bow and arrows of him to whom judgment is not given.

The myth has been cut down to the bare symbols. The first rider only rides forth. After the second rider, peace is lost, strife and war enter the world—really the inner world of the self. After the rider on the black horse, who carries the balances of measure, that weigh out the measures or true proportions of the "elements" in the body, bread becomes scarce, though wine and oil are not hurt. Bread, barley is here the body or flesh which is symbolically sacrificed—as in the barley scattered over the victim in a Greek sacrifice: "Take this bread of my body with thee". The body of flesh is now at famine stage, wasted down. Finally, with the rider on the pale horse, the last, the physical or dynamic self is dead in the "little death" of the initiate, and we enter the Hades or underworld of our being.

We enter the Hades or underworld of our being, for our body is now "dead". But the powers or demons of this underworld can only hurt a fourth part of the earth: that is, a fourth part of the body of flesh: Which means, the death is only mystical, and that which is hurt is only the body that belongs to already-established creation. Hunger and physical woes befall the physical body in this little death, but there is as yet no greater hurt.—There are no plagues: these are divine wrath, and here we have no anger of the Almighty.

There is a crude and superficial explanation of the four horsemen:

but probably it hints at the true meaning. The orthodox commentators who talk about famines in the time of Titus or Vespasian may be reading the bit about barley and wheat correctly, according to a late apocalyptist. The *original* meaning, which was pagan, is smeared over intentionally with a meaning that can fit this "Church of Christ versus the wicked Gentile Powers" business. But none of that touches the horsemen themselves. And perhaps here better than anywhere else in the book can we see the peculiar way in which the old meaning has been cut away and confused and changed, deliberately, while the bones of the structure have been left.

But there are three more seals. What happens when these are opened?

After the fourth seal and the rider on the pale horse, the initiate, in pagan ritual, is bodily dead. There remains, however, the journey through the underworld, where the living "I" must divest itself of soul and spirit, before it can at last emerge naked from the far gate of hell into the new day. For the soul, the spirit, and the living "I" are the three divine natures of man. The four bodily natures are put off on earth. The *two* divine natures can only be divested in Hades. And the last is a stark flame which, on the new day, is clothed anew and successively by the spiritual body, the soul-body, and then the "garment" of flesh, with its fourfold terrestrial natures.

Now no doubt the pagan script recorded this passage through Hades, this divesting of the soul, then of the spirit, till the mystic death is fulfilled six-fold, and the seventh seal is at once the last thunder of death and the first thundrous paean of new birth and tremendous joy.

But the Jewish mind hates the mortal and terrestrial divinity of man: the Christian mind the same. Man is only postponedly divine: when he is dead and gone to glory. He *must not* achieve divinity in the flesh. So the Jewish and Christian apocalyptists abolish the mystery of the individual adventure into Hades and substitute a lot of martyred souls crying under the altar for vengeance—vengeance was a sacred duty with the Jews. These souls are told to wait awhile—always the postponed destiny—until more martyrs are killed; and they are given white robes: which is premature, for the white robes are the new resurrected bodies, and how could these crying "souls" put them on in Hades: in the grave? However—such is the muddle that Jewish and Christian apocalyptists have made of the fifth seal.

The sixth seal, the divesting of the spirit from the last living quick of the "I", this has been turned by the apocalyptist into a muddled cosmic calamity. The sun goes black as sack-cloth of hair: which means that he is a great black orb streaming forth visible darkness; the moon turns to blood, which is one of the horror-reversals of the pagan mind, for the moon is mother of the watery body of men, the blood belongs to the sun, and the moon, like a harlot or demon woman, can only be drunk with red blood in her utterly maleficent aspect of meretrix, blood-drinker, she who should give the cool water of the body's fountain of flesh; the stars fall from the sky, and the heavens depart like a scroll rolled together, and "every mountain and island were moved out of their places". It means the return of chaos, and the end of our cosmic order, or creation. Yet it is not *annihilation*: for the kings of the earth and all the rest of men keep on hiding in the shifted mountains, from the ever-recurrent wrath of the Lamb.

This cosmic calamity no doubt corresponds to the original final death of the initiate, when his very spirit is stripped off him and he knows death indeed, yet still keeps the final flame-point of life, down in Hades.—But it is a pity the apocalyptists were so interfering: the Apocalypse is a string of cosmic calamities, monotonous. We would give the New Jerusalem cheerfully, to have back the pagan record of initiation; and this perpetual "wrath of the Lamb" business exasperates one like endless threats of toothless old men.

However, the six stages of mystic death are over. The seventh stage is a death and birth at once. Then the final flame-point of the eternal self of a man emerges from hell, and at the very instant of extinction becomes a new whole cloven flame of a new-bodied man with golden thighs and a face of glory. But first there is a pause: a natural pause. The action is suspended, and transferred to another world, to the outer cosmos. There is a lesser cycle of ritual to fulfill, before the seventh seal, the crash and the glory.

XI

Creation, we know, is four-square, and the number of creation, or of the created universe, is four. From the four corners of the world four winds can blow, three bad winds, one good one. When all the winds are loosed, it means chaos in the air, and destruction on earth.

So the four angels of the winds are told to hold back their winds and hurt neither earth nor sea nor trees: that is, the actual world.

But there is a mystic wind from the east which lifts the sun and the moon like full-sailed ships, and bears them across the sky like vessels slowly scudding.—This was one of the beliefs, in the second century B.C.—Out of this east rises the angel crying for a pause in the blowing of the winds of destruction, while he shall seal the servants of God in their foreheads. Then the twelve tribes of Jews are tediously enumerated and sealed: a tedious Jewish performance.

The vision changes, and we see a great multitude, clothed in white robes and with palms in their hands, standing before the throne and before the Lamb, and crying with a loud voice: "Salvation to our God which sitteth upon the throne, and to the Lamb". Thereupon angels and elders and the four winged beasts fall on their faces and worship God saying: "Blessing, and glory, and wisdom, and thanksgiving, and honour, and power, and might be unto our God for ever and ever. Amen".—

This suggests that the seventh seal is opened. The angel cries to the four winds to be still, while the blessed, or the new-born appear. And then those who "went through the great tribulation", or initiation into death and re-birth, appear in glory, clothed in the white dazzling robes of their new bodies, carrying branches of the tree of life in their hands, and appearing in a grand blaze of light before the Almighty. They hymn their praise, and the angels take it up.

Here we can see, in spite of the apocalyptist, the pagan initiate, perhaps in a temple of Cybele, suddenly brought forth from the under-dark of the temple into the grand blaze of light in front of the pillars. Dazzled, re-born, he wears white robes and carries the palm-branch, and the flutes sound out their rapture round him, and the dancing women lift the garlands over him. The lights flash, the incense rolls up, the brilliant priests and priestesses throw up their arms and sing the hymn to the new glory of the re-born, as they form around him and exalt him in a kind of ecstasy. The crowd beyond is breathless.

This vivid scene in front of the temple, of the glorification of a new initiate and his identification or assimilation to the god, amid grand brilliance and wonder, and the sound of flutes and the swaying of garlands, in front of the awed crowd of on-lookers was, we know, the end of the ritual of the Mysteries of Isis. Such a scene has been turned by the apocalyptists into a Christian vision. But it really takes place *after* the opening of the seventh seal. The cycle of individual initiation is fulfilled. The great conflict and conquest is over. The initiate is dead, and alive again in a new body. He is sealed in the forehead, like a Buddhist monk, as a sign that he has died the death, and that his seventh self is fulfilled, he is twice-born, his mystic eye or "third eye" is now open. He sees in two worlds. Or, like the Pharaohs with the serpent Uraeus rearing between their brows, he has charge of the last proud power of the sun.

But all this is pagan and impious. No Christian is allowed to rise up new and in a divine body, here on earth and in the midst of life. So we are given a crowd of martyrs in heaven, instead.

The seal in the forehead may be ashes: the seal of the death of the body: or it may be scarlet or glory, the new light or vision. It is, really, in itself the seventh seal.

Now it is finished, and there is silence in heaven for the space of about half an hour.

XII

And here, perhaps, the oldest pagan manuscript ended. At any rate the first cycle of the drama is over. With various hesitations, some old apocalyptist starts the second cycle, this time the cycle of the death and regeneration of earth or world, instead of the individual. And this part, too, we feel is much older than John of Patmos. Nevertheless, it is very Jewish, the curious distortion of paganism through the Jewish moral and cataclysmic vision: the monomaniacal insistence on punishment and woes, which goes right through the Apocalypse. We are now in a real Jewish atmosphere.

But still there are old pagan ideas. Incense rises up to the nostrils of the Almighty in great clouds of smoke. But these clouds of incense-smoke are allegorised, and made to carry up the prayers of the saints. Then the divine fire is cast down to earth, to start the little death and final regeneration of the world, the earth and the multitude. Seven angels, the seven angels of the seven dynamic natures of God, are given seven trumpets to make seven annunciations.

And then the now-Jewish Apocalypse starts to unroll its second cycle of the Seven Trumps.

There is again a division into four and three. We are witnessing the death (the little death) of the cosmos at divine command, and therefore each time there is a trumpet blast, a third part, not a fourth, of the world is destroyed. The divine number is three: the number of the world, four-square, is four.

At the first Trump, a third part of vegetable life is destroyed.

At the second Trump, a third part of all marine life, even ships.

At the third Trump, a third part of the fresh waters of earth are embittered and become poison.

At the fourth Trump, a third part of the heavens, sun, moon and stars, are destroyed.

This corresponds to the four horsemen of the first cycle, in a clumsy Jewish-apocalyptic parallel. The *material* cosmos has now suffered the little death.

What follows are the "three woes", which affect the spirit and soul of the world (symbolised now as men), instead of the material part. A star falls to earth: Jewish figure for an angel descending. He has the key of the abyss—Jewish counterpart of Hades. And the action now moves to the underworld of the cosmos instead of the underworld of the self, as in the first cycle.

It is now all Jewish and allegorical, not symbolical any more. The sun and the moon are darkened because we are in the underworld.

The abyss, like the underworld, is full of malefic powers, injurious to man.

For the abyss, like the underworld, represents the superseded powers of creation.

The old nature of man must yield and give way to a new nature. In yielding, it passes away down into Hades, and there lives on, undying and malefic, superseded, yet malevolent-potent in the underworld.

This very profound truth was embodied in all old religions, and lies at the root of the worship of the underworld powers. The worship of the underworld powers, the chthonioi, was perhaps the very basis of the most ancient Greek religion. When man has neither the strength to subdue his underworld powers—which are really the ancient powers of his old, superseded self; nor the wit to placate them with sacrifice and the burnt holocaust; then they come back at him, and destroy him again. Hence every new conquest of life means a "harrowing of Hell".

In the same way, after every great cosmic change, the power of the *old* cosmos, superseded, becomes demonic and harmful to the new creation. It is a great truth which lies behind the Gea-Ouranos-Kronos-Zeus series of myths.

Therefore the whole cosmos has its malefic aspect. The sun, the great sun, in so far as he is the *old* sun of a superseded cosmic day, is hateful and malevolent to the new-born, tender thing I am. He does me harm, in my struggling self, for he still has power over my old self, and he is hostile.

Likewise the waters of the cosmos, in their *oldness* and their superseded or abysmal nature, are malevolent to life, especially to the life of man. The great Moon and mother of my inner water-streams, in so far as she is the old, dead moon is hostile, hurtful and hateful to my flesh, for she still has a power over my old flesh.

This is the meaning away back of the "two woes": a very deep meaning, too deep for John of Patmos. The famous locusts of the first woe, which emerge from the abyss at the fifth Trump, are complex but not unintelligible symbols. They do not hurt vegetable earth, only the men who have not the new seal on their foreheads. These men they torture, but cannot kill: for it is the little death. And they can torture only for five months, which is a season, the sun's season, and more or less a third part of the year.

Now these locusts are like horses prepared unto battle, which means, horses, horses, that they are hostile potencies or *powers*.

They have hair as the hair of women—the steaming crest of the sun-powers, or sun-rays.

They have the teeth of the lion—the red lion of the sun in his malefic aspect.

They have faces like men: since they are directed only against the *inward* life of men.

They have crowns like gold: they are royal, of the royal orb of the sun.

They have stings in their tails: which means, they are in the reversed or hellish aspect, creatures which once were good, but being superseded, of a past order, are now reversed and hellish, stinging, as it were, backwards.

And their king is Apollyon—which is Apollo, great Lord of the (pagan and therefore hellish) sun.

Having made his weird, muddled composite symbol at last intelligible, the old Jewish apocalyptist declares the first woe is past, and that there are two more still to come.

XIII

The sixth Trump sounds. The voice from the golden altar says: "Loose the four angels which are bound in the great river Euphrates".—

These are evidently four angels of four corners, like those of the four winds. So Euphrates, the evil river of Babylon, will no doubt stand for the waters under the earth, or the abysmal under-ocean, in its hellish aspect.

And the angels are loosed, whereupon, apparently the great army of demon-horsemen, two hundred million, all told, issue from the abyss.

The horses of the two hundred million horsemen have heads as the heads of lions, and out of their mouth issue fire and brimstone. And these kill a third part of men, by the fire, smoke and brimstone which come out of their mouths. Then unexpectedly we are told that their power is in their mouth and in their tails; for their tails are like serpents, and have heads, and with them they do hurt.

These weird creatures are Apocalyptic images, surely: not symbols, but personal images of some old apocalyptist long before John of Patmos. The horses are powers, and divine instruments of woe: for they kill a third part of men, and later we are told they are plagues. Plagues are the whips of God.

Now they ought to be the reversed or malevolent powers of the abysmal or underworld waters. Instead of which they are sulphureous, evidently volcanic beasts of the abysmal or underworld fires, which are the hellish fires of the sun. And they have lions' heads, like powers of the hellish sun.

Then suddenly they are given serpent tails, and they have evil power in their tails. Here we are back at the right thing—the horse-bodied serpent-monster of the salty deeps of hell: the powers of the underworld waters seen in their reversed aspect, malevolent, striking a third of men, probably with some watery and deadly disease; as the locusts of the fifth Trump smote men with some hot and agonising, yet not deadly disease, which ran for a certain number of months.

So that here probably two apocalyptists have been at work. The later one did not understand the scheme. He put in his brimstone horses with their riders having breastplates of fire and jacinth and brimstone (red, dark blue, and yellow), following his own gay fancy, and perhaps influenced by some volcanic disturbance and some sight of splendid red, blue and yellow cavalry of the east. That is a true Jewish method.

But then he had to come back to the old manuscript, with serpent-tailed watery monsters. So he tacked on the serpent tails to his own horses, and let them gallop.

This apocalyptist of the brimstone horses is probably responsible for the "lake of fire burning with brimstone" into which the souls of fallen angels and wicked men are cast to burn for ever and ever more. This pleasant place is the prototype of the Christian hell, specially invented by the Apocalypse. The old Jewish hells of Sheol and Gehenna were fairly mild, uncomfortable abysmal places like Hades, and when a New Jerusalem was created from heaven, they disappeared. They were part of the old cosmos, and did not outlast the old cosmos. They were not eternal.

This was not good enough for the brimstone apocalyptist and John of Patmos. They must have a marvellous, terrific lake of sulphureous fire that could burn for ever and ever, so that the souls of the enemy could be kept writhing. When, after the last Judgment, earth and sky and all creation were swept away, and only glorious heaven remained, still, away down, there remained this burning lake of fire in which the souls were suffering. Brilliant glorious eternal heaven above: and brilliant sulphureous torture-lake away below. This is the vision of eternity of all Patmossers. They could not be happy in heaven unless they *knew* their enemies were unhappy in hell.

And this vision was specially brought into the world with the Apocalypse. It did not exist before.

Before, the waters of the hellish underworld were bitter like the sea. They were the evil aspect of the waters under the earth, which were conceived as some wondrous lake of sweet, lovely water, source of all the springs and streams of earth, lying away down below the rocks.

The waters of the abyss were salt like the sea. Salt had a great hold on the old imagination. It was supposed to be the product of "elemental" injustice. Fire and water, the two great living elements and opposites, gave rise to all substance in their slippery unstable "marriage". But when one triumphed over the other, there was "injustice".—So, when the sun-fire got too strong for the sweet waters, it *burnt* them, and when water was burnt by fire, it produced salt, child of injustice. This child of injustice corrupted the waters and made them bitter. So the sea came into being. And thence the dragon of the sea, leviathan.

And so the bitter waters of hell were the place where souls were drowned: the bitter, anti-life ocean of the end.

There was for ages a resentment against the sea: the bitter, corrupt sea, as Plato calls it. But this seems to have died down in Roman times: so our apocalyptist substitutes a brimstone burning lake, as being more horrific, and able to make the souls suffer more.

A third of men are killed by these brimstone horsemen. But the remaining two-thirds do not refrain from worshipping idols which can "neither see nor hear nor walk".

That sounds as if the Apocalypse here was still quite Jewish and pre-Christian. There is no Lamb about.

Later, this second woe winds up with the usual earthquakes. But since the shiver of the earth must immediately give rise to a new movement, it is postponed awhile.

XIV

Six Trumps are blown, so now there is a pause: just as there was a pause after the Six Seals were opened, to let the angels of the four winds arrange themselves, and the action transfer itself to heaven.

Now, however, come various interruptions. First there comes down a mighty angel, a cosmic lord, something like the Son of Man in the first vision. But the Son of Man, indeed all Messianic reference seems missing in this part of the Apocalypse. This mighty angel sets one burning foot upon the sea and one on earth, and roars like a lion throughout space. Whereupon the seven creative thunders roll out their creative utterances. These seven thunders, we know, are the seven tonal natures of the Almighty, Maker of heaven and earth: and now they are giving voice to seven vast new commands, for a new cosmic day, a new phase in creation. The seer is in a hurry to write down these seven new words, but he is commanded not to do so. He is not allowed to divulge the nature of the new commands, which will bring the new cosmos into being. We must wait for the actuality. Then this great "angel" or cosmic lord raises his hand and swears, by heaven and earth and water under the earth, which is the great Greek oath of the gods, that the old Time is over, the mystery of God is about to be fulfilled.

Then the seer is given the little book to eat. It is the lesser general or universal message of the destruction of the old world and creation of the new: a lesser message than that of the destruction of the old Adam and the creation of new man, which the seven-sealed book told. And it is sweet in the mouth—as revenge is sweet—but bitter in experience.

Then another interruption: the measuring of the temple, a pure Jewish interruption; the measuring or counting of the "chosen of God", before the end of the old world; and the exclusion of the unchosen.

Then comes the most curious interruption of the two witnesses. Orthodox commentators identify these two witnesses with Moses and Elija who were with Jesus in the transfiguration on the mount. They are something much older too. These two witnesses are prophets clothed in sack-cloth: that is, they are in their woeful aspect, hostile or reversed. They are the two candlesticks and the two olive trees which stand before "Adonai", the God of the earth. They have power over the waters of the sky (rain), power to turn water into blood, and to smite the earth with all the plagues. They make their testimony, then the beast out of the Abyss rises and slays them. Their dead bodies lie out in the street of the great city, and the people of the earth rejoice because these two who tormented them are dead. But after three and a half days, the spirit of life from God enters the dead two, they rise to their feet, and a great voice says from heaven "Come up hither". So they rise to heaven on a cloud, and their enemies in fear behold them.

It looks as if we had here a layer of very old myth referring to the mysterious twins, "the little ones", who had such power over the nature of men. But both the Jewish and Christian apocalyptists have balked this bit of Revelation: they have not given it any plain meaning of any sort.

The twins belong to a very old cult which apparently was common to all ancient European peoples; but it seems they were heavenly twins, belonging to the sky. Yet when they were identified by the Greeks with the Tyndarids, Kastor and Polydeukes, already in the Odyssey, they lived alternately in Heaven and in Hades, witnessing to both places. And as such, they may be the candlesticks, or stars of heaven, on the one hand, and the olive trees of the underworld, on the other.

But the older a myth, the deeper it goes in the human consciousness, the more varied will be the forms it takes in the upper consciousness. We have to remember that some symbols, and this of the twins is one of them, can carry even our modern consciousness back for a thousand years, for two thousand years, for three thousand years, for four thousand years, and even beyond that. The power of suggestion is most mysterious. It may not work at all: or it may carry the unconscious mind back in great cyclic swoops through eras of time: or it may go only part way.

If we think of the heroic Dioskouroi, the Greek Twins, the Tyndarids, we go back only half way. The Greek heroic age did a strange thing, it made every cosmic conception anthropomorphic, yet kept a great deal of the cosmic wonder. So that the Dioskouroi are and are not the ancient twins.

But the Greeks themselves were always reverting to the pre-heroic, pre-Olympian gods and potencies. The Olympic-heroic period was only an interlude. The Olympic-heroic vision was always felt to be too shallow, the old Greek soul would drop continually to deeper, older, darker levels of religious consciousness, all through the centuries. So that the mysterious Tritopatores at Athens, who were also called The Twins, and Dioskouroi, were the lords of the winds, and mysterious watchers at the procreation of children. So here again we are back in the old levels.

When the Samothracian cult spread in Hellas, in the third and second centuries B.C., then the twins became the *Kabeiroi*, or the Kabiri, and then again they had an enormous suggestive influence over the minds of men. The Kabiri were a swing back to the old idea of the dark or mysterious twins, connected with the movement of the cloudy skies and the air, and with the movement of fertility, and the perpetual and mysterious balance between these two. The apocalyptist sees them in their woeful aspect, masters of sky-water and the waters of earth, which they can turn into blood, and masters of plagues from Hades: the heavenly and hellish aspects of the twins, malevolent.

But the Kabiri were connected with many things: and it is said their cult is still alive in Mohammedan countries. They were the two secret little ones, the homunculi, and the "rivals". They were also connected with thunder, and with two round black thunder-stones. So they were called the "sons of thunder", and had power over rain: also power to curdle milk, and, malefic, power to turn water into blood. As thunderers they were sunderers, sundering cloud, air and water. And always they have this aspect of rivals, dividers, separaters, for good as well as for ill: balancers.

By another symbolic leap, they were also the ancient gods of gateposts, and then they were the guardians of the gate, and then the twin beasts that guard the altar, or the tree, or the urn, in so many Babylonian and Aegean and Etruscan paintings and sculpture. They were often panthers, leopards, gryphons, earth and night creatures, jealous ones.

It is they who hold things asunder to make a space, a gateway. In this way, they are rain-makers: they open the gates in the sky: perhaps as thunder-stones. In the same way they are the secret lords of sex, for it was early recognised that sex is a holding of two things asunder, that birth may come through between them. In the sexual sense, they can change water into blood: for the phallos itself was the homunculus, and, in one aspect, it was itself the twins of earth, the small one who made water and the small one who was filled with blood: the rivals within a man's own very nature and earthly self: symbolised again in the twin stones of the testes. They are thus the roots of the twin olive trees, producing the olives, and the oil of the procreative sperm. They are also the two candlesticks which stand before the lord of earth, Adonai. For they give the two alternate forms of elemental consciousness, our day-consciousness and our night-consciousness, that which we are in the depths of night, and that other, very different being which we are in bright day. A creature of dual and jealous consciousness is man, and the twins witness jealously to the duality. Physiologically, in the same meaning, it is they who hold apart the two streams of the water and of the blood in our bodies. If the water and blood ever mingled in our bodies, we should be dead. The two streams are kept apart by the little ones, the rivals. And on the two streams depends the dual consciousness.

Now these little ones, these rivals, they are "witnesses" to life, for it is between their opposition that the Tree of Life itself grows, from the earthly root. They testify before the god of earth or fecundity all the time. And all the time, they put a limit on man. They say to him, in every earthly or physical activity: Thus far and no further.—They limit every action, every "earth" action, to its own scope, and counterbalance it with an opposite action. They are gods of gates, but they are also gods of limits: each forever jealous of the other, keeping the other in bounds. They make life possible; but they make life limited. As the testes, they hold the phallic balance forever, they are the two phallic witnesses. They are the enemies of intoxication, of ecstasy, and of licence, of licentious freedom. Always they testify to Adonai. Hence the men in the cities of licence rejoice when the beast from the abyss, which is the hellish dragon or demon of the earth's destruction, or man's bodily destruction, at last kills these two "guardians", regarded as a sort of policemen in "Sodom" and "Egypt". The bodies of the slain two lie unburied for three and a half days: that is, half a week, or half a period of time, when all decency and restraint has departed from among men.

The language of the text, "rejoice and make merry and send gifts to one another" suggests a pagan Saturnalia, like the Hermaia of Crete or the Sakaia at Babylon, the feast of unreason. If this is what the apocalyptist meant, it shows how intimately he follows pagan practice, for the ancient saturnalian feasts all represented the breaking, or at least the interruption of an old order of rule and law: and this time it is the "natural rule" of the two witnesses which is broken. Men escape from the laws even of their own nature for a spell: for three days and a half, which is half the sacred week, or a "little" period of time. Then, as heralding the new earth and the new body of man, the two witnesses stand up again: men are struck with terror: the voice from heaven calls the two witnesses, and they go up in a cloud.

"Two, two for the lily-white boys, clothed all in green-O!—"

Thus the earth, and the body, cannot die its death till these two sacred twins, the rivals, have been killed.

An earthquake comes, the seventh angel blows his trumpet and makes the great announcement: "The kingdoms of this world are become the kingdoms of our Lord and of his Christ, and he shall reign for ever and ever".—So there is again worship and thanksgiving in heaven, that God takes the reign again. And the temple of God is opened in heaven, the holy of holies is revealed, and the ark of the testament. Then there are the lightnings, voices, thunderings, earthquakes and hail which end a period and herald another. The third woe is ended.

And here ends the first part of the Apocalypse: the old half. The little myth that follows stands quite alone in the book, dramatically, and is really out of keeping with the rest. One of the apocalyptists put it in as part of a theoretic scheme: the birth of the Messiah after the little death of earth and man. And the other apocalyptists left it there.

XV

What follows is the myth of the birth of a new sun-god from a great sun-goddess, and her pursuit by the great red dragon. This myth is left as the centre-piece of the Apocalypse, and figures as the birth of the Messiah. Even orthodox commentators admit that it is entirely unchristian, and almost entirely unjewish. We are down pretty well to a pagan bed-rock, and we can see at once how many Jewish and Jewish-Christian overlays there are in the other parts.

But this pagan birth-myth is very brief—as was the other bit of pure myth, that of the four horsemen.

"And there appeared a great wonder in heaven; a woman clothed with the sun, and the moon under her feet, and upon her head a crown of twelve stars: and she being with child cried, travailing in birth, and pained to be delivered.

And there appeared another wonder in heaven: and behold, a great red dragon having seven heads and ten horns, and seven crowns upon his heads. And his tail drew a third part of the stars of heaven, and did cast them to the earth; and the dragon stood before the woman which was ready to be delivered, for to devour her child as soon as it was born.

And she brought forth a man child, who was to rule all nations with a rod of iron; and her child was caught up unto God, and to his throne. And the woman fled into the wilderness, where she hath a place prepared of God, that they should feed her there twelve hundred and sixty days.

And there was war in heaven; Michael and his angels fought against the dragon; and the dragon fought and his angels, and prevailed not; neither was their place found any more in heaven.

And the great dragon was cast out, that old serpent called the Devil, and Satan, which deceiveth the whole world: he was cast forth into the earth, and his angels were cast out with him"—

This fragment is really the pivot of the Apocalypse. It looks like late pagan myth suggested from various Greek, Egyptian and Babylonian myths. Probably the first apocalyptist added it to the original pagan manuscript, many years before the birth of Christ, to give his vision of a Messiah's birth, born of the sun. But connecting with the Four Horsemen, and with the two witnesses, the goddess clothed in the sun and standing upon the moon's crescent is difficult to reconcile with a Jewish vision. The Jews hated pagan gods, but they more than hated the great pagan goddesses: they would not even speak of them, if possible. And this wonder-woman clothed in the sun and standing upon the crescent of the moon was too splendidly suggestive of the great goddess of the east, the great Mother, the Magna Mater as she became to the Romans. This great woman goddess with a child stands looming far, far back in history in the eastern Mediterranean, in the days when matriarchy was still the natural order of the obscure nations. How then does she come to tower as the central figure in a Jewish Apocalypse? We shall never know: unless we accept the old law that when you drive the devil out of the front door he comes in at the back. This great goddess has suggested many pictures of the Virgin Mary. She has brought into the Bible what it lacked before: the great cosmic Mother robed and splendid, but persecuted. And she is, of course, essential to the scheme of power and splendour, which must have a queen: unlike the religions of renunciation, which are womanless. The religions of power must have a great queen and queen mother. So here she stands in the Apocalypse, the book of thwarted power-worship.

After the flight of the great Mother from the dragon, the whole Apocalypse changes tone. Suddenly Michael the archangel is introduced: which is a great jump from the four starry beasts of the Presence, who have been the Cherubim till now. The dragon is identified with Lucifer and Satan, and even then has to give his power to the beast from the sea: alias Nero.

There is a great change. We leave the old cosmic and elemental world, and come to the late Jewish world of angels like policemen and postmen. It is a world essentially uninteresting, save for the great vision of the Scarlet Woman, which has been borrowed from the pagans, and is, of course, the reversal of the great woman clothed in the sun. The late apocalyptists are much more at their ease cursing her and calling her a harlot and other vile names, than in seeing her clothed in the sun and giving her due reverence.

Altogether the latter half of the Apocalypse is a come-down. We see it in the chapter of the seven vials. The seven vials of the wrath of the Lamb are a clumsy imitation of the seven seals and the seven Trumps. The apocalyptist no longer knows what he is about. There is no division into four and three, no re-birth or glory after the seventh vial—just a clumsy succession of plagues. And then the whole thing falls to earth in the prophesying and cursing business which we have met already in the old prophets and in Daniel. The visions are amorphous and have fairly obvious allegorical meanings: treading the winepress of the wrath of the Lord, and so on. It is stolen poetry, stolen from the old prophets. And for the rest, the destruction of Rome is the blatant and rather boring theme. Rome was anyhow more than Jerusalem.

Only the great whore of Babylon rises rather splendid, sitting in her purple and scarlet upon her scarlet beast. She is the Magna Mater in malefic aspect, clothed in the colours of the angry sun, and throned upon the great red dragon of the angry cosmic power. Splendid she sits, and spendid is her Babylon. How the late apocalyptists love mouthing out all about the gold and silver and cinnamon of evil Babylon. How they *want* them all! How they *envy* Babylon her splendour, envy, envy! How they love destroying it all. The harlot sits magnificent with her golden cup of the wine of sensual pleasure in her hand. How the apocalyptists would have loved to drink out of her cup! And since they couldn't, how they loved smashing it!

Gone is the grand pagan calm which can see the woman of the cosmos wrapped in her warm gleam like the sun, and having her feet upon the moon, the moon who gives us our white flesh. Gone is the great Mother of the cosmos, crowned with a diadem of the twelve great stars of the zodiac. She is driven to the desert, and the dragon of the watery chaos spues floods upon her. But kind earth swallows the floods, and the great woman, winged for flight like an eagle, must remain lost in the desert for a time, and times, and half a time. Which is like the three-and-a-half days, or years of other parts of the Apocalypse, and means half of a time-period.

That is the last we have seen of her. She has been in the desert ever since, the great cosmic Mother crowned with all the signs of the zodiac. Since she fled, we have had nothing but virgins and harlots, half-women: the half-women of the Christian era. For the great Woman of the pagan cosmos was driven into the wilderness at the end of the old epoch, and she has never been called back. That Diana of Ephesus, John of Patmos' Ephesus, was already a travesty of the great woman crowned with the stars.

Yet perhaps it was a book of her "mystery" and initiation ritual which gave rise to the existing Apocalypse. But if so, it has been written over and over, till only a last glimpse is left of her: and one other corresponding glimpse, of the great woman of the cosmos "seen red". Oh how weary we get, in the Apocalypse, of all these woes and plagues and deaths! how infinitely weary we are of the mere thought of that jeweller's paradise of a New Jerusalem at the end! All this maniacal anti-life! They can't bear even to let the sun and the moon exist, these horrible salvationists. But it is envy.

XVI

The woman is one of the "wonders". And the other wonder is the Dragon. The Dragon is one of the oldest symbols of the human consciousness. The dragon and serpent symbol goes so deep in every human consciousness, that a rustle in the grass can startle the toughest "modern" to depths he has no control over.

First and foremost, the dragon is the symbol of the fluid, rapid, startling movement of life within us. That startled life which runs through us like a serpent, or coils within us potent and waiting, like a serpent, this is the dragon. And the same with the cosmos.

From earliest times, man has been aware of a "power" or potency within him—and also outside him—which he has no ultimate control over. It is a fluid, rippling potency which can lie quite dormant, sleeping, and yet be ready to leap out unexpectedly. Such are the sudden angers that spring upon us from within ourselves, passionate and terrible in passionate people: and the sudden accesses of violent desire, wild sexual desire, or violent hunger, or a great desire of any sort, even for sleep. The hunger which made Esau sell his birthright would have been called his dragon: later, the Greeks would even have called it a "god" in him. It is something beyond him, yet within him. It is swift and surprising as a serpent, and overmastering as a dragon. It leaps up from somewhere inside him, and has the better of him.

Primitive man, or shall we say early man was in a certain sense afraid of his own nature, it was so violent and unexpected inside him, always "doing things to him". He early recognised the half-divine, half-demonish nature of this "unexpected" potency inside him. Sometimes it came upon him like a glory, as when Samson slew the lion with his hands, or David slew Goliath with a pebble. The Greeks before Homer would have called both these two acts "the god", in recognition of the superhuman nature of the deed, *and of the doer of the deed*, who was *within* the man. This "doer of the deed", the fluid, rapid, invincible, even clairvoyant potency that can surge through the whole body and spirit of a man, this is the dragon, the grand divine dragon of his superhuman potency, or the great demonish dragon of his inward destruction. It is this which surges in us to make us move, to make us act, to make us bring forth something: to make us spring up and live. Modern philosophers may call it Libido or *Elan Vital*, but the words are thin, they carry none of the wild suggestion of the dragon.

And men "worshipped" the dragon. A hero was a hero, in the great past, when he had conquered the hostile dragon, when he had the power of the dragon *with him* in his limbs and breast. When Moses set up the brazen serpent in the wilderness, an act which dominated the imagination of the Jews for many centuries, he was substituting the potency of the good dragon for the sting of the bad dragon, or serpents. That is, man can have the serpent with him or against him. When his serpent is with him, he is almost divine. When his serpent is against him, he is stung and envenomed and defeated from within. The great problem, in the past, was the conquest of the *inimical* serpent, and the liberation within the self of the gleaming bright serpent of gold, golden fluid life within the body, the rousing of the splendid divine dragon within a man, or within a woman.

What ails men today is that thousands of little serpents sting and envenom them all the time, and the great divine dragon is inert. We cannot wake him to life, in modern days. He wakes on the lower planes of life: for a while in an air-man like Lindberg or in a boxer like Dempsey. It is the little serpent of gold that lifts these two men for a brief time into a certain level of heroism. But on the higher planes, there is no glimpse or gleam of the great dragon.

The usual vision of the dragon is, however, not personal but cosmic. It is in the vast cosmos of the stars that the dragon writhes and lashes. We see him in his maleficent aspect, red. But don't let us forget that when he stirs green and flashing on a pure dark night of stars it is he who makes the wonder of the night, it is the full rich coiling of his folds which makes the heavens sumptuously serene, as he glides around and guards the immunity, the precious strength of the planets, and gives lustre and new strength to the fixed stars, and still more serene beauty to the moon. His coils within the sun make the sun glad, till the sun dances in radiance. For in his good aspect, the dragon is the great vivifier, the great enhancer of the whole universe.

So he persists still to the Chinese. The long green dragon with which we are so familiar on Chinese things is the dragon in his good aspect of life-bringer, life-giver, life-maker, vivifier. There he coils, on the breasts of the mandarins' coats, looking very horrific, coiling round the centre of the breast and lashing behind with his tail. But as a matter of fact, proud and strong and grand is the mandarin who is within the folds of the green dragon, lord of the dragon.—It is the same dragon which, according to the Hindus, coils quiescent at the base of the spine of a man, and unfolds sometimes lashing along the spinal way: and the yogi is only trying to set this dragon in controlled motion. Dragon-cult is still active and still potent all over the world, particularly in the east.

But alas, the great green dragon of the stars at their brightest is coiled up tight and silent today, in a long winter sleep. Only the red dragon sometimes shows his head, and the millions of little vipers. The millions of little vipers sting us as they stung the murmuring Israelites, and we want some Moses to set the brazen serpent aloft: the serpent which was "lifted up" even as Jesus later was "lifted up" for the redemption of men.

The red dragon is the kakodaimon, the dragon in his evil or inimical aspect. In the old lore, red is the colour of *man's* splendour, but the colour of evil in the cosmic creatures or the gods. The red lion is the sun in his evil or destructive aspect. The red dragon is the great "potency" of the cosmos in its hostile and destructive activity.

The agathodaimon becomes at last the kakodaimon. The green dragon becomes with time the red dragon. What was our joy and our salvation becomes with time, at the end of the time-era, our bane and our damnation. What was a creative god, Ouranos, Kronos, becomes at the end of the time-period a destroyer and a devourer. The god of the beginning of an era is the evil principle at the end of that era. For time still moves in cycles. What was the green dragon, the good potency, at the beginning of the cycle has by the end gradually changed into the red dragon, the evil potency. The good potency of the beginning of the Christian era is now the evil potency of the end.

This is a piece of very old wisdom, and it will always be true. Time still moves in cycles, not in a straight line. And we are at the end of the Christian cycle. And the Logos, the good dragon of the beginning of the cycle is now the evil dragon of today. It will give its potency to no new thing, only to old and deadly things. It is the red dragon, and it must once more be slain by the heroes, since we can expect no more from the angels.

And, according to old myth, it is woman who falls most absolutely into the power of the dragon, and has no power of escape till man frees her. The new dragon is green or golden, green with the vivid ancient meaning of green which Mohammed took up again, green with that greenish dawn-light which is the quintessence of all new and life-giving light. The dawn of all creation took place in greenish pellucid gleam that was the shine of the very presence of the Creator. John of Patmos harks back to this when he makes the iris or rainbow which screens the face of the Almighty green like smaragd or emerald. And this lovely jewel-green gleam is the very dragon itself, as it moves out wreathing and writhing into the cosmos. It is the power of the Kosmodynamos coiling throughout space, coiling along the spine of a man, leaning forth between his brows like the Uraeus between the brows of a Pharaoh. It makes a man splendid, a king, a hero, a brave man gleaming with the gleam of the dragon, which is golden when it wreathes round a man.

So the Logos came, at the beginning of our era, to give men another sort of splendour. And that same Logos today is the evil snake, the Laocoön which is the death of all of us. The Logos which was like the great green breath of spring-time is now the grey stinging of myriads of deadening little serpents. Now we have to *conquer* the Logos, that the new dragon gleaming green may lean down from among the stars and vivify us and make us great.

And no-one is coiled more bitterly in the folds of the old Logos than woman. It is always so. What was a breath of inspiration becomes in the end a fixed and evil *form*, which coils us round like mummy clothes. And then woman is more tightly coiled even than man. Today, the best part of womanhood is wrapped tight and tense in the folds of the Logos, she is bodiless, abstract, and driven by a self-determination terrible to behold. A strange "spiritual" creature is woman today, driven on and on by the evil demon of the old Logos, never for a moment allowed to escape and be herself. The evil Logos says she must be "significant", she must "make something worth while" of her life. So on and on she goes, making something worth while, piling up the evil forms of our civilisation higher and higher, and never for a second escaping to be wrapped in the brilliant fluid folds of the new green dragon. *All* our present life-forms are evil. But with a persistence that would be angelic if it were not devilish woman insists on the *best* in life, by which she means the *best* of our evil life-forms, unable to realise that the best of evil life-forms are the most evil.

So, tragic and tortured by all the grey little snakes of modern shame and pain, she struggles on, fighting for "the best", which is, alas, the evil best. All women today have a large streak of the police-woman in them. Andromeda was chained naked to a rock, and the dragon of the old form fumed at her. But poor modern Andromeda, she is forced to patrol the streets more or less in police-woman's uniform, with some sort of a banner and some sort of a bludgeon—or is it called a baton!—up her sleeve, and who is going to rescue her from this? Let her dress up fluffy as she likes, or white and virginal, still underneath it all you can see the stiff folds of the modern police-woman, doing her best, her level best.

Ah God, Andromeda at least had her nakedness, and it was beautiful, and Perseus wanted to fight for her. But our modern police-women have no nakedness, they have their uniforms. And who could want to fight the dragon of the old form, the poisonous old Logos, for the sake of a police-woman's uniform?

Ah woman, you have known many bitter experiences. But never, never before have you been condemned by the old dragon to be a police-woman.

Oh lovely green dragon of the new day, the undawned day, come, come in touch, and release us from the horrid grip of the evil-smelling old Logos! Come in silence, and say nothing. Come in touch, in soft new touch like a spring-time breeze, and shed these horrible police-woman sheaths from off our women, let the buds of life come nakedly!

In the days of the Apocalypse the old dragon was red. Today he is grey. He was red, because he represented the old way, the old form of power, kingship, riches, ostentation, and lust. By the days of Nero, this old form of ostentation and sensational lust had truly enough become evil, the foul dragon. And the foul dragon, the red one, had to give way to the white dragon of the Logos—Europe has never known the green dragon. When our era began, it began with the glorification of white: the white dragon. It ends with the same sanitary worship of white, but the white dragon is now a great white worm, dirty and greyish. Our colour is dirty-white, or grey.

But just as our Logos colour began dazzling white—John of Patmos insists on it, in the white robes of the saints—and ends in a soiled colourlessness, so the old red dragon started marvellously red. The oldest of old dragons was a marvellous red, glowing golden and blood-red. He was bright, bright, bright red, like the most dazzling vermilion. This, this vivid gold-red was the first colour of the first dragon, far, far back under the very dawn of history. The farthest-off men looked at the sky and saw in terms of gold and red, not in terms of green and dazzling white. In terms of gold and red, and the reflection of the dragon in a man's face, in the far-off, far-off past, showed glowing brilliant vermilion. Ah then the heroes and the hero-kings glowed in the face red as poppies that the sun shines through. It was the colour of glory: it was the colour of the wild bright blood, which was life itself. The red, racing bright blood, that was the supreme mystery: the slow, purplish, oozing dark blood, the royal mystery.

The ancient kings of Rome, of the ancient Rome, who were really a thousand years behind the civilisation of the eastern Mediterranean, they painted their faces vermilion, to be divinely royal. And the Red Indians of North America do the same. They are not red save by virtue of this very vermilion paint, which they call "medicine". But the Red Indians belong almost to the Neolithic stage of culture, and of religion. Ah the dark vistas of time in the pueblos of New Mexico, when the men come out with faces glistening scarlet! Gods! they look like gods! It is the red dragon, the beautiful red dragon.

But he became old, and his life-forms became fixed. Even in the pueblos of New Mexico, where the old life-forms are the life-forms of the great red dragon, the greatest dragon, even there the life-forms are really evil, and the men have a passion for the colour blue, the blue of the turquoise, to escape the red. Turquoise and silver, these are the colours they yearn for. For gold is of the red dragon. Far-off down the ages gold was the very stuff of the dragon, its soft, gleaming body, prized for the glory of the dragon, and men wore soft gold for glory, like the Aegean and Etruscan warriors in their tombs. And it was not till the red dragon became the kakodaimon, and men began to yearn for the green dragon and the silver arm-bands, that gold fell from glory and became money. What makes gold into money? the Americans ask you. And there you have it. The death of the great gold dragon, the coming of the green and silver dragon—how the Persians and Babylonians loved turquoise blue, the Chaldeans loved lapis lazuli; so far back they had turned from the red dragon! The dragon of Nebuchadnezzar is blue, and is a blue-scaled unicorn stepping proudly. He is very highly developed. The dragon of the Apocalypse is a much more ancient beast: but then, he is kakodaimon.

But the royal colour still was red: the vermilion and the purple, which is not violet but crimson, the true colour of living blood, these were kept for kings and emperors. They became the very colours of the evil dragon. They are the colours in which the apocalyptist clothes the great harlot-woman whom he calls Babylon. The colour of life itself becomes the colour of abomination.

And today, in the day of the dirty-white dragon of the Logos and the steel-age, the socialists have taken up the oldest of life-colours, and the whole world trembles at a suggestion of vermilion. For the majority today, red is the colour of destruction. "Red for danger", as the children say. So the cycle goes round: the red and gold dragons of the Gold Age and the Silver Age, the green dragon of the Bronze Age, the white dragon of the Iron Age, the dirty-white dragon, or grey dragon of the Steel Age: and then a return once more to the first billiant red dragon.

But every heroic epoch turns instinctively to the red dragon, or the gold: every non-heroic epoch instinctively turns away. Like the Apocalypse, where the red and the purple are anathema.

The great red dragon of the Apocalypse has seven heads, each of them crowned: which means his power is royal or supreme in its own manifestation. The seven heads mean he has seven lives, as many lives as a man has natures, or as there are "potencies" to the cosmos. All his seven heads have to be smitten off: that is, man has another great series of seven conquests to make, this time over the dragon. The fight goes on.

The dragon, being cosmic, destroys a third part of the cosmos before he is cast down out of heaven into earth: he draws down a third part of the stars with his tail. Then the woman brings forth the child who is "to shepherd mankind with an iron flail". Alas, if that is a prophecy of the reign of the Messiah, or Jesus, how true it is! For all men today are ruled with a flail of iron. This child is caught up to God: we almost wish the dragon had got him. And the woman fled into the wilderness. That is, the great cosmic mother has no place in the cosmos of men any more. She must hide in the desert since she cannot die.—And there she hides, still, during the weary three and a half mystic years which are still going on, apparently.

Now begins the second half of the Apocalypse. We enter the rather boring process of Danielesque prophecy, concerning the Church of Christ and the fall of the various kingdoms of the earth. We cannot be very much interested in the prophesied collapse of Rome and the Roman Empire.

XVII

But before we look at this second half, let us glance at the dominant symbols, especially at the symbols of number. The whole scheme is so entirely based on the numbers seven, four and three, that we may as well try to find out what these numbers meant to the ancient mind.

Three was the sacred number: it is still, for it is the number of the Trinity: it is the number of the nature of God. It is perhaps from the scientists, or the very early philosophers, that we get the most revealing suggestions of the ancient beliefs. The early scientists took the extant religious symbol-ideas and transmuted them into true "ideas". We know that the ancients saw number concrete—in dots or in rows of pebbles. The number three was three pebbles. And the number three was held by the Pythagoreans to be the perfect number, in their primitive arithmetic, because you could not divide it and leave a gap in the middle. This is obviously true of three pebbles. You cannot destroy the integrity of the three. If you remove one pebble on each side, it still leaves the central stone poised and in perfect balance between the two, like the body of a bird between the two wings. And even as late as the third century, this was felt as the perfect or divine condition of being.

Again, we know that Anaximander, in the fifth century, conceived of the Boundless, the infinite substance, as having its two "elements", the hot and the cold, the dry and the moist, or fire and the dark, the great "pair", on either side of it, in the first primordial creation. These three were the beginning of all things. This idea lies at the back of the very ancient division of the *living* cosmos into three, before the idea of God was separated out.

In parenthesis let us remark that the very ancient world was entirely religious and godless. While men still lived in close physical unison, like flocks of birds on the wing, in a close physical oneness, an ancient tribal unison in which the individual was hardly separated out, then the tribe lived breast to breast, as it were, with the cosmos, in naked contact with the cosmos, the whole cosmos was alive and in contact with the flesh of man, there was no room for the intrusion of the god idea. It was not till the individual began to feel separated off, not till he fell into awareness of himself, and hence into apartness; not, mythologically, till he ate of the Tree of Knowledge instead of the Tree of Life, and knew himself *apart* and separate, that the conception of of a God arose, to intervene between man and the cosmos. The very oldest ideas of man are *purely* religious, and there is no notion of any sort of God or gods. God and gods enter when man has "fallen" into a sense of separateness and loneliness. The oldest philosophers, Anaximander with his divine Boundless and the divine two elements, and Anaximenes with his divine "air", are going back to the great conception of the naked cosmos, before there was God. At the same time, they know all about the gods of the sixth century: but they are not strictly interested in them. Even the first Pythagoreans, who were religious in the conventional way, were more profoundly religious in their conceptions of the two primary forms, Fire and the Night, or Fire and Dark, dark being conceived of as a kind of thick air or vapour. These two were the Limit and the Unlimited, Night, the Unlimited, finding its Limit in Fire. These two primary forms, being in a tension of opposition, prove their oneness by their very *opposedness*. Herakleitos says that all things are an exchange for fire: and that the sun is new every day. "The limit of dawn and evening is the Bear: and opposite the Bear is the boundary of bright Zeus". Bright Zeus is here supposed to be the bright blue sky, so his boundary is the Horizon, and Herakleitos means probably that opposite the Bear, that is down, down in the antipodes, it is always night, and Night lives the death of Day, as Day lives the death of Night.

This is the state of mind of great men in the fifth and fourth centuries before Christ, strange and fascinating and a revelation of the old symbolic mind. Religion was already turning moralistic or ecstatic, with the Orphics the tedious idea of "escaping the wheel of birth" had begun to abstract men from life. But early science is a source of the purest and oldest religion. The mind of man recoiled, there in Ionia, to the oldest religious conception of the cosmos, from which to start thinking out the scientific cosmos. And the thing the oldest philosophers disliked was the new sort of religion, with its ecstasies and its escape and its purely *personal* nature: its loss of the cosmos.

So the first philosophers took up the sacred three-part cosmos of the ancients. It is paralleled in Genesis, where we have a God creation, in the division into heaven, and earth, and water: the first three *created* elements, presupposing a God who creates. The ancient three-fold division of the living heavens, the Chaldean, is made when the heavens themselves are divine, and not merely God-inhabited. Before men felt any need of God or gods, while the vast heavens lived of themselves and lived breast to breast with man, the Chaldeans gazed up in the religious rapture. And then, by some strange intuition, they divided the heavens into three sections. And then they really *knew* the stars, as the stars have never been known since.

Later, when a God or Maker or Ruler of the skies was invented or discovered, then the heavens were divided into the four quarters, the old four quarters that lasted so long. And then, gradually with the invention of a God or a Demiurge, the old star-knowledge and true worship declined with the Babylonians into magic and astrology, the whole system was "worked". But still the old Chaldean cosmic knowledge persisted, and this the Ionians must have picked up again.

Even during the four-quarter centuries, the heavens still had three primary rulers, sun, moon, and morning-star. But the Bible says, sun, moon, and stars.

The morning-star was always a god, from the time when gods began. But when the cult of dying and re-born gods started all over the old world, about 600 B.C., he became symbolic of the new god, because he rules in the twilight, between day and night, and for the same reason he is supposed to be lord of both, and to stand gleaming with one foot on the flood of night and one foot on the world of day, one foot on sea and one on shore. We know that night was a form of vapour or flood.

XVIII

Three is the number of things divine, and four is the number of creation. The world is four, four-square, divided into four quarters which are ruled by four great creatures, the four winged creatures that surround the throne of the Almighty. These four great creatures make up the sum of mighty space, both dark and light, and their wings are the quivering of this space, that trembles all the time with thunderous praise of the Creator: for these are Creation praising their Maker, as Creation shall praise its Maker forever. That their wings (strictly) are full of eyes before and behind, only means that they are the stars of the trembling heavens forever changing and travelling and pulsing. In Ezekiel, muddled and mutilated as the text is, we see the four great creatures amid the wheels of the revolving heavens—a conception which belongs to the seventh, sixth, and fifth centuries—and supporting on their wing-tips the crystal vault of the final heaven of the Throne.

In their origin, the Creatures are probably older than God himself. They were a very grand conception, and some suggestion of them is at the back of most of the great winged Creatures of the East. They belong to the last age of the living cosmos, the cosmos that was not created, that had yet no good in it because it was in itself utterly divine and primal. Away behind all the creation myths lies the grand idea that the Cosmos *always was*, that it could not have had any beginning, because it always was there and always would be there. It could not have a god to start it, because it was itself all god and all divine, the origin of everything.

This living cosmos man first divided into three parts: and then, at some point of great change, we cannot know when, he divided it instead into four quarters, and the four quarters demanded a whole, a conception of the whole, and then a Maker, a Creator. So the four great elemental creatures became subordinate, they surround the supreme central unit, and their wings cover all space. Later still, they are turned from vast and living elements into beasts or Creatures or Cherubim—it is a process of degradation—and given the four elemental or cosmic natures of man, lion, bull and eagle. In Ezekiel, each of the creatures is all four at once, with a different face looking in each direction. But in the Apocalypse each beast has its own face. And as the cosmic idea dwindled, we get the four cosmic natures of the four Creatures applied first to the great Cherubim, then to the personified Archangels, Michael, Gabriel etc., and finally they are applied to the four Evangelists, Matthew, Mark, Luke and John. "Four for the Gospel Natures". It is all a process of degradation or personification of a great old concept.

Parallel to the division of the cosmos into four quarters, four parts, and four dynamic "natures" comes the other division, into four elements. At first, it seems as if there had been only three elements: heaven, earth, and sea, or water: heaven being primarily Light or Fire. The recognition of air came later. But with the elements of Fire, earth and water the cosmos was complete, air being conceived of as a form of vapour, darkness the same.

And the earliest scientists (philosophers) seemed to want to make one element, or at most two, responsible for the cosmos. Anaximenes said all was water. Xenophanes said all was earth and water. Water gave off moist exhalations, and in these moist exhalations were latent sparks, these exhalations blew aloft as clouds, they blew far, far aloft, and condensed *upon their sparks* instead of into water, and thus they produced stars: thus they even produced the sun. The sun was a great "cloud" of assembled sparks from the moist exhalations of the watery earth. This is how science began: far more fantastic than myth, but using processes of reason.

Then came Herakleitos with his: All is Fire, or rather: All is an exchange for Fire—, and his insistence on Strife, which holds things asunder and so holds them integral and makes their existence even possible, as the creative *principle:* Fire being an element.

After which the Four Elements become almost inevitable. With Empedokles in the fifth century the Four Elements of Fire, Earth, Air and Water established themselves in the imagination of men for ever, the four *living* or cosmic elements, the radical elements: the Four Roots Empedokles called them, the four cosmic roots of all existence. And they were controlled by two principles, Love and Strife.—"Fire and Water and Earth and the mighty height of Air; dread Strife, too, apart from these, of equal weight to each, and Love in their midst, equal in length and breadth". And again Empedokles calls the Four: "shining Zeus, life-bringing Hera, Aidoneus and Nestis". So we see the Four also as gods: the Big Four of the ages. When we consider the Four elements, we shall see that they are, now and forever, the four elements of our experience. All that science has taught about fire does not make fire any different. The processes of combustion are not fire, they are thought-forms. H_2O is not water, it is a thought-form derived from experiments with water. Thought-forms are thought-forms, they do not make our life. Our life is made still of elemental fire and water, earth and air: by these we move and live and have our being.

From the four elements we come to the four natures of man himself, based on the conception of blood, bile, lymph and phlegm, and their properties. Man is still a creature that thinks with his blood: "the heart, dwelling in the sea of blood that runs in opposite directions, where chiefly is what men call thought; for the blood round the heart is the thought of men".—And maybe this is true. Maybe all basic thought takes place in the blood around the heart, and is only transferred to the brain. Then there are the Four Ages, based on the four metals gold, silver, bronze and iron. In the sixth century already the Iron Age had set in, and already man laments it. The Golden Age, before the eating of the Fruit of Knowledge, is left far behind.

The first scientists, then, are very near to the old symbolists. And so we see in the Apocalypse, that when St. John is referring to the old primal or divine cosmos, he speaks of a third part of this that or another: as when the dragon, who belongs to the old divine cosmos, draws down a third part of the stars with his tail: or where the divine trumps destroy a third part of things: or the horsemen from the abyss, which are divine demons, destroy a third part of men. But when the destruction is by non-divine agency, it is usually a fourth part that is destroyed.—Anyhow there is far too much destroying in the Apocalypse. It ceases to be fun.

XIX

The numbers four and three together make up the sacred number seven: the cosmos with its god. The Pythagoreans called it "the number of the right time". Man and the cosmos alike have four created natures, and three divine natures. Man has his four earthly natures, then soul, spirit, and the eternal I. The universe has the four quarters and the four elements, then also the three divine quarters of heaven, Hades, and the Whole, and the three divine motions of Love, Strife and Wholeness. The oldest cosmos had no heaven nor Hades. But then it is probable that seven is not a sacred number in the oldest consciousness of man.

It is always, from the beginning, however, a semi-sacred number because it is the number of the seven ancient planets, which began with sun and moon, and included the five great "wandering" stars, Jupiter, Venus, Mercury, Mars and Saturn. The wandering planets were always a great mystery to men, especially in the days when he lived breast to breast with the cosmos, and watched the moving heavens with a profundity of passionate attention quite different from any form of attention today.

The Chaldeans always preserved some of the elemental immediacy of the cosmos, even to the end of Babylonian days. They had, later, their whole mythology of Marduk and the rest, and the whole bag of tricks of their astrologers and magi, but it seems never to have ousted, entirely, the serious star-lore, nor to have broken altogether the breast to breast contact of the star-gazer and the skies of night. The magi continued, apparently, through the ages concerned only in the mysteries of the heavens, without any god or gods dragged in. That the heaven-lore degenerated into tedious forms of divination and magic later on is only part of human history: everything human degenerates, from religion downwards, and must be renewed and revived.

It was this preserving of star-lore naked and without gods that prepared the way for astronomy later, just as in the eastern Mediterranean a great deal of old cosmic lore about water and fire must have lingered and prepared the way for the Ionian philosophers and modern science.

The great control of the life of earth from the living and intertwining heavens was an idea which had far greater hold of the minds of men before the Christian era, than we realise. In spite of all the gods and goddesses, the Jehovah and the dying and redeeming Saviours of many nations, underneath, the old cosmic vision remained, and men believed, perhaps, more radically in the rule of the stars than in any of the gods. Man's consciousness has many layers, and the lowest layers continue to be crudely active, especially down among the common people, for centuries after the cultured consciousness of the nation has passed to higher planes. And the consciousness of man always tends to revert to the original levels; though there are two modes of reversion: by degeneration and decadence; and by deliberate return in order to get back to the roots again, for a new start.

In Roman times there was a great slipping back of the human consciousness to the oldest levels, though it was a form of decadence and a return to superstition. But in the first two centuries after Christ the rule of the heavens returned on man as never before, with a power of superstition stronger than any religious cult. Horoscopy was the rage. Fate, fortune, destiny, character, everything depended on the stars, which meant, on the seven planets. The seven planets were the seven Rulers of the heavens, and they fixed the fate of man irrevocably, inevitably. Their rule became at last a form of insanity, and both the Christians and the Neo-Platonists set their faces against it.

Now this element of superstition bordering on magic and occultism is very strong in the Apocalypse. The Revelation of John is, we must admit it, a book to conjure with. It is full of suggestions for occult use, and it has been used, throughout the ages, for occult purposes, for the purpose of divination and prophecy especially. It lends itself to this. Nay, the book is written, especially the second half, in a spirit of lurid prophecy very like the magical utterances of the occultists of the time. It reflects the spirit of the time: as *The Golden Ass* reflects that of less than a hundred years later, not very different.

So that the number seven ceases almost to be the "divine" number, and becomes the magical number of the Apocalypse. As the book proceeds, the ancient divine element fades out and the "modern", first-century taint of magic, prognostication, and occult practice takes its place. Seven is the number now of divination and conjuring, rather than of real vision.

So the famous "time, times and a half"—which means three-and-a-half years. It comes from Daniel, who already starts the semi-occult business of prophesying the fall of empires. It is supposed to represent the half of a sacred week—all that is ever allowed to the princes of evil, who are never given the full run of the sacred week of seven "days". But with John of Patmos it is a magic number.

In the old days, when the moon was a great power in heaven, ruling men's bodies and swaying the flux of the flesh, then seven was one of the moon's quarters. The moon still sways the flux of the flesh, and still we have a seven-day week. The Greeks of the sea had a nine-day week. That is gone.

But the number seven is no longer divine. Perhaps it is still to some extent magical.

XX

The number ten is the natural number of a series. "It is by nature that the Hellenes count up to ten and then start over again". It is of course the number of the fingers of the two hands. This repetition of five observed throughout nature was one of the things that led the Pythagoreans to assert that "all things are number". In the Apocalypse, ten is the "natural" or complete number of a series. The Pythagoreans, experimenting with pebbles, found that ten pebbles could be laid out in a triangle of $4+3+2+1$: and this sent their minds off in imagination.—But the ten heads or crowned horns of John's two evil beasts probably represent merely a complete series of emperors or kings, horns being a stock symbol for empires or their rulers. The old symbol of horns, of course, is the symbol of power, originally the divine power that came to man from the vivid cosmos, from the starry green dragon of life, but especially from the vivid dragon within the body, that lies coiled at the base of the spine, and flings himself sometimes along the spinal way till he flushes the brow with magnificence, the gold horns of power that bud on Moses' forehead, or the gold serpent, Uraeus, which came down between the brows of the royal Pharaohs of Egypt, and is the dragon of the individual. But for the commonalty, the horn of power was the ithyphallos, the phallos, the cornucopia.

XXI

The final number, twelve, is the number of the established or unchanging cosmos, as contrasted with the seven of the wandering planets, which are the physical (in the old Greek sense) cosmos, always in motion apart from the rest of motion. Twelve is the number of the signs of the zodiac, and of the months of the year. It is three times four, or four times three: the complete correspondence. It is the whole round of the heavens, and the whole round of man. For man had seven natures in the old scheme: that is, $6+1$, the last being the nature of his wholeness. But now he has another quite new nature, as well as the old one: for we admit he still is made up of the old Adam *plus* the new. So now his number is twelve, $6+6$ for his natures, and one for his wholeness. But his wholeness is now in Christ: no longer symbolised between his brows. And now that his number is twelve, man is perfectly rounded and established, established and unchanging, unchanging, for he is now perfect and there is no need for him to change, his wholeness, which is his thirteenth number (unlucky in superstition) being with Christ in heaven. Such was the opinion of the "saved", concerning themselves. Such is still the orthodox opinion: those that are saved in Christ are perfect and unchanging, no need for them to change. They are perfectly individualised.

XXII

When we come to the second half of Revelation, after the newborn child is snatched to heaven and the woman has fled into the wilderness, there is a sudden change, and we feel we are reading purely Jewish and Jewish Christian Apocalypse, with none of the old background.

"And there was war in heaven: Michael and his angels fought against the dragon".—They cast down the dragon out of heaven into the earth, and he becomes Satan, and ceases entirely to be interesting. When the great figures of mythology are turned into rationalised or merely moral forces, then they lose interest. We are acutely bored by moral angels and moral devils. We are acutely bored by a "rationalised" Aphrodite. Soon after 1000 B.C. the world went a little insane about morals and "sin". The Jews had always been tainted.

What we have been looking for in the Apocalypse is something older, grander than the ethical business. The old, flaming love of life and the strange shudder of the presence of the invisible dead made the rhythm of really ancient religion. Moral religion is comparatively modern, even with the Jews.

But the second half of the Apocalypse is all moral: that is to say, it is all sin and salvation. For a moment there is a hint of the old cosmic wonder, when the dragon turns again upon the woman, and she is given wings of an eagle and flies off into the wilderness: but the dragon pursues her and spues out a flood upon her, to overwhelm her: "and the earth helped the woman, and the earth opened her mouth and swallowed up the flood. And the dragon was wroth with the woman, and went to make war on the remnant of her seed, *which keep the commandments of God, and have the testimony of Jesus Christ*".

The last words are, of course, the moral ending tacked on by some Jew-Christian scribe to the fragment of myth. The dragon is here the watery dragon, or the dragon of chaos, and in his evil aspect still. He is resisting with all his might the birth of a new thing, a new era. He turns against the Christians, since they are the only "good" thing left on earth.

The poor dragon henceforth cuts a sorry figure. He gives his power, and his seat, and great authority to the beast that rises out of the sea, the beast with "seven heads and ten horns and upon his head ten crowns, and upon his heads the name of blasphemy. And the beast which I saw was like unto a leopard, and his feet were as the feet of a bear, and his mouth as the mouth of a lion"—

We know this beast already: he comes out of Daniel and is *explained* by Daniel. The beast is the last grand world-empire, the ten horns are ten kingdoms confederated in the empire—which is of course Rome. As for the leopard, bear and lion qualities, these are also explained in Daniel as the three empires that preceded Rome, the Macedonian, swift as a leopard, the Persian, stubborn as a bear, the Babylonian, rapacious as the lion.

We are back again at the level of allegory, and for me, the real interest is gone. Allegory can always be explained: and explained away. The true symbol defies all explanation, so does the true myth. You can give meanings to either—you will never explain them away. Because symbol and myth do not affect us only mentally, they move the deep emotional centres every time. The great quality of the mind is finality. The mind "understands", and there's an end of it.

But the emotional consciousness of man has a life and movement quite different from the mental consciousness. The mind knows in part, in part and parcel, with full stop after every sentence. But the emotional soul knows in full, like a river or a flood. For example, the symbol of the dragon—look at it, on a Chinese tea-cup or in an old wood-cut, read it in a fairy-tale—and what is the result? If you are alive in the old emotional self, the more you look at the dragon, and think of it, the farther and farther flushes out your emotional awareness, on and on into dim regions of the soul aeons and aeons back. But if you are dead in the old feeling-knowing way, as so many moderns are, then the dragon just "stands for" this that and the other—all the things it stand for in Frazer's *Golden Bough:* it is just a kind of glyph or label, like the gilt pestle and mortar outside a chemist's shop.—Or take better still the Egyptian symbol called the *ankh*, the symbol of life etc. ♀ which the goddesses hold in their hands. Any child "knows what it means". But a man who is *really* alive feels his soul begin to throb and expand at the mere sight of the symbol. Modern men, however, are nearly all half dead, modern women too. So they just look at the *ankh* and know all about it, and that's that. They are proud of their own emotional impotence.

Naturally, then, the Apocalypse has appealed to men through the ages as an "allegorical" work. Everything just "meant something"—and something moral at that. You can put down the meaning flat.

The beast from the sea means Roman Empire—and later Nero, number 666. The beast from the earth means the pagan sacerdotal power, the priestly power which made the emperors divine and made Christians even "worship" them. For the beast from the earth has two horns like a lamb, a false Lamb indeed, an Antichrist, and it teaches its wicked followers to perform marvels and even miracles—of witchcraft, like Simon Magus and the rest.

So we have the Church of Christ—or of the Messiah—being martyred by the beast, till pretty well all good Christians are martyred. Then at last, after not so very long a time—say forty years—the Messiah descends from heaven and makes war on the beast, the Roman Empire, and on the kings who are with him. There is a grand fall of Rome, called Babylon, and a grand triumph over her downfall—though the best poetry is all the time lifted from Jeremiah or Ezekiel or Isaiah, it is not original. The sainted Christians gloat over fallen Rome: and then the Victorious Rider appears, his shirt bloody with the blood of dead kings. After this, a New Jerusalem descends to be his Bride, and these precious martyrs all get their thrones, and for a thousand years (John was not going to be put off with Enoch's meagre forty) for a thousand years, the grand Millennium, the Lamb reigns over the earth, assisted by all the risen martyrs. And if the martyrs in the Millennium are going to be as bloodthirsty and ferocious as John the Divine in the Apocalypse—Revenge Timotheus cries—then somebody's going to get it hot during the thousand years of the rule of Saints.

But this is not enough. After the thousand years the whole universe must be wiped out, earth, sun, moon, stars and sea. These early Christians fairly lusted after the end of the world. They wanted their own grand turn first—Revenge Timotheus cries!—But after that, they insisted that the whole universe must be wiped out, sun, stars and all—and a *new* New-Jerusalem should appear, with the same old saints and martyrs in glory, and everything else should have disappeared except the lake of burning brimstone in which devils, demons, beasts, and bad men should frizzle and suffer for ever and ever and ever, Amen!

So ends this glorious work: surely a rather repulsive work. Revenge was indeed a sacred duty to the Jerusalem Jews: and it is not the revenge one minds so much as the perpetual self-glorification of these saints and martyrs, and their profound impudence. How one loathes them, in their "new white garments". How disgusting their priggish rule must be! How vile is their spirit, really, insisting, simply insisting on wiping out the whole universe, bird and blossom, star and river, and above all, everybody except *themselves* and their precious "saved" brothers. How beastly their new Jerusalem, where the flowers never fade, but stand in everlasting sameness! How terribly bourgeois to have unfading flowers!

No wonder the pagans were horrified at the "impious" Christian desire to destroy the universe. How horrified even the old Jews of the Old Testament would have been. For even to them, earth and sun and stars were eternal, created in the grand creation by Almighty God. But no, these impudent martyrs must see it all go up in smoke.

Oh, it is the Christianity of the middling masses, this Christianity of the Apocalypse. And we must confess, it is hideous. Self-righteousness, self-conceit, self-importance, and secret *envy* underlie it all.

By the time of Jesus, all the lowest classes and mediocre people had realised that *never* would they get a chance to be kings, *never* would they go in chariots, never would they drink wine from gold vessels. Very well then—they would have their revenge by *destroying* it all. "Babylon the great is fallen, is fallen, and is become the habitation of devils". And then all the gold and silver and pearls and precious stones and fine linen and purple, and silk, and scarlet—and cinnamon and frankincense, wheat, beasts, sheep, horses, chariots, slaves, souls of men—all these that are destroyed, destroyed, destroyed in Babylon the great—! how one hears the envy, the endless envy screeching through this song of triumph!

No, we can understand that the Fathers of the Church in the East wanted Apocalypse left out of the New Testament. But like Judas among the disciples, it was inevitable that it should be included. The Apocalypse is the feet of clay to the grand Christian image. And down crashes the image, on the weakness of these very feet.

There is Jesus—but there is also John the Divine. There is Christian love—and there is Christian envy. The former would "save" the world—the latter will never be satisfied till it has destroyed the world. They are two sides of the same medal.

XXIII

Because, as a matter of fact, when you start to teach individual self-realisation to the great masses of people, who when all is said and done are only *fragmentary* beings, *incapable* of whole individuality, you end by making them all envious, grudging, spiteful creatures. Anyone who is kind to man knows the fragmentariness of most men, and wants to arrange a society of power in which men fall naturally into a collective wholeness, since they *cannot* have an individual wholeness. In this collective wholeness they will be fulfilled. But if they make efforts at individual fulfilment, they *must* fail, for they are by nature fragmentary. Then, failures, having no wholeness anywhere, they fall into envy and spite. Jesus knew all about it when he said: "To them that have shall be given" etc.—But he had forgotten to reckon with the mass of the mediocre, whose motto is: we have nothing and therefore nobody shall have anything!

But Jesus gave the ideal for the Christian individual, and deliberately avoided giving an ideal for the State or the Nation. When he said "Render unto Caesar that which is Caesar's", he left to Caesar the rule of men's bodies, willy-nilly: and this threatened terrible danger to a man's mind and soul. Already by the year 60 A.D. the Christians were an accursed sect; and they were compelled, like all men, to sacrifice, that is, to give worship to the living Caesar. In giving Caesar the power over men's bodies, Jesus gave him the power to compel men to make the act of worship to Caesar. Now I doubt if Jesus himself could have performed this act of worship, to a Nero or a Domitian. No doubt he would have preferred death. As did so many early Christian martyrs. So there, at the very beginning, was a monstrous dilemma. To be a Christian meant death at the hands of the Roman State; since to submit to the cult of the Emperor and worship the divine man, Caesar, was impossible to a Christian. No wonder, then, that John of Patmos saw the day not far off when *every* Christian would be martyred. The day would have come, if the imperial cult had been absolutely enforced on the people. And then when *every* Christian was martyred, what could a Christian expect but a Second Advent, resurrection, and an absolute revenge! There was a condition for the Christian community to be in, sixty years after the death of the Saviour.

Jesus made it inevitable, when he said that the money belonged to Caesar. It was a mistake. Money means bread, and the bread of men belongs to no man. Money means also power, and it is monstrous to give power to the virtual enemy. Caesar was *bound*, sooner or later, to violate the soul of the Christians. But Jesus saw the individual only, and considered only the individual. He left it to John of Patmos, who was up against the Roman State, to formulate the Christian vision of the Christian State. John did it in the Apocalypse. It entails the destruction of the whole world, and the reign of saints in ultimate bodiless glory. Or it entails the destruction of all earthly power, and the rule of an oligarchy of martyrs (the Millennium).

This destruction of all earthly power we are now moving towards. The oligarchy of martyrs began with Lenin, and apparently Mussolini is also a martyr. Strange, strange people they are, the martyrs, with weird cold morality. When every country has its martyr-ruler, either like Lenin or like Mussolini, what a strange, unthinkable world it will be! But it is coming: the Apocalypse is still a book to conjure with.

A few vastly important points have been missed by Christian doctrine and Christian thought. Christian fantasy alone has grasped them.

1. No man is or can be a pure individual. The mass of men have only the tiniest touch of individuality: if any. The mass of men live and move, think and feel collectively, and have practically no individual emotions, feelings or thoughts at all. They are fragments of the collective or social consciousness. It has always been so, and will always be so.

2. The State, or what we call Society as a collective whole *cannot* have the psychology of an individual. Also it is a mistake to say that the State is made up of individuals. It is not. It is made up of a collection of fragmentary beings. And *no* collective act, even so private an act as voting, is made from the individual self. It is made from the collective self, and has another psychological background, non-individual.

3. The State *cannot* be Christian. Every State is a Power. It cannot be otherwise. Every State must guard its own boundaries and guard its own prosperity. If it fails to do so, it betrays all its individual citizens.

4. Every *citizen* is a unit of worldly power. A *man* may wish to be a pure Christian and a pure individual. But since he *must* be a member of some political State, or Nation, he is forced to be a unit of worldly power.

5. As a citizen, as a collective being, man has his fulfilment in the gratification of his power-sense. If he belongs to one of the so-called "ruling nations", his soul is fulfilled in the sense of his country's power or strength. If his country mounts up aristocratically to a zenith of splendour and power, in a hierarchy, he will be all the more fulfilled, having his place in the hierarchy. But if his country is powerful and democratic, then he will be obsessed with a perpetual will to assert his power in interfering and *preventing* other people from doing as they wish, since no man must do more than another man. This is the condition of modern democracies, a condition of perpetual bullying.

In democracy, bullying inevitably takes the place of power. Bullying is the negative form of power. The modern Christian State is a soul-destroying force, for it is made up of fragments which have no organic whole, only a collective whole. In a hierarchy, each part is organic and vital, as my finger is an organic and vital part of me. But a democracy is bound in the end to be obscene, for it is composed of myriad dis-united fragments, each fragment assuming to itself a false wholeness, a false individuality. Modern democracy is made up of millions of frictional parts all asserting their own wholeness.

6. To have an ideal for the individual which regards only his individual self and ignores his collective self is in the long run fatal. To have a creed of individuality which denies the reality of the hierarchy makes at last for mere anarchy. Democratic man lives by cohesion and resistance, the cohesive force of "love" and the resistant force of the individual "freedom". To yield entirely to love would be to be absorbed, which is the death of the individual: for the individual must hold his own, or he ceases to be "free" and individual. So that we see, what our age has proved to its astonishment and dismay, that the individual *cannot* love. The individual cannot love: let that be an axiom. And the modern man or woman *cannot* conceive of himself, herself, save as an individual. And the individual in man or woman is *bound* to kill, at last, the lover in himself, or herself. It is not that each man kills the thing he loves, but that each man, by insisting on his own individuality, kills the lover in himself, as the woman kills the lover in herself. The Christian *dare not love:* for love kills that which is Christian, democratic and modern, the individual. The individual

cannot love. When the individual loves, he ceases to be purely individual. And so he *must* recover himself, and cease to love. It is one of the most amazing lessons of our day: that the individual, the Christian, the democrat *cannot* love. Or, when he loves, when she loves, he *must* take it back, she *must* take it back.

So much for private or personal love. Then what about that other love, "caritas", loving your neighbour as yourself?

It works out the same. You love your neighbour. Immediately you run the risk of being absorbed by him: you must draw back, you must hold your own. The love becomes resistance. In the end, it is all resistance and no love: which is the history of democracy.

If you are taking the path of individual self-realisation, you had better, like Buddha, go off and be by yourself, and give a thought to nobody. Then you may achieve your Nirvana. Christ's way of loving your neighbour leads to the hideous anomaly of having to live by sheer resistance to your neighbour, in the end.

The Apocalypse, strange book, makes this clear. It shows us the Christian in his relation to the State: which the Gospels and Epistles avoid doing. It shows us the Christian in relation to the State, to the world, and to the cosmos. It shows him in mad hostility to all of them, having, in the end, to will the destruction of them all.

It is the dark side of Christianity, of individualism, and of democracy, the side the world at large now shows us. And it is, simply, suicide. Suicide individual and *en masse*. If man could will it, it would be cosmic suicide. But the cosmos is not at man's mercy, and the sun will not perish to please us.

We do not want to perish, either. We have to give up a false position. Let us give up our false position as Christians, as individuals, and as democrats. Let us find some conception of ourselves that will allow us to be peaceful and happy, instead of tormented and unhappy.

The Apocalypse shows us what we are resisting, unnaturally. We are unnaturally resisting our connection with the cosmos, with the world, with mankind, with the nation, with the family. All these connections are, in the Apocalypse, anathema, and they are anathema to us. We *cannot bear connection*. That is our malady. We *must* break away, and be isolate. We call that being free, being individual. Beyond a certain point, which we have reached, it is suicide. Perhaps we have chosen suicide. Well and good. The Apocalypse too chose suicide, with subsequent self-glorification.

But the Apocalypse shows, by its very resistance, the things that the human heart secretly yearns after. By the very frenzy with which the Apocalypse destroys the sun and the stars, the world, and all kings and all rulers, all scarlet and purple and cinnamon, all harlots, finally all men altogether who are not "sealed", we can see how deeply the apocalyptists are yearning for the sun and the stars and the earth and the waters of the earth, for nobility and lordship and might, and scarlet and gold, splendour, for passionate love, and a proper unison with men, apart from this sealing business. What man most passionately wants is his living wholeness and his living unison, not his own isolate salvation of his "soul". Man wants his physical fulfilment first and foremost, since now, once and once only, he is in the flesh and potent. For man, the vast marvel is to be alive. For man, as for flower and beast and bird, the supreme triumph is to be most vividly, most perfectly alive. Whatever the unborn and the dead may know, they cannot know the beauty, the marvel of being alive in the flesh. The dead may look after the afterwards. But the magnificent here and now of life in the flesh is ours, and ours alone, and ours only for a time. We ought to dance with rapture that we should be alive and in the flesh, and part of the living, incarnate cosmos. I am part of the sun as my eye is part of me. That I am part of the earth my feet know perfectly, and my blood is part of the sea. My soul knows that I am part of the human race, my soul is an organic part of the great human soul, as my spirit is part of my nation. In my own very self, I am part of my family. There is nothing of me that is alone and absolute except my mind, and we shall find that the mind has no existence by itself, it is only the glitter of the sun on the surface of the waters.

So that my individualism is really an illusion. I am a part of the great whole, and I can never escape. But I *can* deny my connections, break them, and become a fragment. Then I am wretched.

What we want is to destroy our false, inorganic connections, especially those related to money, and re-establish the living organic connections, with the cosmos, the sun and earth, with mankind and nation and family. Start with the sun, and the rest will slowly, slowly happen.

Apocalypse: *Appendixes I, II, III*

Apocalypse, *Fragment I*

After reading the Old Testament, and then Revelation, one is forced to the conclusion that the Jews hated their neighbours one and all with such an obsession of hatred, that Jesus was bound to come with his new gospel: Thou shalt love thy neighbour as thyself.

Myself I am very grateful to the new translations of the Bible. A translation like Moffatt's frees the book from the pompous snoring of the old Elizabethan language and the parson's voice combined. The Bible language is wonderful, granted. But like all the much-vaunted Elizabethan English, it tends to be more full of sound than of sense, and to stupify some part of the intelligence with gorgeous noise. This gorgeous noise at last becomes almost unbearable, and between it and the parson's voice and the Sunday School teacher's moral expoundings, Scripture sounds at last entirely mechanical and empty.

But take a simple new translation, and the spell is broken. The beauty of Isaiah is even greater, now it is more intelligible, the loss of that Elizabethan gilding gives it its own poetry. And the Gospels and the Epistles lose that curious theatrical quality which is for us inseparable from the Elizabethan style, they cease to be something to mouth out, histrionically, and they take on their own true tenderness, their strange and manly gentleness. After all, how interesting the Bible is, when we can come to it fresh and find it human and alive, alive with all the emotions of the human soul, even the smallest and most unpleasant, as well as the deepest. How strange the religious note is, varying so much and still having sincere intimacy all the time! How truly beautiful the Psalms, many of them, and the magnificent poetry of Isaiah! Even the Jewish form of poetry that they call "parallelism", because the second line re-echoes the first in a parallel image, how curiously satisfying it can be, once one enters the image-rhythm of it!

"Except the Lord build the house, they labour in vain that build it:
except the Lord keep the city, the watchman waketh but in vain..."

There is the perpetual yet unexpected antiphony, like the strong heart-beat followed by the weak.

To me, the Bible had gone dead because it was cut and dried: its noise was a fixed noise, its meaning a fixed meaning. And not only was it dead, it was antipathetic. Arriving at manhood, one felt that the Bible had been bullied into one, and by second-rate minds at that. Its whole meaning was second-rate, because it had been expounded by these second-rate orthodox people, parsons and teachers, who would not and perhaps could not extract anything from the book but a sort of glorified grocery-shop morality and book-keeping.

After twenty years and more, after some little study of old literature, of ancient history touching Babylon and Persia and Egypt, Crete, Mycenae, and the Ionian sea-board, at last one can come back and discover the Bible afresh, entirely afresh, and rescue it from parsons and Sunday School teachers and Elizabethan theatrical obscurity. It is a question of recovering the true background. Recover the real background, put the book into natural relationship with its time and place and spirit, and it lives again with a fine new life. We have it cut and dried. Set the strange flower on its stem again.

I think the Bible goes so deep in our consciousness, that if the Bible dies, or becomes dead and fixed and repellant to us, then something very important in our responsive soul also goes dead and fixed, and we set into a sort of general resistance. By origin we are Christians, we have been brought up Christians. But what do we mean, after all, by Christians? Religion is a question of ritual and of belief. But as Protestants we have known almost no religious ritual. And what do we believe?

As a matter of fact, we don't know. As far as religion goes, we don't know what we believe. And it doesn't really matter. When you see a churchful of people all repeating the same *Credo*, it is obviously a merely superficial repetition. Look at the faces of these people, and you can see written there very plain and very contrasting beliefs. They are all Christians, and verbally they all believe alike. But actually, their beliefs are as different as beliefs can be. And why not! It must be so.

Religion is not a question of belief, it is a question of feeling. It is a certain deep feeling which seems to soothe and reassure the whole soul. But Christianity is very curious. It seems to have two distinct sets of feeling, one focussing in Jesus and in the command: Love one another!—the other focussing, not in Paul or Peter or John the Beloved, but in the Apocalypse. And this second sort of Christianity is weird. It is a doctrine of the chosen people, of the elect: it is based on everlasting hatred of worldly power, and of people in power: it looks for the end of the world, and the destruction of everybody except the *Saved*. And nearly all Christians and teachers of the Bible today teach *this* sort of Christianity, the Apocalypse sort.

And this has really killed the Bible for us. The one thing we loathe is this "salvation" business, and especially the people who are "saved". These horrible "saved" people and all the good godly ones who are *right*, always *right*, they have become so repulsive to us that they have made the Bible itself repulsive, and they have killed all our religious responses in us. And when our religious responses are dead, or inactive, we are really cut off from life, because the deepest part of our consciousness is not functioning. We try to take refuge in art. But to my mind, the essential feeling in all art is religious, and art is a form of religion without dogma. The *feeling* in art is religious, always. Whenever the soul is moved to a certain fullness of experience, that is religion. Every sincere and genuine feeling is a religious feeling. And the point of every work of art is that it achieves a state of feeling which becomes true experience, and so is religious. Everything that puts us into connection, into vivid touch, is religious. And this would apply to Dickens or Rabelais or *Alice in Wonderland* even, as much as to *Macbeth* or Keats. Every one of them puts us curiously into touch with life, achieves thereby certain religious feeling, and gives a certain religious experience. For in spite of all our doctrine and dogma, there are all kinds of gods, forever. There are gods of the hearth and the orchard, underworld gods, fantastic gods, even cloacal gods, as well as dying gods and phallic gods and moral gods. Once you have a real glimpse of religion, you realise that all that is *truly* felt, every feeling that is felt in true relation, every vivid feeling of connection, is religious, be it what it may, and the only irreligious thing is the death of feeling, the causing of nullity; the frictional irritation which, carried far, leads to nullity.

So that, since essentially the feeling in every real work of art is religious in its quality, because it links us up or connects us with life, you can't substitute art for religion, the two being essentially the same. The man who has lost his religious response *cannot* respond to literature or to any form of art, fully: because the call of every work of art, spiritual or physical, is religious, and demands a religious response. The people who, having lost their religious connection, turn to literature and art, find there a great deal of pleasure, aesthetic, intellectual, many kinds of pleasure, even curiously sensual. But it is the pleasure of entertainment, not of experience. So that they gradually get tired out. They cannot give to literature the one thing it really requires—if it be important at all—and that is the religious response; and they cannot take from it the one thing it gives, the religious experience of linking up or making a new connection. For the religious experience one gets from Dickens belongs to Baal or Ashtaroth, but still is religious: and in *Wuthering Heights* we feel the peculiar presence of Pluto and the spirit of Hades, but that too is of the gods. In *Macbeth* Saturn reigns rather than Jesus. But it is religious just the same.

Now the Bible, we know well, is a great religious book. It is full of God. But not, we find at last, to our unspeakable relief, not the chapel God of the grocery-store keepers. The Jews did a wonderful thing when they focussed the whole religious feeling of man upon One God. But that does not prevent their Bible from being full of all the gods. It is this discovery which a man can make in his maturity, to his unspeakable relief.

The Bible is full of all the gods. Nay, even, the Jahveh of the Old Testament *is* all the gods, except the dying and redeeming gods. But surely the Jehovah of Genesis and Numbers, Samuel, Psalms, Isaiah, Ezekiel, surely he is all the gods in turn, Dionysic, Apollo-like, strange like Ra, and grim like Baal or Bel. You can't make an idol to Jehovah because he has the qualities of all the ancient gods in turn, Ouranos or Kronos or Saturn, even the old Osiris, or the mysterious gods of the first Sumerians. He is One because he is all of them, not because he is different from any of them. He does not sit absolute and apart, while all the other gods topple, mere fallen idols. He is in himself all the gods and all the idols, savage and fertile, and even he is all the unknown gods that are yet to come.

To me, it was an immense relief when I read a new translation and realised this. We have been brought up to believe: If this God exists, One and Eternal, then none of the other gods exist, and all the rest is hollow.—But now, having really read the Bible as a *book*, not as a one-sided pronouncement, I realise the very truth of the Bible: If this God exists, One and Eternal, then all the other gods exist too. For all the gods are only "sides" of the One God. We say of a man: Oh, you only know one side of him!—We can say the same of God. We only know one side of him, and a very small side. If we are to know God well, we must know all the gods: which means knowing God on all possible sides.

"Shriek for sorrow, ships of Tartessus
for your haven is no more.—"

When I was young, and heard the chapel gloating that Babylon was fallen, and Assyria was no more, and Persia was but a name, and Moab had left not so much as a mark on the ground, I was always profoundly depressed. I felt it would be so wonderful if one could go to Babylon, or to Nineveh, or if one could meet the Moabitish women. But now I find the Bible is full of Moab and Babylon, Nineveh and Susa, and that without the gods of Egypt and the gods of the Chaldeans, the God of Israel would have been more uninteresting than a block of wood. So much of the splendour of the Bible is Egyptian splendour, and Babylonian, so much of the beauty, the *reality* comes from Amalek and Moab. The Jews were able to make a One God because they came into contact with so many peoples and so many civilisations, so many alien gods, each of which lent something to the Jewish mind, and to the Jewish soul. All the old Jewish poetry is the poetry of adventure with strange peoples and strange gods, and the Bible is perhaps more profoundly a book of roaming than is Herodotus or the Odyssey.

And the influence, of course, is dual. The Jews *loved* roaming, they loved meeting strange peoples, learning from strange cultures, which meant strange religions. The Jews from the very start down to this day have always *loved* to be with gentiles, to learn gentile ways and wisdom. In a sense, they are a people that always has lived and always will live on the culture of other races. The Jewish mind is simply an amalgam of all the cultures of the ages. And today, wherever there is a new culture, there will the Jew hasten, fascinated.

So, of course, in the past he was always having to be *whipped* back to Jerusalem: as he is today. The Jew has such a curious duality. His real delight is centrifugal: he *loves* to go to strange peoples and to assimilate strange cultures: he always did. But his fear of losing himself in slavery made him, after Egypt, react savagely against all strange peoples, and pivot himself on his One God, whose Chosen People he belonged to.

The Bible contains more of the whipping back to Jerusalem than the excursion into the wonder-world of other races and cultures. The Jewish prophets hated their neighbours so bitterly because the Jewish people were all too prone to like their neighbours overmuch, and merge too easily. Jews on the whole are bored by Jews. Gentiles are more interesting. It is obvious from the Book of Daniel and from

Esther that the Jews had a most thrilling time in Babylonia, in Chaldea, and that they learned all there was to be learned from the Chaldeans. They probably enjoyed Egypt and Babylon, even in captivity, as they now enjoy New York and London, in freedom: perhaps even more. And the splendid thing about the Bible is the wideness of its contact and the bigness of its intelligence and its secret sympathy. It is obvious that the Jews were intensely attracted by Egypt and Amalek, Moab, Chaldea, Assyria, Phoenicia and Persia. The attraction appears in the Bible in marvellous poetry of cursing and commination and prophecy of doom, as a rule. But under the words of hate comes the poetry of the lure.

So now, after all these years of narrow monotheism, and a Bible that had become a very prison of the soul and the mind, suddenly we realise that we have been deceived. We have taken the Bible out of its setting, cut it off from the contact with history and the living races it plays amongst, and set it in unreal isolation, as an absolute. We have been wrong. We have taken the Old Testament at its own value of a One God of a Chosen People cursing and annihilating everybody else, whereas it is a strange and fascinating Odyssey of a whole race wandering among strange races that attracted them intensely, and threatened to absorb them, would have absorbed them but for the violent, frenzied resistance of the prophets, from Moses onwards.

The Bible evolved from centuries of vivid contact with strange races and strange gods. Even Jehovah himself was so evolved. Now we have to put both God and the Bible back into the enormous historical setting. Everything back into contact. Nothing absolute and detached. All things in vivid, interweaving contact, the gods of Egypt and Chaldea with the God of Israel, all understood in contact with one another.

As with the Old Testament, so with the New. Put it back into its contacts, its vital relationships. The world is vast, the experience of mankind is vast. Let us get back into contact. We have imprisoned ourselves unnecessarily in an isolated religion, tethered ourselves to an isolated god, and listened too long to the language of isolation and exclusiveness. And a state of isolation is a state of falsity and death.

What we need is to get back into contact, into religious contact. Taking the Bible as our religious basis, we too need to get back into contact with Egypt and Babylon, we need to know again as the Chaldeans knew, and the Egyptians. Our consciousness is crippled and maimed, we only live with a fragment of ourselves.

Turning from the Old Testament to the New, we do turn actually into a new world. It is like coming into the fresh air. It is a strange thing, the liberating effect of a new feeling in mankind. When Jesus said: Love one another.—Thou shalt love thy neighbour as thyself.— Love your enemies.—he did suddenly open wide a great door from the weary house of strife into the fresh air of a new life.

Again we must get back the context, re-establish the contact with the "world" of the first century of Christ. It was a world, as we know *ad nauseam*, of conquest and of civil war. From 700 B.C. to the year 1 A.D. the great waves of conquest swept over Asia Minor and Eastern Europe. The Jews, from their little Jerusalem, kept being swept away, though they had, so far, still managed to creep back and restore the temple. By the time of Augustus there was comparative peace. But the lands of the Mediterranean, especially the east, were a great churned debris of wreckage, from "conquests" of Assyrians, of Medes, and Persians, of Alexander the Great with his Macedonians, and of the Roman generals. "How old were you when the Mede appeared?" men asked one another in the sixth century before Christ. But by the end of the century it changed to "How old were you when Darius of the Persians conquered us?"

Conflict was in the air. From the year 1000 B.C. onwards, the so-called civilised world has been in a mad whirl of war and conquest. But before Christ it was even worse than since. The enemy was always either imminent or present. Destruction and hostility swept over men. Whole races were shifted, like great herds of cattle, from their own lands to far-off countries. Now that war is almost universally in the air again, today, we can sympathise somewhat with the men of the last centuries before Christ, and understand why the Jews hated everybody, and why the Greeks were so suicidally irritable and quarrelsome. Men were beside themselves, owing to the centuries of remorseless friction and conquest, they were in a state of chronic irritation amounting to hysteria. The Jews of Jesus' day were in this condition. The Greeks were already sinking into hopeless fidgettiness.

It needed the Roman "peace", very much an "armed peace", to restore a measure of calm. But it needed much more. It needed the new emotion which Jesus brought into the world. "Love one another! Love your enemies!" The message was a miracle, in that world of irritation and hysteria. Even today we feel the great soothing and balm of it. The implication of the message was: Strive no more to be top dog. Don't struggle any more to master somebody else. Don't fight any more to be first. Be content to be last, and humblest. For in the final kingdom, the last shall be first.—

This was Jesus' message, familiar to us now, but by no means assimilated or accepted, even today. By no means. Everybody wants to be top dog: and certainly every nation wants to crow loudest on its own muck-heap.

But in Jesus' day, the message was just madness. Man could not *conceive* of anything except the struggle of every man to be top dog. To ninety-nine percent of the people, Jesus' teaching was just creeping and repulsive idiocy. I think, as a matter of fact, it is so to most people today: say sixty-percent, instead of ninety-nine. Yet even in Jesus' day, a few great minds, like Paul's, and the Apostle John's, recognised the fundamental truth of the new teaching, and felt the quickening of the new *feeling*. That was the great point, the quickening of the new feeling. We have to recognise it. If we read the Greek and Roman literature of the first centuries, we feel there is something missing in it, there is a certain staleness. There is nothing of the new breath of life that blows through the Gospels and the great Epistles. The tenderness of Paul in some of the Epistles, expressing his tender concern for his distant brothers, and exhorting them above all things to love one another, not to quarrel, and not to *harden*: this brings a new human relationship into the world, a new sort of love. Perhaps Epicurus had tried for something similar, but there was a touch of resignation in Epicurus, no vivid hope.

With Jesus, a new thing came into the world. And we can say with confidence, that no further new thing will ever come into the world again, without a further new breath of love, and of tenderness. Another new breath of love, and another new courage of tenderness, coupled with a courage of power, this alone will release us from the weary world that imprisons us. For we are as much imprisoned in war, in conflict, in that mean form of conflict called competition, in the mean fight for money, for a mere living: we are as much shut up in the stale prison of all this, as the men of Jesus' day were shut up in the prison of conquest.

Jesus gave the key-word by which men might slip out of the prison of conquest, individually, or in little communities. But alas, it is a terrible fact of human psychology, that what is true for the individual is not necessarily true for a community such as a nation or an empire. A man may perhaps love his enemy, in the Christian or charitable sense of love, because by so doing, nine times out of ten he can escape from his enemy, or at least escape from the wearisome necessity of keeping up an enmity. But a nation that loves its enemy will be destroyed or absorbed by that enemy. This is a truth that is enshrined in the whole of the Old Testament. The Jews as a nation—or a tribe—tended to be fascinated by alien nations and so make themselves and their nation a victim of the alien people. It nearly happened in Egypt and Babylon, and would have happened easily save for the other profound Jewish instinct of national self-preservation through a religion hostile to all other religions. The prophets and leaders *whipped* the people back into isolation.

Now perhaps we may say that a nation which tends to let itself be absorbed should let itself be absorbed. But men and nations are strange things. Man has needs which are obvious, and deep, obscure needs. A man who is tremendously attracted and tempted by strange races may at the same time have a profound need to adhere to his own race, or nation, at any cost, and even to sacrifice himself to that need. We may say that truth, or right, or religion is greater than race or nation, and superficially, it is so. A priest may sacrifice his nationality entirely to his Church. But this only makes the Church the final enemy of the nation, and, for some men, forces a choice between church or nation.

Truth as a matter of fact is nothing but the profound and compelling feeling of the human heart. The real truth lies in the things we do, not in the things we say or believe.

The great question is, how deep is the need in men to belong to a nation, a self-governing group? It seems as if it were a shallow need. It seems as if we moderns might all of us be citizens of the world; as if, when asked what country we belong to, we might say: The world!—

But I doubt if it is really so. Man has several beings, not only one being. When I get to heaven, no doubt I shall have no passport, I shall be a naked soul indistinguishable from the naked soul of a negro or a Chinaman. But that is a grand abstraction, and abstractions get us nowhere. Here, in the complex being that I am, there lives a me which is simply an individual, just a man like any other man, negro or Tartar. But there lives also a me which is European, which is at home in Europe, which feels and thinks as a European feels and thinks. Further, there is a me which is an Englishman, which has its final group-connection with England, and its fulfilment in *power* in the acts of the English nation. And it is useless to say these things don't matter, the individual alone counts. It is not true.

One of the obscurest but profoundest needs of man is this need to belong to a group, a group called a church, or a nation, or an empire, and to feel the power thereof. And the chief reason for the profound dissatisfaction of today is that man is unhappy in his collective self. Modern nations no longer give adequate expression to the deeper, collective feelings of the men of the nation. They no longer express our true nature, the nature of power which is in us. Modern nations, in their present activity, have become curiously meaningless, really powerless, in the creative sense, and the men of the nation suffer accordingly, from a sense of meaningless living and of powerlessness. Modern nations need smashing and remaking: the unit is too big, the carcase is too unwieldy, the power is dead.

Hence the great attraction of America. It is a new nation. It has not reached a final form. All things are possible to it. It seems full of power. And therefore men transfer themselves from the old group to the new. A man who goes to America and takes up citizenship does actually sever his old connection, and form a new one. If I go to America and become naturalised, I do, *in myself*, throughout my whole consciousness, undergo a subtle change, and take on a new being. Also I cease from being what I have been, an Englishman.

This need for a new group-connection was profound, in the men who embraced Christianity during the first centuries. A man who became a Christian ceased, really, to be a Jew, or ceased to be a Roman. He had discovered a new "nation", the nation of Christians. And the sense of community was intense, in the early church.

But Jesus had repudiated all empire on earth. He left it to the devil. The power of the world was Satan's. Render unto Caesar those things which are Caesar's. A man, a Christian was a *pure* individual, an embodied soul belonging to God, and no more.

This is good Christianity, but it turns out to be fallacy, when applied to mankind at large. The vast bulk of men are not pure individuals, and never will be, for the pure individual is a rarity, almost a kind of freak. The vast bulk of men need to belong to a self-governing group, a tribe, a nation, an empire. It is a necessity like the necessity to eat food.

And the psychology of a nation or tribe or empire is not and cannot be the same as the psychology of the individual. The nation is made up of individuals—or rather, of individual human beings. But the psychology of a nation is made up of *certain* basic instincts, *certain* basic needs, *certain* basic aspirations of these individuals, and not of *all* the individual instincts or aspirations. The basic instincts and needs of the individual which belong to his group soul are almost impossible to determine. They are revealed in action, they cannot rise direct into consciousness because the individual consciousness is individual, and these instincts and needs are really collective. So no one man can embody them or know them. They must be expressed before they can be known. Hence the utter uncertainty of the future.

Jesus, as the pure idealist, wanted to free men from the collective self, the tribal or national self. But strange as it may seem, he might as well have tried to free men from breathing. The problem of the *collective* activity of Christianity was left entirely to be solved by time. And it has never been solved.

Men were tired to death of their old group allegiance, tired to death of being Jews or Greeks or Egyptians or Romans, tired to death of state and nation and empire. Those that became Christians cut the old allegiance. But they immediately founded new groups, new communities, with a new rule of presbyters. And these groups quickly fused into a new State, a Church with a gradually elaborating rule of presbyters and bishops, a new authority and a new *power*. In spite of Jesus, *power* came back. It must be so. In the deeper instinctive self, man is a being of power, and must feel himself powerful, powerful beyond himself, in his community or nation or, in the Christian case, his Church. The Christian Church grew into the Catholic Church, with its supreme Pope as divine as ever Augustus was, or Nero, in the pomp of Rome. The Church became a great power indeed, it established the ritual and religious life of the people, it was building up a fine philosophy, and then, alas, the old, old lust for power and wealth conquered the spirit of love and growth, and by the time of the Borgia popes the Church was back in the old position of Mammon or Babylon the great harlot.

Man is a being of power, and then a being of love. The pure individual tries either for sheer power, like Alexander, or sheer love, like Christ. But mankind forever will have its dual nature, the old Adam of power, the new Adam of love. And there must be a balance between the two. Man will achieve his highest nature and his highest achievements when he tries to get a living balance between his nature of power and his nature of love, without denying either. It is a balance that can never be established, save in moments, but every flower only flowers for a moment, then dies. That makes it a flower.

Nevertheless man can be a little more intelligent about himself and his destiny when he realises his dual nature, his nature of power, which is really collective, and his nature of love, which is individual.

Jesus came to establish the nature of love in the world. The apostles took up the task. They wanted to do it by avoiding any conflict with power, and the powers that be. Yet the conflict came. And gradually the Church itself became the great power, and by the time of the Reformation it was a power peculiarly devoid of love. So the pendulum swings.

In that early church of Christians, however, in the first century, there were plenty of men who became Christians in the belief that here was the *new* great Power. We have to realise that to a big portion of early Christians, Jesus was not love at all, he was just the name of a new power. He signified no tenderness nor gentleness, he signified rather a semi-magic potency that was going to destroy the world, wipe out the hated Romans, and establish the new saints in a reign of glory. As in the beginning of every new movement, Christianity was embraced by men who were the purest anti-Christ in spirit. There was an inordinate amount of subtilised sheer hate in the world, in the first century. A good deal of this sheer hate found its way into the Christian communities. These Christians of extraordinary subtilised hate are always revealed by their mad craving to destroy the world and to gain inordinate power for themselves. To them Jesus, "the Fish" was rather a supreme maleficent power that was going to wipe out the whole phenomenal world, leave only these spirits of pure lust for power to reign over a void sort of world, than any spirit of divine love. St. Paul and St. John the Apostle must have had bitter, bitter fights already with this sort of diabolical Christian, and it is a great wonder the early Church saved itself and emerged truly as the Church of the breath of love. Perverted power-lust threatened the early Church as it threatens every great revolution, and even every idealist movement. Many men are socialists out of perverted power-lust. And this form of lust is diabolical, deadly, it is a fearsome form of hate. Even Lenin was pure hate, really: but pure. The rest of the bolshevists are usually impure hate. It comes from the perversion of the nature of power in a man.

And now we can turn to the Apocalypse. For the Apocalypse, the last book in the Bible, is a book of power. It is a book of power-lust, written by a man who is a prisoner, denied all power.

Now we must free ourselves from the superficial contempt for power which most of us feel and express today. We only know dead power, which is force. Mere force does not command our respect. But power is not mere force. It is divine like love. Love and power are the two divine things in life. This is what Nietzsche meant.

But love is only divine when it is in harmonious relation to power: and power is only divine when it is in harmony with love. Jesus plainly said he only came to fulfil, to make complete, the old Law of power. The early Church, and a great Pope like Gregory, knew and gave perhaps the best example of love in harmony with power, and power in harmony with love. The following popes only too soon lost the love in striving for power, and the antithesis was Francis of Assisi and similar saints, who wanted to destroy all power in the name of love.

In the last century, Shelley sang over and over again of the perfection to which men would arrive when all "power" had been wiped off the face of the earth. But we feel, about Shelley as about Francis, there is a certain basic falseness in it all. We feel, moreover, in both men the same lack of warmth and of real kindly love, in both is the death of love. The death of power is the death of love: and vice versa.

The war against power culminated actually in Lenin. Lenin was pure, as Francis and Shelley were pure. In fact, Francis, Shelley and Lenin are the three great figures of history, men of pure spirit single in their fight against power. Lenin fulfilled what Shelley preached. Lenin was as pure a poet of action as Shelley was of words. And he accomplished the great feat of the Christian ages, he destroyed power in the name of love. Lenin accomplished for the State what Christ preached only for the individual. For the individual, the ideal is love. But you cannot have love as an ideal for a State. Values are different. The State has a lower scale of values. What is love in the individual is well-being in the State. Lenin sincerely wanted the well-being of every individual in the State. He was, in a sense, the god of the common people of Russia, and they are quite right, in the modern sense, to worship him. "Give us this day our daily bread". And Lenin wanted above all things to give them their daily bread. And he could not do even that. What was love in theory became hate in practice. He loved the people because he saw them powerless—and he was determined that power should not exist on earth. He himself was the final power which should destroy power. It was the Church of Christ in practical politics. And it was anomaly, it was horrible. Because it was un-natural.

Jesus was very careful, really, *not* to assume power, and not to destroy power. The great God of Power, of Might, was the Father.

And even Caesar was, in a sense, the Father. Render unto Caesar that which is Caesar's. And Jesus himself taught us the Lord's prayer.

> "Our Father, which art in heaven, hallowed be thy name,
>   thy kingdom come,
>   they will be done on earth as it is in heaven—"

We observe, Jesus himself never said: "*My* kingdom come," nor even: "*My* will be done on earth as it is in heaven". Jesus truly claimed no kingdom: the kingdom was the Father's: and the law, the *will* was the Father's. Jesus only came to supplement or complete this will, to make the kingdom of the *Father* perfect. Jesus has no kingdom: he insists all the time that the kingdom is the Father's, it belongs to the Lord Almighty, the Lord of Hosts, the God of power, to him who gives life and strength and potency.—And so the Church of Christ *cannot* have temporal power. But the Church of God can.

Jesus has no "power", and seeks no power. His is the mystery of love, and it is another mystery. The mystery of love has a great potency, indeed. But it is not the potency of rule, it is the potency of no-rule.

Power is a definite and positive thing, an enrichening which comes to us from Rule, from a Ruler, an Almighty, a Lord of Hosts. Try to get away from it as we may, ultimately we must come back to the ancient fact that the universe, the cosmos is swayed by a great Ruler, an Almighty. There is Rule in the cosmos, there is Mind in the cosmos, there is even Will in the cosmos. It is a pity Jesus called it "the Father"—it does so suggest the old gentleman with a beard. But Jesus spoke in purely human terms. And Jesus was most careful always to do homage to the Father.

A Kosmokrator there is, in spite of all our efforts at denial. There is a great and terrible Ruler of the cosmos, who gives forth life, and takes back life. The Kosmokrator gives us fresh life every day. But if we refuse the Almighty, the Ruler, we refuse the life. And whoever cuts us off from the Almighty cuts us off from life. Whoever gets between me and the Lord of Life, the Kosmokrator, Lord of Hosts and giver of might, source of our strength and power and our glory as far as we can be glorious, whoever gets between me and this, or Him, if you like, is my enemy, and *hates* me. So that St. Francis of Assisi, and Shelley, and Lenin all three hated men who lived in the might and splendour of life, who ruled and accepted rule. And since all common men live and want to live in the might and the splendour of life, Francis, and Shelley, and Lenin hated all common, upstanding, free and dauntless men. This is peculiarly and viciously true of the socialists everywhere: they hate all free, upstanding and dauntless men.

The most free, the most upstanding, the most dauntless men are happy, splendidly happy to accept the rule of a real man of power, who draws vitality from the cosmos. And they are unhappy, wretched when cut off from rule and from power, and forced to be democratic.

Now the fact that the Lord's prayer says first of all: Thy kingdom come, shows that men first and foremost want *rule*, the sense of power, power in the rulers above them. They want it even before they want bread. The common man wants to be consummated in the splendour and might of the rulers above him. It is a primary, paramount need, old and yet still unrecognised. When rulers have no cosmic splendour and might, then the common man tears them to pieces. It is a crime that a ruler should be impotent and without cosmic splendour, it is a great crime against the manhood of men. What does a man care about good food and good plumbing, if his life is inglorious and meaningless! Men like Lenin and the socialists, and Shelley and the "spiritists" would steal away from man his most precious treasure of all, his sense of solid splendour in life, his share in the glory of the cosmos. For first and foremost the cosmos is glorious, and man is part of the cosmos.

But the might, and the splendour, and the glory must all be tempered by love. Which means, we must be willing to submit, upon necessity, to the death of our individual splendour and might, as individuals we must upon occasion be willing to be weak and insignificant, humble, meek, mournful, poor in spirit, in order that a greater, a completer glory may come among men. For one man cannot be truly glorious unless all men, according to their degree, are glorified. This is the supreme truth that men like Caesar, or like Napoleon, have failed to grasp.

Before Jesus, before the period in which Jesus came, men sought only glory and might, let it cost what it would. Every man sought his own splendour, no matter what other men might suffer. Or if individual men were not quite so overweening, nations were. Every nation sought its own glory, at the cost of all its neighbours.

But already in the sixth century before Christ came the first signs of the other necessity in man, the need to die in the immediate self, and be re-born in a greater self. Men had been very blind to one another. It needed an experience as of death to make them aware, a little more aware of one another, and of the other man's needs.

It was in the sixth century men began, almost universally in the "known" world, to practice the cults of the dying god. It was then that the Orphic mysteries began. The dying god may have symbolised the death and re-birth of vegetation, of corn, the rousing again with spring of the phallic power of fertility, throughout "nature". But it meant much more than this. It meant also, from far-off centuries, before Plato, long before Jesus, the need man felt of death, the death-wish, so that a man might experience mystically, or ritually, the death in the body, the death of the known desires, and a resurrection in a new self, a more spiritual or highly-conscious self. The great death-wish of the centuries following the sixth century B.C., which brought the tragic conception into life, and which has lasted to this day, was the wish for escape from the old way of consciousness, the way of Might and of Cosmic Power, into a new way of consciousness, the way of knowledge. Man has two supreme forms of consciousness, the consciousness that I AM, and that I am full of power; then the other way of consciousness, the awareness that IT IS, and that IT, which is the objective universe or the other person, has a separate existence from mine, even preponderant over mine. This latter is the way of knowledge: the loss of the sense of I AM, and the gaining of knowledge, or awareness, of the other thing, the other creature.

About 600 B.C., the wish for pure knowledge became dominant in man, and carried with it the death wish. Men wanted to experience death, and come out on the other side, and know what was on the other side of death, all the time while they were still alive. This great wish for death and the adventure through death into the beyond took on many different shapes in many different religions. The Olympians perhaps knew nothing of it. But into the Olympian religion came the Orphic mystery and the Dionysic ecstasy, ways of getting out of the body and of obtaining experience beyond, in the beyond of this world: ways of knowing as the gods knew, which is the same as knowing what lies beyond death. For the gods lie beyond death. That world where the gods live is the world that men call death, and that world where men live is the world of the death of the gods.

In all known countries sprang up the strange rituals called mysteries, which were first and foremost the ritual in which a man experienced death, and went through the dark horror of Hades, to rise again in a new body, with a new consciousness and a new glory, god-like. These mysteries went far beyond any fertility cult, though they might embody that too. The ear of corn that was born was also the new body of a man with its new consciousness, god-like.

In Greece it was the Orphic mystery, the mysteries of Dionysos, Iacchos, the Eleusinian mystery: in Egypt it was the mystery of Osiris and Isis: in the near East, the mysteries of Tammuz, the mysteries of Attis: and in Persia, the mystery of Mithras. In India, Buddha took his mystery to a different conclusion, to Nirvana. But it was in the same spirit, with the same nostalgic wish for death in the body, and in the old way of consciousness, and the complete passing away of the old self into a final state of complete being, called Nirvana. With the Hindus, something the same happened. But with them it was a way through death to a new *power*, a new control of the vitalistic forces.

So the whole world went religious mad, if we may dare to say so, about the same time. The Greeks who resisted the Orphic and Dionysic "madness"—to use their own words—none the less took a similar road, seeking the loss of self and the gaining of *pure knowledge*. The pure knowledge that the Ionian Greeks began to thirst for, in the sixth century B.C., is not ultimately very different from Buddha's Nirvana or even St. John's New Jerusalem. Pure knowledge, pure science, Nirvana, Pradhana, the sheer ecstasy of Iacchos, the transport of the initiate re-born of Isis, or re-born at Eleusis, or re-born from the blood of the Mithraic bull, all these are *states of consciousness* which are almost identical. The modern physicist is on the brink of Nirvana, the man who follows Einstein right through achieves in the end a state of ecstasy which is the culmination of the way of knowledge. There is a short-cut, through ritual, through yoga practice. And there is the long, long way from Thales and Anaximander down to Einstein. But the final state of consciousness achieved is almost the same, in each case. *And it is the goal*, in each case. The modern physicist is on the brink of the culminating ecstasy, when his search for *knowledge* will consummate itself in the final and inexplicable *experience*, which will be mystic jargon if put into words. All roads lead to Rome: and all search for knowledge, *whatever the knowledge*, leads to the same result, the mystic experience of ecstasy in re-birth, the experience of Nirvana, the achievement of the state of Pradhana, one or the other of the ultimate experiences which are all alike, but reached by different roads.

Men achieved, in the fifth century B.C., by ritual, what men are now at last achieving by science, the science of physics. Ritual comes first: then dogmatic religion: finally science. And they all three at last achieve the same end, the same state of consciousness. Einstein himself is in the same state of consciousness, essentially, as an Orphic initiate was in, four centuries before Christ.

So, following the fulfilment of the experience by ritual, came the recording of the mystic experience. Now every Mystery was secret, profoundly secret. The ritual might never be revealed, nor even the experience. Every initiate must experience the Mystery for himself, in his own body. He must die his own death. At the same time, the priests of each religion did apparently elaborate a theory or an explanation of the Mysteries, and this, divulged to the initiates, must have passed into the common consciousness in exoteric forms. Anyhow we know enough of the Eleusinian Mysteries to know roughly what they were about: about the mystery of death, and the passage through Hades, and the re-birth in a higher world, or state: a glory. But unfortunately no pagan apocalypse remains to us, only a Mithraic fragment. For the rest, every Apocalypse is Jewish, and by far the most famous is that of John of Patmos. But there are others: the Apocalypse of Enoch, and the visions in the Book of Daniel are also counted as apocalypse. An Apocalypse is really a vision, a revelation of heavenly things, and it takes the place of the older form of prophecy, in which the voice of God was heard, while God remained unseen, or seen only in a burning bush.

The Apocalypse of John is unique. It is undeniably Jewish, intensely Jewish, though written in the name of Christ. At the same time, there is something very unjewish about it, and it is, we might say, entirely unchristian. At the very beginning, it suggests the esoteric symbols of the pagans, and as we read on, we realise that here is a document that has a scheme far too complex for a Jewish revelation. This is an esoteric document, elaborate, complex, and concealed, and there is nothing Christian in it but the name of Christ. For Christianity brought first and foremost a new feeling into the world, rather than a new idea: a feeling of brotherly or spiritual love, as contrasted with the old carnal love. And it was not, as with Epicurus and the Greeks of his school, a feeling of affection tinged with resignation and hopelessness, the affectionate tolerance of those who have really lost hope. It was a fresh and triumphant feeling, that through brotherly, spiritual love man would be saved throughout eternity. Brotherly love without any form of desire was in itself a new feeling. But that God Himself, or at least, the Son of God, was such a lover, the supreme desireless lover, this was a new religious conception. And that the resurrection would be an entering into immortality in the great desireless love of Christ, this too was a new conception, a new inspiration. We can judge the Christianity of any work, or any individual, by the presence or absence of this "pure", desireless love, selfless, esteemed as divine. And we can find none of it in the vengeful chapters of John's Apocalypse. John of Patmos wants his revenge, final, heaven after. Neither the pagans nor the Jews nor even the Christian gnostics grasped the new feeling and the new concept of desireless, immortal love, a love which was basically a love of the other man, a love of the neighbour, loving one's neighbour being conceived as part of the divine desireless love of Christ. Even the mind of Plato contained no such concept, and his emotional self knew no such feeling. Plato wished sincerely for the human "good". He did not realise that what humanity needed was a little "pure" love. He still thought it wanted Rule: wise rule, benevolent rule, but still, loveless rule.

The pagan religions, the Jewish religion never got beyond the great conception of power. In the beginning, the cosmos itself was the great Power that Is. The cosmos was alive, and its power was a great living effluence. Looking into the sky was like looking into the eyes of some mighty living creature, or being: and even today, we cannot look into the eyes even of a cat or a baby without quivering from the naked contact with life and the power of life. The universe was all power, and man derived power from the cosmos. At his maximum, he was full of power, and like a bridegroom, vivid with potency. So that, towards the end of the great pagan era, though long before Christianity or Plato, cosmic power came to be conceived as phallic power, and the act of marriage was the consummation of man's divinity. But this was only towards the *end* of the pagan era: or shall we say, with the Greeks, towards the end of the barbaric era. The almost universal phallic worship of the last centuries before true history begins, the worship which left the phallic stones standing everywhere in southern Europe, was perhaps the last phase of the great cosmic worship of power. Power was in the cosmos, power was in the sun and moon, power was in the phallos. Our anthropologists abandon the sun-myth for the fertility-myth, and they will no doubt abandon the fertility-myth for something else. But any way, they have at last accepted the army of phallic stones that even yet stand erect and forbid the honest anthropologist to ignore them.

When the cult of dying gods came into the ancient worship of cosmic power, the two great aims of worship did not change essentially. The aim of the worship was still the acquiring of the splendid phallic power or fertility which man recognises as his best and fullest physical state, and further, the acquiring of the higher power which, when attained, gives man his immortality. To have the fullest phallic potency man must undergo a temporary winter-death and transit through Hades, like the plants. This is an old cosmic truth lost sight of today, yet lingering in the fertile nations. And again, to enter into that higher power wherein man has his immortality, a man must die an even deeper death, a death of the consciousness, and emerge with a new consciousness. So that from the dual mystic death he emerges with a new body and a new consciousness or spirit, and the consummation of the initiation is based on the "marriage" of these two, the re-union.

So I think we can safely say, the old pagan Mysteries all consisted in a death, first of the body and then of the spirit or consciousness: a passage through the underworld of the dead, in which the spirit or consciousness achieved death step by step: then a sudden emergence into life again, when a new body, like a babe, is born, and a new spirit emerges: then the meeting of the new-born frail spirit with the Great Spirit of the god, which descends from heaven for the consummation: and then the final marriage again of a new body and new spirit.

None of this, as we see, is Christian exactly. It is too physical and too self-glorious. It is, if you like, a grand self-glorification which Christianity absolutely discouraged. Christianity is based above all on *communal* love, and communion must be a communal act. Even Pentecost is not individual—the Spirit descends on the members of the Church, while they are together, not upon some special *initiate*. In Christianity, a man might never really forget his neighbour, for the very love of Christ was a love of the neighbour. In Christianity, a man lost his own *self* for ever, and became only a vessel of the divine love.

This obliteration of self *entirely* was obnoxious to all pagans, and even Jews; and the self-glorification consummated in the pagan and Jewish ritual was obnoxious to all Christians. To the pagans, as to the Jews, the lack of a certain pride and assumption in a man was repugnant. To the Christians, pride and assumption were the devil. Even the Epicureans, who practised a sort of affectionate resignation and a sort of humility, were really very unpopular in the pagan world. The Stoics, with their pride, their insolence almost in enduring misery or misfortune, carried on the old pagan spirit, and won the day with the pagans. The great split had started long before Christ, between the way of pride and power, and the way of mildness and gentleness. Christianity made the breach absolute.

Now on which side of the breach is John of Patmos? First we must be clear that John of Patmos is not the same man as the Apostle John, John the beloved disciple, John who wrote the Fourth Gospel. The Fourth Gospel is perhaps the greatest of Christian documents, and John the Apostle is one of the great religious spirits of all time. John of Patmos is quite another man. He is said to have been already an old man when he was exiled from Ephesus to Patmos by the Roman magistrates of the city of Ephesus, for some offence against the Roman State, perhaps refusing to perform the ritual act of worship to the Emperor. For the date when Revelation is supposed to have been finished is fairly late, about 96 A.D., after the Christians had been recognised by Rome as a hostile sect. Again, because of the peculiar and ungrammatical, "bad" Greek in which Revelation is written, later critics have decided that John of Patmos did not know much Greek, that he had probably emigrated quite late in life from Galilee to Ephesus, that his natural language was Aramaic, but that in a religious connection he even *thought* in Hebrew. Hence his Revelation is a mental translation from good old Hebrew into bad Greek. All of which is very plausible except the bad Greek: which is so peculiar and special in its form, that one cannot help suspecting that John of Patmos invented his own lingo for his own highly esoteric work, his Revelation which was a sheer mystification to anyone who didn't have the key. So that we absolutely cannot swallow the idea that John of Patmos was a rustic old Rabbinical Jew who emigrated late from Galilee, and stammered naïvely in bad Greek, and got himself exiled for some years to Patmos, for some naïve fault or other. Revelation is a sophisticated work if ever there was one.

And is it in the Christian spirit of meekness and gentleness that it is written? The reader of the Apocalypse can answer for himself. But since the book begins with the seven famous "messages" to the seven churches in Asia, and since each message ends with a promise of reward, if we look at the seven rewards we can roughly judge what the man who wrote the book wanted. The rewards are:

1. To him that overcometh will I give to eat of the tree of life, which is in the midst of the paradise of God.

2. He that overcometh shall not be hurt by the second death.

3. To him that overcometh will I give to eat of the hidden manna, and will give him a white stone, and in the stone a new name written, which no man knoweth saving he that receiveth it.

4. And he that overcometh, and keepeth my works unto the end,

to him will I give power over the nations: And he shall rule them with a rod of iron; as the vessels of a potter shall they be broken to shivers: even as I received of my Father. And I will give him the Morning Star.

5. He that overcometh, the same shall be clothed in white raiment, and I will not blot out his name out of the book of life, but I will confess his name before my Father and before his angels.

6. He that overcometh will I make a pillar in the temple of my God, and he shall go no more out: and I will write upon him the name of my God, and the name of the city of my God, which is new Jerusalem, which cometh down out of heaven from my God: and *I will write upon him* my new name.

7. To him that overcometh will I grant to sit with me in my throne, even as I also overcame, and am set down with my Father in his throne.—

This is a mysterious scale of promises which goes very high indeed. For "he that overcometh" shall at last sit in the throne alongside of the Messiah and even of Almighty God, sharing the throne even of the Lord of Hosts. The very thought is enough to make one tremble, and disclaim any such awful ambition. For whatever our conception of Almighty God may be, and even if we cannot form any conception, and are content with a last wild feeling of awe and delight, still the presumption of sharing the eternal throne frightens us and shocks us. I am not and never shall be equal to Almighty God, or able to sit on a throne beside him. My very soul tells me this. My very soul tells me that if the Kosmokrator, the Unknown, at last gives me the kiss of acceptance, that is my happiness.

Jesus himself did not expect to sit on the throne of the Father. The angel of Annunciation promised Mary: "He shall be great, and shall be called the Son of the Highest: and the Lord God shall give unto him the throne of his father David: And he shall reign over the house of Jacob for ever: and of his kingdom there shall be no end.—"

Or again: "And Jesus said unto them: Verily I say unto you, That ye which have followed me, in the regeneration when the Son of Man shall sit in the throne of his glory, ye also shall sit upon twelve thrones, judging the twelve tribes of Israel".—And it is David who says: "The Lord said unto my Lord, sit thou on my right hand. Until I make thy foes thy footstool".—And even this does not seat Jesus upon the throne of the Father, even in David's poetic song. And Paul goes on plainly to say of Jesus: "God hath made that same Jesus, whom ye have crucified, both Lord and Christ".

The seventh promise, to the Church of Laodicea, is quite clear, and quite definite. Moffatt's translation gives: "The conqueror I will allow to sit beside me on my throne, as I myself have conquered and sat down beside my Father on his throne". It is a stupendous, and, we must feel, non-Christian promise. It is however pagan: for an initiate might sit down with Dionysos or with Isis, in the full consummation and glory of initiation. But both Dionysos and Isis, also Mithras and Attis, they are all mediator gods, who go between heaven and earth; they are not Almighty God himself. It is strange even for a man to *think* of sitting down beside Almighty God: somehow terrifying.

Now lest there seem an element of sentimentality or falsity in this feeling, let us ask ourselves again, do we really *believe* in Almighty God, anyhow? Are not the words cant words, nowadays?

From the last far corner of the soul comes the confession: There is Almighty God.—With the reason, we think: Ah, in the cosmos of the astronomists, where then is this Almighty God?—But the reason answers herself: The cosmos brought forth all the world, and brought forth me. It brought forth my mind, my will, and my soul. Therefore there must be that in the cosmos which can bring forth all things, including mind and will and feeling. Therefore there must be that in the cosmos which contains the essence, at least, or the potentiality, of all things, known and unknown. That in the universe which contains the potentiality of all things, contains the potency also of thought and act and feeling and will, along with the rest. And this terrific and frightening and delighted potency I call Almighty God. I think of it, and am filled with fear—fear of my own crass presumptuousness,—and filled with a sense of delight and liberation. If there is Almighty God, I care about nothing else. There is Almighty God, and I am delighted, the whole burden of my fear shifts over.

There is Almighty God. The next question, still more serious, is how to come into living contact.

How did men in the past come into Contact? The way of Jesus is good, but we want a greater way, a more ample contact. I do not want to be safe in the arms of Jesus. I am not safe in the arms of Jesus, for my soul cries out to seek Almighty God. And I will seek down any avenue.

The seven promises to the seven churches ought to be the real clue to the Apocalypse. But as a matter of fact, taken in detail the work is incomprehensible. Only roughly can we gather what it means. But from the start, it is obvious it cannot be taken at its face meaning. The words are not intended to mean just what they say. They are intended to have a wrapped-up meaning, or perhaps a whole series of wrapped-up meanings: three or four separate meanings wrapped up in the same sentence, like creatures tied up in a cloth. And it is now impossible for us to unfold the cloth and let out all the meanings. Because John of Patmos tied the knots too tight, for one thing, and for another, we feel that the manuscript had been tampered with, messed about, before it became really public.

Anyhow we know from the first chapter that we are reading a book quite different from any other Christian book of the New Testament. In fact, it is difficult to believe that John of Patmos had ever read any of the Gospels or of the Epistles, or even that he knew anything of the canonical life-story of Jesus. The Jesus of Revelation is simply incomprehensible from the Gospel point of view. The Gospels, especially the Fourth, are so very careful to insist

[The MS fragment ends here in mid-sentence]

Apocalypse, *Fragment 2*

The tenderness of Paul in some of the Epistles, expressing his tender concern for his distant brothers, and exhorting them above all things to love one another, not to quarrel, and not to *harden*: this brings a new human relationship into the world, a new sort of love. Perhaps Epicurus had tried for something similar, but there was a touch of resignation in Epicurus, no vivid hope. The Epicureans felt that the gods cared no more about the world of man. The Christians taught that God cared supremely: but that man showed his love of God by loving his fellow-men.

Now the pagans of Jesus' day did not care very much about their fellowmen. The world was full of religion, even religions of dying gods who rose to life and gave new life also to men. But in the mysteries, the initiate gained a new life, a re-birth, a "glory" for himself, and he was supposed to keep it to himself. He must not even tell anybody. The aim of the mysteries, of initiation, was to make a man glorious along with the God, Isis, Osiris, or Orphic Dionysos, or Mithras: to make a man glorious, to take him through the symbolic death, and so free him from the terrors of actual death, which would be the "second death" of the initiate: and also, by teaching him to die in the immediate or greedy self, and to rise in a higher or nobler self, thus free him from the chain of "mistakes" which the pagans did not call "sins", as we do.

Thus the pagans were religious, and their religion was also moral: the Stoic severely so. But there was no very definite sense of sin. And also there was no particular concern about the other person. The Christians transferred some of the Jewish passion of "a Chosen People" into their brotherly love, Christians fell at once into communities and "churches", Christian love was collective, and the duty of every Christian in saving himself was to help save his neighbour. *Every* soul was precious, and so every man should concern himself in saving every soul. The pagans did not think that every soul was precious—far from it—and it was a man's business to save himself alone. His other duties were duties of citizenship, moral duties, not concerned with the soul.

The first great split between Christianity and paganism came in here: in the intense feeling of community which Christianity at once inspired in the early "Churches", a new collective oneness, apart from, and even hostile to race or State or local culture. It was partly a transfer of the Jewish feeling of the Chosen People, watched over by God, to peoples who were not Jewish.

The second great difference was the great split which the Christians made with the Cosmos. The Christian saw nothing in the world but the soul of man, the love of Christ, and sin. The sun ceased to matter, or the moon, and harvest and spring-time were of no concern. It was not till after the Dark Ages that the Catholic Church brought back into human life the great rhythm of the seasons, and re-established the great pagan festivals of Christmas, Easter, Midsummer, and the Day of All the Dead, which set the calendar of the year and the calendar of the soul in harmony again. Then later Christianity reverted in Protestantism, and particularly Puritanism, to the old abstraction which cared for nothing but the soul of man, and sin, and summer and winter were lost, the sacred moments of the equinoxes were forgotten, the great festivals became times of eating only, the cosmic connection was less than a myth.

But in Jesus' day the connection with the cosmos was still strong, in all the old religions, even the Jewish. Jesus came from Galilee, not from Judea. Galilee was an open land of mixed races, subject to every influence. It had none of the shut-in intensity of fanaticism of Jerusalem and Judea, so blackly Jewish. Jesus came from a spiritually free country, probably even a kindly country. The peasants and artizans were perhaps mostly Jews, speaking, presumably Aramaic. And these, of course, focussed in the synagogues, just like the Jews in Europe. But most of the higher workmen and shop-keepers and the property-owning classes of Galilee must have been Greek-speaking, and by race Greek or Asiatic or Egyptian, almost anything. They had their summer villas on the Lake of Galilee, just as rich people have villas on the Italian Lakes. And apparently they lived without friction. Nay, one feels they must even have been friendly, kindly, even as the English or American owners of villas on Lake Como are mostly kindly towards the Italian peasants and fishermen today. Jesus grew up in no unfriendly atmosphere in Galilee. We feel it in all the Gospels. And we feel the change, when he goes into Judea among the Jews. Indeed, his rather beautiful trust of his fellow men in Galilee only makes the Jews of Jerusalem more dangerous to him, later on. It may be that the rich pagan Greeks of Galilee were Epicurean by tendency, gentle in manners and indulgent to their inferiors, and that this gentleness helped to beget Christianity. For it is not words that beget new things, it is feeling. And without knowing one word of Epicurean doctrine, Jesus may have been profoundly influenced by Greek Epicureans, merely by contact with their refined gentleness and tolerance, and their unassuming affectionateness of people of old breeding or culture. It is old culture that counts, not old breeding. And one cannot help feeling in Jesus the result of that diffident kindliness which is characteristic of old and tried culture. But in Jesus, a religious young Jew of the working-class, the diffidence is burned out and the kindliness kindled to love by religious passion.

The Greek world of Jesus' day was tired. There was too much to cope with. There had been too much war, too much disaster. And there was now too much consciousness. Into the Greek-speaking world was gathered the consciousness of every living culture, every extant religion, whether Hellenic or Egyptian, Chaldean or Persian or Roman or even, probably, Hindu. The Greeks knew of *all* the religions: as we do today. They knew of all the cults and philosophies, all the problems, all the solutions. And it was too much for them. They knew too much, and it paralysed them, dissipated their energy. Jesus probably spoke some Greek, even if not much. We presume he naturally spoke Aramaic, a language which spread over the Near East. He was preserved by his Jewishness and his synagogue from enquiring after strange gods. Yet he must have been familiar with the pagan temples, temples to Isis, temples to Mithras and Bacchus. They must have been part of his landscape, as must the pagans carrying flowers and sacrifice to the gods, and the open-air ritual of sacrifice. Jesus must have seen it all, all his life, familiar and not unfriendly. We cannot feel that he hated it: surely it had its beauty for him too. He was a country boy, not bred up in the narrowness of a city set. In the country things which are are accepted more naturally. And probably it was the charm of the small pagan temples in the Galilean countryside which made him resent so hotly the trafficking in the great temple of Jerusalem.

The temples were there, the pagan worship was in the air. How should Jesus be insensitive to it! It is only stupid, mechanical people who are not aware of things felt by others. Jesus may not have known anything definite about the Mysteries of Mithras, or Isis, or the Orphic Mysteries. Yet since some of them were practised in his neighbourhood how could [he] be unaware of them, and of their supposed significance? A great nature like that of Jesus is sensitively *aware*. And who is going to tell me that he was totally unaware of Dionysos and the Orphic Mysteries, or the mysteries of Isis or Mithras? for the temples of these deities must have stood by the Sea of Galilee. Only a stupid nature is unaware of things that are vital to others. Could I be unaware of a Catholic procession if I met it in the street, or fail to ask what it was about?

And in the same way that he must have known something of the pagan Mysteries, even by breathing them in the air, since he lived in a pagan province, Jesus must have known also something of the ancient star-lore, and the ancient symbols. The old, old Chaldeans of the oldest Babylon began reading the stars, and the Jews very often read with them, from the earliest days. The stars were in the Jewish consciousness, despite the fact that the scribes expurgated them so often. You can't easily make a people unaware of something which it is profoundly aware of. Even by turning the chief stars into archangels, you don't escape them entirely.

The stars are very remote to us: thinly scattered in enormous, enormous space: comparatively, so lonely and few. But that is how we see them objectively, scientifically. The first way of seeing the stars was purely subjective.

It seems to me, man has had, as far as we can tell, three great phases of consciousness, each carrying its own culture. The first was a far-off phase of purely collective consciousness, when men thought and felt instinctively *together*, like a great flock of birds or pack of wolves. They did not think single thoughts or feel single feelings, but their great thoughts and their great feelings were tribal, felt all at once by a mass of men, but culminating or focussing in some leader.

This feeling-in-unison is profound and is religious. At its highest, it is purely religious: taking "religious" to mean the feeling of being *in connection*. And at its deepest, the early *unison* consciousness of man was aware of the cosmos, and aware of the immediate connection between itself and the vast, potent, terrible cosmos, that lived with all life. Naked tribal man breast to breast with the naked cosmos, pouring his consciousness collectively into the cosmos, and in ritual, in naked superb ritual alone taking from the cosmos life, vitality, potency, prowess, and power: *pouvoir*, *Macht*, might. The tribe or nation culminated in one man, the leader or chief, the tip of the great collective body. And this tip of the tribe touched the very heart of the cosmos, the core of the sun, and drew down the life of the potent heavens to man, potent yet yearning man.

This was the condition of pre-historic, or shadow-historic civilised man. It was the civilisation of the tumulus and the pyramid, pyramidical to symbolise the broad basis of the people culminating in the living tip of the leader or hero. It was a culture absolutely religious, for *all* was religious, every act was performed in connection with the great cosmos, and at the same time, there were no gods. Man, tribal or collective man was nakedly breast to breast with the cosmos, and the need for God had not arisen in the human soul.

It did not arise till man felt himself cut off from the cosmos, till he became aware of himself apart, as an apart, fragmentary, unfinished thing. This is the Fall, the fall into knowledge, or self-awareness, the fall into tragedy and into "sin". For a man's sex is his fragmentariness. The phallos is the point at which man is broken off from his context, and at which he can be re-joined. In his awareness of sex, which is awareness of separateness and fragmentariness, lies man's sense of shame and sin.

How man came to be cut off in consciousness from the cosmos we do not know. But we can see that it is the same thing as knowledge: knowledge is only possible in a separation of subject and object. We can also see that it is tragedy. And we can see that it may be called "sin", since it is a "fall" from unison or at-oneness.

We can also see that it makes a God, or gods necessary to the consciousness. There must be an intermediary between man and the "lost" cosmos. There must be an intermediary consciousness which understands both sides, both the great, creative, incomprehensible cosmos and the soul of man. In short, the cosmos must have a great man in it—a soul, or God.

Then follows the great history of the gods, the overthrow of Ouranos the Demiurge or Creator by Kronos the Kosmokrator, then the overthrow of the Kosmokrator or Ruler of the Cosmos by Zeus the Thunderer or Father who speaks to his children. And finally, the potential overthrow, or at least supplementing of Zeus by Dionysos, semi-substitution of Jesus for the Father, the Spirit for the Almighty.

This is the history of man's repeated "falls" in self-consciousness: from Creator to Ruler, from Ruler to Father, from Father to Son, and from Son or Spirit to mind alone, godless once more. The last state is the same as the first, godless. But now, instead of being naked vital man breast to breast with the vital cosmos, it is naked, disembodied mind losing itself in a naked and disembodied universe, a strange Nirvana. This is the final condition of science, of modern physics and modern physicists. Really to "understand" the last theories in physics needs a mystic *experience* like that of the ecstatic saints, or like that of Nirvana, or the state of *samadhi* in Brahmin saints, or the ecstatic state of an Orphic initiate.

These are the three states of man, cosmic-religious, god-religious and philosophic-scientific. Jesus was the last manifestation of the god-religious state. We are at the end of the philosophic state. What next? We don't know.

The tribes that exist as tribes on earth today are only degenerate fragments of the great old cosmic-religious humanity. So also were the cave-men; degenerate fragments, left isolated by some geological cataclysm. These are not the human beginnings at all, but fag ends of a previous human greatness.

Similarly the pagan religions of Jesus' day were the vast decadence of the Zeus or Father stage of religion, mingled with strange echoes of all the other past, the Kosmokrator, the Creator, and even the naked Cosmos.

Now when man first "fell" into knowledge or self-consciousness, I believe the first thing he did was to lie down and gaze at the stars. Then he felt himself back in his old oneness: he was again at one with the mighty and living cosmos. But alas, now he was doomed to view it objectively.

So I believe the stars are the very oldest religion. And I believe the oldest of all old historical civilisations, the great River civilisations of the Euphrates, the Nile, the Indus were all primarily "star" civilisations, cosmic in the astronomical sense.

This star-cult never died. It outlived all the gods, and lingers even today. In Jesus' day it was immeasurably degraded and mixed up with horoscopy and witch-craft. But it was star-cult still, the heavens were still terrific and marvellous, the planets were still tremendously potent Rulers.

And did Jesus know absolutely nothing of star-cult? Impossible. To an imaginative, vivid nature, impossible. The Jews had been shifted twice into Babylonia. They had learned all they could of Chaldean star-lore. The Jewish priests, scribes, lawyers who fixed the law of Moses in the Pentateuch, about 400 B.C. apparently, they no doubt suppressed all the star-lore they could from the Scriptures. Later scribes, editing later books, from Isaiah and Ezekiel down to Daniel no doubt suppressed still more. But enough remains to take us continually to the ancient Babylon, long before Belshazzar's. And the "wheels" of Ezekiel are surely Anaximander's wheels. They are very much botched, but there they are surely Anaximander's wheels. Now Anaximander was an Ionian Hellene or Greek born just before the year 600 B.C. He is one of the most shadowy fathers of science, but his wheels of the heavens are stupendous, and fascinating to this day. And Ezekiel, or Ezekiel's transcriber has got them all mixed up with the vision of the Almighty, which the Prophet saw at the beginning of his prophetic days.

Now Anaximander is supposed to have invented the wheels, but surely the Chaldeans, the Babylonians invented them, after thousands of starry years, against Ionian decades. Modern science hates to go one step beyond the Greeks: but it seems to me that Chaldea taught Ionia before Ionia could stammer in Greek. Why be afraid of the great ancient pre-Greek world! It goes deeper and deeper into time.

The Jews always had a lot of star-lore up their sleeve—lots of pagan lore, really. The savage old orthodox priests of the Jerusalem temple fixed the law, and suppressed stars and strange gods, but throughout the centuries Jews have thought and dreamed outside the Mosaic law.

Jesus was such a dreamer: but the early Christian fathers were good suppressers. Already the apostles Paul and John had realised that Christianity must be a cult to itself—they were Jews—; and they were both educated in pagan lore, so they knew how to suppress all they wished to suppress. Paul was not only a Jew, he came from a city of Stoics and was a good deal a Stoic, and ancient Puritan. The Apostle John reads strangely like a chastened pagan. It is obvious that both he and St. Paul know the Orphic Mysteries—or at least, a good deal about them. Both men knew by instinct what they wanted to suppress from the new religion. And this was: first, star-lore, for star-lore had become a burden, a superstition of horoscopy and "fate"; then, blood-rites, for these had become tangled up with magic; then, the peculiar apotheosis of the individual which was the glory of the pagan initiate; then, the cult of "powers", for the pagan initiates were supposed to acquire all sorts of powers; then, the cult of vision and prophecy, which tended to break up a brotherhood; and finally, all the pagan symbolism possible, for it tended to set men on the old paths.

The early fathers, from the Apostles downwards, tended to suppress all these things. Yet in the second century A.D., having cast out the old pagan and starry devil bit by bit, they let him in whole again at the very last minute, and there he is, the old demon, sitting at the very end of the Bible, in the Apocalypse. But then the door was slammed, and the work of destruction went on wholesale. The Christians destroyed all pagan evidence, and the destruction was carried on even to our day. Fifty years ago, in remote Catholic villages, or Puritan villages, every strange-seeming book or manuscript was carried to the parish priest or clergyman, and if he smelled anything that wasn't Christian, he promptly burned it. Nineteen hundred years of burning! Almost everything is lost, and we have to go by hints.

The Apocalypse was almost lost. The eastern Fathers, in Antioch and Byzantium and Alexandria, they fought hard to exclude Revelation from the Bible. Naturally! for in those old countries they knew what it was about. But the more barbarous Latin Fathers of Italy and Africa wanted it included, first, because it was supposed to have been written by the great Apostle John, second because it was such a good hammer against the Roman Empire, identified with Babylon. Well, it turned out just as good a hammer against the Roman Church, and it turned out that John of Patmos was not the Apostle John at all, but quite another man.

There were three Johns: John the Baptist, who had really a great following with curious doctrines lasting long after Jesus' day; then John the Apostle, who wrote the Fourth Gospel and some Epistles: then John of Patmos, called the Divine.

John of Patmos is supposed to have been already an old man, when he composed his Revelation on the island of Patmos. There had been other Jewish apocalypses before his: even the later part of the Book of Daniel is an apocalypse. An apocalypse is a revelation of what lies beyond this world: really, it is a journey into heaven. John's Revelation is obviously this.

The work is written in curious, ungrammatical, almost enigmatical Greek. Modern critics have supposed that John of Patmos, like Jesus, was a native of Galilee: that he emigrated late in life to Ephesus: that he gave offence to the Roman government in Ephesus owing to some religious difference, and that he was exiled to Patmos for a term of years, returning, however, at last to Ephesus, and living, according to tradition, to a great old age.

But there seems no reason at all for supposing that John came from Galilee, or that he was rustic and unlettered, arriving from the country in the city of Greeks when he was already old. The writer of Revelation was no naïve spirit from the rural countryside. He was a Jew of Jews, and surely a city Jew who had spent most of his years in reading "religion" and discussing it. Surely he was one of those Jews of the Dispersion who remained intensely Jewish, but who none the less interested himself in the cults of the pagans: a-sort of new Jew fascinated by the mysteries and the symbolic ritual and perhaps, more remotely, by the many forms of sorcery extant in the pagan world of Ephesus. There is a touch of the sorcerer about him, and his mind is, perhaps, partly the mind of the conjuror.

One thing is certain: he is very little of a true Christian. He had almost none of the new spirit of "loving his fellow-man in Christ", which was the clue to the other, greater John the Apostle, and to St. Paul. Neither is he a "prophet" as Jesus was. He is that new thing, a "seer" who sees terrific and occult visions, and his processes are the processes of magic and of occult science.

It may be this Apocalypse is older than the date usually assigned to it from internal evidence: viz. 96 A.D. It certainly is much older in spirit and design: though that is no test of date. One cannot help feeling, after reading the work several times, that it is not Christian at all: which means, that its author knew nothing of the Gospels or the great Epistles, nor of the Apostles, but that merely the *name* of Jesus is put in, in place of the old word Messiah. The work is certainly Messianic: but the Messiah is that strange semi-magical figure of Jewish imagination, a terrific magical apparition that should turn the world inside out. The Messiah is never for a moment the "gentle Jesus". There seems to be even no inkling of such a Jesus. Time after time appears the terrific vision of the Son of Man, and the Son of Man is always a slightly monstrous marvel-apparition which is the same as that of the Almighty and very like that of the pagan Time Spirit and Demiurge and Kosmokrator. But it has nothing whatsoever to do with the Jesus of the Gospels. Neither has the Lamb that shall save the world. The Lamb is entirely esoteric, and Jewish-pagan. And, if we must admit it, a trifle ridiculous.

It is possible that the accepted date of 96 A.D. is correct, for the finishing of the Apocalypse. It is also possible that the destruction of the Temple referred to may be the second destruction, by Herod Antipas, and not the Third, by Titus; and that therefore the Apocalypse may be considerably earlier, say even 50 A.D., and previous to the Gospels and the Epistles. It may be, the Apostles knew the Apocalypse, before the Gospels were written. And if they did, it would certainly point them a road to be avoided at all costs.

We must believe that St. John the Apostle and St. Paul, both of them Greeks by culture, had not only a sure *instinct* what to avoid in current religion, but also a highly educated philosophical knowledge of what was dangerous. Brought up as they were in the welter of religions, beset by the innumerable semi-magical cults and sects, they did as men must do who want fresh air for the soul, they set their faces against magical cult and esoteric cult, absolutely. St. John did indeed leave the miracles: but there was no magical practice connected with them. The idea is that pure belief will heal. And he even introduced the story of the wine at the marriage at Cana, and this is very suggestive of Orphic ritual. But he wanted, no doubt, to establish *at the very first* that Jesus *had* the miracle-working powers, that they were part of the divine nature: and then to proceed to the new doctrine: where Jesus says: I have not taught in secret; what I have taught, I have taught openly—

For the rest, there is an astonishing absence of any suggestion of magic, of transformation or transmigration, and of star-influence, in the New Testament, and this must be because St. Paul especially, being of stoical education, set his face against such things. We cannot help feeling that by the time the Gospels had achieved their present form, all the loose ends of paganism possible had been removed from them by Christian teachers who knew well what they were doing.

And we cannot help feeling that the same happened, more ineffectually, to the Apocalypse. St. Paul would surely have suppressed the book. But it appealed, and appeals today powerfully to the lower strata of religious imagination, bordering on sorcery and magic. The early Christians could not forego it. So that what happened, probably, is that his unkown "editor" of whom the critics complain was not an editor at all, but that for years the manuscripts of the Apocalypse were expurgated and amended, bit by bit, to remove the more glaring paganisms and to substitute a more Christian note. The seven letters to the seven churches have surely been cooked up in this way, till they are almost meaningless. The seven rewards may be more or less original: they suggest a certain scheme of rewards attending on the conquest of the seven natures of man by the "spirit": but even they are confused. There has been deliberate confusion made in the Apocalypse, no doubt by Christian scribes and teachers up to the year 150 A.D. or thereabouts, and for the definite purpose of covering up the pagan trail in the book. And when finally one manuscript was chosen by the Fathers as authoritative, it would be one in which the original thread was sufficiently broken and tangled to make the scheme irrecoverable. Since the scheme is no longer there, it is no longer to be recovered entire.

But at least sections of the Apocalypse seem to be intact. Myself, I feel the whole work as John of Patmos left it was probably quite complete; but afterwards, it had to be watered down, and doctored up, to make it fit the Christian scheme. And the greatest havoc was played at the beginning and at the end of the book: the middle fared rather better.

Even as it is, anyone who is at all acquainted with the old use of symbols must feel at once that here we have an esoteric work, a secret "plan" of regeneration: really, the description of the processes of initiation into a higher form of life, through the way of mystic death, the journey through the underworld or Hades, the re-emergence of the spirit into the new light of a higher world, or heaven, then the re-birth of the body (perhaps as a babe) and then the "re-birth" of the spirit through fusion with the Saviour, and finally, the re-marriage of the new body with the new spirit in the deathless glory of the gods: or heaven.

Orthodox critics have a very ingenious interpretation of the scheme of Revelation. They look on the book as "prophecy", following the rather feeble historical-prophecy method of the latter part of the Book of Daniel. The Apocalypse is supposed to be the prophecy of what will happen to the Church of Christ. First, there is the early Church under Roman persecution: persecution increases and increases till the blood of the martyrs is *all* shed, and the Church is *destroyed*: this may be under the Romans, or, if you are a modern Protestant, the Church of Christ is now *almost* destroyed by the Babylon of Mammon, commerce, luxury etc., after a run of two thousand years. When the blood of all the martyrs is shed, then Christ will appear again, and destroy the world, kings, emperors and all. After that, follows the millennium, when the saints and the martyrs are resurrected and, from their numerous thrones, actually govern the earth: emperors, kings and princes are no more, but the saints rule, and do not allow commerce or any woe. This goes on marvellously for a thousand years, and then all is over. The world is finished. Souls are summoned from paradise, earth and hell, to be judged. This is the Last Judgment, and the Second Death of the wicked. But the righteous do not suffer the Second Death at the Last Judgment. They rise to the new jewel-city of Jerusalem.

This interpretation is as good as one can get, taking the point of view of the Church, and taking the book as it stands. But the book seems hopelessly messed up at the end, and also at the beginning. And the "Church" interpretation leaves a good deal of the middle of the work meaningless.

We have to admit that while John of Patmos did no doubt have a Church in mind, a "body" of Christian men: he was too much a Jew of the Chosen People to escape the collective idea: at the same time he had the idea of the individual redemption or regeneration of the body and spirit perhaps even more deeply in mind. The Apocalypse equates rather better to the individual than to the Church. The individual dies the mystic death. Now this is not done in a moment. It is a process of seven stages. Man has seven "natures", seven "levels" of being, seven dynamic centres of consciousness. These centres are conquered one by one, by the higher consciousness or spirit. It is like seven "stages of the Cross". Man conquers his "nature" in seven stages, by seven great degrees.

This *conquest* of the natural man is in the reverse of the *growth* of the natural man. Man grows up stage by stage, from babe to child, from child to adolescent, from adolescence to manhood, from manhood to husband, from husband to fatherhood, from fatherhood or ruler of the household, to mature authority in the clan or State. This is a mere shallow instance of the seven stages of man's development, and his seven levels of consciousness.

When he starts the great self-conquest which constitutes the mystic death, he travels in the reverse direction of life and growth: that is, he goes counter-sunwise, widdershins. He conquers himself first as an elder, or magistrate, an authority in the world, then as a father or ruler of young life, then as a bridegroom or sexual being, then as an adolescent, with the adolescent curiosity and egoism, then as a boy, with a child's calm assurance of self, and finally as a babe, or physical-functioning entity. He conquers his nature stage by stage, in the reverse direction of growth. At each stage there is a death. At the seventh stage, or it may be the *sixth*, there is a final death; and then follows a liberation of some sort, a re-emergence of the true ego, the irreducible witness, and then a process of re-birth and a marriage.

In the old psychology, man considered himself really as a dual entity, a creature of soul and spirit, anima and animus, blood and "water". The body was a third thing, caused by the fusing of the blood and the "water", the anima and animus, the soul and spirit: and so, as the soul and spirit separate, the body disappears. In the "trinity" of a human entity, it is the body itself which is the "ghost", being merely the manifestation of the "marriage" of the great "two", the blood and water, the moist and the dry, the soul and the spirit.

Hence a full Mystery would contain a dual death: of soul and spirit. But since soul was really conceived of as being the blood itself, we tend easily to say, the death is of the body and the spirit, and the resurrection is of the body and the spirit. Whereas truly, the death is of the soul and spirit, and on consummation of this death, the body (the world) dissolves: and the resurrection is of the soul and spirit, and when these two rise and fuse again, new, the new body descends upon them—the new Jerusalem. The new Jerusalem, esoterically, is the new body of a re-born man. It is also the new body of the community, the Church of Christ, the Bride.

This may seem all nonsense to modern minds. But it is the honest and passionate attempt of man to understand his own mysterious and complex nature, and I must say, it seems to me even now more satisfactory, more *dynamic* than our so-called science of psychology. Of course I don't mean to say that as I put it, crude and bald, it is very significant. But if we really try to grasp the pagan symbolic psychology, in its great range and its great depth of understanding— symbolic understanding—it does make our modern conception of the human being look small and trashy. And we really *are* smaller and sillier, as understanding emotional beings, than the pagans were. We are cleverer mentally. But physically, emotionally, vitally we are smaller and sillier than the intelligent pagans of St. John's day.

Besides, if we take the very earliest "scientists", we do not jeer at them for saying the very things the old religions say. "Water is the material cause of all things", says Thales, and modern scientists refrain from jeering. But it needs a close study of the pagan conception of the universe in the sixth century B.C. to know what was really meant by water. And at the same time the scientists hate it when Thales is supposed to have said: All things are full of gods.—They consider he never would have said it. Yet it seems exactly the thing a "scientific" mind might have said at the end of the seventh century, and leads us in to a profoundly interesting and revealing study of what Thales can have meant by "gods". Anaximander taught that all things come into being owing to the "strife" of opposites, the moist and the dry, the cold and the wet. *As soon as there is creation, there is duality.* This appears to be one of the very oldest and deepest notions, of religion and science alike. The third thing is the Boundless, the

Infinite, which is increate. The great wheels of the heavens, of Anaximander, are great rings of fire enclosed in dark envelopes of air (or cloud): the whole universe is made up of these two, the hot and the cold, the moist and the dry. And these elements, in the body, are blood and water, soul and spirit. And the body, the third thing, is an apparition from the boundless, the infinite. "All things are earth and water, that come into being and grow", says Xenophanes. "All things are an exchange for Fire", says Herakleitos. And again: "Fire lives the death of air, and air lives the death of fire".

All this "impious pagan duality" was taken over by philosophy from religion. In fact all the oldest ideas were taken over from religion. Then they were pulled to pieces, or unravelled, by philosophy, and science began.

But man has two ways of knowing the universe: religious and scientific. The religious way of knowledge means that we accept our sense-impressions, our perceptions, in the full sense of the word, complete, and we tend instinctively to link them up with other impressions, working towards a whole. The process is a process of association, linking up, binding back (religio) or referring back towards a centre and a wholeness. This is the way of poetic and religious consciousness, the instinctive act of synthesis. "O my love is like a red red rose" is an act of synthesis and fusing of the love and the red rose, a movement towards a unison through poetic association. This is a religious act, a binding back (religio) or connection, but it is spontaneous. In definite religion the perceptions are referred back consciously till they reach the clue which holds all things together, God.—"Lord, thou hast been our dwelling place in all generations—". There we have ourselves and our generations and our dwelling-place all suddenly fused in the Lord. It is poetry, but it is specific, religious poetry. All poetry is religious in its *movement*, let its teaching be what it may. And we can just as safely say, that no religion is truly religious, a binding back and a connection into a wholeness, unless it is poetic, for poetry is in itself the movement of vivid association which is the movement of religion. The only difference between poetry and religion is that the one has a specific goal or centre to which all things are to be related, namely God; whereas poetry does the magical linking-up without any specific goal or end. Sufficient that the new relations spring up, as it were, that the new connections are made.

Science is only the contrary method, the opposite working of the consciousness. Yet how strange the contraries are. The scientific instinct breaks up or analyses the direct impression: that is the first step: and then logical reason enters, and makes inferences. Religion starts from impressions accepted whole and referred back to other impressions. Science starts from questioning an impression, and comparing it, *contrasting* it with another impression.

At dawn we see the sun, red and slow, emerge over the horizon and beginning to sparkle: religion and poetry at once say: like a bridegroom coming forth from his chamber: or like the gold lion from his lair: something similar. But the scientific spirit says: What *is* the shining thing? Does it really rise up from behind the hill every day?—and if so, how does it get back behind the hill, in order to be ready for the next dawn? How does it *work?*—

There we see the two processes of the human consciousness. Whenever I see the sun going down, I shall say to myself: The sun is leaving us: he is looking back at us and departing: he is setting over the edge of the world, taking his way into another place.—That is the inevitable feeling of every man who looks at the sun setting, be he the greatest scientist living. And it will be the feeling of every man, while men remain men. It is our *immediate* awareness of sunset. To remove or "correct" this awareness, we have deliberately to change our state of mind, and say: No, the sun is not sinking. It is the earth which is turning round and cutting with her sharp edge, called the horizon, over the face of the really motionless planet, the sun.—There we have our second or cognitive awareness of sunset: and we believe the second awareness to be the "truth".

But it is obvious there are two forms of truth. To our senses, the red sun slowly sinks like a drowning thing. This is the truth, and perhaps the more vital truth, since it is our everyday *experience*. On the other hand, we know by a long, long chain of inference that sunset is caused by the earth's diurnal rotation on her axis. This is the other truth, the truth of explanations. To obtain the realisation of this second truth we have to cut off our sense-impressions of sunset. But also, in our sense-impression of sunset, we have to forget other sense-impressions, other phenomena, which somehow contradict this "sinking like a drowning thing" impression.

There we are, with two sets of truth, because we have two ways of consciousness. Nothing on earth will prevent us from *feeling*, and from knowing by feeling, that the sun at evening sinks down like a drowning thing. And nothing on earth will now alter our knowledge, our knowledge by inference, that the sun does not sink at all, but that the earth turns her back on him. At least, I suppose nothing will ever alter this "fact".

So there we are, dual in consciousness. And as in this matter of sunset, one stream of consciousness excludes the other. When I see the sun sink I *can't* see him stand still while the earth spins round to hide me from him. It can't be done. When I *know* that the earth spins round at sunset and carries me away from the motionless sun, it is impossible for me to *see* the sunset: my senses are abstracted, and must be. If they weren't, I should see a red sun slowly merging down behind the world's horizon, taking his way to other skies. Contradictions!

The impious duality of the pagans returns full upon us, when we realise how dual is our consciousness itself. Man is a creature of dual consciousness. It is his glory and his pain. Because though the two streams of consciousness can never be identified with one another, though we are divided between them, very often torn between them, still we are whole and integral beings in which the two streams can be harmonised and reconciled, each being left to its own full flowing. There *need* be no war-fare. Why should I not have two entirely different sunset-conceptions, or two ways of sunset-knowledge, since both are natural to me?

If we can accept the *unquestioning* way of consciousness, the way of direct impression, which proceeds from affirmation to affirmation, we shall be much better able to understand the older form of the pagan consciousness. Long before Christ, the questioning method of consciousness had arisen, in India and in Ionia particularly. But everywhere it had to struggle against the older form of consciousness, to which the "question" was obnoxious, or even impious, when applied to vital things or concepts. It was impious to question the gods. The feeling lasts to this day, and will always last, since the primitive consciousness, shall we say the primal way of consciousness in man is the unquestioning way of affirmation, and movement from affirmation to affirmation by way of image. Even the scientists of the last century *saw* all their science, built up their systems of images in answer to the scientific questions. Lord Kelvin couldn't grasp anything unless he could make an image of it: a model, he said. And Darwin *saw* his evolution theories, like a seer, in successive images. The images came in answer to his questions, but images they were, none the less, built up from bones and fossils. Even our very view of the cosmos, the earth going round the sun and the planets obeying their own laws of motion, even this is only a mental image re-constructed from our visual image of the heavens. It is a composite photograph instead of a direct photograph.

But today, science, even the science of physics, is said to have moved beyond the image, the atom is now imageless and utterly unimaginable. Therefore, to most minds, to mine certainly, it has turned into nothingness. The modern atom is to my mind a desperate nothingness, and science has really ceased to be. I give it up. The physicists today seem to me to be in a state of mind of supreme *contemplation*, they have gazed upon the atom, like a Buddhist on the navel, till they are translated into a state comparable to Nirvana or Samadhi, or the mystic ecstasy of the initiate, and there we must leave them.

So that whether we follow the way of affirmation or the way of question, we proceed from image to image. The motion is the only thing that is different: the mind can only come to rest upon an image. But in the way of affirmation, image adds itself to image in a humming unison like a swarm of bees, till at last the individual consciousness consummates itself, the swarm is completed upon the clue, the God-idea, the humming unison of the consciousness rises to a pitch where it transcends, and the whole consciousness swoops into a pure state of conscious awareness which is at the same time like a swoon of pure oblivion, and the crisis of the religious consciousness is reached. Even a great poem brings the same supreme state of at-oneness, in its own degree.

But the process of question, the process of philosophy and science, even exact science like physics, at last reaches the same state, or a state exactly comparable. Anyone who knows the condition of supreme religious consciousness knows that the true modern physicist and mathematician—it is now the same—is in a precisely similar state of mind or soul, or has passed through such a state, and builds his science on a description of this state: imageless, unimaginable. Both the religious and the scientific states of mind are at last imageless and unimaginable, to be known only by transcription: and modern physics are an attempt to transcribe such a state.

Both ways end in the same place, the absolute somewhere or the absolute nowhere. But the method of approach is different. There is the method of association and unison, and the method of contrast and distinction. The whole way of spiritual, rational, and mental consciousness is a way of contrast. The Son of God is himself a question directed against the Father, and a complement in opposition.

The point of all this is that there need be no quarrel between our two ways of consciousness. There *is* a quarrel, there always has been, perhaps there always will be, since human nature is *ab ovo* quarrelsome. But there need not be.

So let us leave the way of question, and try to take again the older way of affirmation. We shall find that our mind now definitely moves in images, from image to image, and no longer is there a logical process, but a curious flitting motion from image to image according to some power of attraction, some *sensuous* association between images.

Apocalypsis II

probably began the Psalm: Ah, why is there such antagonism to God?—He would have said almost all in those few words. But he would at the same time have lost almost all the emotional reactions. So there we are.

The language of the remote ancients—and not so very remote, either—is to me incomprehensible, or nearly so, even when it is translated into our own speech. The Psalms are really antipathetic to the modern mind, because the modern mind is so abstracted and logical, it cannot bear the non-logical imagery of the Hebrew hymns, the sort of confusion, the never going straight ahead. But there *was* no straight ahead to the ancient mind. An image, an emotional conception completed itself, then gave place to another, and sometimes even the emotional sequence is puzzling, because the images started different trains of feeling then, from those they start now.

We can understand the terrific delight of the early Greeks when they really found out how to think, when they got away from the concrete and invented the abstract, when they got away from the object itself and discovered laws and principles. A number was once *actually* a row of pebbles. There was no *seven*, only seven pebbles or counters. To the early Pythagoreans three was a perfect number, because when you divided it, it left a central guardian, with one number on either hand: a perfect balance. Whereas four—the even numbers—were imperfect, because when you divided them it left a gap in the middle. This, we see, is just three pebbles in a row, or four pebbles in a row. And arithmetic sprang into being when Pythagoras—or whoever it was—thought of arranging the pebbles in squares and in triangles, instead of in rows, long rows. An arrangement of pebbles in squares immediately gave the idea of multiplication, and the arrangement of a triangle on a base of four gave the dekad, the ten: made up of $1+2+3+4$: and this became the number that was called the "natural" number. "All the Hellenes and barbarians count up to ten, by nature, and then begin again".

Pythagoras lived in the fifth century B.C.—and until his day, apparently, arithmetic slumbered in the bosom of the eternal. The delight men took in discovering actual number, the laws of number, and so escaping from the inevitable pebbles, was intense. It was so all through the field of consciousness. The enormous and tyrannous heavens of stars and Rulers were now examined objectively, to see how they *were governed* instead of how they ruled. Till now, till about 600 B.C., when the *real* change in the direction of man's consciousness definitely set in, the cosmos had consisted of Powers and Rulers. Now, it was to be proved subordinate and subject in itself to a greater rule. There was a new wild instinct on earth: to prove that all the great Rulers were subject to One Rule. The rule of kings was over, in the consciousness of man. The immediate connection with the cosmos was broken. Man and the cosmos came out of touch, they became, in a sense, enemies. Man set himself to *find out* the cosmos, and at last to dominate it. Henceforth the grand idea was no longer the living sway of the cosmos over man, through the rule of kings. Henceforth it was the dominion of man over the cosmos, through the collective effort of Mind. Men must love one another, so that collectively Man could conquer the cosmos. And the conqueror was Mind. And Mind was One and indivisible.

This terrific *volte face* of the human consciousness had a dual effect on man himself. It thrilled him with the highest happiness, or bliss, the sense of escape from the cosmos and from the body, which is part of the cosmos, into Mind, immortal Mind. And at the same time, it filled him with a great ennui and a great despair, as he felt death inside himself, the death of the body. Plato, who thrills with the greatest thrill of all, perhaps, is ultimately filled with a great pessimism. The thrill of the discovery of the laws of mind, the laws of thought, logic, grammar, made men wild with intoxicated delight. Socrates, in Plato, is simply drunk with the triumph of being able to reason. Drunk! In some of the dialogues we see Socrates disgustingly false and tricky, tricking his opponent with arguments palpably specious and puerile, so that we wonder the opponent swallowed such stuff. Then we remember that argument, real dialectic was such a new thing on the face of the earth, that when the purest nonsense was arrived at logically, or with apparent logic, it was mutely accepted. A great deal of the argumentative side of early Greek philosophy—and later—results in pure nonsense. But it was mental, *rational* nonsense, so it was found acceptable. Irrational truths became nonsensical, and rational nonsense became truth. So it was in the field of pure philosophy, *human* philosophy. Even Plato's *Ideas* are really rationalised nonsense. But they are still accepted, under the convention of: Reason at any price, the Ideal, cost what it may!

It is obvious to us now that Reason is only a function, like any other, and the Idea, even the Platonic Idea, argue as we will, is only an abstraction from direct sensual experience. However brilliant the conclusion drawn from certain premisses, the premiss itself is drawn from an experience of the senses. All our consciousness starts with sensual experience, call them perceptions or what you will, and ends with abstractions from this experience, conceptions or ideas or whatever we like.

Everything is based on sense-experience; in our consciousness, the atom, the electron itself is experienced, perceived or felt by the senses, or it is nothing at all. Spirit, as far as it is *experience*, is only a more subtle form of sense-experience. And even God, as far as he is real, is our experience of the senses. The whole great basis of our consciousness is sensual, and this field of consciousness is immense, illimitable. But man sets limits to his sensual consciousness, and then he atrophies and dies.

There is the sensual consciousness, enormous and potent: and then there is Mind. Mind is the function of abstraction from sensual experience, and in abstraction it established another world of reality for man. If we make a square of pebbles, with four pebbles on each side, it contains sixteen pebbles. It will always be so, forever: and the same whether it is pebbles or people or houses. $4 \times 4 = 16$. Now then, which is reality—the square of pebbles, or the eternal law that the square of four is sixteen? Which is the real eternal, the sixteen pebbles lying on the ground in a square, or the immutable law or idea, $4 \times 4 = 16$? Wherein do you see God, in the sixteen pebbles on the floor, or in the intangible truth, $4 \times 4 = 16$? Which "rules", the law, or the substantial object?

The answer is, of course, that neither rules. The "laws" don't "govern" the universe. The "laws" of the universe are only the more subtle properties of "things". It is a law of pebbles, that $4 \times 4 = 16$. It is also a law of houses and men, $4 \times 4 = 16$. Indeed it is a law of all things. For all things it is true, $4 \times 4 = 16$. The law is without exception. There is no exception to the rule. The rule rules all things, for $4 \times 4 = 16$ yesterday and today and forever. This then is the eternal Ruler. Such are the immutable, eternal and unanswerable Rulers of the universe: such Laws. And since they are things of the mind, they must proceed from a great Mind. Hence the one eternal and infinite Ruler of the universe is a supreme Mind, and the Supreme Mind rules by uttering eternal Ideas, or Laws. This is the Logos, and the Platonic Idea, and the modern conception of God. To this supreme Mind the body must submit, even unto death. And this is Jesus. For the body that is sacrificed to Mind will rise up a new body, to a new life. When Mind triumphs, then sin and sorrow, confusion and strife will pass away. Or when the Spirit triumphs: Spirit being the great impulse of yielding to Mind, the Spirit of self-sacrifice and rising beyond the body: then all men will be good, and heaven will be on earth.

Plato believed that the only happiness for man was the rule of Mind over the body. That is, he believed in a philosopher-king, one of the old tyrants—in the Greek sense—governed and swayed by reason, by philosophy, by the eternal Mind. The king governing, but himself governed by Mind: this would produce a perfect state. Well, Plato was adviser to a king, a tyrant, and it was a terrible fiasco. Mind ruling over a king didn't seem to work. In fact, during history, the kings that have been ruled by mind, either their own or somebody else's have usually made the greatest mess: or left the greatest mess behind. The necessary quality in a king seems to be character, of which Mind forms only a part.

So, kingdoms ruled by Mind are nearly as unhappy as kingdoms ruled without mind. So—it is kingdoms that are wrong, and rule which is the mistake. Let there be no kings, no rulers, and no rule, but let every man be governed from within by the Spirit. Now spirit, we know, is the will to submit, to sacrifice the self to Mind, or to Law, or to the other person. The Mind says that Sweet Reason shall rule, and the body cries its glad assent. And this is Shelley. All physical kings and rulers are evil. There shall be no rule, but the rule of "love"—which means submission, submission to the sweet reason of the spirit.

The process is one long process: the destruction of the last vestige of the rule of kings, the destruction of all the great Rulers from the consciousness of man, the separation of man from the cosmos, from the old cosmic sway, and finally, the reversal of the Rule of the ages: the rule of Man, collectively, over the cosmos, the rule of Mind over Matter, the rule of the Son of Man, which is of course the spirit or mind of man, over all the world. This is to bring the grand Millennium.

We are very near this Millennium. The ancient rule of kings has fizzled down to almost nothing. There are no ruling men: men are collected in masses, and the masses occasionally come into collision.

The triumph of Mind over the cosmos progresses in small spasms: aeroplanes, radio, motor-traffic. It is high time for the Millennium.

And alas, everything has gone wrong. The destruction of the world seems not very far off, but the happiness of mankind has never been so remote.

Man has made an enormous mistake. Mind is not a Ruler, mind is only an instrument. The natural laws don't "govern", they are only, to put it briefly, the more general properties of Matter. It is just a general property of Matter that it occupies space. $4 \times 4 = 16$ is not "reality": that is to say, it has no existence in itself. It is merely a permanent property of all things, which the mind recognises as permanent: as sweetness is a property of sugar. Ideas are not Rulers, or creators: they are just the properties or qualities recognised in certain things. The Logos itself is the same: it is the faculty which recognises the abiding property in things, and remembers these properties. God is the same. God as we think him could no more create anything than the Logos could create anything. God as we conceive him is the great know-all and perhaps be-all, but he could never *do* anything. He is without form or substance, he is Mind; he is the great *derivative*. God is derived from the cosmos, not the cosmos from him. God is derived from the cosmos as every idea is derived from the cosmos.

The cosmos is not God. God is a conception, and the cosmos is *real*. The pebble is real, and $4 \times 4 = 16$ is a property of the pebble. Man is real, and Mind is a property of man. The cosmos is certainly conscious, but it is conscious with the consciousness of tigers and kangaroos, fishes, polyps, seaweed, dandelions, lilies, slugs, and men: to say nothing of the consciousness of water, rock, sun and stars. Real consciousness is touch. Thought is getting out of touch.

The crux of the whole problem lies here, in the duality of man's consciousness. Touch, the being in touch, is the basis of all consciousness, and it is the basis of enduring happiness. Thought is a secondary form of consciousness, Mind is a secondary form of existence, a getting out of touch, a standing clear, in order to come to a better adjustment in touch.

Man, poor man, has to learn to function in these two ways of consciousness. When a man is *in touch*, he is non-mental, his mind is quiescent, his bodily centres are active. When a man's *mind* is active in real mental activity, the bodily centres are quiescent, switched off, the man is out of touch. The animals remain always in touch. And man, poor modern man, with his worship of his own god, which is his own mind glorified, is permanently out of touch. To be always irrevocably in touch is to feel sometimes imprisoned. But to be permanently out of touch is at last excruciatingly painful, it is a state of being nothing, and being nowhere, and at the same time being conscious and capable of extreme discomfort and *ennui*.

God, what is God? The cosmos is alive, but it is not God. Nevertheless, when we are in touch with it, it gives us life. It is forever the grand voluted reality, Life itself, the great Ruler. We are part of it, when we partake in it. But when we want to dominate it with Mind, then we are enemies of the great Cosmos, and woe betide us. Then indeed the wheeling of the stars becomes the turning of the millstones of God, which grind us exceeding small, before they grant us extinction. We live *by* the cosmos, as well as in the cosmos. And whoever can come into the closest touch with the cosmos is a bringer of life and a veritable Ruler; but whoever denies the Cosmos and tries to dominate it, by Mind or Spirit or Mechanism, is a death-bringer and a true enemy of man. St. John, in the Apocalypse, is working for the dominion of Mind over the Cosmos: that is the Millennium. First, the *whole* Church of Christ, the Logos or Mind, will be martyred by the Rulers of the world. Then Christ will come again, and the martyrs shall be themselves princes, princes, princes over all men, for a thousand years: for all Rulers will have been destroyed and cast into hell. Finally, after these thousand years of Millennium and rule of Martyrs, the grand end shall come, the end of the cosmos entirely, and the Last Judgment.

How they long for the destruction of the cosmos, secretly, these men of mind and spirit! How they work for its domination and final annihilation! But alas, they only succeed in spoiling the earth, spoiling life, and in the end destroying mankind, instead of the cosmos. Man cannot destroy the cosmos: that is obvious. But it is obvious that the cosmos can destroy man. Man must inevitably destroy himself, in conflict with the cosmos. It is perhaps his fate.

Before men had cultivated the Mind, they were not fools.

Explanatory Notes

Bible quotations are from the King James Bible (1611) unless otherwise specified (as in note on 73:17–26).

A REVIEW OF *THE BOOK OF REVELATION*
BY DR. JOHN OMAN

41:1 The Apocalypse Written by John of Patmos, the Book of Revelation is the last book of the New Testament and records his dream-vision of the mysteries of the cosmos and the final end of creation.

41:17 the four Prophets of the Old Testament The Prophets are traditionally Isaiah, Jeremiah and Ezekiel; Daniel is added here because of his apocalyptic writings.

42:5 L. H. Davidson A variant of DHL's pseudonym 'L. H. Davison', first used on the title page of *Movements in European History* (1921).

INTRODUCTION TO *THE DRAGON OF THE APOCALYPSE*
BY FREDERICK CARTER

45:2 Dragon of the Apocalypse DHL read an early version of Carter's book, then titled *The Dragon of the Alchemists* (and later published in 1926), in June 1923 and a longer and much-revised version in 1929. This later manuscript became *The Dragon of the Apocalypse*, eventually published as *The Dragon of Revelation* (1931), for which DHL wrote this introduction.

47:25 Millennium The belief in a future thousand-year period of blessedness. See Revelation xx.

47:29 New Jerusalem The holy city of God which descends from heaven in John's symbolic vision, representing the Second Coming of Christ, who will establish a New Church which will be eternal.

47:39–40 And I saw . . . A white horse! Revelation xix. 11.

48:17 *Pilgrim's Progress* . . . Dante An allegory (1678) in the form of a dream-vision by John Bunyan (1628–88) . . . Dante Alighieri (1265–1321), Italian poet, whose *Divina Commedia* (*Inferno*, *Purgatorio*, *Paradiso*) was begun *c.* 1300.

48:35–6 Mr. Facing-both-ways . . . Janus [48:37] A character in Bunyan's *Pilgrim's Progress* . . . The Roman god of gates and beginnings whose Festival was held in January and whose temple gates signified peace when closed, war when opened. He was represented with two faces looking in opposite directions.

49:8 **Kronos** In Greek mythology Chronos (meaning 'time') was the youngest of the Titans, offspring of Heaven and Earth, who fathered the Olympian deities who supplanted him. See note on 109:27.

50:30 **sodom-apples** See Deuteronomy xxxii. 32 where the 'fruits of Sodom', the city accursed by God, turn into ashes. See note on 117:31–2.

51:11 **Chaldean** Ancient Kaldu, part of Babylonia, traditionally the home of astronomy, astrology and magic.

51:17 **Baal** Chief god of the Assyrians and Babylonians, also called Marduk.

51:28 **Euphrates ... Mesopotamia** The longest river of western Asia and traditionally one of the rivers of Eden (Genesis ii. 14) ... the alluvial plain between the rivers Euphrates and Tigris was ancient Babylonia or Mesopotamia, now part of modern Iraq.

52:9 **strong man to run a race?** See Psalms xix. 4–5.

52:14 **Belshazzar's day** The son of Nebuchadnezzar (see note on 128:34) and last king of Babylonia, killed in the sack of Babylon by Cyrus in 538 BC.

52:30–31 **Artemis and Cybele** In Greek mythology Artemis was the virgin goddess of nature and wildlife, daughter of Zeus and sister of Apollo, who became identified with the Roman goddess Diana. Cybele was the ancient Phrygian goddess of nature and fertility, later identified with Rhea as the wife of Chronos and mother of Zeus. However, neither Artemis nor Cybele were originally moon goddesses, though the former came to be equated with Selene, moon goddess in Greek mythology.

53:17 **Astarte** Also Ashtoreth, the mother goddess of Phoenicia, deity of sexuality and war and sometimes also erroneously identified as a moon goddess.

54:38 **Chapel ... Christian Endeavour** [54:39] The young DHL was a member of the Congregationalist Chapel and participated in the Christian Endeavour movement, which especially encouraged young people to serve actively in the local church.

55:57 **'I was ... Omega'** Revelation i. 10. Alpha and Omega, the first and last letters of the Greek alphabet, hence the beginning and the end.

55:9–10 **'Alleluia ... reigneth'** Revelation xix. 6.

55:11–13 **'And he treadeth ... God'** Revelation xix. 15.

55:21 **Moffatt's** James Moffatt, *The New Testament: A New Translation* (1913). (Hereafter referred to as Moffatt.)

55:28 **Assyria** The principal Mesopotamian power from the twelfth to the seventh centuries BC.

55:29 **the Seleucids** The dynasty, founded by one of Alexander the

Explanatory Notes

Great's generals, Seleucus Nicator, which ruled Syria from 312 to 65 BC and dominated the greater part of western Asia.

55:30 **Pompey and Anthony** Gnaeus Pompey (106–48 BC), the Roman general who with Julius Caesar and Crassus formed the first triumvirate in 60 BC but was defeated by Caesar in the ensuing civil war in 49–48 BC. Mark Antony (*c.* 83–30 BC) and Octavian (later Augustus) defeated Brutus and Cassius after the murder of Caesar and divided the Roman Empire: Antony ruled the eastern half, but his relationship with Cleopatra caused his later breach with Octavian, and in the civil war that followed Antony was defeated. He committed suicide in 30 BC.

55:32 **Homer** The Greek epic poet who is thought to have lived some time before 700 BC and is traditionally believed to be the author of the *Iliad* and the *Odyssey.*

55:34 **Ur ... Nineveh ... Sheba to Tarshish** Ur was the ancient city where Abraham settled, on the Persian Gulf near one of the mouths of the Euphrates, and seat of three Sumerian dynasties, the last of which ended *c.* 2300 BC ... Nineveh was an ancient Assyrian city on the Tigris river, which flourished under Sennacherib and Ashurbanipal in the seventh century BC ... Sheba probably refers to the biblical town of Beersheba (Genesis xxvi. 30). Tarshish, or Tartessus, in southern Spain, is a region which grew wealthy through its trade with the Phoenicians and Carthaginians.

56:2 **Mithraic** The worship of Mithras, ancient Aryan god of light and truth whose cult spread over the empire of Alexander the Great and reached Rome in 67 BC, from whence it spread throughout the Roman Empire.

APOCALYPSE

59:8 **nonconformist ... Band of Hope or Christian Endeavour** [59:24–5] Generally used of Protestant dissenters such as Presbyterians, Congregationalists, Methodists, Quakers and Baptists ... See note on 54:38.

60:9 **War and Peace** Epic novel by Leo Tolstoy (1828–1910), written between 1865 and 1872.

61:8 **pie-pie** Sanctimonious (slang).

61:15–16 **'And I saw ... was called'** Revelation xix. 11.

61:20 *Pilgrim's Progress* See note on 48:17.

61:21–2 **Euclid ... the part'** The teaching of geometry in DHL's day was based on the *Elements* of Eucleides, the Greek mathematician who taught *c.* 300 BC.

61:27 *Faerie Queen* Long poem by Edmund Spenser (1552–99), *The Faerie Queene,* published 1589–96.

61:30–40 **'And before the throne ... to come—'** Revelation iv. 6–8.

62:8–9 wadings in blood . . . the Lamb . . . 'the wrath of the Lamb'
[62:10] See Revelation vii. 14; xiv. 20; xvi. 3–4; xix. 13 . . . Revelation
vi. 16–17.

62:13 Salvation armies The Salvation Army was founded by W. Booth
in 1865, and is widely known as an international Christian organization
for evangelistic and social work.

62:21 Pentecost chapel The Pentecostal Movement began in the early
years of the twentieth century. Believers sought a baptism in the Holy
Spirit accompanied by speaking in tongues.

62:21–3 MYSTERY . . . THE EARTH Revelation xvii. 5. One of the greatest
cities of the ancient world and once the capital of the Chaldean empire,
Babylon was where the Jews were deported to after the conquest of
Jerusalem by Nebuchadnezzar in 597 BC.

62:32–4 'Babylon the great . . . bird—' Revelation xviii. 2.

63:6 Pharisee The Pharisees were a Jewish religious group who appear
as the chief adversaries of Christ in the Gospels. Christ denounced their
self-righteousness and purely external observance of the law.

63:14–15 a city that 'had . . . in it' Revelation xxi. 23.

64:3–4 Primitive Methodist Chapels . . . Congregationalist
[64:17] Begun in 1811 in association with the Wesleyan Methodist
Church, and 'primitive' in the sense that they attempted to re-create the
earliest form of church order . . . Nonconformists who believe in the
autonomy of each local church, with a democratic Church government
which recognizes only Christ as its head. See 'Hymns in a Man's Life',
in *Phoenix II*, p. 600.

64:27 Beauvale Chapel DHL occasionally attended this chapel in Eastwood, Nottinghamshire. See *Letters*, i. 23.

64:32 'Lead kindly Light' Hymn by Cardinal J. Newman which for
DHL represented sentimentality. See 'Hymns in a Man's Life', in
Phoenix II, p. 600.

65:12 Love one another John xiii. 34.

66:3–4 'internal evidence' DHL had been reading *A Critical and Exegetical Commentary on the Revelation of St. John* by R. H. Charles (Clark,
1920, 2 volumes), which establishes this date. See vol. i. p. xci.

67:7 Temple of Jerusalem The national shrine of the Jews, destroyed by
the Babylonians in 586 BC and rebuilt in 520 BC. This second temple was
desecrated by Antiochus Epiphanes in 167 BC.

67:14 Millennium See note on 47:25.

68:13 Buddha . . . Plato [68:13] 'The Enlightened One', variously named
Sakyamuni, Gautama or Siddhartha, who flourished in northern India in the
fifth century BC . . . The Athenian philosopher (*c.* 427–348 BC) and pupil
of Socrates, whose teachings Plato recorded in his *Dialogues*. DHL read
Benjamin Jowett's classic translation of the *Dialogues* (1871).

68:20 Francis of Assisi (1181?–1226). Founder of the Franciscan Order, and saint.

68:23 Lenin Vladimir Ilyich Ulyanov (1870–1924). Russian politician who established the dictatorship of the Communist Party in 1917.

69:5 Abraham Lincoln ... President Wilson [69:6] Lincoln (1809–65), President of the United States (1861–5) ... Woodrow Wilson (1856–1924), President of the United States (1913–21).

69:19 the late Tsar Tsar Nicholas II (1868–1918), the last emperor of Russia (1894–1917), was forced to abdicate after the February 1917 Revolution. He was imprisoned and shot by order of the Soviet authorities.

71:6 any rule of 'Beasts' See Revelation xiii.

73:3 'superiority' goal Alfred Adler (1870–1937), Austrian psychiatrist, emphasized the way that an inferiority complex develops when an individual feels deficient in comparison with others (e.g. physically) and must therefore strive for superiority in order to compensate.

73:17 'John to ... Amen' ... Moffatt's translation [73:26] ... **authorised version** [73:27] Revelation i. 4–7 ... See note on 55:21 ... the King James Bible of 1611.

73:29 wandering by the lake See Matthew iv. 18ff. and Mark ii. 10ff.

73:29–74:16 'On the Lord's day ... golden lampstands—"' Revelation i. 10–ii. 1 (Moffatt).

74:17 the sword of the Logos The Word of God. See Hebrews iv. 12.

74:20–21 'My heart ... and watch' Mark xiv. 34 (Moffatt).

74:24 the visions of Ezekiel and Daniel See Ezekiel i. 26–8 and Daniel vii. 9–10 and x. 5.

75:14–17 holocaust ... Chthonioi DHL had read Gilbert Murray's *Five Stages of Greek Religion* (1925), which explains that the holocaust was a ritual in which a sacrifice was completely burned to appease the dead and the lords of death, the Chthonioi.

76:21 Helios ... Chaldeans [76:22] The sun god ... See note on 51:11.

77:14 Artemis ... Cybele [77:18] ... **Astarte** [77:18] None of these was originally a moon goddess, as Selene was, but all became associated with the moon. See notes on 52:31 and 53:17.

77:40 Aldebaran A red star of the first magnitude which forms the bull's eye in the constellation Taurus.

78:1–2 He who is not with me is against me Matthew xii. 30 (Moffatt).

79:27 the Book of Daniel ... the Apocalypse of Enoch [79:28] Believed to have been written around the middle of the second century BC ... The Book of Enoch, which DHL was reading in December 1929, was written by several authors and consists of a series of revelations of good and evil, the angelic hosts, destiny, the nature of Gehenna and Paradise.

79:32-3 Antiochus Epiphanes King of Syria from 175 BC (d. 163 BC) who in 167 BC attacked Jerusalem and desecrated the temple.

81:9 *King of Kings and Lord of Lords* Revelation xix. 16.

81:15-16 Pompey or Alexander or Cyrus Here synonyms for power and conquest; all three were surnamed 'the Great'. See note on 55:30. Alexander (356-323 BC) became King of Macedon in 336 BC. One of the great military geniuses of history, he conquered the Persian empire, invaded Egypt, Turkestan and India. Cyrus II was Emperor of Persia (reigned *c.* 559-530 BC), the greatest empire the world had seen. After conquering Babylon, he allowed the Jews exiled there to return to Judah.

81:32 the Aegean civilisation . . . a Christian work [81:37] The cultural area in the pre-Hellenic period (before 1200 BC) which included the Greek mainland, Crete, Cyprus, the Cyclades and the coastal areas of Asia Minor and Syria . . . DHL has adapted the account in Charles, vol. i. pp. xxii–xxiii, of the Old Testament sources and writers of Revelation.

82:2-4 the trampling . . . the horses . . . 'Come, Lord Jesus, Come!' [82:7] Cf. Revelation xiv. 19-20 . . . Revelation xxii. 20 (Moffatt).

82:16 post-David period David (d. *c.* 970 BC), first king of the Judean dynasty.

82:21 Ezekiel's great vision Ezekiel, prophet of the Old Testament, whose visions of the divine throne and glory influenced apocalyptic writings and Revelation.

82:23 the Time Spirit DHL was probably recalling his reading of Frederick Carter's *The Dragon of the Alchemists* (1926) which discusses this concept: 'There are certain ancient images of Time, Mithraic and Gnostic, and Orphic . . . the figure usually named Æon' (p. 45).

82:25 Anaximander . . . Anaximander's wheels in Ezekiel [82:30] Greek astronomer and philosopher (*c.* 610-540 BC) who taught that the primary substance is eternal and indestructible matter which he called the Boundless or the Infinite; it contained within itself all contraries, such as heat and cold, moist and dry, and he believed that the universe consists of the alternate separation of these contraries and their creative union . . . Burnet quotes an ancient Greek commentator on the wheels of Anaximander: 'The heavenly bodies are a wheel of fire, separated off from the fire of the world, and surrounded by air. And there are breathing-holes, certain pipe-like passages, at which the heavenly bodies show themselves . . . We do not see the wheels of fire as complete circles; for the vapour or mist which formed them encloses the fire, and forms an outer ring except at one point in their circumference, through which the fire escapes, and that is the heavenly body we actually see' (pp. 66-8). Cf. Ezekiel i. 15-21.

83:8 the four Creatures . . . Michael and Gabriel [83:13] The cherubim, originally Assyrian or Akkadian in origin, influenced accounts in Genesis and other Old Testament books. See note on 133:12 . . . Michael ranks as the greatest of all the angels in Jewish, Christian and Islamic writings; Gabriel is the second-highest-ranking angel.

83:22 **Demiurge** From the Greek for 'craftsman', used by Plato of the Divine Being in his account of the formation of the universe, and by later Greek Christian writers of God as the Creator. The Gnostics, however, used the word to describe the lesser deity responsible for creating the material universe, and distinguished this power from the supreme God. Cf. 'The Body of God' and 'Demiurge', *The Complete Poems* pp. 691 and 689.

83:26–30 **Archdeacon Charles ... in mind** Rather unfair to Charles, who is here making a linguistic point about the text, not commenting on its sources. (See Charles, vol. i. p. 30.) Charles's commentary is primarily concerned with the sources of Revelation in ancient Hebrew texts but he was also aware of the pagan derivation of much of the Bible (see vol. i. p. clxxxvi).

85:22 **Orphic** Orphics believed that the soul could survive death if it were kept pure, and conceived a mythology with either Dionysus or Orpheus as the central figure to exemplify that belief. The sect had appeared by the fifth century BC but the formal organization of the sacred literature came in about the third century BC.

85:29 **the dispersion** The Diaspora, or Dispersion of the Jews, began with the Assyrian and Babylonian deportations (722 and 597 BC) to Armenia and Iran, but eventually spread throughout the Roman Empire to Egypt, Asia Minor, Greece and Italy.

86:18 **Nero, or Nero redivivus** The last Roman emperor (AD 54–68) of the Julio-Claudian dynasty, Nero was proverbial for his tyranny and brutality. It was believed that he would return as the dragon of Revelation xiii and the beast of xvii.

87:11 **Rheims Cathedral** The Cathedral of Notre-Dame, in Rheims, one of the finest examples of French classical gothic architecture, suffered badly during the First World War, but was restored and reopened in 1927.

87:26 **Minoans ... Etruscans** The Bronze Age civilization of Crete (*c.* 3000–1000 BC) ... A confederation of politically independent city-states in Italy which flourished *c.* 500 BC but was conquered by the Romans. See D. H. Lawrence, *Sketches of Etruscan Places*, ed. S. de Filippis (Cambridge University Press, 1992).

87:27 *Urdummheit* Gilbert Murray writes in *Five Stages of Greek Religion*: 'The progress of Greek religion falls naturally into three stages ... First there is the primitive Euêtheia or Age of Ignorance, before Zeus came to trouble men's minds, a stage to which our anthropologists and explorers have found parallels in every part of the world. Dr. Preuss applies to it the charming word "Urdummheit", or "Primal Stupidity" ... one is tempted to regard it as the normal beginning of all religion, or almost as the normal raw material out of which religion is made' (p. 16).

87:36 **Thales ... Pythagoras** [87:37]   Greek philosopher and scientist, Thales (640–546 BC) was the founder of Greek geometry, astronomy and philosophy. He taught that water, or moisture, was the primary substance from which the world was created ... Greek mathematician and philosopher born in Samos (flourished *c.* 530 BC), whose doctrines of metempsychosis and that earthly life is only a purification of the soul are known only through his disciples.

88:12 *Neufrecheit*   New impertinence (German).

88:22–89:18 'a marvellous ... destroying the earth'   Charles is referring to the historical resilience of Revelation since each age applies the prophecies of Antichrist and Apocalypse to itself. See Revelation xi. 18.

90:6 **Indus ... Mycene** [90:9]   The civilization of the Indus Valley dates from the first part of the third millennium BC ... The ancient Greek city-state in the Peloponnese, first occupied by Greek-speaking peoples *c.* 2000 BC. It dominated mainland Greece and the Aegean from the sixteenth to the thirteenth centuries.

90:18 **Rameses ... Assiburnipal** [90:18] **... Darius** [90:19]   A variant of Ramses, the name of twelve kings of the nineteenth and twentieth dynasties of ancient Egypt ... A version of Ashurbanipal, King of Assyria (669–626 BC) ... Darius I (558?–485 BC), King of Persia (521–485 BC), who built Persepolis, extended the Persian empire and initiated the great war between the Persians and the Greeks.

91:23 **Herakleitos ... Empedokles ... Anaxagoras**   Of these pre-Socratic philosophers, Heraclitus of Ephesus (flourished *c.* 500 BC) most influenced DHL's thought. Heraclitus taught that all things are in a ceaseless state of flux, a conflict of opposites, coming into and passing out of existence, and that fire, or energy, is the type and origin of this continual change ... A disciple of Pythagoras, the Greek philosopher and statesman Empedokles (*c.* 493–433 BC) maintained that the universe was a plenum composed of four 'roots' or kinds – fire, air, water and earth – which unite and separate under the contrary forces of Love and Strife, thus causing the creation and dissolution of all things ... Anaxagoras (*c.* 500–428 BC) taught that all matter is composed of minute particles which contain mixtures of all qualities and that the mind or intelligence acts upon masses of these particles to produce the objects we see. Cf. 'Anaxagoras', *The Complete Poems*, p. 708.

91:24 **Socrates and Aristotle**   DHL is making an idiosyncratic distinction here between these two Greek philosophers (whose dates are 469–399 BC and 384–322 BC, respectively) and the pre-Socratics cited above.

92:5 **sphinx conundrum**   The sphinx, a mythological creature with a human head and a lion's body, was sent to ancient Thebes by Hera, Queen of Heaven, to ask the Thebans the riddle about the three ages of man, which was finally solved by Oedipus.

92:26 **Hector . . . Menelaus**   The eldest son of Priam and Hecuba, King and Queen of Troy, slain by Achilles, whose lover Patroclus he had killed on the battlefield . . . Menelaus was the King of Sparta and younger brother of Agamemnon. His wife, Helen, was abducted by Paris, a son of Priam, and thus began the Trojan War.

95:7 **the birth of the Child**   See Revelation xii. 5.

95:23 **And all this is God**   Cf. 'God is Born' and 'The Body of God', *The Complete Poems*, pp. 682 and 691.

95:24–96:6 **Today . . . did things**   DHL derived the ideas in this paragraph from Murray, p. 27.

96:11 **scientists . . . Hesiod** [96:19] **. . . Professor Jowett's Plato** [96:23]   In the original sense of a man who has knowledge of any branch of learning . . . Greek poet (*c.* 800 BC) who wrote the *Works and Days*, a collection of maxims, and the *Theogony*, an account of the origins of the universe from chaos and the history of the gods . . . Benjamin Jowett (1817–93), Regius Professor of Greek and Master of Balliol College, Oxford (1855–93), best known for his translation of Plato's *Dialogues* (1871).

97:11 *epos*   DHL uses this Greek word (which refers to an epic poem or epic poetry in general) incorrectly, confusing it with epoch, a cycle or period of time.

97:12–14 **The 'world' is established . . . sevens**   DHL was indebted for this number symbolism to Charles and to Carter's *The Dragon of the Alchemists* (1926), p. 52.

97:20–28 **twenty-four elders . . . temple**   See Revelation iv. 4–6.

97:37–8 **eastern Fathers**   Origen, Basil, St John Crysotom, from centres such as Alexandria, Constantinople and Antioch, as distinct from the western fathers such as Augustine, based in the cities of north Africa and Rome.

97:38 **Cromwellian . . . Christian iconoclast** [98:8]   Oliver Cromwell (1599–1658), Lord Protector of England (1653–8) . . . A breaker or destroyers of images, a participant in the movement of the eighth and ninth centuries to abolish images in the Christian churches of the East and hence also used of Cromwell and his followers.

98:13 **'Iris too is a cloud'**   DHL paraphrases from Burnet who quotes Xenophanes (Greek poet, *c.* 576–480 BC): 'She that they call Iris is a cloud likewise, purple, scarlet and green to behold . . . "Iris too" is a cloud' (pp. 120–21).

98:14–15 **sardine stone . . . commentators**   Revelation iv. 3; possibly jasper, topaz or sardius, a variety of carnelian . . . Charles, vol. i. pp. 113–14.

98:18–19 **a new era**   DHL was fascinated by the notion of the great dance of the heavens; cf. 'Dawn is no longer in the House of the Fish' in 'Astronomical Changes', *The Complete Poems*, p. 616.

98:19 **The Fish**   In Christian art and literature, the symbol of Christ,

Explanatory Notes

possibly pagan in origin or else derived from the Greek acrostic ΙΧΘΥΣ ('Jesus Christ, Son of God, Saviour').

98:23–5 **Thunder . . . creation** Cf. 'Silence' and 'Kissing and Horrid Strife', *The Complete Poems*, pp. 698 and 709.

98:26 **Logos of the beginning** See John i. 1 and Revelation xix. 13.

98:32–3 **Then before . . . seven Spirits of God** See Revelation iv. 5.

99:10 **The Almighty has a book in his hand . . . how the book is to be** *opened* [99:14] See Revelation v. 1 . . . See Revelation v. 2. DHL is forgetting John Oman's *Book of Revelation* (1923), which he had reviewed in 1924, where Oman writes that some first-century books were indeed no longer scrolls but leaves fastened together into a kind of notebook.

99:19–21 **The Lion of Judah . . . with seven horns.** See Revelation v. 5–6.

99:33 **Mithras, a bull** See note on 56:2. Central to the myth was the sacrifice of a bull, from whose blood was said to have sprung all living creatures. The cult offered immortality to its initiates but was almost entirely superseded by Christianity in the fourth century.

99:36–7 **'Wash me . . . whiter than snow—'** Chorus written by E. R. Latta to the Salvation Army hymn by Samuel H. Hodges 'Blessed be the fountain of blood' (1899). Cf. Revelation vii. 14.

100:10 **by their bite ye shall know them . . . 'as it were slain'** [100:11] Cf. Matthew vii. 20. . . . Revelation v. 6.

100:18–24 **There follows . . . the drama begins** DHL's exposition of Revelation v. 8–14. For Joseph and the sheaves, see Genesis xxxvii. 5–8.

101:1 **the famous four horsemen** Revelation vi. 1–8.

101:9–16 **the seven seals . . . transfigured** DHL was indebted for the notion of Apocalypse as a manual of spiritual enlightenment to James Pryse's *The Apocalypse Unsealed* (1910) which he read in 1917. Pryse suggested that the seven seals are the seven 'chakras' (centres of psychic energy in the physical body) and that their opening represents the transcendental conquest of the self, leading to a mystic rebirth.

101:19–20 **the four dynamic natures . . . the three 'higher' natures** Pryse writes that 'the body has four principal life-centres' (p. 14) and that the four horses correspond to these divisions.

101:30–32 **The sons of God . . . says Enoch** See 1 Enoch vi–vii and 2 Enoch xviii. 1–6. Cf. Genesis vi. 1–4.

102:37 *mana* According to Murray the word 'comprises force, vitality, prestige, holiness, and power of magic, and . . . may belong equally to a lion, a chief, a medicine-man, or a battle-axe' (p. 34). Cf. 'Mana of the Sea' and 'Lord's Prayer', *The Complete Poems*, pp. 705 and 704.

103:4 **bended bow of the body, like the crescent moon . . . Pythagoras show his golden thigh** [103:15] As is the body of cosmic man in the apocalyptic Zodiac described by Pryse in *The Apocalypse Unsealed* . . . According to Greek legend, Pythagoras had a golden thigh given him by the gods. The thigh was the seat of male strength and majesty and was sometimes a euphemism for the phallus, e.g. Genesis xxiv. 2.

103:27–8 **'Take this bread of my body with thee'** Recalling Christ's words to his disciples at the Last Supper. See Matthew xxvi. 26; Mark xiv. 22; Luke xxii. 19.

104:1 **The orthodox commentators . . . Titus or Vespasian [104:2]** See Charles, vol. i. pp. 155 ff . . . Vespasian (AD 9–79), first of the Flavian emperors of Rome (AD 69–79), was succeeded by his eldest son Titus (AD 39–81), who reigned AD 79–81.

105:9–10 **'every mountain . . . out of their places'** Revelation vi. 14.

106:1–2 **Creation . . . is four . . . the four angels of the winds [106:5] . . . mystic wind from the east [106:7]** Cf. 'The Two Principles', in *Phoenix II*, pp. 225–37, where DHL writes of the 'fourfold division of the cosmos' and the 'fourfold activity [which] is the root activity of the universe' (p. 233). See also Carter, who explains how in ancient times the world was seen as a square, 'at each angle of which were the supports of the heaven's pillars or mountains. These four quarters have their iconographic symbols in the four living creatures' (*The Dragon of the Alchemists*, pp. 52–3) . . . The west wind was, traditionally, the good wind. The angels of the four winds were: Uriel (south), Michael (east), Raphael (west), Gabriel (north) . . . The wind from the east is the sirocco, the wind of God.

106:16–17 **'Salvation . . . to the Lamb'** Revelation vii. 10.

106:20–22 **'Blessing . . . Amen'** Revelation vii. 12.

106:24 **'went through the great tribulation'** Revelation vii. 14.

107:10 **Mysteries of Isis** The principal goddess of ancient Egypt, sister and wife of Osiris (see note on 156:23) and mother of Horus, Isis was the type of the faithful wife and mother. Her statue bore the inscription: 'I am that which is, has been, and shall be. My veil no one has lifted'; hence to lift the veil of Isis is to uncover a great mystery. DHL's knowledge of her initiation rites may have come from his reading of Murray, who tells of Apuleius's initiation (p. 182), and also from his reading of *Isis Unveiled* (1877) by the theosophist Madame Blavatsky.

107:16 **'third eye' . . . Uraeus [107:18]** In Buddhist belief, all men possess a third eye, the focus of great occult power, said to be in the middle of the forehead . . . The sacred serpent, emblem of supreme power, worn on the head-dress of ancient Egyptian divinities and sovereigns. The uraeus also becomes a symbol of strength transformed into spiritual power.

107:26–7 **there is silence . . . half an hour** Revelation viii. 1.

108:15 **seven angels . . . of God** The seven angels of the Presence, represented by the seven planets, named in 1 Enoch.

109:23 **'harrowing of Hell'** The medieval English term for Christ's defeat of the powers of hell and its plundering after his death, and a widespread theme in art and drama in the Middle Ages.

109:26–7 **the Gea-Ouranos-Kronos-Zeus series of myths** In Greek mythology, Gea the earth goddess emerged from Chaos as the first of the heavenly beings. From her came the heavens, Uranus, and the sea, Pontus. Mating with Uranus, she bore many offspring and, mindful of their safety, made the sickle with which her youngest son, Chronus (or Chronos), castrated Uranus. Chronus then mated with his sister Rhea who gave birth to the Olympians – Hestia, Demeter, Hera, Hades, Zeus and Poseidon. Chronus, warned that one of his children would depose him, swallowed each of his offspring as it was born, but Rhea hid Zeus and gave Chronus a stone to swallow instead. Finally, with the help of the Titans, Zeus overthrew Chronus.

109:38 **'two woes'** See Revelation ix. 3–12.

110:20 **Apollyon . . . two more still to come** [110:24] The Greek version of the Hebrew Abaddon, meaning 'destroyer'; the angel of the bottomless pit in Revelation ix. 11 and thus a good power, a servant of God. In occult and noncanonical writings, however, he is depicted as evil; for example in John Bunyan's *Pilgrim's Progress* (1678) he is the devil . . . Cf. Revelation ix. 12.

111:2–3 **'Loose the four angels . . . Euphrates'** Revelation ix. 14.

111:11–16 **The horses . . . they do hurt** A paraphrase of Revelation ix. 17–19.

112:11 **'lake of fire burning with brimstone'** Revelation xix. 20.

112:35–113:3 **Salt had . . . them bitter** Anaximander's doctrine (see Burnet, pp. 53–4, 64–5). Cf. 'Salt', 'The Four' and 'The Boundary Stone', *The Complete Poems*, pp. 705–6.

113:7–8 **the bitter, corrupt sea, as Plato calls it** A reference to Plato's *Laws*, iv. 705, which DHL has misunderstood. Plato writes of the dishonest social and business habits which sea commerce breeds.

113:13 **"neither see nor hear nor walk"** Revelation ix. 20.

114:9 **the seven creative thunders** Cf. 'Silence', *The Complete Poems*, p. 698.

114:17–19 **this great 'angel' . . . oath of the gods** A paraphrase of Revelation x. 6. However, in Greek mythology the gods were bound by their oath on the river Styx, which flowed around the underworld.

114:32 **Orthodox commentators . . . Moses and Elija . . . the mount** [114:32–3] See John Oman, *Book of Revelation*, p. 12 and Charles, vol. i. pp. 281–3 . . . Christ appeared with the Old Testament prophets Moses and Elijah on the Mount (variously interpreted as the Mount of Olives, Mount Hermon or Mount Tabor) to Peter, James and John; see Matthew xvii. 1–13, Mark ix. 2–13, Luke ix. 28–36.

115:4 **'Adonai', the God of the earth** The plural of the Semitic word 'adon', meaning lord; in Hebrew religion the most usual substitute for the hidden name of God. See note on 156:17.

115:22 **the Tyndarids, Kastor and Polydeukes . . . Dioskouroi** [115:25] In Greek mythology Castor and Pollux were the twin sons of

Tyndareus and Leda, according to Homer, although other legends say that Pollux was fathered by Zeus and is immortal, while Castor was mortal. When Castor died, Pollux begged Zeus to be allowed to die too. Tradition says that the brothers live one day on the earth and the next among the gods of Olympus. They are also the constellation Gemini and protecting deities of sailors and travellers.

116:5 **Tritopatores ... the Samothracian cult ... the Kabiri** [116:9–11] Attic deities said to be the ancestors of mankind, often referred to as lords of the winds and gatekeepers to whom sacrifices were due: not, however, associated with the Dioskouroi ... The Cabiri were originally chthonian, non-Hellenic deities, whose cult spread throughout Greece and was especially important at Samothrace where mysteries were held. They formed a pair and were later confused with the Dioskouroi. DHL may have been familiar with them from his reading of *Faust* (1808 and 1832) by Goethe (1749–1932) or of *Psychology of the Unconscious* (1915) by the Swiss psychiatrist Carl Gustav Jung (1875–1961), p. 130 ff.

116:27 **balancers** Cf. 'Walk Warily' and 'Kissing and Horrid Strife', *The Complete Poems*, pp. 707 and 709.

117:9–10 **A creature ... duality** Cf. 'On Being a Man', in *Phoenix II*, pp. 616–22, where DHL writes of 'the self which darkly inhabits our blood and bone, and for which the ithyphallos is but a symbol. This self which lives darkly in my blood and bone is my *alter ego*, my other self, the homunculus, the second one of the Kabiri, the second of the Twins, the Gemini' (p. 619).

117:31–2 **'Sodom' and 'Egypt'** Revelation xi. 8. An allusion to the cities Sodom and Gomorrah which God destroyed (see Genesis xviii, xix) and hence, by analogy, any place regarded as a centre of immorality.

117:35–7 **'rejoice ... Babylon** In ancient Roman times the Festival of Saturn was a time of general merrymaking, even for the slaves. The Hermaia was a similar festival in Crete in honour of the god Hermes, and the Sakaia feast-day in Babylonia was also a time of licence, revelry and feasting.

118:7 **'Two, two ... green-O!—'** A very old folksong that has appeared in many versions in ancient and modern languages. In England it is best known as 'The Twelve Apostles' or 'The Ten Commandments' or, from the refrain, 'Green grow the rushes, O!'

118:11–13 **'The kingdoms of this world ... and ever'** Revelation xi. 15.

119:10–30 **'And there appeared ... cast out with him'** Revelation xii. 1–9.

120:32 **the Scarlet Woman** See Revelation xvii. 4–5.

121:36–7 **Diana of Ephesus** The temple of Diana at Ephesus was one of the Seven Wonders of the World. Diana was an ancient Italian goddess who came to be identified with Artemis. See Acts xix. 24–35.

123:17 **Esau sell his birthright** See Genesis xxv. 29–34. Jacob and Esau were the twin sons of Rebecca and Isaac; coming in faint from the field one day, Esau sold his birthright to Jacob for a mess of pottage.

123:26 **Samson ... David slew Goliath** [123:27] Hebrew hero (*c.* eleventh century BC) and enemy of the Philistines (see Judges xiii. 2–xvi. 31), whose great strength enabled him to perform remarkable feats ... David (d. *c.* 970 BC), first king of the Judean dynasty, who slew the Philistine giant Goliath with a pebble and a sling in battle; see 1 Samuel xvii.

124:3 **Libido or *Elan Vital*** According to Sigmund Freud (1856–1939), libido is the energy of instinctive desires, especially sexual ones, but Jung saw it as the source of all creative impulses, a notion much closer to DHL's beliefs. *Élan vital*, 'life force', was a term used by the philosopher Henri Bergson (1859–1941) to designate the force of creative evolution in the universe.

124:8–9 **When Moses set up the brazen serpent** See Numbers xxi. 4–11.

124:22 **Lindberg ... Dempsey** [124:23] Charles Augustus Lindbergh (1902–74), the American aviator who made the first non-stop transatlantic flight from New York to Paris, 20–21 May 1927 ... William Harrison ('Jack') Dempsey (1895–1982), American heavyweight boxer, who on 4 July 1919 won the world heavyweight championship.

125:21 **agathodaimon ... kakodaimon** Good spirit ... evil genius. Jung's *Psychology of the Unconscious* (1915) explains how in mythology 'the hero is himself a serpent, himself a sacrificer and a sacrificed. The hero himself is of *serpent nature* ... The serpent is the Agatho and Kako demon' (p. 417).

126:16 **Laocoön** A Trojan priest of Apollo who tried to prevent the Trojans from bringing the Wooden Horse into the city. As he was about to offer a sacrifice to Apollo, two sea serpents encircled him and his two sons and killed them. The Trojans, taking this as an omen, drew the Horse into the city.

127:1 **Andromeda** Andromeda's mother, Cassiopeia, boasted that she was more beautiful than the Nereids; they appealed to Poseidon who sent a monster to ravage the country. Andromeda was chained to a rock as a sacrifice but was rescued by Perseus who slew the monster and married Andromeda.

128:34 **Nebuchadnezzar** King of Babylonia (605–562 BC) who first captured Jerusalem.

129:8–10 **the Gold Age ... the Steel Age** The five ages of man in Greek mythology were the Golden, or the age of Saturn (or Chronus), when happiness and fertility were universal and men lived in innocence without sin; the Silver, when men ceased to revere the gods, knew evil, and began killing one another; the Bronze, in which a warlike race of cruel men lived who used metal tools and weapons; the Iron, the age of sin, in which Zeus let loose the Deluge which drowned everyone except Deucalion and

Pyrrha. The present age, called the Steel or the Stone, is the last and most degraded era of the human race.

129:25 'to shepherd mankind with an iron flail' Revelation xii. 5 (Moffatt).

130:4–5 the numbers seven, four and three In ancient numerology seven was the number of creation, the cosmos, space, and was represented by a square plus a triangle. The Pythagoreans equated the world with four and the supreme deity with three.

130:12–20 And the number three ... condition of being See Burnet, p. 289 on the Pythagorean system of numbers.

130:22–4 the Boundless ... primordial creation According to Burnet this Boundless substance is not one of the opposites but the body from which our world emerged. Strictly speaking the opposites to which DHL refers are not 'elements', an idea which came later with Empedokles. See Burnet, p. 58.

131:10 Anaximenes with his divine 'air' Anaximenes (flourished *c.* 546 BC), a younger associate or pupil of Anaximander, believed that the primary substance of the universe was a form of vapour or air.

131:20–21 exchange ... every day Burnet cites Heraclitus: 'All things are an exchange for Fire' and 'The sun is new every day' (p. 135). The primary substance, Fire, is in constant flux so that 'All things are in motion like streams' (p. 146). Heraclitus's notion of 'exchange' is illustrated when fire takes in fuel and gives out heat and smoke instead (p. 147).

131:21–2 'The limit ... bright Zeus' Heraclitus, quoted in Burnet, p. 135.

131:25–6 Night lives ... the death of Night Cf. Heraclitus: 'Fire lives the death of air, and air lives the death of fire; water lives the death of earth, earth that of water' (Burnet, p. 135).

131:30 'escaping the wheel of birth' The cult of Orphicism held that the soul was a fallen god and the main purpose of its rites was to release the soul from the 'wheel of birth', i.e. from reincarnation in animal or vegetable forms. Philosophy and meditation were means of purification and escape from the 'wheel'. See Burnet, pp. 81–3.

132:24–5 We know ... flood From Burnet: 'in the sixth century darkness was supposed to be a sort of vapour, while in the fifth its true nature was known' (p. 109).

133:12 the wheels of the revolving heavens ... Cherubim [133:33] See note on 82:25 ... Originally Assyrian, the cherubim appear in the Old Testament (Genesis iii. 24) as huge, winged creatures with either leonine or human faces and the bodies of bulls, sphinxes or eagles. Four cherubim, each with four faces and four wings, appeared to the Hebrew prophet Ezekiel (x. 14). In Revelation (iv. 8) they are living creatures who render unceasing praise to their Maker.

134:8 'Four for the Gospel Natures'   All extant versions of this ancient folksong (see note on 118:7) have 'Gospel makers', 'writers' or 'preachers', never 'natures'. However, see 'The Evangelistic Beasts', McDonald, ed., *Phoenix*, p. 66 and 'The Two Principles', Roberts and Moore, eds., *Phoenix II*, pp. 225–37: 'In religion we still accept the Four Gospel Natures, the Four Evangels, with their symbols of man, eagle, lion and bull, symbols parallel to the Four Elements, and to the Four Activities, and to the Four Natures' (p. 233).

134:12–13 At first . . . Fire   Burnet however states that the earliest Ionian cosmologists (*c.* sixth century BC) established only one primary substance.

134:18–19 Anaximenes said all was water . . . Xenophanes . . . water [134:19]   Anaximenes gave the name 'air' to the one and infinite substance; it was Thales who called it water . . . 'All things are earth and water that come into being and grow', Xenophanes, quoted by Burnet, p. 120.

134:27–30 Herakleitos . . . an element   According to Heraclitus Strife separates the primary substance into its manifestations and hence is the creative principle which causes the world to exist. 'Homer was wrong in saying: "Would that strife might perish from among gods and men!" He did not see that he was praying for the destruction of the universe; for, if his prayer were heard, all things would pass away' (Burnet, p. 136). Cf. 'Strife', *The Complete Poems*, p. 713. DHL incorrectly calls Fire an element here: it is the One, the Boundless. The notion of elements arose with Empedokles.

134:34–5 the Four Roots   'Hear first the four roots of all things' (Burnet, p. 205). Cf. 'The Four', *The Complete Poems*, p. 706.

134:36–9 'Fire and Water . . . breadth'   Burnet, p. 205.

134:40 'shining Zeus . . . Nestis'   'Empedokles also called the "four roots" by the names of certain divinities' (Burnet, p. 229).

135:1–2 the Four . . . elements   'Empedokles called the elements gods; for all the early thinkers had spoken in this way of whatever they regarded as the primary substance. We must only remember that the word is not used in its religious sense. Empedokles did not pray or sacrifice to the elements' (Burnet, p. 230).

135:7–9 Our life . . . our being.   See Acts xvii. 28 and cf. 'The Four', *The Complete Poems*, p. 706.

135:10 the four natures of man . . . 'the heart . . . thought of men' [135:13–15]   Empedokles was influential in traditional medicine, where the 'identification of the four elements with the hot and the cold, the moist and the dry' (Burnet, p. 201) eventually gave rise to the four temperaments, each with its element: air, sanguinary; fire, nervous; water, lymphatic; earth, bilious . . . Empedokles, quoted in Burnet, p. 220.

135:24–9 the dragon . . . is destroyed   See Revelation xii. 4, viii. 7–12, ix. 17–18, vi. 1–8.

136:1–3 **four and three ... the right time** The Neopythagoreans created many analogies between things and numbers. Aristotle believed that 'according to them the "right time" ... was seven, justice was four, and marriage three' (Burnet, pp. 107–8). See note on 130:4–5.

137:31 *The Golden Ass* ... **'time, times and a half'** [137:39] A satire by Apuleius (b. *c*. AD 123), supposedly an autobiography, in which the author is changed into an ass by the error of an enchantress's servant. The ass passes from one master to another, observing the follies and vices of humanity, and is finally restored to human form by the goddess Isis ... Revelation xii. 14.

139:1–2 **'It is ... over again'** ... **'all things are number'** [139:5] Burnet writes of Pythagoras: 'we are probably justified in referring to him the conclusion that it is "according to nature" that all Hellenes and barbarians count up to ten and then begin over again' (p. 103) ... It was not the repetition of five but the discovery of the harmonic intervals – the fourth, the fifth and the octave – 'that led Pythagoras to say all things were numbers' (Burnet, p. 107). Cf. also 'Tortoise Shell', *The Complete Poems*, p. 354.

139:6–9 **The Pythagoreans ... imagination** According to Burnet, Pythagoras 'used to give the number of all sorts of things ... [and] demonstrated these by arranging pebbles in a certain way ... Aristotle compares his procedure to that of those who bring numbers into figures ... like the triangle and the square' (p. 100). Traditionally, it was Pythagoras who first revealed the 'tetraktys of the dekad', a figure representing the number ten as the triangle of four:

139:17–18 **Moses' forehead** Moses is represented with horns owing to a mis-translation of Exodus xxxiv. 29–30. When Moses came down from Mount Sinai 'the skin of his face shone', but the Hebrew for 'shone' may be translated as 'sent forth *beams*' or '*horns*' and the Vulgate accepted the latter.

141:5–6 **'And there was ... the dragon'** Revelation xii. 7.

141:11 **Aphrodite** In classical mythology, the goddess of love and beauty who sprang from sea foam near the island of Cythera.

141:22–6 **'and the earth ... *Jesus Christ*'** Revelation xii. 16–17.

142:2–5 **'seven heads ... a lion'** ... **explained** by Daniel [142:6–7] Revelation xiii. 1–2 ... See Daniel vii. 7–8, 19–27.

142:11 **Macedonian ... Frazer's *Golden Bough*** [142:31] The intermediary between Greek and Hellenistic culture, Macedon under Philip and

Alexander became a world power, but was annexed as a province by Rome in 146 BC . . . Published 1890–1915 in 12 vols. by Sir James Frazer (1854–1941).

143:4 **number 666** . . . **Simon Magus** [143:9] . . . **Revenge Timotheus cries** [143:25]   Revelation xiii. 18 . . . Sorcerer of Samaria (see Acts viii. 9–13), who attempted to buy miraculous powers from the Apostles (Acts viii. 18–19) . . . Timotheus (447–357 BC) of Miletus, famous musician and poet, cited in Dryden's 'Alexander's Feast' (1697): 'Revenge, Revenge, Timotheus cries' (l. 131). See also D. H. Lawrence, *Kangaroo* (1923), chap. xiii.

144:1 **'new white garments'**   Revelation vi. 11.

144:21–2 **'Babylon . . . habitation of devils'** . . . **And then all the gold . . . Babylon the great** [144:22–6]   Revelation viii. 2 . . . Paraphrase of Revelation xviii. 11–13.

145:11–12 **'To them that have shall be given'** . . . **'Render unto Caesar that which is Caesar's'** [145:17]   See Matthew xxv. 29 . . . See Matthew xxii. 21; Mark xii. 17; Luke xx. 25.

145:24 **Nero** . . . **Domitian**   See note on 86:18 . . . Son of the Roman emperor Vespasian, Domitian (AD 51–96) succeeded his brother Titus in AD 81. He became a despot and demanded public worship of himself as a god. Towards the end of his reign both Jews and Christians were persecuted and, according to tradition, it was during that persecution that John, in exile on Patmos, received the visions recorded in Apocalypse.

146:16 **Lenin** . . . **Mussolini**   See note on 68:23 . . . Benito Mussolini (1883–1945) became dictator in Italy in 1925.

147:37 **each man . . . loves**   'The Ballad of Reading Gaol' (1898) by Oscar Wilde (1856–1900), ll. 37, 53.

148:7 **'caritas'**   Christian charity, the love of God and of one's neighbour (Latin).

APPENDIX I, *APOCALYPSE*, FRAGMENT I

153:4 **Thou shalt . . . thyself**   Matthew xxii. 39; Mark xii. 31.

153:6 **Moffatt's**   See note on 73:17.

153:29–30 **'Except the Lord . . . in vain . . .'**   Psalm cxxvii. 1.

154:10 **Babylon . . . Mycenae** [154:11]   See notes on 62:21–3 and 90:6.

154:28 *Credo*   I believe (Latin); part of the Nicene Creed said or sung as part of the Mass.

154:36–7 **Love one another!**   John xiii. 34.

155:19–20 **Dickens** . . . **Rabelais** . . . *Alice in Wonderland* . . . *Macbeth* . . . **Keats**   Charles Dickens (1812–70), English novelist . . . François Rabelais (1494?–1553), French humanist and satirist . . . *Alice's Adventures in Wonderland* (1865) by Lewis Carroll (1832–98) . . . *Macbeth* (c. 1604) by William Shakespeare (1564–1616) . . . John Keats (1795–1821), English Romantic poet.

156:6 *Wuthering Heights*   Novel (1847) by Emily Brontë (1818–48).

156:7 **Pluto and the spirit of Hades . . . Saturn** [156:8]   In Greek mythology Pluto, or Hades, was god of the netherworld; the name Hades was transferred to his kingdom . . . Italian name for Chronus. See note on 109:26–7.

156:17 **Jahveh**   Jehovah, the sacred name of God.

156:20 **Dionysic, Apollo-like . . . Ra** [156:21]   In Greek mythology Dionysus, the son of Zeus and Semele, was the god of wine; Apollo, son of Zeus and Latona, was the god of music and poetry who later became identified with the sun . . . In Egyptian mythology Ra was the sun god and supreme deity, often identified with Horus.

156:23 **Ouranos or Kronos or Saturn . . . Osiris** [156:23] **. . . Sumerians** [156:24]   See note on 109:26–7 . . . The great deity of the ancient Egyptians, the god of the dead whose son Horus was the god of renewed life. In Greek mythology Osiris was equated with Dionysus . . . People of the south Mesopotamian civilization which flourished during the third millennium BC.

157:1–2 **'Shriek . . . no more.—'**   Isaiah xxiii. 1 (Moffatt).

157:4 **Assyria . . . Moab** [157:5]   See note on 55:28 . . . Enemies of Israel in the biblical period (see Deuteronomy xxiii. 3–5).

157:7 **Nineveh . . . Susa** [157:9]   See note on 55:34 . . . The capital of Elam and afterwards of the Achaemenids, where Darius I built his palace.

157:10 **Chaldeans . . . Amalek** [157:13]   See note on 51:11 . . . An ancient nomadic people who lived in the Sinai desert between Egypt and Canaan (see Genesis xxxvi. 12).

157:18 **Herodotus . . . the Odyssey** [157:19]   The Greek historian (*c.* 480–425 BC) born at Halicarnassus, who travelled widely in Europe, Asia and Africa . . . Greek epic poem attributed to Homer.

159:4–5 **Thou shalt love . . . your enemies**   See Matthew v. 43–4 and John xiii. 34.

159:12–13 **restore the temple . . . Augustus** [159:13]   See note on 67:7 . . . Nephew of Julius Caesar and the first Roman emperor (from 27 BC till his death), Gaius Julius Caesar Octavianus (63 BC–AD 14) had the title Augustus conferred on him in 27 BC by the Senate. See note on 55:30.

159:19–20 **'How old . . . conquered us?'**   Burnet quotes Xenophanes: '"Of what country are you, and how old are you, good sir? And how old were you when the Mede appeared?"' (p. 114).

160:1–2 **For . . . first**   Matthew xix. 30 and xx. 16.

160:23 **Epicurus**   The founder of a school of philosophy, Epicurus (341–270 BC) taught that repose, or the absence of pain, is the greatest good. Since repose is produced by virtue, it follows that we should pursue virtue.

162:26–7 **Render . . . Caesar's**   See note on 145:11–12.

163:28 **the Borgia popes . . . Mammon** [163:29]   Rodrigo Borgia (1431–1503) fathered Cesare and Lucrezia Borgia and became Pope Alexander VI in 1492 . . . Originally the Aramaic word for 'riches' (and occurring in the Greek text of Matthew vi. 24 and Luke xvi. 9–13), taken by medieval writers to be the name of the devil of covetousness.

164:22 **'the Fish' . . . Lenin** [164:32]   See note on 98:19 . . . See note on 68:23.

165:2 **Nietzsche . . . Gregory** [165:6] **. . . Francis of Assisi** [165:9]   Friedrich Nietzsche (1844–1900), German philosopher, who was contemptuous of Christianity's ethical teaching of compassion for the weak . . . Gregory I, saint and titled 'The Great', was Pope from 590 to 604 and a zealous reformer of clerical and monastic discipline . . . See note on 68:20.

165:31 **'Give us . . . bread'**   Matthew vi. 11.

166:3–5 **'Our Father . . . heaven—'**   Matthew vi. 9–10.

167:29 **Caesar . . . Napoleon**   Caius Julius Caesar (102?–44 BC), Roman general and statesman, conqueror of Gaul and dictator of Rome until his assassination . . . Napoleon Bonaparte (1769–1821), Corsican general who became First Consul of France in 1799 and Emperor in 1804.

168:3 **Orphic mysteries**   See note on 85:22.

168:7 **Plato**   See note on 68:13.

168:33–5 **That world . . . death of the gods**   A paraphrase of Heraclitus: 'Mortals are immortals and immortals are mortals, the one living the others' death and dying the others' life' (Burnet, p. 138).

169:4 **Eleusinian mystery . . . Osiris and Isis** [169:4–5] **. . . Tammuz** [169:5]   Religious rites in honour of Ceres, or Demeter, first performed at Eleusis in Attica and later partly celebrated at Athens . . . See notes on 107:10 and 156:23 . . . Babylonian deity originally associated with sun-worship, who became the divine personification of the annual death and revival of vegetation.

169:6 **Attis . . . Mithras** [169:6]   A Phrygian deity who became a symbol of the death and revival of plant life. Originally the great goddess drove him mad because he wished to marry a mortal woman, but after his death his spirit passed into a pine tree and violets sprang from his blood. The myth is similar to that of Adonis in Greek legend . . . See notes on 56:2 and 99:33.

169:20 **Pradhana . . . Einstein** [169:24]   DHL may mean 'pranidhana', in Buddhist theology a commitment to gain enlightenment, or 'sadhana', a spiritual exercise which is a way of attaining an inner mystical state. Neither of these, however, is equivalent to Nirvana . . . Albert Einstein (1879–1955), the discoverer of the theory of relativity.

169:27 **Thales and Anaximander**   See notes on 87:36 and 82:25.

170:14–15 **a Mithraic fragment**   See notes on 56:2 and 81:32.

171:6 **Christian gnostics**   Derived from the Greek word for 'knowledge', gnosticism was a religious movement which in its Christian form flourished in the second century. Central importance was attached to the idea of 'gnosis', the revealed knowledge of God and of the origin and destiny of humanity, by means of which the spiritual aspect of mankind could be redeemed. See note on 83:22.

172:24 **Pentecost ... Stoics** [172:36]   The Greek name for the feast which falls on the fiftieth day after Passover; it celebrates the descent of the Holy Ghost on the Apostles (Acts ii. 1–4). Also popularly known as Whit Sunday ... School of Greek philosophers, founded by Zeno in about 310 BC, who believed that happiness and virtue consist in liberating the self from the passions and appetites. Virtue is the highest good and suffering is, or should be, a matter of indifference.

173:18–27 **All of which ... was one**   DHL knew no Greek and derived this argument from Charles, vol. i. pp. x–xi and xxi.

173:34–9 **To him ... his throne**   Revelation ii. 7; ii. 11; ii. 17.

174:1–7 **And he ... angels**   Revelation ii. 26–8; iii. 5.

174:8–12 **He that ... new name**   Revelation iii. 12.

174:13–15 **To him ... throne**   Revelation iii. 21.

174:29–33 **He shall ... no end.**   Luke i. 32–3.

174:34–7 **'And Jesus said ... Israel'**   Matthew xix. 28.

174:37–9 **'The Lord said ... thy footstool'**   Psalm cx. 1. See also Acts ii. 35; Mark xii. 36; Luke xx. 41–4.

175:1–2 **'God hath made ... Christ'**   Acts ii. 36.

175:4–6 **'The conqueror ... his throne'**   Revelation iii. 21 (Moffatt).

APPENDIX II, *APOCALYPSE*, FRAGMENT 2

177:5 **Epicurus ... Isis** [177:16]   See note on 160:23 ... See note on 107:10.

177:16 **Osiris, or Orphic Dionysos, or Mithras ... Stoic** [177:23]   See notes on 156:23, 85:22, 56:2 and 99:33 ... See note on 172:24.

178:14 **Day of All the Dead**   All Souls Day, 2 November. The phrase is a translation of the Italian 'il giorno dei Morti', which DHL came across in Italy in 1912. See *Letters*, i. 467 and *The Complete Poems*, p. 232.

179:26 **Bacchus**   Another name for the Greek god Dionysus.

181:30–35 **the great history ... Almighty**   See note on 109:26–7.

182:5 **samadhi ... the three states of man** [182:7] **... into Babylonia** [182:36]   The state of concentration or higher trance achieved through meditation, used by both Hindu and Buddhist believers ... DHL's version of Comte's 'Law of three stages' in human intellectual development, in which humanity progresses from a theological stage (in which the meaning of things is explained in terms of gods and spirits), to a transitional metaphysical stage (where essences, final causes and other abstract ideas replace the religious), to the positivist, which seeks to discover the laws governing phenomena in the universe . . . See note on 85:29.

182:38 **Pentateuch** The first five books of the Old Testament – Genesis, Exodus, Leviticus, Numbers and Deuteronomy – traditionally attributed to Moses.

183:2 **Belshazzar's** See note on 52:14.

183:3 **'wheels' of Ezekiel** See note on 82:25; Ezekiel i. 15–21.

183:25–6 **a city of Stoics** Paul came from the city of Tarsus in Cicilia, which was also the home of a famous philosophical school of Stoics.

184:10 **eastern Fathers** See note on 97:37–8.

185:3 **Dispersion** See note on 85:29.

185:21 **Messiah** From the Hebrew word for 'anointed'; a person invested by God with special powers, usually a king who, as 'the Lord's anointed', was held to be sacrosanct.

185:35–6 **Herod Antipas** DHL is mistaken; the temple was desecrated by Antiochus Epiphanes in 167 BC (see note on 67:7). Herod Antipas (4 BC–AD 39), who beheaded John the Baptist, and lived during the time of Christ's ministry, was the son of Herod the Great, who had been appointed King of the Jews by the Romans in 40 BC.

186:10 **the marriage at Cana** See John ii. 1–11 for the account of the miracle of the water turned to wine.

186:14–15 **I have not . . . openly** Paraphrase of John xviii. 20.

186:28 **his unknown 'editor'** See note on 81:32.

188:15 **seven 'stages of the Cross' . . . anima and animus** [188:37] Actually, the seven stations of the Cross, pictures or carvings showing incidents in the last journey of Christ from Pilate's house to his entombment . . . Jung saw these as the female and male aspects of the unconscious self. DHL has adapted the terms for his discussion of early Greek philosophical accounts of the spirit and soul.

189:27–8 **'Water is . . . says Thales . . . what Thales can have meant by 'gods'** [189:35–6] Thales believed that 'water was the stuff of which all other things were transient forms' (Burnet, pp. 47–8) . . . Θεόῳ 'god' could also describe natural phenomena and even human passions (Burnet, pp. 14, 48–9). See also note on 95:24–96:6.

190:6–9 **'All things . . . of fire'** Burnet, pp. 120, 135.

190:21–2 **'O my . . . red rose'** 'A red, red Rose' (1794), poem by Robert Burns (1759–96).

190:27–8 **'Lord . . . all generations—'** Psalm xc. 1.

191:8–9 **like a bridegroom . . . his chamber** Psalm xix. 5.

192:35 **Lord Kelvin . . . Darwin** [192:36] Sir William Thomson, first Baron Kelvin (1824–1907), Professor of Natural Philosophy at Glasgow University, best known for his work on thermodynamics and electricity

... Charles Robert Darwin (1809–82), author of *On the Origin of Species* (1859) and *The Descent of Man* (1871).

194:3 *ab ovo*   From the egg (Latin), i.e. from the beginning.

APPENDIX III, *APOCALYPSIS II*

195:20–34 **A number ... begin again**   See notes on 139:1–2, 139:1–2 and 139:6–9; see also Burnet, pp. 102–3 and 288–9.

196:30–38 **In some of the dialogues ... nonsense**   DHL here conflates the Socratic method, in which Socrates enquired into ethics by questioning people, with that of the Sophists, itinerant teachers who went from city to city giving instruction for a fee. They emphasized the ability to argue for any point of view irrespective of its truth, hence the negative associations of Sophist and sophistry.

198:16 **terrible fiasco**   Plato was invited by Dion of Syracuse in 367 BC to teach Dionysius II to be the ideal philosopher-king, but the new ruler banished Dion and kept Plato a virtual prisoner. However, in 357 Dion returned and expelled Dionysius.

199:29 **Thought is getting out of touch**   Cf. 'Thought', *The Complete Poems*, p. 673.

Further Reading

Armytage, W. H. G., *Heavens Below: Utopian Experiments in England 1560–1960*, Routledge, 1961. (*Useful historical account.*)

Auerbach, E., *Mimesis*, Princeton University Press, 1953. (*Classic analysis of Western literature and thought from the Bible to Joyce.*)

Black, M., *D. H. Lawrence: The Early Philosophical Works*, Macmillan, 1991. (*Fine description of the genesis of DHL's philosophical thought.*)

Clarke, L. D., 'The Apocalypse of Lorenzo', *D. H. Lawrence Review* 3. ii. (1970). (*Useful early essay.*)

Cohn, N., *The Pursuit of the Millennium*, Secker & Warburg, 1957. (*Very full, scholarly account.*)

Fernihough, A., *D. H. Lawrence: Aesthetics and Ideology*, Oxford University Press, 1993. (*Fine study of DHL's literary and art criticism, with reference to the philosophical thinking that informs it.*)

Fjågesund, P., *The Apocalyptic World of D. H. Lawrence*, Norwegian University Press, 1991. (*Useful summary of Continental apocalyptic thought in the first third; thereafter disappointing.*)

Gilbert, A., *Religion and Society in Industrial England*, Longman, 1976. (*Sound general study.*)

Goodheart, E., *The Utopian Vision of D. H. Lawrence*, University of Chicago Press, 1971. (*Dated, but some valuable insights.*)

Kermode, F., 'Lawrence and the Apocalyptic Types', *Critical Quarterly* x (Spring, 1968). (*Seminal essay on apocalyptic thought in DHL.*)

    The Genesis of Secrecy, Harvard University Press, 1978. (*Stimulating enquiry into hermeneutics and the interpretation of biblical narrative.*)

    The Sense of an Ending, Oxford University Press, 1968. (*Classic study of fin de siècle and apocalyptic writing.*)

    Modern Essays, Fontana, 1971. (*Excellent study.*)

    Poetry, Narrative, History, Blackwell, 1990. (*Excellent chapter on biblical narrative.*)

Manuel, F. E. and F. P., *Utopian Thought in the Western World*, Oxford University Press, 1979. (*Exhaustive scholarly account.*)

Montgomery, R. E., *The Visionary D. H. Lawrence*, Cambridge University Press, 1994. (*Draws interesting parallels between DHL's thought and that of philosophers and mystics.*)

O'Leary, S., *Arguing the Apocalypse*, Oxford University Press, 1994. (*Interesting study of contemporary apocalyptic rhetoric.*)

Further Reading

Urang, S., *Kindled in the Flame: The Apocalyptic Scene in D. H. Lawrence*, University of Michigan Press, 1983. (*Worthy description of apocalyptic elements in DHL's writings, focusing on the major fiction.*)

Worthen, J., *D. H. Lawrence: The Early Years 1885–1912*, Cambridge University Press, 1992. (*Lucid biography.*)

READ MORE IN PENGUIN

In every corner of the world, on every subject under the sun, Penguin represents quality and variety – the very best in publishing today.

For complete information about books available from Penguin – including Puffins, Penguin Classics and Arkana – and how to order them, write to us at the appropriate address below. Please note that for copyright reasons the selection of books varies from country to country.

In the United Kingdom: Please write to *Dept. JC, Penguin Books Ltd, FREEPOST, West Drayton, Middlesex UB7 OBR.*

If you have any difficulty in obtaining a title, please send your order with the correct money, plus ten per cent for postage and packaging, to *PO Box No. 11, West Drayton, Middlesex UB7 OBR*

In the United States: Please write to *Consumer Sales, Penguin USA, P.O. Box 999, Dept. 17109, Bergenfield, New Jersey 07621-0120.* VISA and MasterCard holders call 1-800-253-6476 to order all Penguin titles

In Canada: Please write to *Penguin Books Canada Ltd, 10 Alcorn Avenue, Suite 300, Toronto, Ontario M4V 3B2*

In Australia: Please write to *Penguin Books Australia Ltd, P.O. Box 257, Ringwood, Victoria 3134*

In New Zealand: Please write to *Penguin Books (NZ) Ltd, Private Bag 102902, North Shore Mail Centre, Auckland 10*

In India: Please write to *Penguin Books India Pvt Ltd, 706 Eros Apartments, 56 Nehru Place, New Delhi 110 019*

In the Netherlands: Please write to *Penguin Books Netherlands bv, Postbus 3507, NL-1001 AH Amsterdam*

In Germany: Please write to *Penguin Books Deutschland GmbH, Metzlerstrasse 26, 60594 Frankfurt am Main*

In Spain: Please write to.*Penguin Books S. A., Bravo Murillo 19, 1° B, 28015 Madrid*

In Italy: Please write to *Penguin Italia s.r.l., Via Felice Casati 20, I–20124 Milano*

In France: Please write to *Penguin France S. A., 17 rue Lejeune, F–31000 Toulouse*

In Japan: Please write to *Penguin Books Japan, Ishikiribashi Building, 2–5–4, Suido, Bunkyo-ku, Tokyo 112*

In Greece: Please write to *Penguin Hellas Ltd, Dimocritou 3, GR–106 71 Athens*

In South Africa: Please write to *Longman Penguin Southern Africa (Pty) Ltd, Private Bag X08, Bertsham 2013*

READ MORE IN PENGUIN

Penguin Twentieth-Century Classics offer a selection of the finest works of literature published this century. Spanning the globe from Argentina to America, from France to India, the masters of prose and poetry are represented in by the Penguin.

If you would like a catalogue of the Twentieth-Century Classics library, please write to:

Penguin Marketing, 27 Wrights Lane, London W8 5TZ

(Available while stocks last)

READ MORE IN PENGUIN

A CHOICE OF TWENTIETH-CENTURY CLASSICS

Ulysses   James Joyce

Ulysses is unquestionably one of the supreme masterpieces, in any artistic form, of the twentieth century. A modernist classic, its ceaseless verbal inventiveness and astonishingly wide-ranging allusions confirm its standing as an imperishable monument to the human condition. 'It is the book to which we are all indebted and from which none of us can escape' – T. S. Eliot

The Heart of the Matter   Graham Greene

Scobie is a highly principled police officer in a war-torn West African state. When he is passed over for promotion he is forced to borrow money to send his despairing wife on holiday. With a duty to repay his debts and an inability to distinguish between love, pity and responsibility to others and to God, Scobie moves inexorably towards his final damnation.

The Age of Innocence   Edith Wharton

Into the world of propriety which composed the rigid world of Old New York society returns the Countess Olenska. Separated from her European husband and bearing with her an independence and impulsive awareness of life, she stirs the educated sensitivity of Newland Archer, who is engaged to be married to young May Welland.

The Worm Forgives the Plough   John Stewart Collis

'The precise nature of an ancient country task and its tools, the characters of different trees and undergrowths, the solitudes and silences, the whole experience can seldom have been better or more lovingly described' – John Fowles

The End of the Chapter   John Galsworthy

Here Galsworthy writes about the lives and loves of the Cherrells, cousins of the Forsytes. Galsworthy's grasp of political and social change and its effect on a family, as well as his incisive sense of character, make this a fine trilogy with which to end *The Forsyte Saga*.

READ MORE IN PENGUIN

A CHOICE OF TWENTIETH-CENTURY CLASSICS

Three Soldiers   John Dos Passos

Stemming directly from Dos Passos's experience as an ambulance driver in the First World War, *Three Soldiers* is a powerful onslaught against the mindless war machine.

The Certificate   Isaac Bashevis Singer

Penniless and without work, eighteen-year-old David Bendiner arrives in the big city, Warsaw, in 1922, determined to become a writer. But the path from innocence to experience is a slippery one. Within days, Singer's enjoyable hero is uncerebrally entangled with three women and has obtained a certificate to emigrate to Palestine with one of them.

The Quiet American   Graham Greene

The Quiet American is a terrifying portrait of innocence at large. While the French Army in Indo-China is grappling with the Vietminh, back at Saigon a young and high-minded American begins to channel economic aid to a 'Third Force'. 'There has been no novel of any political scope about Vietnam since Graham Greene wrote *The Quiet American*' – *Harper's*

Wide Sargasso Sea   Jean Rhys

After twenty-seven years' silence, Jean Rhys made a sensational literary reappearance with *Wide Sargasso Sea*, her story of the first Mrs Rochester, the mad wife in Charlotte Brontë's *Jane Eyre*. It took her nine years to write it, and in its tragic power, psychological truth and magnificent poetic vision it stands out as one of the great novels of our time.

The Desert of Love   François Mauriac

Two men, father and son, share a passion for the same woman. Maria Cross is attractive, intelligent and proud, but her position as a 'kept woman' makes her an outcast from society. Many years later, in very different circumstances, the two men encounter Maria again and once more feel the power of this enigmatic woman who has indelibly marked their lives.

READ MORE IN PENGUIN

A CHOICE OF TWENTIETH-CENTURY CLASSICS

Details of a Sunset and Other Stories Vladimir Nabokov

More than mere footnotes to the masterly novels of his maturity, these early Russian stories are rich in the glittering surfaces and deep undercurrents of Nabokov's genius. '*Details of a Sunset* is much concerned with different kinds of loss ... and yet the effects of these stories are mainly exhilarating, even affirmative' – *The New York Times Book Review*

Jean Santeuil Marcel Proust

Drawing on the intense emotional experiences of his youth, Proust tells the story of boyhood summers of strawberries and cream cheese, of garlands of pink blossom under branches of white may, of love and its lies, of political scandal and of his deep feeling for his parents.

The Shadow-Line Joseph Conrad

A young and inexperienced sea captain's first command finds him with a ship becalmed in tropical seas and a crew smitten with fever. As he wrestles with his conscience and with the sense of isolation that his position imposes, the captain crosses the 'shadow-line' between youth and adulthood.

The Reef Edith Wharton

Anna Leath, an American widow living in France, has renewed her relationship with her first love, diplomat George Darrow. But on his way to her beautiful French château, where he hopes to consolidate his marriage plans, Darrow encounters Sophy Viner, who is as vibrant and spontaneous as Anna is reserved and restrained.

The Claudine Novels Colette

Seldom have the experiences of a young girl growing to maturity been evoked with such lyricism and candour, and in Colette's hands Claudine emerges as a true original, first and most beguiling of this century's emancipated women.

PENGUIN AUDIOBOOKS

A Quality of Writing that Speaks for Itself

Penguin Books has always led the field in quality publishing. Now you can listen at leisure to your favourite books, read to you by familiar voices from radio, stage and screen. Penguin Audiobooks are ideal as gifts, for when you are travelling or simply to enjoy at home. They are produced to an excellent standard, and abridgements are always faithful to the original texts. From thrillers to classic literature, biography to humour, with a wealth of titles in between, Penguin Audiobooks offer you quality, entertainment and the chance to rediscover the pleasure of listening.

You can order Penguin Audiobooks through Penguin Direct by telephoning (0181) 899 4036. The lines are open 24 hours every day. Ask for Penguin Direct, quoting your credit card details.

Published or forthcoming:

Emma by Jane Austen, read by Fiona Shaw

Persuasion by Jane Austen, read by Joanna David

Pride and Prejudice by Jane Austen, read by Geraldine McEwan

The Tenant of Wildfell Hall by Anne Brontë, read by Juliet Stevenson

Jane Eyre by Charlotte Brontë, read by Juliet Stevenson

Villette by Charlotte Brontë, read by Juliet Stevenson

Wuthering Heights by Emily Brontë, read by Juliet Stevenson

The Woman in White by Wilkie Collins, read by Nigel Anthony and Susan Jameson

Heart of Darkness by Joseph Conrad, read by David Threlfall

Tales from the One Thousand and One Nights, read by Souad Faress and Raad Rawi

Moll Flanders by Daniel Defoe, read by Frances Barber

Great Expectations by Charles Dickens, read by Hugh Laurie

Hard Times by Charles Dickens, read by Michael Pennington

Martin Chuzzlewit by Charles Dickens, read by John Wells

The Old Curiosity Shop by Charles Dickens, read by Alec McCowen

PENGUIN AUDIOBOOKS

Crime and Punishment by Fyodor Dostoyevsky, read by Alex Jennings

Middlemarch by George Eliot, read by Harriet Walter

Silas Marner by George Eliot, read by Tim Pigott-Smith

The Great Gatsby by F. Scott Fitzgerald, read by Marcus D'Amico

Madame Bovary by Gustave Flaubert, read by Claire Bloom

Jude the Obscure by Thomas Hardy, read by Samuel West

The Return of the Native by Thomas Hardy, read by Steven Pacey

Tess of the D'Urbervilles by Thomas Hardy, read by Eleanor Bron

The Iliad by Homer, read by Derek Jacobi

Dubliners by James Joyce, read by Gerard McSorley

The Dead and Other Stories by James Joyce, read by Gerard McSorley

On the Road by Jack Kerouac, read by David Carradine

Sons and Lovers by D. H. Lawrence, read by Paul Copley

The Fall of the House of Usher by Edgar Allan Poe, read by Andrew Sachs

Wide Sargasso Sea by Jean Rhys, read by Jane Lapotaire and Michael Kitchen

The Little Prince by Antoine de Saint-Exupéry, read by Michael Maloney

Frankenstein by Mary Shelley, read by Richard Pasco

Of Mice and Men by John Steinbeck, read by Gary Sinise

Travels with Charley by John Steinbeck, read by Gary Sinise

The Pearl by John Steinbeck, read by Hector Elizondo

Dr Jekyll and Mr Hyde by Robert Louis Stevenson, read by Jonathan Hyde

Kidnapped by Robert Louis Stevenson, read by Robbie Coltrane

The Age of Innocence by Edith Wharton, read by Kerry Shale

The Buccaneers by Edith Wharton, read by Dana Ivey

Mrs Dalloway by Virginia Woolf, read by Eileen Atkins

READ MORE IN PENGUIN

D. H. LAWRENCE

NOVELS

Aaron's Rod
The Lost Girl
The Rainbow
The Trespasser
Women in Love
The First Lady Chatterley
The Boy in the Bush
(with M. L. Skinner)

Lady Chatterley's Lover
The Plumed Serpent
Sons and Lovers
The White Peacock
Kangaroo
John Thomas and Lady Jane

SHORT STORIES

Three Novellas: The Fox/
   The Ladybird/The Captain's
   Doll
St Mawr *and* The Virgin and
   the Gipsy
Selected Short Stories
The Complete Short Novels

The Prussian Officer
Love Among the Haystacks
The Princess
England, My England
The Woman Who Rode
   Away
The Mortal Coil

TRAVEL BOOKS AND OTHER WORKS

Mornings in Mexico
Studies in Classic
   American Literature
Apocalypse
Selected Essays

Fantasia of the Unconscious
   and Psychoanalysis and the
   Unconscious
D. H. Lawrence and Italy

POETRY

D. H. Lawrence: Selected Poetry
Edited and Introduced by Keith Sagar
Complete Poems

PLAYS

Three Plays

Penguin are now publishing the Cambridge editions of D. H. Lawrence's
texts. These are as close as can now be determined to those he would have
intended.